THE
DARK
DIDN'T
CATCH
ME

THE DARK DIDN'T CATCH ME

Crystal Thrasher

A MARGARET K. MC ELDERRY BOOK

Atheneum 1975 *New York*

Library of Congress Cataloging in Publication Data

Thrasher, Crystal.
The dark didn't catch me.
"A Margaret K. McElderry Book."
SUMMARY: Able to find beauty in the hills of
southern Indiana, Seeley withstands the work, troubles,
and sorrows that encompass her family during the depression.
[1. Indiana—Fiction. 2. Depressions—1929—
Fiction] I. Title.
PZ7.T4Dar [Fic] 74-18193
ISBN 0-689-50025-4

Copyright © 1975 by Crystal Thrasher
Published simultaneously in Canada by McClelland & Stewart, Ltd.
Manufactured in the United States of America by
The Book Press, Inc.
Brattleboro, Vermont
Designed by Harriett Barton
First Edition

THE
DARK
DIDN'T
CATCH
ME

chapter one

Julie,   Jamie,   and   I
climbed up the tailgate of the truck and over the furniture, digging down among the barrels and boxes to find
a place where the cold November wind wouldn't hit us
directly and where we wouldn't be likely to bounce out.
I stumbled and fell over the rolled carpet and landed with
my feet up in the air.

"Straighten up, Seely, and put your skirt down," Julie
said.

I tucked my legs under me and made room for her and
Jamie just as the truck gave a coughing lunge and started
moving unsteadily down the lane to the main road.

Jase Perry drove the old rattletrap truck. He had been
at the farm since daylight, loading and unloading the
things Mom wanted to take with her to Greene County.

The only thing he hadn't taken off the truck at least once was the big cast-iron cooking stove. He mumbled under his breath that he knew she was taking that cook stove whether anything else moved or not.

The Perrys had been neighbors to us ever since I could remember. But for a time now, they had been living down in the Indiana hills, and we hardly ever saw them. When we were younger, we had thought Jase and Dicie were our aunt and uncle. Then, one day, Julie came home crying because Floyd Perry, their oldest, had told her she wasn't his cousin. Mom explained to us the difference between friends and relations. She ended by saying, "God gave us our relations, but thank God we can pick our own friends."

I don't know if we chose the Perrys for friends or if it was just something that grew with time. At our house we didn't seem overly blessed with friends *or* relations. The Perry kids had a grandma and an Aunt Lulu, but the only relation of ours that I ever heard tell of was our Great-grandmother Curry; and she was dead.

Floyd Perry, Mom, and the baby, Robert, who was four, sat in the front seat now with Jase. Floyd folded up his long legs, his bony knees nearly under his chin, and straddled the gear shift. Mom held Robert on her lap and sat next to the window in case she got carsick from the long drive.

If Mom didn't want to go someplace but had to go anyway, she was apt to get carsick. We would stop and wait until she guessed she was able to go on.

In the first place, Mom said, Dad had bought that

house in Greene County without ever telling her a thing about it. She had thought he was just taking a load of corn in to the grain elevator and would be home before dark.

But it had been late that night when Dad got home. Mom had walked the floor and sworn up and down that Dad had been knocked on the head and robbed of all his money. Or else the team of horses had run away with him, and he was lying hurt or maybe dead somewhere between home and the granary. I think she favored the first explanation. She mentioned it the most often.

Mom had been close to crying when we heard his step on the porch. She hurried to open the door before he'd had time to reach it.

"Where on earth have you been? Are you all right? Have you still got the money?" Mom had to stop to catch her breath.

Dad said, "You didn't ask if I was hungry or if I'd had any supper, Zel. Set out a bite for me, and we'll talk while I eat." He seemed to notice then that Julie, Jamie, and I were still up. "Why aren't you kids in bed? You'll all be late for school in the morning."

Julie said, "There's no school tomorrow. It's Saturday."

"School or no—you'll not lay abed later than six o'clock; and it's near midnight right now."

Before Julie closed our bedroom door, I heard Mom say, "I hear you note the time, Rob. Now, let's hear what kept you out till this hour of the night."

Mom woke us the next morning banging the stove lids

and dragging the iron skillet and coffee pot across the top of the stove as she started breakfast. The kitchen door slammed when she went out to gather eggs, and the oven door closed with a loud whoosh after she shoved the pan of biscuits in to bake.

"Wonder why Mom is upset this early in the morning?" I said to Julie. "We're not even up yet."

Julie smiled and nudged me toward the edge of the bed. "Suppose you get up and find out what's bothering her. I'll stay here till you think it's safe to venture in to breakfast."

I got out of my nightgown and put on the same gingham dress I'd worn the day before. Just as I stepped into the hall, Jamie opened his bedroom door. His hair, dark as a buckeye bean, fell in a mass of tousled curls over his ears and down on his forehead. I knew he'd been waiting for me. I took his hand and we went to the kitchen to wash up for breakfast.

Jamie was nine and a half, a year and a half younger than me, but small and shy for his age. He and I were Mom's in-between kids. Not old enough to be treated like grownups yet, and too big to be fussed over and babied. Mom made over Robert and went out of her way to cater to his every want, trying to keep him a baby, I guess; and she fussed at Julie, telling her to grow up and act her age. Jamie and I were left alone. We were at the stage where no one seems to expect much of kids.

At the breakfast table, Dad said, "I'll load the wagon first thing in the morning and take the livestock on ahead. That gives you a week to pack. It's a small house,

Zel, so take only the things you'll need to set up house-keeping."

Mom said, "I won't step a foot out of this house. I don't know how you can expect me to just pack up and leave everything."

"Jase says I can get work down there. There's a good stand of timber on the place and money to be made cutting props and rail ties for the mines. Art Sudlow is taking the team of horses off my hands. He'll pick them up at Jase's. After I get the stock settled in the barn, I'll stay at the Perrys'. Their place is just a little ways back in the hills from your house."

"Don't call it my house," Mom said. "I want no part of it."

Dad went on talking as if Mom hadn't opened her mouth.

"Jase will be here next Saturday morning with his truck. You have things ready to go when he gets here. I'll be at the house to help Jase unload the truck and set up the stoves when you all get there."

Dad left for Greene County the next morning. He took the pigs, our pet lambs, crates of squawking chickens, and feed for the animals in the farm wagon. The cow was tied to the back of the wagon with a lead rope. She bawled and swung her head as if to say she wouldn't go either. As the wheels began to turn, she braced all four feet, and when the rope tightened, first one leg and then the other gave way and buckled under her. She stumbled, then got to her feet, and lumbered along after the wagon.

We had watched until Dad and the wagon were out

of sight. Julie had said, "It would make more sense to take the heating stove along on this first load with the animals. Then the house would be warm when we got there."

But the fat black monster with the isinglass face and cast-iron ruffle around its hips was riding here on the loaded truck with us.

Jase stayed on the back roads and bypassed all the towns. The roads had been graded and tarred sometime in the past, but now the chuckholes were deep enough to bury one of our hogs, and they lay as close together as a man's tracks. I think Jase hit nearly every one of them.

We bounced up and down on the back of the truck, scraping our knees and elbows on the rough edges of the barrels and Mom's bedsprings. It seemed like every time we got warm and comfortable, Jase would hit another chuckhole or swerve to miss one, and we would go tumbling from side to side.

Soon after we crossed the fork of White River, Jase stuck his head out the window and yelled, "You kids back there, hang on tight! You're in Greene County now."

As if that was the signal it had been waiting for, the pockmarked blacktop turned into a barely passable road of shallow gravel and frozen ruts of red clay.

Suddenly the truck seemed to stand on its nose. All the boxes shifted and slid forward making our cramped space even smaller. I caught hold of the sideboard and pulled myself up, then braced against the rail; I looked over the top. The road went straight down with a sharp bend at the foot of the hill.

Jase changed the gears, and I fell back on the carpet roll. Then as I tried to sit up, the gears clashed again, slowing the truck to a jerking near standstill. When Jase shifted the gears again, the truck groaned and shook itself like a dog after a rainstorm. I was sure it was falling apart, but it held together, and we slowed to a crawl for the sharp turn.

After we had rounded the bend, we could see that the road had many such twists and turns as it climbed to the top of another hill and meandered off through the woods, to lose itself among the trees. The truck labored and nearly stalled on the steep grades. Julie said if the back was heavier than the front, the truck would tip on end going up the steep hills. Jamie and I crept forward until we touched the cab and clung to the slat sides with both hands, adding our weight to that of the front end.

Huge trees grew near the tracks we followed through the woods. Branches and bare limbs spread across the way and threatened to sweep us off the heaped load. On one side we looked down into wooded ravines a hundred feet deep. On the other side, hills, slashed through with ragged, red-edged gullies, rose just as high. First the hill would be on one side of the road, then pretty soon it would be on the other. Whichever way Jase turned, there was always a hill and a hollow on either side of us.

The hills grew higher and the ruts in the road got deeper as we crept farther into the strange, unknown county soon to be our home. We saw a few run-down, shabby houses framed by toothless picket fences along the way. Ragged kids, followed by slat-sided hounds, ran to peek from behind trees and watch us go by. We raised our hands and called out to them, but nobody waved back at us.

Our lunch was gingersnap cookies from a brown paper sack. We didn't have anything to wash them down with, so we played a game to see who could make the most spit for swallowing them. Jamie choked on his last gingersnap, and I slapped his back until he could get his breath. His face was still purple.

Julie said, "Jamie, don't you dare have one of your spells. There isn't room in here for you to have a fit."

Jamie giggled. We wrapped a quilt around him and pulled him down between us to share our warm place.

It was nearly dusk when Jase called out the window and said, "There's your house up ahead. You're home."

The pale winter sun disappeared behind hovering dark clouds and distant hills. We could barely make out the small, weather-beaten house in the clearing.

Julie, looking at the hills surrounding us, said, "Lord, you'll have to lie on your back at high noon to ever see the sun from down here."

She was probably right. She usually was. At sixteen, Julie wasn't very big, but she knew almost everything.

I wondered what it would be like to climb to the top of the highest hill before daylight and watch the sun come out of the earth and rise to meet me. I knew it would surely be warm and sunny up there while it was still night and pitch black around this house.

Jase stopped the truck near the open-air front porch, which slumped toward the road. Its carved posts leaned forward under the weight of the tin roof, and it looked as if one step on it would bring the whole porch tumbling down upon us.

Julie and I jumped from the truck, skirted the rickety porch, and picked our way carefully through knee-high brown ragweed and many seasons of dried grass to the back door. The house looked better on the inside than it had appeared to be from the road. The room we entered ran the full width of the house with windows all along one wall and across one end. Worn blue-figured linoleum covered the area in front of the flue hole, but the rest of the floor was bare pine boards. A wide unpainted shelf was built along the wall where the stove would sit, and beneath it was a big woodbox heaped full of kindling and stove wood.

Julie waved her hand toward the shelf and woodbox. "It looks like Dad made good use of his time while he was waiting for us."

"He wasted his time if he did it for Mom. She'll see the bare floor and not even notice that it's clean."

I opened the solid oak door that separated the kitchen from a good-sized living room and one bedroom in the front part of the house. From the living room four steps led up to a small plank door; then four more steps led up to the attic. It covered the whole house and had one long narrow window at each end.

Julie and I used the brick chimney that passed through the center of the attic as a dividing line. We chose the left side next to the stairs for our bed and dresser and allowed the boys the right side for theirs.

We were tired and hungry but most of all thirsty for a drink of water. Mom said the water had to be boiled before we could drink it. No telling how long it had been since anyone had lived here. Anything could have fallen into the well. We gagged and shuddered.

Mom ordered us away from the rotten boards that covered the mouth of the well. She said it looked to be wide enough to swallow us all without leaving a trace.

"The first thing tomorrow, your dad is going to clean that well and make a decent cover for it, or I'll not stay in this godforsaken hole. And if you kids want a bed to sleep on tonight," she added, "you'll take those straw ticks out to the barn and stuff them."

We were glad for any reason to get away. The house was no place for us right then or any time when Mom felt that way.

Mom had made the straw ticks by sewing feed sacks together, leaving a slit down the center for stuffing in the straw. While Dad and Jase set up the stoves to heat the house and cook supper, we filled the ticks in the barn with clean straw for our beds.

The first night or so, the beds would be so high we'd have to take a running jump to get in, but by the end of the week the mattresses would be mashed down flat and hard on the wooden bed slats.

Only Mom and Dad had springs on their bed. And the way those wire coils screeched and brayed every time one of them turned over, I was glad we didn't have springs. Sometimes a spring would break and poke up through their feather tick. Then Dad would take the bed apart and tie the coils down with bailing wire. He would skin his knuckles and swear that bedsprings were a contraption invented by the devil to test a man's soul. But he'd fix them and wrestle them back in place before bedtime.

All the way to the barn we could hear the men cussing the stovepipes as they banged them together to get a tight fit in the flues. We stayed there in the hayloft, waiting for things to quiet down in the house.

Floyd and Julie lugged the straw-filled mattresses to the wide door of the hayloft and heaved them down to the frozen barnyard below, while Jamie and I rolled in the high straw stacks and scattered it over the loft floor. Floyd tried his best to put straw down the front of Julie's blouse, but she squealed and wiggled out of reach. Then he chased her across the loft and fell headfirst into the hay, which was stacked from the eaves to the ridgepole.

Floyd was nearly as tall as Dad and Jase but not as thick and heavy. He seemed to be all knees and elbows with a long stretch of nothing in between. Dad said Floyd was just skin and bones now, but he would be a giant when he got his growth, if he didn't stumble over his big feet and break his neck. Floyd had chipped a big piece off a front tooth, once, when he tripped and fell on the wood pile.

I was just burying Jamie under a pile of straw when I heard Mom calling us to bring the mattresses and come to supper. I dug him out and brushed away the straw as best I could. Floyd was still picking straw out of Julie's hair at the supper table.

Before they left that night, Jase said, "On Monday morning, you kids take the first mud lane you come to and follow it straight to the schoolhouse door. Come home with my young'uns. Dicie'll show you the short cut through the woods and the path across Lick Crick. Julie, you can catch the school bus with Floyd. It comes right by here."

Julie smiled at Floyd, then took a lamp and went up the attic steps to make our bed.

After Jamie and Robert had gone to sleep on their side of the attic, Julie and I put our things away and got into our outing flannel nightgowns. Before we put out the light, I turned to the stitched center of my notebook. Lines were crossed out and penciled through where I had made a mistake or changed my mind later. If I tore a sheet from the book, a clean page would fall out on the other side, so I just crossed things out.

Starting on a clean page, I wrote, "Today we traveled all the way from home to the end of the world. Dad says we will make a home here because he can find work and there is no place else to go."

Mom hollered up the steps and said, "Seely, blow out that lamp and go to sleep. You're wasting coal oil."

I turned the wick as low as it would go and still make light.

"Blow it out, I said!"

I blew; and the attic was so black I couldn't see across the room. I stuck my notebook under the straw tick, shut my eyes, and scooted up close to Julie's back.

chapter two

*J*ase came down early Sunday morning to help Dad build a platform and cover for the well. He said there was a cold mist blowing in from the east and it felt like it might snow. He didn't know if Dad would want to work on the well or not.

Mom left the room to get a warm wrap, and Dad said, "I know it's not a fit day to be working on that damn well, but if I don't get it done today, I'll never hear the last of it."

While Dad and Jase were talking over the best way to get the job done, Jamie and I grabbed our sweaters and ran outside.

The mist had turned into big wet snowflakes, which melted away as soon as they hit the ground. We lifted our faces to the snow and stuck out our tongue to catch the cold, tasteless slush in our mouth.

Before long, the snow stopped, and a cold drizzle of rain fell in its place.

Mom went to the well with Dad and Jase. "I won't know a moment's peace until that well is braced and covered."

She stood over the men, telling them what she wanted done, but finally the cold drizzle sent her back to the warmth of the kitchen. "By rights," she said, as she was leaving, "I ought to have a pump right there in the house."

Jamie and I moved closer to the well so we could watch Dad and Jase measure and cut the two-by-fours.

Dad said, "You kids stand back."

We stepped away, then crowded up close when he took the old boards off the opening to measure and fit the new cover.

"Damn it! I told you kids to get back. All your mother needs right now is to have you two young'uns fall in this well."

We sought shelter in the barn. It was dim and shadowy, with a heavy, still coldness, not the least bit like the cozy place it had seemed last night when we stuffed our mattresses.

Jamie began to rummage through an old chest full of broken harness, tools, and other farm junk. He complained it was too dark to see if anything was worth keeping. I found a lantern hanging on a peg just inside the door and a tin box of matches on the wide beam beside it. I stood on a feed box and lifted them down. Jamie said we shouldn't strike matches, but I lit the lantern, anyway, and carried it with us as we looked around the barn.

On the very bottom of the chest of old trash, Jamie found a small Indian arrowhead. He piled the junk and trash back in the chest, then searched through every corner and cubbyhole in the barn, but he didn't find another arrowhead.

I blew out the lantern and hung it back on the peg. Then we ran back to the well to show Dad Jamie's find.

While we had explored the barn, Dad and Jase had been busy. They had built an open shed over the well, shingled its roof, and laid a railing around the middle. They were nailing boards from the ground to the railing, closing in the lower half of the shed, by the time we got back.

When they heard a car drive up, Dad and Jase put their hammers down and turned to see who was coming to our house. The only man we knew in Greene County was Jase; and he was here already.

"I'll bet it's the preacher," I whispered to Jamie.

Preachers were the only people I ever saw in black suits, with hats set square across their heads. If Dad had to wear a hat, he'd tilt it a little over one eye. "Like a roving gambler," Mom said.

Jase said, real low, to Dad, "That's George Brent. On his way home from church. Wife drags him there every Sunday."

Then he raised his voice and called heartily, "Howdy, George."

The man stopped, then came on, more sure of himself

after seeing Jase. "Morning, Jase. Nasty weather." He turned to Dad and said, "I'm your neighbor from down the road there a-piece. Bud Watson over at the McVille general store told me he had sold this place, but I didn't expect to see the new owners moving in so soon."

Dad shook his hand, then drew his pipe and tobacco from the bib pocket of his overalls. He cupped his hands around the pipe and tamped the tobacco down with his thumb. Then he bent away from the weather to shield a match and light it. The pipe went out, but he sucked on it anyhow and fiddled with it while he talked.

"I couldn't see no reason to wait till winter was upon us to make the change. Wanted to be settled in before it turned off cold, but there's a lot to be done around here."

George said, "I see you didn't waste any time getting started on it."

"This well had to be taken care of, first thing," Dad replied. "Bad as I hate to be working on the Sabbath, it had to be done."

I thought to myself, Dad didn't have much choice in the matter. It was either displease the Lord or please Mom. And he had to live with Mom.

George had a friendly face, what we could see of it. The hat seemed to rest on his bushy black eyebrows. It shaded his eyes, and a thick black mustache drooped across his upper lip and hid his mouth. It was hard to tell if he was smiling, but he had laughter in his voice.

"Hello there, little one," he said to me. "Who is that big-eyed girl hiding behind you?"

Jamie slipped his hand in mine and tugged lightly. I held his hand and stood firm.

18

"This is Jamie," I said. "He's a brother."

Dad said, "I thought I told you kids to get in the house, out of this rain."

He didn't say it like he was angry with us for not minding him the first time, just reminding us we had no business there and should play somewhere else.

The car horn sounded in two long blasts, then a short beep-beep. George turned and waved in the general direction of the noise and called, "I'm coming, dear. I'm coming."

Then he turned his back to the road and said to Dad, "That's my wife, Clara. Good woman, but curious as a coon and impatient as a baby. Can't abide waiting."

The horn blared again, and George said, "Well, we just stopped by to see if there was anything we could do to help you folks get settled. If you need anything, give us a holler, or send one of these big-eyed young'uns down to the house to fetch us."

Dad was smiling, pleased by the offer of help from a neighbor in this strange county.

There's no doubt about Dad's smiles. They cover his whole face. His lips turn up at the corners, and deep lines crease his cheeks. Wrinkles fan out from his eyes and pucker the skin between his sandy eyebrows and high cheekbones, drawing his eyes half shut. Even his hump-backed Roman nose loses its sternness. I noticed Dad's smile was catching. Jase and George were smiling, too.

Jamie tugged at me again, urgently this time. I copied the man's voice and said, "All right, Jamie. I'm coming! I'm coming!"

The cold drizzle had changed to a steady rain by now that hit us hard when we stepped from the shelter of the covered well. We made a dash for the kitchen door.

Not much later, Dad and Jase came in soaked to the skin. Jase said to Mom that he guessed she had the only roofed wishing well in Greene County. His guess was close to the truth. Mom wished it was in the kitchen, and Dad said he wished he'd never heard of the damn thing.

It rained all Sunday night and was still sprinkling on Monday morning when we left for school. We had to be flat on our back sick and the house quarantined before we ever missed a day. I never knew for sure if they wanted us to have an education or just couldn't stand having us around underfoot.

That first day in school sticks in my mind like the red clay mud that clung to my shoes that morning and sucked them off my feet with every step I took. While I struggled to get my feet and shoes back together and take another step, I lost my balance and fell. I threw my hands out to break my fall, and both hands slapped into the clay mud up to my elbows.

Jamie, who had walked on ahead, came back and pulled me out of the mud and on to the road bank. The rain dripping from the tall weeds mixed with the tears that were running down my face.

Jamie said I looked like a mud crybaby. I laughed, then cried again when I saw the mud caked on my hands and feet and coat sleeves. He took off his cap and wiped my face and hands, then he stuck it on my head and pulled the flaps down over my ears.

"Don't cry because you got all muddy, Seely. All the other kids will be muddy, too." He smiled and added, "Unless they can fly!"

He took my hand to steady me along the slick road and held it all the way to school.

The schoolhouse was a one-room frame building that had been painted white, but the paint had cracked and washed away, leaving it a dirty, faded gray. A pencil could be dropped through the wide cracks in the board floor, and the cold wind whistled up through the openings, chilling our feet and legs. Even when I stood next to the red-hot stove in the middle of the room, my feet and legs didn't get warm.

I didn't like this school, and I didn't want to stay here with all these skinny, scrawny kids. Maybe after a while, I would shrivel up and shrink to their size, and then my eyes would be the biggest part of me, too. I cornered Jamie and whispered, "Let's go home. I don't like it here."

He shook his head, then stepped far enough away so that my whispers wouldn't reach him.

That first day, I sat at a desk in the very last row. Mr. Thompson, the teacher, said I should sit there until he could put me in my place. I thought, "That settles it." He would never be able to place me here, so he would have to send me home.

But I wouldn't leave without Jamie, I'd get him, then we would go right down that mud road, straight home. I would leave this school where no one spoke or smiled at me.

There was one tall, bony girl with dark hair hanging

straight to her shoulders from a middle part and held back from her face with a scrap of flowered gingham. She had a split place in her upper lip that looked as if it had been sewed together by a six-year-old child and had puckered.

She smiled crookedly as she moved about the room helping the little kids out of their coats and fastening or pinning their clothes together to hide their nakedness. When she spoke to them, her words slurred together, and I couldn't understand what she said. But her soft brown eyes were pretty, and I thought she looked kindly at me as she walked by.

I liked her at once. But when I smiled at her, she lowered her eyes and turned away. I didn't know what to do. Out of the two dozen or more kids in the school room, she was the only girl anyways near my size.

At midmorning, we had a twenty-minute recess. Children stood around in bunches like cows in a hailstorm, looking at Jamie and me as if they expected us to disappear into thin air. And I would have if I had known how.

Once my eyes met those of a tall boy with mussed-up red hair and clothes that looked as if he'd slept in them. I stared right back at him, daring him to speak, to say anything at all. A fight would have been better than this quiet, staring stand-off.

After recess, the teacher assigned a desk to me. "Ah, you girl," he said. "Take the seat behind Clarence," pointing to the gawky redhead who had stared so steadily at me earlier.

I couldn't see over Clarence's head, so I stared at the

back of it. "If he lived at our house, his hair wouldn't be allowed to grow that long," I thought. "Dad would cut it, if he had to take the sheepshears to do it."

When Clarence moved his head, a little gray bug scurried to the tip of his hair, fell to his shoulder and burrowed underneath his wrinkled shirt collar. His tousled hair seemed to be alive and crawling with the little bugs. I forgot the open book on my desk as I watched them and waited for each one to complete the journey from his scalp to his shirt collar.

Clarence fidgeted and scratched his head. Then he turned around in his seat and caught me staring at him.

Mom had told us and told us about staring at people.

"In the first place," she said, "it's rude. And if you stare long enough, they will turn and catch you at it."

I kept my eyes on my desk after that and pretended to read. I swore that Clarence would never again catch me looking at him; not even if he taught his bugs how to do tricks.

At last school was over. Jamie and I walked with the little Perry girls as far as their house. Dicie showed us a path, a shortcut through the woods, and gave us chocolate-covered cupcakes to eat on the way home.

"You kids stay on the path and you'll come to a foot-log across Lick Crick. Climb the bank on the other side, and you'll come out of the woods behind your barn."

We started walking slowly down the faint path through the sedge brush to the woods. Dicie called after us, "Don't poke along or stop to play, now, or the dark will catch you in the woods, for sure."

I hurried along and Jamie ran to keep up with me. At

the edge of the woods, I hesitated. The ground ahead of us was covered with leaves, and the path we were supposed to follow was hidden somewhere underneath them. Jamie stopped beside me and just stood there looking at the trees that grew tall and thick all around us.

The pale sun, which had been shining down through a hole in the clouds, slipped behind a heavier cloud and brought the dark a little closer to us.

We put off going into the woods until Jamie said, "Look, Seely. Not at the ground, but away up ahead. See how the trees part and make a road through there?"

I looked to where his hand was pointing. He was right. Up close, the ground all seemed the same, but at a distance, I could tell where the path passed through the trees.

It was twilight under the trees, and the deeper we went into the woods, the darker it got to be. The wind whistled and whined amongst the top branches. We crossed the ridge and took another bearing on our path. We were about midway down when I stepped on a patch of wet, slick leaves. My feet flew out from under me, and I slid down the muddy hill on my rump and elbows, my hands flailing thin air as they grabbed for a root or a young sapling to break my fall. Now that I needed one, the trees stood far apart and back from the path.

A rotten log lying across the way stopped my sliding, and Jamie slammed into me from behind. He grabbed me around the waist and hung on for dear life. I loosened his hands to get up. Then I saw he was crying.

"For heaven's sake, Jamie, what are you crying about? I slid down the same hill and I'm not crying."

He wiped at his tears with his sleeve and said, "I know you did. But you didn't come down as fast as I did."

Our slide downhill had taken us off the path and brought us to the top of a huge rock that jutted from the hillside. Patches of gray moss the size of a dishpan spotted it, and greenbriars grew in a tangled mass along one whole side.

From there, we could see a creek running between clay banks at the foot of the hill and a log wedged in place over the water for fording it.

"There's the footlog, Jamie. We're almost home."

We squatted on our heels and inched our way down the sloping side, away from the greenbriars, and jumped from the edge of the rock to the ground.

The face of the overhanging rock was nearly hidden by vine-covered trees and broken branches that lay snagged at a slant on the side of the hill. To dodge the dangling brown vines, we stepped close to the rock—and walked into a large dry space under the overhang.

I forgot Dicie's warning to hurry when I saw a cave going back into the ground. Jamie refused to go through the wide opening to the cave with me. He said it might fall in on us, even though there were layers of flat rocks packed into the dirt on either side of the cave opening, so it couldn't possibly fall. I started to go into the cave, but he grabbed my arm.

"Let's go, Seely. We'll come back some other time and bring a light with us."

"I'll bet the Indians hid in this cave, sometimes, when they used to live in these woods," I said.

Jamie moved away from me, toward the woods. "Let's

go home, Seely. For all we know, Indians may still live here."

I left the cave, and we struck off downhill in the direction of the creek. It was further away than it had looked from up there. I held onto the trees and Jamie hung onto me, as we slipped and skidded down the hill.

At the creek, we stopped and cleaned the mud and leaves off each other as best we could. Mom would probably raise Cain anyway about our muddy clothes and say we must have rolled in every mudhole we came to, to get so dirty.

Jamie crossed the footlog on his hands and knees. I looked back at the big rock to place it firmly in my mind, then dropped to my knees, and followed him across the creek.

Tree roots made steps for us to hang onto as we climbed the slick river bank on the other side. We were puffing and out of breath when we ran from the cluster of trees into a clearing and saw our barn just a little way ahead.

For just a moment before disappearing behind the hills, the sun came out of the clouds and showed its face above the tree tops.

Jamie smiled happily at me. "We're home, and the dark didn't catch us. Seely, we've outrun the dark."

chapter three

*E*very week, Mr. Thompson picked two pupils to carry the water from Old Man Bishop's well into the school. He chose me and Frieda Walters to carry water my first week there. Frieda was the girl with the harelip.

The Bishop house was empty, Frieda told me on our first day. Old Man Bishop had been dead and buried a long time, but the people down here still called it his place and his well.

"In the fall of the year," she added, "pears ripen and rot on the trees in his backyard because the kids aren't allowed to pick his pears."

"But they drink his water," I said.

"That's different," Frieda said, and didn't say anything more until we were on our way back to school with the water.

Then she shifted the bucket to her other hand and whispered, as if sharing a secret, "I don't really have to go to school. When you're sixteen, like me, you can quit any time you want to."

I was surprised she was that old, because Frieda was in the sixth grade with me. She told me that before Mr. Thompson came, the teachers didn't want to be bothered with her, because of her lisp. She finally just sat in whichever grade she had books for.

"It's mostly the slow learners who don't finish school before they're sixteen," she added.

I prayed a silent prayer that I wouldn't be a slow learner and still be in the sixth grade when I was sixteen.

Frieda hardly ever spoke in class because of her harelip, but on our way to and from Old Man Bishop's place that week she chattered like a blue jay. Friday morning, though, she seemed to be worried about something. She didn't say anything. We were crossing the playground on our way back from the well, when she asked, "Seely, do you like to carry water with me?"

I said, "Sure. Why wouldn't I? I like you. Besides, I get out of doing school work for a while each day."

She brightened up right away. Her dark eyes were shining and she looked pretty. "Let's ask the teacher if you and me can carry water all the time. We'll have to carry it when it's cold and snowing and wade through mud when it rains, but we'll get out of school work." Mr. Thompson looked surprised when we suggested it, but he agreed.

One morning as we were banging and clanging the

water buckets to Old Man Bishop's, she said, "My brother Teddy likes you. He thinks you're a cute little blond girl."

I didn't know which one was Teddy, but he must be the stupidest boy in school, I figured. Probably ugly, too, with big feet and overalls that struck him halfway to his knees, like all the other boys; and a dirty shirttail flapping out. To please Frieda, I listened when Mr. Thompson called classes up front to recite and looked at all the boys as they walked by to see which one was Teddy.

He was in the fourth grade. That was the largest class in school and took up two full rows when they recited their lessons. Everyone could get through the first three grades, but they seemed to bog down in the fourth and stay there. Each year the class grew, Frieda said, and no one seemed to mind the least bit. Some of the kids were going through for the third or fourth time.

Teddy was one of the slow learners. He was thirteen years old, and Frieda said he'd probably never get beyond fourth grade.

He was a shy, slightly built boy with dark curls that fell over his forehead, nearly hiding his solemn brown eyes. Teddy seldom smiled, but when he did, his face and eyes lit up like a freshly trimmed coal-oil lamp.

I was a homely, rough-and-tumble, towheaded tomboy, but he chose me for his best girl, anyway. After he gave me his two agate taws during the noon marble game and said I could keep them forever, the whole school knew I was his girl.

During recess, if we played hide-and-seek, Teddy let

me get home free. If I was put on the end of crack-the-whip, he ran to catch my hand and drag his feet so we wouldn't go sprawling in the dirt and dust of the playground.

For my birthday, he gave me a pen and pencil set. The pen didn't work and the pencil had been mashed on the end until lead wouldn't fit in it, but I flaunted the pen and pencil in front of the kids at school as if they were pure gold with a lifetime guarantee. But I swore Jamie to secrecy, and I never mentioned Teddy or his gift to anyone at home.

Winter came early in December and stayed. The first snow lay on the ground like a dirty white blanket and waited for fresh snow to fall and cover it. Then a blizzard, bringing more snow, froze over everything. We had to break ice on the water buckets in the kitchen to wash our face and hands before breakfast each morning.

That was a time when the fires never went out in the kitchen cook stove or the Hot Blast Florence heater in the middle of the living room floor. Dad got up in the middle of the night to lay chunks of wood on the fires to keep them going until morning.

One bitter cold day, while we were in school, Dad and Jase Perry butchered the hogs and our two pet lambs. I cried over my lamb, but Mom said it had to be done. There wasn't enough feed for them and the cow. And we needed the cow for milk.

George Brent, the farmer who lived around the bend on the gravel road, brought his tackle chain and pulley and helped with the butchering. Dad and Jase shared the meat and gave Mr. Brent pork tenderloin and lamb chops for his help and the use of his tackle.

Later on, Dad went to the Brents' and helped George cut and cord wood. George gave Dad money for it, but I think Dad would've rather had a cord of wood. He said that big heating stove ate wood faster than he could cut it by himself.

The attic room never got warm. Dad didn't believe in wasting heat or using up stove wood to heat a bedroom. When Mom called us to get up for school, we'd grab our clothes in our arms and race downstairs to crowd around the roaring red-hot stove to get dressed. The heat didn't spread far from the stove, so we had to stand close to get any benefit from the fire.

I was always the first one down the steps to find a spot next to the stove to put on my clothes.

One morning, I was standing too near the stove when I bent over to pull on my underwear. I yelled, leaped away like a scalded cat, and fell over Robert, who was sitting on the floor with his blanket around him. He began bawling and squalling, making more noise than I was.

Mom yelled, "My God, the baby!" and came running in from the kitchen to grab him up in her arms.

I was screaming, "Christ! I'm on fire! I've burned my butt off."

Mom slapped me across the mouth with the back of her hand. "You shut up and hush that talk, right now! Can't you see you're scaring the baby half to death? Get some clothes on and cover yourself. You're too big to be running around the house naked, showing everything you've got."

Julie grabbed a handful of lard out of the big can in the kitchen and rubbed it over the blisters. "Now it won't burn so bad and probably won't even scar." She giggled and patted on more lard. "Oh, Seely, it's a shame you ain't wider across the rear end. If you were, you'd have 'Hot Blast Air-Tight Florence' tattooed for life on your fanny."

The blistered bottom gave me a good excuse to lean forward at my desk that day and watch Clarence play with his little gray bugs, though. I tried not to look directly at him. It seemed to me that he had always sat in front of me. Any time I raised my eyes, I could see his thick red hair curling down over his dirty shirt collar. I don't think he ever washed his hair or took a bath. I know he never studied his lessons during study period, either.

He would sit at his desk and open his notebook; then he would lean way over and shake his hair to make the bugs fall out onto the paper. He kept a sharp lead pencil handy to jab and poke at them. If the teacher came down our aisle, Clarence would slam the book shut and mash all the bugs inside.

I don't know why, but that very evening, Clarence followed us home from school. No one asked him to, he just walked along behind us. When we opened the back door at home, he walked in and sat down.

Mom didn't know him. I suppose she thought we had finally found one friend in school and had brought him home with us. She added another potato and onion to the soup and set another plate on the table. Next to my place.

We each had our own place at the table, and we sat there for every meal. If one of us was absent, the chair was pushed up to the table. Tonight, Clarence had my chair and the kitchen step stool was in my place.

Mom had baked cornbread in a big round iron skillet, and a raspberry cobbler was cooling on the sideboard by the stove. Mom canned hundreds of quarts of berries in the summer, and we ate them one way or another all winter. Dad was partial to raspberry cobbler, and Mom usually made it as a special treat for him. I guess she figured if he had got a job that day it would be a celebration, and if he hadn't, it could be a consolation to him.

Clarence took a case knife from the table and measured the cuts of cobbler. Then he stuck his finger in the largest slice so no one else would eat it. He licked his finger and smacked his lips with pleasure afterwards.

Dad hadn't come home yet, but when supper was ready, Mom said, "You kids wash your hands and don't forget to use the soap. That's what we have it for."

Clarence splashed and sloshed the water in the wash basin and came to the table with his red curly hair slick as clay mud and his round freckled face shining in the lamp light.

Mom treated him like company and expected me to. She said, "Seely, talk to Clarence. You haven't said a word since you sat down at the table."

I said, "Hi, Clarence." As if I hadn't sat behind him

all day and walked home with him following along behind me.

He kept on chewing and didn't answer me.

"Stupid!" Julie said to me in a whisper.

Clarence stopped chewing, with his spoon halfway to
his mouth and said, "Huh?"

I started giggling and Jamie caught the giggles from
me; soon the whole table was in an uproar, with Clarence
laughing as loud as the rest of us.

We wouldn't have dared to carry on that way if Dad
had been home. He would have made quick work of
clearing the lot of us from the table.

"You kids straighten up this minute," Mom finally
said. "Do you want Clarence to think you act this way
all the time?"

Clarence said, "No, ma'am," and slurped his soup.

I covered my face with my hands to hide my laughter,
and my stool tipped over backward, knocking my bowl
off the table as I fell.

Mom said, "Seely, go to the attic!"

I went.

Jamie came up after supper and said he would have
brought me some cobbler, but there wasn't any left.
Clarence had eaten two pieces, and Mom had offered him
more. Then after Clarence had cleaned his plate, he
handed it to Mom and said, "I dry the dishes at home.
Dad says I can't wash them to suit him, and I don't have
a mother to do it. If you like, I can dry your dishes for
my supper."

Jamie said Clarence was stuttering and red as a beet,
but his offer must have pleased Mom. She took to him

right off the bat. She let him dry dishes for her and asked him to come back again when he left.

When I fell asleep, I was still trying to figure out ways to keep him from ever coming back to our house.

But the next night when I got home from school, there was Clarence in the kitchen dropping Mom's homemade noodles into a pot of boiling blackberries. I stood watching until the last noodle fell in the pot. Then Clarence excused himself and went outdoors.

I said, "Yuk . . . I'm not going to eat any dessert tonight. Not after that dirty old Clarence handled all the noodles."

Mom didn't turn from stirring the berries. "Many's the time I've had to send you away from the table with dirty hands."

"But he's different. All the kids laugh and make fun of him. Even the teacher says Clarence is a shame to the school."

"I don't ever want to hear tell of one of you kids making fun of someone because they're different. That day, I'll take a strap to you. Clarence never had a ma to care for him or see that he was raised properly. He's been shifted from pillar to post ever since he was a baby, living first with one relative and then another all his life, and not one of them wanting him. That would tend to make a body different."

"But does he have to come here ?. . ."

"Hush, he's coming in. Just keep quiet and eat your supper like everyone else."

I didn't tell Mom about the bugs Clarence grew in his hair. She would've taken lye soap and sulfur to all of us,

Clarence included, if she'd known. Mom couldn't bear to have any kind of bugs or a spider on the place.

I thought he had probably drowned them when he washed and slicked his hair down with water. But the next day at school, his hair had dried out and the bugs came alive and scurried across his notebook like tiny caged mice.

My hair had grown almost as long as Clarence's, so on Saturday Dad lined the boys and me up on a bench in the far end of the kitchen and started cutting our hair.

He cut mine last. He had barely begun cutting on one side when he commenced cussing. Dad usually cussed and roared when he had to cut my hair. He said it was like corn silk. It wouldn't lay down or stay in one place when he combed it or turn loose of the comb so he could clip it. But this time it was a different kind of swearing.

"Good diddlely damn, Zel. This kid is as lousy as a pet coon."

The other kids came running in to look.

"Damn it, you young'uns get in the other room. Can't have the whole bunch of you getting them. Wouldn't you know," he said to Mom, "if there was one louse in the county, this kid would find it and bring it home?"

Dad doused my head with coal oil, sulfur, and bacon grease, and Mom tied a hot towel around my head and pinned it so it wouldn't come loose. I figured that greasy mess was just feeding the little beasts, but I didn't care. Let them eat and grow fat!

I told Jamie, who was staring open-mouthed at me, "Now all my hair will probably fall out by the roots, and I'll be as slick bald-headed as old Bud Watson. I hope it does! Then I won't have to get my hair cut by that . . . that big baboon ever again."

Jamie turned and ran toward the other room. "Tattle-tale," I thought. "Go ahead and tell!" That wasn't any worse than some of the things Mom called Dad when she didn't like him. And today, I didn't like him.

Mom went up to Dicie Perry's to borrow a fine-tooth comb and was gone all afternoon. Dad said she could have made a comb in the time it took her to borrow one. When she got back, Julie held the lamp close, and Mom went over my head, hair by hair. When each strand was free and clear of bugs, Mom made us cross our hearts and raise our right hands and swear we wouldn't mention lice at school.

She said, "Dicie and me took care of the other buggy head in school, so we won't have to worry about you bringing more of them home."

She lifted a stove lid and threw the towels that had been around my head into the fire. "Everyone else's kids can carry lice, but I'll not have it said that one of mine ever did."

Monday morning, when I took my seat at school, Clarence was all ready seated at his desk. His hair was cut to a stubble, and his clean, pink scalp shone through where the scissors had taken big bites out of his hair. He turned and smiled at me as if we had something in common, and I noticed his plaid shirt had been washed and ironed for the first time.

chapter four

Jase Perry had said, when he moved us down to Greene County, that Dad could go to work cutting mine props and railroad ties for the mines like he did. But after Dad got there, he was told they were laying off men, not hiring them.

Dad cut wood for George Brent until he filled the woodshed, but other than that, Dad didn't go to work at all. It wasn't because he didn't look for it. He tried every rumor of work and went on from there. At the breakfast table he would say to Mom, "Zel, you'd better pack a clean shirt and a few things for me. It may be a spell before I get back."

Dad had been gone for nearly a week this time. Mom said she didn't expect him before Christmas, but every time she passed by the window, she pulled the lace curtain to one side and looked down the road toward town.

I guess Dad's being out of work was the reason the Women's Circle from the Flat Hollow Methodist Church brought the bushel basket of food stuff to our house on Christmas Eve. I don't know how they decide who needs a basket on Christmas, but however they figured it, Mom figured differently.

We had been trimming the Christmas tree when they came to our front door. Mom had said, right up to the last day, we couldn't have a tree. "There won't be a stitch of anything, no gifts of any kind to put under one this year," she said. "It's nonsense to have a bare tree and nothing to put under it."

But she changed her mind and gave in to us when she saw all the colored paper chains we had made and the angels we had cut from magazines and old greeting cards to hang on it. She even popped corn and threaded it on a long string, while Julie and Floyd Perry took a handsaw and went to the ridge to find a good cedar tree.

Cedar trees were about the only thing that would grow on the red clay knobs that rose out of the hills, jutting up between the oak and beech trees like a scab on the hillside. The cedars were scrubby, lopsided little trees with sharp spines and spurs that nipped and stung like a bee when we touched them. Everyone hated the cedars until Christmas; then they cut them and carried them home to set in a place of honor until the middle of January.

The Perrys had cut one for their Christmas tree, and Floyd said he knew right where to find another good one for us. But it took him and Julie a long time to find it. It was nearly dark before they came dragging it through the barnyard to the house.

Floyd nailed two flat boards crossways on the bottom of the tree and stood it in the corner of the front room. It wobbled back and forth and fell over. He stuck chips from the woodbox under the boards to level it, and laid big rocks on top of it all to keep the tree from tilting to one side.

Mom brought out an old white shirt of Dad's and spread it under the tree. She said it covered the rocks and boards and gave a natural look of snow for Christmas. We laughed when she buttoned the collar around the base of the tree and tucked the sleeves under the edges.

Mom lit two lamps and set one at each side of the tree, so we could see to trim it. We only decorated the front side where it showed. Mom was helping and seemed to be enjoying it as much as we were when someone knocked at the front door.

She handed Julie the string of popcorn and turned to open it. We should have barred the door or refused to answer, because Mom's Christmas spirit fled through the open door and away into the night.

Mom took the offered basket and held it in both hands, blocking the doorway. The women whispered a few words to her, and she thanked them as if they were all deaf. As soon as the door was slammed shut behind them, Mom flung the basket across the room and burst out crying.

"I'm not going to be treated like one of their shiftless,

no-good, hillbilly tribes. They don't need to think for one minute just because Rob ain't working regular, I can't manage. We'd have plenty right now if the root cellar hadn't frozen up solid and ruined the whole lot."

She wiped at her wet face with her apron tail and bent to gather up the scattered groceries. Jamie picked up six oranges that had rolled across the room and held them out to her. She looked at them as if she didn't know what they were. Then she said, "You kids eat them. And give one to Floyd."

Jamie passed the oranges around and put the one that was left over under the Christmas tree.

"Maybe Jase and Dicie would come down and eat dinner with us, tomorrow," she said more quietly. "Lord knows, there's enough here for both families. They might as well help us eat it."

She sent word home with Floyd that she was expecting them all to come to dinner next day.

As soon as Floyd left the house, Mom sent the boys upstairs to bed. She told Julie and me to rid up the front room before we went to bed, while she put the charity stuff out of her sight and got rid of the basket. "If I have to look at that tomorrow," she said, "I won't be able to eat a bite."

We gave the room a lick and a promise and then watched Mom as she moved between the basket on the table and the kitchen cabinet. She had loaded her arms with cans and boxes and turned toward the cabinet when Dad opened the kitchen door and stepped into the light.

He must have walked all the way from town. He

41

moved slowly like he could hardly put one foot in front of the other. He lifted the wooden box he was carrying on his shoulder, set it on the floor next to the woodbox, and heaved a great sigh of relief when he straightened.

He put his hands on the church charity basket. "What's all this?" he asked Mom.

"A poor box—" Her voice rose and broke.

I thought she was going to start crying again. She closed the cabinet door and started over, her voice flat and steady.

"The women from the church left it here earlier this evening. Floyd was here, so I told him to tell his folks to come for dinner tomorrow. Maybe I'll feel better about using it if I share it with Dicie."

"No reason for you to feel that way, Zel," Dad said. "It was given in good faith. We'll use it with that thought in mind, and share it if that's what you want."

"But Rob, it's for the poor!"

"I know." He moved nearer to her, but he didn't touch her. "I bought a crate of winesaps for the kids' Christmas. It was the only thing I could find for the money I had."

"Set them under the tree," Mom said. "We'll all enjoy them."

I didn't know we were poor. I knew we didn't have any money—Dad said so often enough—but we had food to eat and warm coats and shoes to wear. I thought the kids I went to school with were poor because they didn't have these things.

Julie and I each took one of the small, deep red apples

and went upstairs. They were hard and tangy and cracked like ice on a tree limb when we bit into them. The deep red of the skin faded and ran all the way to the core.

The next day, Dicie brought a fruit jar full of her homemade wine and two quarts of canned peaches to add to the meal Mom had fixed.

The little girls brought tin whistles that Jase had picked up some place to give them. The only time the whistles were out of their mouths was while they were eating.

To add to the racket, Floyd gave Jamie an old harmonica he had. Jamie breathed in and out, on the same keys—e-e-e-o-o-o, e-e-e-o-o-o— all day long.

Mom and Dicie talked quietly while they set the hot dishes on the table. Jase sat brooding with his feet propped on the apron of the heating stove and drank wine. Dad tried to talk to him, but Jase didn't seem to want to talk. He'd answer Dad, then go back to his brooding. Julie and Floyd held hands and walked close together in the yard. I seemed to be the only one who heard the shrill whistles and off-key whine of the harmonica as the kids raced through the house and jumped up and down the steps leading to the attic door.

Grownups must have an unspoken agreement that if your company's kids misbehave you'll yell at your own. I didn't think Mom or Dicie were paying any attention to the kids, but every time one of the Perry girls screamed, Mom hollered at me.

The Perrys went home as soon as they had finished

eating. The stillness they left behind seemed to press on my eardrums. Jamie sat on the attic steps, with his back resting against the door, and played his harmonica. But the sounds he made were soft and faint, almost like music. Dad sat quietly with Robert on his knees and smoked, while Mom and us girls cleaned up the kitchen. He seemed almost content. Not a bit the way he usually was since he'd been out of a steady job. I'd heard Mom tell Dicie that living with Dad lately was like sitting on a powder keg with a lit fuse; you never knew when he would blow up.

Mom was right about him blowing up. Dad would yell at us kids about things he didn't used to pay any attention to. No matter where we were or what we were doing, we were always in his way. He'd tell us to go to bed, then slam the attic door behind us. He'd blow up just at the sight of that attic door swinging open.

We'd hear Dad pacing from the kitchen to the front room for a while, then he'd slam the kitchen door behind him and walk hurriedly off toward the woods. Sometimes, he'd walk in the woods until after dark, or else he'd go to the Perrys' and talk to Jase and come home when we were asleep.

Jase had been laid off cutting timber nearly a month before Christmas, but he didn't go out looking for work, like Dad. He just lay around home or came over to our house. Jase was at our house a lot that winter. If he didn't come by for the long-green smoking tobacco, left hanging in the barn by the last people who had lived here, Dad would take the short cut and carry some to him. Dad's pipe tobacco came out of a cotton pouch with a drawstring top. He said long-green was too strong for him. It bit his tongue.

Dad and Jase went rabbit hunting if they had shells for the shotguns, or sat around drinking the homemade wine Dicie worked up during the summer, if they didn't. We could always tell which it had been. If Dad was asleep when we got home from school, they'd been in Dicie's wine; but if we had rabbit for supper, they had been hunting.

At the start of the second semester, Frieda and I recited lessons with the seventh grade, and Jamie was moved to the fourth, on condition. Teddy stayed where he was. He said he didn't mind. He liked the fourth grade. If the teacher had moved him to another class, he wouldn't have known anything.

Teddy knew his reader by heart and could do all the problems from the fourth-grade arithmetic book in his head. When we had ciphering matches on Friday afternoon, if Mr. Thompson stayed with adding and subtracting, Teddy could give the answers while the other kids were still writing the figures on the blackboard. Then he'd smile shyly at me from the front of the room.

Sometime during February, I had scarlet fever and we were quarantined at home. No one else caught it, but I had a red, blotchy rash and itched all over. After the rash and the redness went away, the skin peeled and flaked off my hands and feet like a snake shedding its winter skin in warm weather.

We worried about missing school for so long. Jamie fumed and fussed the most. Now that he was in the fourth grade, he was afraid he'd never get out. He said, "That grade is a jinx to the kids. If I don't pass this year, I'll still be there when I start to grow whiskers."

Eventually, the quarantine was lifted and we went back to school. Half the seats in the room were empty. It seemed a lot of the kids had caught the fever. Teddy's seat was among the empty ones, his books and papers were gone from his desk.

I waited until we were on our way to fill the water buckets. Then I asked Frieda where he was. She said Teddy had taken sick with the fever and died. He hadn't once complained of feeling bad. No one had even known he was sick.

"One morning Mama went to wake him for school and there he was, dead as a doorknob. I guess the Lord knew Teddy would never get past the fourth grade, so He took him out of school for good." Frieda's voice was flat and toneless as if death was not strange or unusual to her.

I had never known anyone who died. The nearest death had ever come to me had been when Dad butchered my pet lamb. I had cried then, and Dad said if I didn't hush my bawling he'd give me something to cry about.

I missed Teddy, but I didn't cry for him. It wasn't the same thing, at all.

Mr. Thompson moved another boy into Teddy's seat to fill out the row. Before long, it was as if Teddy had never been there. Nobody said his name. Only in my mind, he ran after me at recess and smiled shyly across the room during school hours.

chapter five

We'd gotten into the habit of stopping by the Perry house on the way to school to pick up the girls. One morning Dicie said we needn't bother for a spell. She didn't have anything fit to put in their dinner buckets, so she wasn't sending them to school.

I thought everyone had peanut butter and oleo they could put on biscuits or homemade bread, like Mom did for us. We nearly choked to death on it, but we had something in the lunch pail. Sometimes, when I couldn't swallow another bite, I'd feed a peanut-buttered biscuit to the old three-legged dog that hung around the schoolhouse begging food from the kids, just to see him try to get the peanut butter off the roof of his mouth. He seemed to know that all I had was peanut butter, and he didn't come near me. He didn't like it any better than I did.

Before long Jase and Dicie sent Floyd and the girls to live at their grandmother's in Sullivan County. Dicie said the girls could go to school there, until Jase went back to work. Floyd said he was going to quit school and sign up for the CCC as soon as he was seventeen and send the money home to help his folks.

We had heard President Roosevelt make a speech over our battery radio about the CCC just a few nights ago. I guess Floyd had heard the same fireside chat. The President said he had formed the Civilian Conservation Corps to take the jobless boys off the streets and highways, put spending money in their pockets, and supplement their families' incomes. Meanwhile, these boys would be building the roads and bridges our country so desperately needed and protecting our national parks.

Dad had said he thought it was a good thing the President had done. The three C's taught the boys discipline and kept them out of trouble. "A lot of folks would be starving right now," he said, "if they didn't have a boy sending money home from camp every month for them to live on."

But still he tried to talk Floyd out of quitting school and joining the three C's. If a man was ever going to amount to anything, he had to have an education, Dad said. Money wasn't everything.

"When you ain't got it, it is," was Floyd's answer.

With Floyd and the girls away, Jase did more drinking than hunting. Jamie and I quit using the shortcut by their house. Every time we went by, Jase was staggering around in the yard trying to get his bearings or asleep and snoring on the cot on their screened-in porch. We never saw Dicie.

One night after Dad had been drinking wine all day with Jase, we heard a shotgun blast that echoed all through the hills before settling in the hollows. Dad jumped up and said, "That sounded like it came from Jase Perry's. I'd better get up there and see what has happened."

He grabbed his sheepskin coat from a hook by the back door and pulled his cap low over his eyes. "I'll be back as soon as I can," he told Mom. "No need to wait up for me."

Mom made us go to bed early, but I lay there for hours. The sound of low hushed voices woke me. It was dark outside, but Mom hadn't closed the attic door and a path of light came up the steps. Dad was saying, ". . . had wedged the double-barreled shotgun under his chin and used his bare big toe to pull the trigger. He blew his brains all over the bedroom wall where him and Dicie slept."

Mom murmured something I couldn't hear, and Dad said, "They took her away, too."

I heard him strike a match, and a few moments later I could smell the pipe smoke as it wafted up the stairs.

"She broke down, completely out of her head. When the sheriff and me got back to the house, Dicie was sitting flat on the floor beside Jase, humming and singing, them long black braids of hers swinging back and forth

49

as she kept time to the tune. Crooning to him, as if she was lulling a weary child to sleep."

"What's to become of those poor kids?" Mom asked.

"They'll be all right where they are. Their aunt and granny will see to their needs."

I heard him knock the doddle out of his pipe. "Better be sure our kids go by the road to school today. It'll be a spell before they finish up at the house."

The lights went out. I heard the long sigh of the bed springs and went back to sleep.

I felt like I had just closed my eyes when Mom called us to get ready for school. In the rush and confusion of getting dressed and in to breakfast, no one asked what had happened the night before.

I told Jamie on the way to school. "The reason Mom made sure we went around the road to school this morning is that Jase Perry blowed his head off last night with a shotgun."

He said, "I don't believe it. Seely, if you don't stop making up stories like that, no one is ever going to believe a word you say. People will say you're just a liar!"

"I am not lying! He did so, and there was blood and brains all over the place."

Jamie looked kind of greenish, like he was about to throw up. "I'm not going to walk with you today. You're . . . you're making me sick." He ran ahead and left me to walk the rest of the way alone.

I didn't really believe Jase had killed himself, either. I suspected if Jamie and I cut through the woods on our way home, we'd see Jase stumbling off toward the outhouse with his shoe strings untied and overall galluses hanging down around his hips, the same as usual.

Maybe I'd just dreamed I heard Dad and Mom talking last night, and Jase and Dicie would still be at their house if we stopped by.

But what if they weren't there? That was a chance I couldn't take, not with Jamie—and certainly not alone.

Eventually, the talk died down about Jase and Dicie. The men blamed it all on the Depression. They talked a lot about the Depression. They blamed the President and every man who had money when they didn't.

All I knew about the Depression was what I read in the dictionary. There were six definitions of depression, so I picked the second and last ones because they seemed to fit the way things were in Greene County, Indiana. "The state of being depressed," and "A period during which there is a decline in business."

In early April, Dad put out a truck garden patch, all in beans, back of the barn. He said, "If this Depression lasts much longer, we'll be eating beans three times a day."

School was out and the beans had started sprouting green leaves the size of a squirrel's ear above the red clay ground when Dad came home one evening and told Mom he'd heard tell that the government was starting up a factory at Crowe. Every man who showed up there ready for work had a job. "It may mean moving again," he said, "but I'm going to be the first man in the line to get a job."

"Seems a shame, don't it, Rob?" Mom said. "Jase Perry moved us down here where neither of you could work. If he'd only held out a while longer, he'd be moving us out to where there's a promise of work for everyone."

chapter six

Dad left before day-
light the next morning, walking to Crowe, and was gone
for nearly a week. Mom sang as she cleaned the house
from top to bottom and wondered aloud what kind of
place Dad would find for us in Crowe. She was sure he'd
get a job. "If there's work to be had," she said, "your
daddy will find it."

Dad found a job. He told us all about it as soon as he
got home. He said he had walked most of the way down
there, but he'd hitched a ride back home with another
man who had gone to Crowe for a job. "He'll pick me
up here early Monday morning," Dad said, "but I don't
know when I'll be able to get home again."

"What about a house for us, Rob?" Mom asked.
"Couldn't you find a place for us to live there?"

Dad said the government had thrown together some shacks for the workers to live in, but they weren't fit for a man's wife and children. "The only people who will live in them are hillbillies from Kentucky," Dad said, "and painted streetwalkers."

I waited for Mom to ask which state streetwalkers came from, but she didn't. She never said much of anything, but her lips turned down at the corners and her eyes lost the happy, expectant shine they had worn for the past few days.

I knew she had been counting the days until we could bid good-bye to the hills and hollows and live, as she put it, like civilized human beings again. Mom told Dad it was hard for her to stay behind with us kids while he shook the red clay from his feet and went out of the hills to live.

"Zel, it's a job. A man has to go where the work is. And I'll feel better about it if I know you and the young'uns are here in your own house."

"All right, Rob," Mom said. "I'll stay. But I'll tell you right now, I don't like it."

No more was said about moving. Mom got Dad's things together so he'd be ready to leave when his ride to Crowe came by on Monday morning. When we tried to help her, she snapped, "Get out from under my feet and leave me be. You kids are more hinder than help."

We spoke softly and moved quietly out of her way.

We didn't see Dad before he left, and we didn't see him again for a long time. But we kids didn't miss him very much. There was a lot to see and do in the woods around us.

Spring seemed to come to Greene County at the same time Dad got the job in Crowe. It seemed like just overnight the trees leafed out in their many shades of green, and in the woods dogwood and rosebud bloomed. Their deep pink and white blossoms blazed a colorful trail haphazardly up and down the hills. I could understand how the county had got its name; even the grass looked greener here than anywhere else.

The singing and chirping of birds awoke us at first light, and we'd go out and wade through heavy morning dew, exploring the country around us. Wild yellow canaries, with dabs of black painted on their wings, darted and swooped overhead. We ran into the thickets and buckbrush after them, trying to find where they nested and hatched their young. We told Mom if we could find their nest, we'd bring her a canary.

She said, "You leave them wild things be. If you put your hands in a nest, the mother won't come back, and the little ones will starve to death."

Paths and trails, which had lain hidden on the bare red ground, appeared when the grass started growing beside them. We followed the paths to wild strawberry patches and thickets of wild plum, white with blossoms. Up near the empty Perry house, we found spearmint, thick and fragrant, growing wild around an ever-flowing pool of clear, cold spring water gushing out of the hillside. We chewed sprigs of spearmint leaves and cupped the spring water in our hands for a drink. The water was always colder and sweeter after chewing the mint leaves.

We found the first wild flowers in the woods and carried crowfoots, lamb's-tongues and white kitten britches, limp and wilted, home to Mom. We gathered moss, soft and thick as lamb's wool, and held it close to our faces, just to touch something beautiful. Then we placed it back on the ground and packed the grainy black woods' earth gently around it so it wouldn't die and we could come back to it another day.

Jamie and I wandered along the creek bank where touch-me-nots made a patchwork quilt of yellow, orange, and green down to the water's edge. We skirted the mass of flowers and fished broken limbs and twigs from the creek, then waited for the muddied water to clear so we could see the slate and sandstone that lay on the riverbed.

When we came to the footlog, we saw that dead leaves and broken branches had drifted and collected there, forming a dam under the footlog. Small streams of water were flowing slowly at each side, but the main stream was being held back, making a pool above the footlog. Soon it would overflow and cover our makeshift bridge.

The next day, Jamie and I went to Lick Crick to clear away the rubbish that had lodged under the log and free the trapped river. Before long, the water was rushing downstream again and out of the hills to join White River in the bottom lands.

All the rivers that ran through the hills of Greene County were clean, clear, and fast running, as if in a hurry to get out of the hills and see the world; a world not hemmed in on all sides by tall trees and small mountains.

We would get home after dark, our clothes wet and muddy from playing along the creek bank and covered with sticktights and cockle burs. We'd stop at the barn, light the lantern, and hurriedly strip the burrs from our clothes before going on to the house for supper.

Once we asked Mom to bring Robert and walk in the woods with us, but she said she was as close to the woods as she ever wanted to be. "I don't see what you two kids can find to do in them hills and hollows," she said.

One morning, Julie came with us. I gathered bunches of redbud and dogwood blossoms, and Julie broke long branches of waxy paw-paw leaves and scarlet-veined sumac to add greenery. Then we hurried home to give the fruit jar full of flowers to Mom.

She accepted, silent and tight-lipped. Not even springtime could lessen Mom's dissatisfaction with the place or make her any happier to be there without Dad. She didn't see the beauty of green things growing from the red dirt. All she ever saw was the mud we tracked into the house from the clay paths that led up to the door.

She said she didn't know how Dad could go away and leave her in these hills with nothing but trees around her and mud underfoot. He could have found a place out of this dark hollow, if he'd tried.

She blamed the hills for Jase's death and Dicie's breakdown. "If they had been any place except in these godforsaken hills, they could've faced these hard times and seen them through," she said. "They'd known trouble before and stood up to it." Now that Dicie was gone, she was all alone down here. She guessed she didn't have a friend in the world. She clung to her aloneness and refused to make friends. The ones who came to call and pass the time of day with her seldom came back after the first time.

George and Clara Brent came by faithfully, once or twice a week, when they were driving to McVille or to the city. Mom spoke civil enough to them, but she was brusque with her answers and cut their visits short with excuses of work to be done. After they'd gone, Mom would mutter, "I've got better things to do than listen to Clara Brent's gossip and tall tales."

We gave up trying to make Mom feel better.

The leaves Julie had picked for Mom from the sumac bush had given her a bright red rash from wrists to elbows. In no time at all, her arms were swollen to nearly twice their normal size and covered with a mass of tiny water blisters. Mom smeared a baking soda paste over Julie's arms and wrapped strips torn from an old sheet around each one.

Before the end of the week, Julie had the poison on both legs, too, all the way up to her straddle. Mom said Julie was too big and too old to be traipsing around the country. She'd had no business out in the woods in the first place!

Mom fussed and complained as she gently washed the open sores, applied salve, and changed the bandages.

I said Julie looked like one of the Egyptian mummies I'd seen in my history book, only they were bandaged neater. They didn't have lumps and knots with long strings hanging out on their arms and legs.

Mom snapped at me. "Missy, if you don't like the way I do this, maybe you'd better get one of them Egyptians to show me how they do it! Lord knows, I could use some help."

I guess He did. Early on Monday morning, He sent the Brents by our house on their way to the county seat. They asked, the way they always did, if we needed anything brought out from town. We never did, because anything Mom needed she could get on credit at Bud Watson's general store in McVille.

Clara took one look at Julie and said, "Zel, you'd better get ready and take this girl in to see a doctor. My trading can wait. There ain't room in that car for all four of us, so I'll stay here with your young'uns until you and George get back."

Julie looked ready to cry. Robert was bawling and hanging on to Mom's skirt. Jamie came and stood close by me, and I put my arm around him. His brown eyes were wide with fright. To take someone to a doctor's office was enough to scare anybody. The only time one of the hill families ever saw a doctor was when he came, after all the homemade remedies had failed, to write or sign a death certificate. We were sure we would never see Julie again. The doctor would sign the papers, and they would bury her.

Clara took Robert on her lap in the rocking chair and talked and rocked until he quieted down. He cuddled into her soft rolls of flesh and listened to her stories. Robert would be five years old in the fall, but he was small for his age and acted a lot younger.

Clara didn't know what to do with us kids. She held Robert on her lap and wouldn't let Jamie and me out of her sight. When she went to the kitchen to make peanut butter and bread for us, we had to be there with her.

She opened the cupboard doors and clucked over the dishes Great-grandmother Curry had left to Mom and handled them as carefully as fresh-laid eggs. Mom wouldn't have liked her going through things in the house while she was away. I didn't know what she'd say when she noticed that Clara had cleaned the pie safe in the kitchen and polished the dull turquoise door panels until they shone like a pewter pot in a mudhole.

Clara had lit the coal-oil lamps and started supper before we heard George's car throwing gravel as it turned into the barnyard, bringing Mom and Julie home.

We weren't allowed to touch Julie or use anything she touched. I had to sleep in Jamie's bed with him and Robert so I wouldn't catch her poisoning. I told Mom I wouldn't show my straddle to a doctor or anyone else, even if I did get poisoned.

She said, "I don't think we have to worry about you, Seely; poison kills poison."

I guess she was right. Nothing ever poisoned me.

We had an old two-holer outhouse down the path past the root cellar, but while Julie had the poison, she had to use the china chamber pot, the rose-flowered one that matched the bowl and pitcher on Mom's dresser. Every evening Julie carried the pot at arm's length to empty it Then she washed it and brought it back upstairs. Mom cautioned her daily to be careful of how she handled it, but Julie still swung it by two fingers like a tin slop bucket.

One morning Julie rushed over and sat with all her weight on the pot. The pot split and left her sitting in the middle of a puddle and broken china.

I laughed, but I thought Mom would probably bust a blood vessel or else beat Julie to death when she saw the mess on the floor.

She didn't. She cleaned the floor and didn't say a word or lay a hand on Julie.

But Julie couldn't keep quiet. "That old pot was cracked long before I ever sat on it."

Mom pressed her lips tighter than ever and gave an extra hard swipe with the mop. "That old pot, as you call it, was your Great-grandmother Curry's chamber pot. I carried the set with me when I married your father. I might have known you kids couldn't keep your hands off it, and it would get broken."

Great-grandmother Curry had been dead for a hundred years, I'll bet, but Mom still took care of her things and spoke of her as if she expected Great-grandmother Curry to walk through the door at any time and find a chip in one of her dishes or a speck of dust on the walnut stand table.

Julie said, "My hands didn't touch it. All I did—"

Mom whirled around, the mop still clutched threateningly in her hands. I ducked my head and ran from the room.

chapter seven

*M*om resigned herself to staying in Greene County, but she was a changed person. I could hear her walking the floor and moving about at night, long after us kids were in bed. Each morning she would look even more tired and worn than she had the day before. Her body seemed to shrink and bend in the middle like an old woman's.

She said she was trapped in these everlasting hills and there was no way out for her. Day and night she could feel the hills closing in on her, squeezing the very life from her body. Once her eyes filled with tears, and she said, "I have nothing to look forward to, nothing at all."

Dad stayed at Crowe. He came home whenever he could bum a ride with one of the men who was driving up our way. The first time he came home, Jamie ran to him as soon as he walked through the door and began to tell him all the things we'd been doing since he'd been away. Dad shushed him and asked Mom, "Doesn't this kid ever hush up?" He pushed Jamie away impatiently and began to talk to Mom.

He never stayed long. He would give Mom some money and his dirty clothes to wash and be gone before noon the next day. He never seemed to notice us kids unless we walked between him and the lamplight while he was reading the newspaper. We were just as happy that he didn't. We knew we were more apt to get the back of his hand than a pat on the head if we were within touching distance. Only Robert dared to approach him. He would climb on Dad's lap and sit quietly content, while Dad read or smoked his pipe and talked about his work.

Mom's eyes and face were soft and tender when Dad kissed her good-bye, but by the time she had finished scrubbing his heavy pants and shirts on the board and put them out to dry on the line, her lips would be drawn to a thin slit and her dark eyes hard and snapping beneath a frowning brow.

In the early part of May, Mom said with more spirit and determination than we had heard in a long time, "Maybe we'll eat beans all winter, but we're going to have fresh green vegetables this summer."

I looked at the field of burdock, dandelions, and ragweed that was our yard and wondered how on earth she could ever get a garden planted there.

She sent Jamie and me to clear the fence row where some rhubarb had gone to seed, its bushy yellow blossoms standing higher than the crooked old pickets, and the smartweed and wild geranium crawled across the ground and lay heavily underfoot.

Then, while she was still fired with the vision of green vegetables growing plentifully at hand, she asked George Brent to bring his horse and plow a garden spot for her. There was no offer of pay and none was asked. When the weeds were turned under, he worked the plowed ground with a harrow. But there were still big lumps and clods left where the harrow had missed them.

Mom and Julie took turns with the spade and hoe, breaking the hard clods of dirt, and I raked the ground into a pliable patch ready for planting as soon as George brought the seeds out from the city.

Mom traded a handmade quilt she had spent years piecing and sewing together to Clara for enough money to pay for the seed potatoes, corn, and tomato plants George brought to her.

Ever since the day Clara had stayed with us kids while Mom took Julie to a doctor in town, Clara had tried to wheedle Mom out of our junky old furniture or sometimes a dish that had taken her fancy. I couldn't imagine why she'd want them. She had the money to go and buy anything she fancied, brand new.

While George was laying out the garden rows, Clara sat in the front room and rocked and talked. She ran her hands over the cool marble top of the old black walnut stand table and said, "Now, Zel, if you ever want to get rid of this, let me know. Not that I'd have any earthly use for it, but I'd like to have this lovely old piece."

Mom smiled, pleased that Clara admired the table or else because she knew she had something Clara didn't have and couldn't get. She had carried in two cups of coffee from the pot on the back of the stove and set one near Clara's hand.

"Oh, I don't think I'll ever have need to part with that stand table. I expect to give it to one of my girls when they marry."

I looked at the old table and thought to myself, "I don't have to worry. It won't last that long!"

Jamie came running across the porch, dodging the loose boards, and in the front door. He was so excited and out of breath he couldn't speak.

Mom said, "Settle down, Jamie, and take a deep breath before you have a spell. Whatever it is can wait that long."

"George found a whole nest of copperheads," he said. "He's killing them with the hoe. You should see, they're all over the garden. Big ones and little ones crawling everywhere!"

He turned and ran back to the garden.

Mom said, "I'd better see about him. He's apt to be sick from all the commotion going on."

Clara pulled her weight from the rocker, and we followed Mom to the plowed ground. Jamie stood watching, pale and tense, as George gave a final whack with the hoe to one rusty spotted snake still moving near his feet. One by one, he lifted the dead snakes on the hoe blade and threw them over the fence onto the gravel road. The last and largest one of all, he picked up by the tip of its tail and snapped its head off before he tossed it onto the road with the others.

He rubbed his hands on his coveralls, then pulled a big handkerchief from his pocket and wiped the sweat off his face. "I probably plowed them buggers up yesterday. But they were sluggish and didn't start moving around until the sun came up this morning and warmed their bed. You kids will have to watch where you're tramping. When you run onto one nest of copperheads, there's bound to be another nearby."

There seemed to be no end to the hidden dangers just lying in wait for us kids behind every tree and beneath each blade of grass. Mom warned us about the five-leaf poison ivy vine, the bottomless sinkholes that could swallow us and never leave a trace of our whereabouts, and snakes. We were to be especially cautious about watching for snakes.

She said, "If you kids see a snake, listen for a rattle. A rattler will warn you, but a copperhead is blind and sneaky. They'll strike without warning."

Last summer, Julie's cat had been bitten by a snake, and it swelled up and died. Dad said he didn't know where the damn cat could've gone to get snake bit. All the snakes on the farm were harmless, caught more mice around the barn than the damn cat.

Now, from the way Mom spoke, there were only two kinds of snakes in Greene County, both deadly poison; and if one didn't make any noise, it was a copperhead.

After George stepped off the garden rows, staked them, and strung binder twine so we could plant in a straight line, he and Clara went home. He left most of his garden tools, in case we needed them to finish working the garden.

I know Mom must have had other gardens; she knew all about raising vegetables. But I couldn't ever remember another one. She had to tell us kids everything that had to be done and how to do it.

She showed Julie and me how to set out tomato and cabbage plants. I dug the holes, Julie poured water for the roots to drink; and on her hands and knees, Mom set the plants and tamped the soft earth around them. Every so often, she would stand and place both hands flat to the small of her back and stretch as far as she could reach. She would smile at us and say, "Well, this ain't plantin' peas, is it?"

Then she would kneel and set the next plant.

We sowed lettuce, radishes, green onions, and two rows of sweet corn close to the house. Mom said, "The sweet corn is going to be right handy up here. I can get a mess of roastin' ears just by reaching through the kitchen window." Then she laughed.

I guess that's what made the garden so special to us. Mom didn't laugh much or smile on us often these times. But that day, she did both.

At dusk, Mom called Jamie and Robert from where they were playing in wet clay, and the five of us walked to the house together. Mom was the happiest I'd seen her since the day we moved down here.

Late the next day, Mom marked rows at one end of the plowed ground for the potato patch. Then she showed Jamie and me how to cut the eyes and peelings for seed and save the rest for soup. "It's a blessing that school is out." Mom said. "I'd never get this garden planted without your help."

Mom gave us two dull paring knives and left us with a gunny sack full of potatoes. "When you get the kettle full for cooking, quit cutting, and start planting. Do it like I showed you—a couple of feet apart and cover them well."

When they were all cut and sorted, Mom took the pan of potatoes to the house to start supper, and we started planting the sprouts and peelings. I dug shallow holes about a foot apart, and Jamie dropped in the seeds. Then we covered them with a thin layer of dirt and stamped it down with our bare feet.

We worked at a snail's pace, trying to time it so we would finish planting about the same time the potato soup was done. We figured if we took small mouthfuls and swallowed slowly, it would be too dark to work in the garden after supper.

Every morning by first light, we were out in the garden in our nightclothes, checking the rows to see if anything had come up, long before it was time for us or the plants to be up. It seemed like the weeds popped up overnight. At the first sight of green growing in the garden, we ran to tell Mom the corn was coming up. She took one look and said it wasn't corn, it was ragweed. We wanted to pull all the weeds, but she said she'd pull the weeds until we could tell the difference between them and a stalk of corn. She shook her head as if she couldn't believe our ignorance and went to the kitchen to fix our breakfast.

One morning Mom called us, and Julie and Jamie went in to the house at once. Breakfast was ready. I could smell the ham and biscuits, and I knew Mom would have thick, creamy ham gravy to put over the biscuits; but I had to go to the outhouse first. Instead of going back to the house and taking the path from the kitchen door, past the root cellar, to the outhouse, I lifted my nightgown above my knees and cut catty-cornered through the tall, dewy weeds.

I was watching for prickly thistles, trying to miss the nettles, and didn't see the snakes until I stepped on them. A big brown snake was coiled like a piece of rope protectively over a nest of soft-skinned white eggs. Baby snakes, the size of overgrown fishing worms, were slowly working their way through small cracks in the shells.

I didn't breathe and I didn't hear a sound from the snakes. "My God, I thought, copperheads!" and started screaming.

I forgot I had to go to the toilet. I whirled around and started running through the weeds and thistles straight for the kitchen door. I was midway through the high weeds when I saw Jamie. He had run out of the kitchen door, and his bare arms were covered with scalding hot ham gravy. Almost at once, he dropped down and began to wipe it off frantically on the grass.

I didn't know what had happened, but I caught his hands and lifted him to his feet. Mom rushed to help him.

69

The burns from the gravy were deep and raw where Jamie's arms bent at the elbow. Mom wrapped clothes soaked in soda and cold well water around them. She said all her children would probably be crippled one way or another, living down in this hellhole, where a body couldn't get a doctor until he died nor a preacher to read over him when he did.

After she finished dressing Jamie's burns, she said, "Now, Missy, what were you screaming and yelling about? You scared Jamie something fierce, so he knocked over that hot gravy. He could've been scalded to death. It's just a miracle he's not burned a lot worse than he is. Well?..."

She was waiting for me to answer. I had forgotten the snakes. "I stepped on a bunch of snakes hatching in the high weeds." It was little more than a whisper.

"If this is one of your stories, I'll take a strap to you, Seely." Mom opened the screen door. "Come and show me where you saw them."

We walked by the garden where Mom took a hoe from the fence to clear the thistles from our way and kill the snakes, if she found any.

They were still lying just as I'd seen them. The parent snake sluggish and sleepy with the small ones squirming over and under it as they left the soft white egg sacks.

Mom took one look, snorted, and turned back the way we had come. "All that fuss and pother over a little garter snake and a nestful of babies." She tossed the hoe toward the garden fence where it caught and swung a few times before it fell to the ground, blade side up. It was no time

70

to remind her that we'd been told never to leave a hoe with the blade bare.

I put the hoe back on the fence and ran after her in time to catch the tail end of her words. "You've got to control yourself, Seely, or you'll send me to an early grave with your tomfoolery."

It seemed like I was forever promising to behave myself, not to yell at Robert, not to scream at field mice, lower my voice, and stop telling big stories! Mom said the truth was good enough, I didn't need to embroider everything I said.

"I thought they were copperheads. I really did. They didn't make a sound, and there could have been a whole colony of them just waiting for me."

"You thought? Seely, you don't think. You speak without thinking and yell before you're hurt. This time it was Jamie who got hurt. Maybe if you have to take care of him, it will teach you to think the next time. From now on, you're to be responsible for Jamie."

She talked and I listened to her. For once, I paid strict attention to every word. A bad scare like this might bring on one of Jamie's fits, she said, and I was old enough to help him and should know what to do if he had one when we were alone. "There's nothing to be afraid of. Just be sure he can't bite his tongue or choke on it. The fits don't last more than a minute, and most of the time he knows they're coming on and can tell you."

Jamie didn't have fits often, and I hoped my yelling wouldn't make that kind of trouble for him now.

It didn't.

Though Mom was afraid Jamie's arms would be stiff or crooked because she couldn't take him to a doctor, they healed fast and straight. In time, only a few pink scars remained to remind me of my foolishness.

chapter eight

*B*eginning that morning, Jamie was my responsibility. I stayed with him and took care of him. I did my share of the chores and his, too, as long as his arms were bandaged. While I cut and raked weeds along the fence row and fed the chickens, Jamie sat in the shade of the big maple tree, rubbing Clover Leaf salve on his arms. And while I carried buckets of water down the garden row, watering the plants as I went, Jamie's shadow lay alongside mine as he followed silently, waiting for me to be done with the work.

I would hurry through our chores so we could roam the hills and hollows together. There was always a new stand of woods Jamie wanted to explore, or a red clay bank to dig into for Indian arrowheads. Jamie had a cigar box almost full of arrowheads now, but still he searched for more. On a ledge, away under the big rock on the other side of the creek, he kept his cigar box of treasures. My notebook was stuck between two rocks a little to one side of Jamie's ledge. I had taken it with me once to write in while we watched the day change colors, and I left it there when we went back to the house.

As the days grew longer, Jamie and I spent more and more time in the woods or in the room under the big rock. The woods were our playground, and the cave was our resting place till it was time to go home.

On some of the trees near our cave, dried black grapevines the size of a man's arm hung free from the top branches or twisted over the larger limbs and down the trunk of the tree. We found by holding a vine in both hands, like a baseball bat, and taking a running jump into the air, the grapevine would lift us high off the ground. Then we'd wrap our legs around the vine and fly through the air like great wingless birds, far out and over the gully behind Lick Crick.

We had discovered that people around these parts threw their junk and trash into the gully. Sometimes good junk. Jamie and I rummaged through the junk hole and found bright amber bottles, pretty colored dishes that were cracked only a little, and old books that we carried up to the cave. We set the amber bottles on the flat rocks up and down each side of the opening, and late in the day they caught the light of the sun and reflected on every side of the cave.

One hot day followed the other with no sign of a break in the heat. After the sun went down behind the hills, we'd draw water from the well and water the garden. Sometimes, we would lug the buckets from Lick Crick and fill the rain barrel and wash tubs. With every bucket of water drawn from the well, Mom would say, "If this hot spell doesn't break soon, I'm afraid this old well will go dry or get too low for us to use. I don't know what we'd do without drinking water."

The cow had gone dry during the first hot spell of spring, and we didn't have any milk to drink. Mom bought canned milk and complained that "feeding a dry cow was as bad as paying for a dead horse. Neither one was of any earthly good to anybody."

Once in a while, thunder clouds, black and rumbling, would roll in from the west, and we'd have a gully-washer of a storm. Water roared down from the hills and rain stood ankle deep in the garden rows. But by nightfall, the dry, cracked red clay had absorbed all the moisture.

After these cloudbursts, steam rose from the ground and the muggy heat sapped our strength. We sat in the shade or catnapped while Mom rocked and fanned herself on the front porch.

Most of the gardening was done late in the day after the sun had lost its power to scorch us or burn the fresh-turned earth. Fighting bugs off the plants and keeping the weeds from taking over the garden was a job for everybody. One day we killed bugs, and for the next two days we cut weeds.

It was our day to weed the beans. Jamie and I worked until we couldn't see the end of the bean row for the sweat in our eyes. Then Jamie laid the hoe, blade down, in the dirt along the unfinished row, and we ran down the path to Lick Crick.

The wide swimming hole under the willow trees was the promised coolness we had waited for all day. We stripped off our clothes and dived into the creek, head first and bare naked.

Jamie splashed me and shoved my head under the surface. I came up spluttering, spitting muddy water, and trying to duck him.

"That's not fair! I wasn't ready yet!"

He laughed and swam out of my reach, turned and splashed water in my face. He caught hold of a willow limb that hung low over the water and pulled himself into the tree. Then he made a belly whopper into the creek beside me.

I went under again.

I gagged and gasped for breath and wiped the creek water from my eyes. When I could see, I waded to the shallows and climbed the slick, red bank to fall breathlessly into the tall horseweeds that grew thick along Lick Crick.

Jamie splashed and whooped his way out and lay laughing on the ground beside me. He picked up his shirt and dried my hair before we dressed. If Mom saw my wet hair, she'd know I'd gone in swimming naked. She'd harp on it for a week and might forbid me to go swimming in the creek, dressed or not, if she knew.

Dressed again, we ran through the dusk trying to catch the flickering, green-tailed lightning bugs that flitted just overhead, and choked on our laughter when we tripped and fell.

Mom said we were growing wild as a couple of woods' colts, but she didn't say stay home. She just said, "Stay with your brother, Seely." And she never noticed when we left.

Once when we were hunting a different place to swing on a grapevine—a longer, stronger one with a deeper hollow to span—we crossed the ridge and saw a big white house sitting all by itself between two hills. There was no smoke coming from the chimney and not a soul around the place. Just another big empty house.

I wanted to get closer, to look inside, but Jamie wouldn't hear of it. He said he'd heard in school there were a lot of empty houses back in the hills. People just packed up and moved away overnight, leaving behind what they couldn't carry out on their backs.

I wondered where all the others lived who came to school. Somehow, I'd never talked to them much. We hadn't seen them since school let out in April. I wished someone would move into one of the empty houses in the hills near us. I felt as if Jamie and I were the only kids around. I missed Frieda and her talking to and from the well. I'd had to listen closely to understand everything she said, but she knew an awful lot I couldn't find in books. Even if Frieda had come to see me and asked me to go to her house, Mom wouldn't have let me go there.

Julie's friend, Nancy Ann Arthur, came to see her once or twice a week, but we seldom saw anyone else.

We didn't see many cars on the road in front of our

house, either. When the Brents' car passed by our place, Jamie and I ran to the picket fence to watch it out of sight, just as we'd seen other kids do the day we had moved in.

The mailman drove by every day, and sometimes an old beat-up truck, with its springs sagging under a load of battered household stuff being moved in or out of the hills, would stop and get water for the steaming radiator.

We would run and hide behind the house, in case they were gypsies, until we heard the truck chugging on down the road.

Mom was sure every stranger who stopped was a gypsy, spying out families where they could steal the kids. Dad said gypsies weren't stupid. They wouldn't want her kids! "A lot you know about it," Mom snapped, and continued to watch us like a chicken hawk at a brooder house door whenever a stranger came by.

I think I would've talked to these strangers if Mom hadn't kept us away from them. I wanted someone who would talk to me. Mom talked, but she said, "Seely, do this," or, "Seely, don't do that." And she never told me why. I needed someone who could give me a reason for things.

Jamie didn't talk much at all. He was just there in case I had something to say. We could be together all day and not speak three words. But I could touch Jamie; like Teddy, we could communicate.

Sometimes, Jamie reminded me of Teddy with his quiet ways and gentle manner. I knew Teddy had liked the hills, and I often wished he could have stayed here a little longer to roam the hills and hollows with Jamie and me. Once, I remarked to Jamie that I bet Teddy could've got out of the fourth grade all by himself, if God had kept his nose out of it.

Jamie had said, "Seely, you'll go to hell for finding fault with God. And if Mom ever hears you, you'll get worse than that for it."

chapter nine

We left the front gate at daylight on Sunday and walked fast all the way to get to church before the last bell rang for service. Mom had sworn she'd never set foot inside the church after the Flat Hollow Methodist Church women left the Christmas basket at our house, but not a Sunday passed that we weren't there. As we hurried along the dusty, graveled road, other women and children joined us. By the time we reached the church house, there would be more than a dozen kids running, fighting, falling, and crying, while their moms and mine calmly exchanged bits of news and the latest gossip.

Clara Brent would smile and wave as she and George passed us in a cloud of dust. He'd slow down and nod at the women as if apologizing for riding while they walked or else for the choking dust his automobile stirred up on the road.

The women smiled and waved back, then said nice things about the Brents. No one seemed to blame them for being well off or driving a car while the others had to walk to church.

I guess most of the people knew they would be riding with the Brents if George had room in the car to carry them. They were glad George and Clara had money and a car, because any time they needed anything they knew they could always borrow from the Brents.

No one could have been more surprised than Mom when Clara came to our house early one morning to borrow from her.

I had just started down the first row of potato vines, knocking the bugs off with a stick and burying them in the soft dirt with my big toe, when George and Clara drove into the barnyard. George helped Clara out of the car, then he went to the barn, and Clara came to the potato patch.

"Seely, how would you like to come over to my house and help out for a spell? This heat has got me plumb tuckered, and I'm behind with everything."

I smiled and dug my toes in the soft dirt. "If I had my druthers, I guess I'd druther do anything than bug potatoes."

She laughed and said, "I'll speak to your mom about it," and went on to the house.

I guess the idea of Clara Brent borrowing something from her stunned Mom long enough for her to say I could go. Jamie could bug potatoes by himself for a while. And she supposed she could spare me for an hour or so.

Jamie hung on the gate, looking as if he had lost his last friend, and I climbed into the car with George and Clara and bounced off down the road to their house.

That first day, Clara showed me how to make a bed: to fold the corners of the sheet under the mattress; lay the pillows end to end so the lacy border would hang over the side; then spread the silky coverlet neatly over the whole thing. I changed the same bed three times before I finally did it to suit her.

Clara showed me how to set her table, and while she taught me, she talked. My wish had come true. Clara had a vast store of information, and she gave it all to me. She told me about everyone and everything in our neck of the county. I didn't even have to ask.

My head was spinning as I tried to digest everything she had told me. After the dishes were washed and put away, Clara gave me a quarter and said, "Run along home, now. But come back in a couple of days. I want you to help me do some cooking."

I went out the back door, past the barn and woodpile, and cut through their cornfield. Their corn was a lot higher than ours, but it was full of weeds. Mom said our corn should be knee high by the Fourth of July. It only had about a week to make it.

Most of the time, I was just glad to be with Clara. As long as I was helping her, I didn't have to work in the garden. Luckily, there wasn't much to do in the garden now or Mom might not have let me go. We were using the lettuce, radishes, and green onions. I even carried some to Clara when I went to her house to help with whatever she was doing that day.

We had fresh green peas, too, and we liked them creamed. Dad hadn't been home once for creamed peas or fresh garden salad, but today was the Fourth of July, and he was home from Crowe for the weekend. Mom said it was a good thing Dad had come home today. The vines had dried up so fast, this would be the last mess of peas she'd be able to get this summer.

Whenever Dad came home, Mom fixed something special for him and used her good dishes on the table. When he was away, we had soup and cornbread or biscuits and beef gravy from chipped plates and bowls that came in the big sacks of Robin Hood flour.

Today, Mom dug a few potatoes, no bigger than marbles, and creamed peas and potatoes together for supper. She said they would go further that way. There was fried chicken and wilted lettuce on the table; green onions and red and white radishes lay side by side in great-grandmother Curry's old cut-crystal relish dish. The wild strawberries that Julie and I had picked during the morning were soaking in simple syrup, ready for the tiny shortcake biscuits warming in the oven.

Dad had no more than got seated at the table when he said to Mom, "You couldn't keep your hands off the potatoes and wait for them to get big enough to eat before you dug into them, could you? It's the same thing every year."

83

I don't know why he was scolding her. He knew as well as we did that Mom had dug into the potatoes today especially for him.

She pretended not to hear him. "Let's say grace, children, and thank God our garden has given us food for today."

We bowed our heads. Since Mom had been going to prayer meeting every Wednesday night with Clara and dragging us to church on Sunday, we had to give thanks for every bite we swallowed, whether we felt thankful or not.

When thanks had been given and every plate around the table was filled to the brim, Dad said to Mom, partly in jest but mostly in earnest, "You'd do better to thank the good Lord your back held up to hoe the weeds. Seems to me you could've found a more likely piece of ground if you wanted to grow vegetables. But no, you had to pick the weediest damn spot I've ever laid eyes on to put out your garden."

He said it lightly, but Julie didn't take it lightly. She pushed her chair back from the table. Tears of anger spilled over on her face as she ran toward the stairs.

Dad called, "Where do you think you're going? Come back here and finish your supper."

Julie didn't hold back or hesitate for a moment. He left the table and went after her. She stopped on the steps and turned to face him, her back to the attic door.

"I won't sit at that table and listen to you find fault with everything Mom has done." Her words trembled and broke, but she didn't back down. "Who are you to find fault with Mom's judgment? You weren't here to pick a garden spot nor to work in it. She's had it all to do."

Julie wiped angrily at her tears, but she was determined to have her say if it killed her. "I have seen Mom do the work of a man and his horse to raise that garden. If she wants to bless and use those puny potatoes, that's her privilege."

The light from the coal-oil lamp cast flickering shadows around the two of them. She was small and dark, and he a threatening giant towering over her. Supper was forgotten as we sat silent and big-eyed, watching the two on the steps. Mom made a motion as if to rise, then sank back in her chair, and covered her face with her hands, as if she couldn't bear to look.

I thought Dad surely would kill Julie for defying him. I'd never known him to raise his hand to Mom or ever to hit Julie, but this was different. This was the first time one of his children had dared to stand up to him. Mom didn't often talk back to Dad or argue with him. And now Julie was talking to him just the way she did to one of us kids when we got out of line.

Dad lifted his hand and shook his finger in her face, but he didn't strike her. "Don't you dare to sass me, young lady! You're not so big that I can't turn you across my knee."

Where the light caught Dad's face, it looked red and swollen with held-in anger. Yet, when Julie stepped down as if to move away from him, he put his arm across her path and said quietly, "Look, girl, I . . ."

"You look!" she shouted. "You never see Mom and us kids any more."

She slipped by his upraised arm and ran out the door. He followed at her heels, swearing under his breath with every step he took. When Julie passed through the gate, she swung it shut so hard a loose paling fell, striking Dad on the shinbone.

He bent and picked it up, then stood slapping it against his leg while he looked down the road after her. We watched until Julie faded into the shadows and we couldn't see her any longer.

Our Fourth of July that had started out to be such a good day had ended with harsh words and bitterness. Julie was alone out there somewhere in the dark. And downstairs, Mom and Dad raised their voices to each other.

I cried myself to sleep. In the bed on the other side of the room, Jamie had nightmares and groaned in his sleep. All the grief and sorrow of the world seemed to have settled in our attic room.

I never knew when Julie slipped quietly into bed with me nor heard her get up the next morning; but when I went downstairs for breakfast, Julie was in the kitchen with Mom. They were both ready for church.

Dad was gone. I didn't ask where he was; it was enough just to know he wasn't there. Maybe it wasn't all his fault, but when he wasn't around, we were sure of peace and quiet. It would be two, maybe three or four weeks before he ran out of clean clothes and came home again.

Mom said, "Seely, get your brothers up for church and dress yourself. The others will have gone on without us if we don't hurry."

It was as if the night before had never happened. Just another bad dream to think on, then tuck away and forget. Mom never mentioned it. And if Julie spoke of it, Mom ignored her and changed the subject.

chapter ten

*N*ot long afterward, the mining people came into the hills with big Mack trucks and bulldozers, just as Jase Perry had said they would. We had something new to think about.

Jamie and I watched from a distance as they tramped through the forest slashing and marking the big trees they could use for crossties and props in the mines.

The same trucks that moved the machines into the hills brought Ben Collier and his sawmill and set it up in the hollow about a mile from the gravel road. When the huge trees were cut and trimmed, they were hauled off in trucks or dragged with chains and pulleys to Ben Collier's sawmill.

I didn't like the noisy mill or the loud, groaning trucks and machinery that tore and ripped the hills and ruined the woods. "If these trucks keep going," I told Jamie, "we'll have to stay in the yard near our house. There won't be any place left in the woods to run and play."

Jamie said, "They had to put the mill there. It's the only flat, level place with a dirt road leading to it, except the schoolyard."

The way I felt about that schoolhouse, I thought that would have been the ideal place for them to put the saw-mill. And I told Jamie so.

He looked at me as if I had suddenly sprouted horns and long pointed ears. "Why, Seely, where would we go to school if they did that?"

We wandered through the hills to the ridge above the big white house to see if anyone had moved into it. When we topped the rise, we saw smoke coming from the chimney and people walking in the yard. We lay belly down on the ground and parted the high tickle-grass so we could spy on them and not be seen.

While we watched, Ben Collier moved away from the others and went into the house. We heard the woman call to the boy and girl but not what she said to them. As they passed from sight around the corner of the big house, Jamie and I got to our feet and followed the path we'd made back to the sawmill.

I didn't say a word on the way back. I was too busy figuring out how to get acquainted with the blond Collier girl. She was about my size and looked to be about my age. She would have to go to our school—it was the only one anywhere near—and I would see her there. But I hated to waste the month or more until school started. I thought maybe she would come to her dad's mill and we would see her there, but only the boy came to work with his dad.

We saw the first fallen trees slide down the ground chute and watched as the big circle saw sliced the logs into long, rough boards as thin as a shingle. The men didn't pay any attention to us, and nobody said we couldn't hang around and watch them. Every day, we went by the sawmill to see if it was still standing and if the men were still working there.

When we tired of listening to the singing blade and counting the rough boards as they slid past it, we climbed the hills to the ridge above the Colliers' house and spied down the slope on them. We never once went down to the house or spoke to the kids. In the short time we had lived here, we had grown as shy and backward as the kids who had been born in the hills and never been beyond them.

Sometimes we would dare each other to call out to the yellow-haired girl while she walked alone in the yard, but we could never quite bring ourselves to yell loud enough for her to hear us.

It didn't take long after the trees were cut down for the tall sprouts and sucker limbs to grow thick around the raw edge of the stump, leaving plenty of room inside for a cool, shaded playhouse. We found one about four feet wide near the path leading toward the abandoned house where Jase and Dicie Perry and their kids had lived.

We would sit for hours on the tree stump in plain sight

90

of the Perry place, telling each other ghost stories. We never went any nearer the place and we always sat facing the house. Late in the afternoon when the sun filtered down through the trees making long, wavy shadows around us was the best time for telling stories, but it didn't leave us much time to get home before dark.

Jamie could tell better ghost stories than I, but I could scare him to tears with my tales about the long-dead Indians who had lived in these woods.

One day, when we were telling ghost stories, we heard people—live ones—coming up our path.

"Shut up!" Jamie told me. "Be quiet until we can see who it is."

We held our breath as the blond girl and her brother walked by our hideout. They were speaking in whispers and walking so softly their feet barely touched the ground. Soon after they passed us, they left the path and struck off through the woods toward their dad's mill.

"We missed our chance to talk to them," I told Jamie. "We should have called out to them as they walked by us."

"Couldn't you tell they were scared half to death, Seely?" Jamie said. "If we'd moved or called out to them, they never would've stopped running." After a moment's thought, he added, "Besides, they would have hated us forever for scaring them."

I had forgotten how it had been the first time Jamie and I had walked home through these woods. That day, we would've bolted and run at the slightest sound. But now, the woods were as familiar as our own back yard, and it was hard for me to imagine anyone being afraid of them.

It was just a few days later that Dad came home again. It had been nearly a month since his last time home. I guess he ran out of clean clothes or else he figured Mom was about out of money. He piled his dirty clothes in a stack on the kitchen floor and laid a bunch of money on the table.

Mom kind of laughed and said she felt like she was taking in washing and getting paid in advance for the work. She and Dad acted like they had forgotten what had happened the last time he was home.

But I could tell Julie hadn't forgotten. As soon as she saw Dad, she went upstairs to our bedroom. When I went up to tell her supper was ready, come and eat, she was writing a letter to Floyd Perry.

Floyd had gone into the three C's as soon as he could after Jase had killed himself and Dicie had been sent to the insane asylum over at Richmond. He'd written to Dad that he couldn't get a job, and he wasn't helping his mom and the little girls by mooning around the house all day. The last time he wrote to Dad he was somewhere in Idaho and was sending his checks to his grandma for the little girls' keep.

Floyd had written to Julie almost every week. She had bought ten cents' worth of penny postcards from the mailman and sent little notes back to him.

Then one night Dad had picked up and opened one of Floyd's letters to Julie before she found it, and he read it out loud at the supper table. I don't know why she got so angry about it. The letter didn't say much. Just that he couldn't make any plans for his future while he was taking care of his whole family.

When Dad handed the letter over to Julie, she wadded it up in a ball and threw it on the live coals in the cookstove.

The next morning Julie told Mom that Dad had no right to open her mail. She was entitled to a little privacy.

"Your daddy meant no harm by it," Mom told her. "He looks on Floyd Perry like one of his own."

"But he's not!" Julie flared out at Mom.

Although I hadn't seen any more of his letters, I guess Floyd had kept on writing to Julie because she wrote to him faithfully.

"Julie, Mom said for you to come to the table," I repeated.

"I heard you," she said.

"Well, come on!"

Reluctantly, she put the pencil and paper away and went down to the supper table. Dad didn't speak directly to Julie, or she to him. Mostly they acted as if the other one wasn't there.

When Dad left the house to walk over to the sawmill to talk to Ben Collier, Mom told Julie that she was just as stubborn and hard-headed as her dad. Neither one of them would give an inch in any direction.

"Maybe so," Julie said. "But I won't stay in the same room with him."

"We'll see about that," Mom said. And I guess she did.

Because Julie sat at the table and kept the peace until Dad went back to Crowe.

Before he left, Dad told Mom he wouldn't be home again before Labor Day. But if she'd make a list for him, he'd bring our school shoes and other things we needed when he came.

Usually Jamie and I would have been counting the days and couldn't wait until our new school things came, and we could start back to school again. But Jamie didn't seem to care this year. He had dark smudges under his eyes and cried easily. I don't think he was getting a full night's sleep often. I could hear him tossing and turning in his bed across the room from me. Sometimes he called out in his sleep and never knew when I answered him.

Mom said he'd worn himself out running all over the hills and hollows from daylight till dark. So we stopped going to the sawmill or over the ridge to spy on the Collier place. Seemed like every time we'd leave our yard, Mom called us back to the house.

On the days when I went to help Clara, Mom kept Jamie close to her so she could keep an eye on him.

chapter eleven

I was at Clara's on the Friday afternoon that Dad came home for the Labor Day weekend. By the time I got there, the school things he brought had been sorted out. On the bed I shared with Julie, tablets, pencils, ink, and pen were stacked on top of my school shoes. I cracked the back of the yellow tablet and wrote my name on the first line. Then I ran downstairs to see Jamie and Robert's new things. Even though Robert wouldn't be going to school, he got the same as Jamie. Just as Julie and I always got the same.

Jamie had a new jacket with a zipper, and he was trying it on for fit. He had never worked a zipper before, and he was having trouble getting the jacket to close.

"Let me do it, Jamie," I said. "I'll fasten it for you."

"Leave the boy alone," Dad said. "Let him do it for himself."

I stepped away from Jamie but stood waiting, ready to help him if he asked.

He quit trying to fasten the jacket and took it off. His face was pale and his hands trembled as he hung it up. Dad said I was making a sissy out of Jamie. He told Mom if she ever expected him to be a man or act like one, she'd better start treating him like one. He scuffled with Jamie and roughed him up until he ran crying out of the house.

When I would have gone after him, Dad said, "Leave him be!"

I ran out of the house anyhow and didn't stop running until I was in the cave under the big rock. There, in my notebook, I wrote down all my mixed-up feelings about Dad and wondered why it hurt so bad. Why did he have to come home? He didn't care about us, or he wouldn't do the things he did. He made Mom unhappy and fought with Julie, and now he'd hurt Jamie and made him cry. I hated him. I wished he would go back to Crowe and never come home.

At the supper table Jamie barely touched his food and excused himself as soon as I did, following me up the steps to our bedroom.

Julie went to Nancy Ann's early Saturday morning. Nancy Ann's mother had a dress shop in her home, and Julie had been helping her there every Saturday. She spent nearly every weekend at her house.

The morning was cool and overcast, so Jamie and I played in our room and wrote in our new yellow tablets.

After lunch, we went outside. Dad was working on the fence in front of the house, so we started around to the backyard.

"I've fixed the hinges on that gate and oiled them," Dad said. "And replaced the missing palings. So you kids watch how you use it."

We walked over to the gate and opened and closed it. Sure enough, it didn't squeak. I swung it back and forth a few times, testing it. "Don't swing on that gate!" We moved away from the gate and sat on the porch steps watching him.

He was fixing the picket fence out by the road when the mailman stopped and handed him a letter.

Dad turned it over in his hands, read the return address, then slowly tore the narrow end off the sealed envelope, took out the message, and read it. Then he returned the letter to the envelope and slipped it into the bib pocket of his overalls.

At the supper table he said to Mom, "Floyd Perry will probably be home any day now. He wrote Julie that any kind of a job would pay him better than the three C's."

Mom said, "Do you think a kid like that can even find a job nowadays?"

"I don't know," Dad replied. "Ben Collier was telling me just yesterday he could use a regular hand over at the sawmill. I thought I'd go over and speak to him tonight about giving Floyd the job. Floyd would make him a good, steady worker, if he hasn't found someone already."

Dad put the letter, addressed to Julie, on the stand table when he left for Crowe. She found it there when she got home later that Sunday. She picked it up, then threw it down again. She started to walk away, but turned back, and took the letter with her to the attic.

When Mom sent me to the attic to make the boys' bed and pick up things, Julie had my geography book spread across our bed, opened to the big map of the United States, and she was pencil-marking the shortest way home to Greene County from Idaho.

Dad came home the weekend school started, and the week after that. I heard him tell Mom that he'd try to get home every week and get the place ready for winter. After bad weather set in, he might not be able to make it home for two or three months.

I watched the clouds swinging low over the hills and waited impatiently for winter.

When school started, Doris and Carney Collier came to our school, but Doris was quiet and standoffish. The very first day, Frieda and I asked her to come play with us, but she just shook her head and turned away.

She always got to school just in time to take her seat before the bell rang and was the first one to leave the room when school was out.

Doris wore two or three different dresses that first week. They were always starched slick and hardly faded at all. I thought she felt like she was too good to play with us because we had only one or two dresses to our names, and they had been washed and faded until they hung limply around our knees.

Dad said he bet Ben Collier made a good living from his sawmill. He ought to; if he didn't, he wasn't out any money for hired hands. Most of his help were men working off a debt for raw slab lumber. All of them but Floyd Perry. He said Ben was lucky to get Floyd for any amount of money.

Floyd had come to our house the first week after school started. He was a lot bigger than when he went away. He slung the canvas bag that held all his stuff into a corner of the kitchen and lifted Mom plumb off her feet in a bear hug. Her eyes had been wet when he finally put her down.

Then he had turned and gathered the boys up in his arms and smiled at Julie over their heads. Floyd slept on a pallet on the kitchen floor that night and set off early in the morning to see Ben at the mill. He went to work for Ben that morning and got a room with board at the teacher's house.

Floyd didn't come over often, he was kept too busy working at the mill. He said people came from all over the county and bought the rough planks and built houses. Or they would build on another room or porch to the house they lived in. Dad said the lumber was green and unseasoned. It would warp all out of shape in a year's time. A man was a fool or worse, who would waste his time and money building a house with green boards.

I thought a warped barn and porch would be better than the ones we had, but, wisely, I never said so. Every time the wind came up, I expected to see our porch go flying through the air. The holes and loose boards had to be skirted like a game of hop-scotch whenever we used the front door. But if Dad said a hole in the floor was better than a solid, warped board, I'd better believe it, even if I fell through the hole.

I supposed that was the reason Doris wouldn't have anything to do with Frieda and me. She lived in a big house with a solid porch, and her papa made a lot of money at the sawmill.

Doris was a small-boned girl with long yellow hair and the bluest eyes. Not deep blue like the violets that bloomed thick in the woods, but blue like the skies in summer. Her skin was so pale and thin I could see every vein like fine blue threads on a white quilt top. When she bent forward over her desk, her hair covered her face, and all I could see was her starched dress and fine dandelion hair. She reminded me of an ear of unshucked corn, its bright silk tassel sprouting from one end. I thought the reason she sat in the room and read during the noon hour was probably because she was too frail to mix in our games and would break into a million pieces if she ever fell.

Last year Frieda and I had sat together at noon and traded sandwiches. But this year she walked home for her lunch every day. Her mother was expecting a baby, and Frieda had to help her. She lived a ways from school and sometimes she barely made it back before the bell rang. I sat on one side of the school room to eat lunch and Doris sat on the other.

Sometimes, when I would glance her way, I would surprise her looking in my direction. But she never smiled or even acted like she saw me. She would quick drop her head or look out the window next to her desk.

Maybe, if we had gone down to her house just once last summer, Doris and I would be friends right now. I wished Jamie and I had leaped from our hiding place in the woods that day and made ourselves known to her and Carney. Even if it had scared them, they would've been over it by now.

The boys yelled, "Stuck-up! Stuck-up! Hair like a buttercup." But Doris sat quietly at her desk and read, as if she was the only one in the room and hadn't heard a word they said.

Then one day while we sat reading with an empty room between us. Doris asked to borrow the book I had when I was finished with it.

I said, "Sure, if you like Gene Stratton Porter's books. This one is about a girl named Amaryllis who lives in a magic garden."

She smiled at me. "I know. I read a lot of her books. Whenever I can find one."

From then on, we exchanged books, helped each other on book reports for English class, and swapped our family history.

She had an older sister. But her sister Della was a lot older than Julie and had been out of school a long time. Doris said Della had worked in the city until she began to get fat, then she quit her job and came home to stay.

She said, "Della hardly ever leaves the house. Papa built a room onto the big house for her, and she stays in there most of the time. Della doesn't like living back in the hills, but Mama told her it wasn't what she liked that made her fat, but what she got. So she never says much about it anymore."

As the days grew shorter, the noon hours seemed to grow shorter. Our class assignments became easier when Doris and I did them together. We whispered and giggled as we bent our heads over the huge encyclopedia to look up assignments for history. We both hated that class, but together we made it fun instead of a distasteful task.

We found out we were the same age, liked a lot of the same things, and disliked some people for the same reasons. We talked a lot, but she didn't say much more about her family or where they had lived before they moved to Greene County. I didn't ask her any questions. I figured if she wanted me to know about it, she would tell me.

She seemed to be starved for someone to talk to and as eager as I was to be friends. I wondered how I could have thought her stuck-up. She was nice.

chapter twelve

*D*oris was in the eighth grade with Frieda and me. Carney was older than Doris but a grade behind her in school. He wasn't dim-witted or stupid; he just wasn't interested. Doris said that once her papa had sworn Carney was going to get an education and amount to something if it killed the both of them. From the way it looked to me, most likely it would.

One evening, Doris asked me to walk home with her. The day was cloudy and overcast, and dusk had fallen earlier than usual. The hills with their tall trees and dark thickets of hazelnut frightened her. She had lived in the hills all fall and part of the summer, but her mama made her stay close to home.

"I guess if it wasn't for school," Doris said, "she'd never let me out of her sight."

I wanted to tell her that Jamie and I had spied on her and watched her house from the top of the ridge that summer, but I wasn't sure she would understand. Our friendship was too new, and the thought of losing her for a friend scared me to death.

Doris always stayed after school now and helped me clean the room. Since Frieda had got her new baby brother and had to hurry home every day, I had been doing it alone. Every night I'd walk home with Doris when we'd finished and cut back above the sawmill on the path Jamie and I had made over the ridge and through the woods. I would still get home about the same time, so no one knew I took Doris home; and I didn't tell them.

One evening when we were done earlier than usual, I took Doris down the path that led to our house. At the footlog I told her, "If you ever want to come to my house, just cross the creek there, and when you get to the top of the bank on the other side, you can see our barn. Jamie and I have made a clear path from the barn to the footlog and up to our hidden cave."

I pointed to the big flat rock that jutted out from the hillside. The trees that had shielded it from sight all summer were nearly bare, and the rock stood out in plain view for all to see. I had never taken Frieda to the cave, but now I said to Doris, "Would you like to see my secret place? No one else knows about it but Jamie. We share it. But he won't mind if I share it with you."

She came eagerly, kicking the yellow and red beech

and maple leaves that lay thick on the ground as she walked. The smoky purple haze of Indian summer still hovered over the hills, but dusk had already settled in the room under the big flat rock.

Doris hesitated at the mouth of the cave, then ducked her head and followed me into the deep shadows of the place Jamie and I claimed for our own.

No matter how hard or how long it rained, the space under the rock was always dry. The stone ledge where Jamie set his cigar box of treasures never drew dampness or mildew.

I showed Doris where I kept my diary notebook stuck in a crack between the rocks. The pages were coming loose from the backstitching, and I had to watch how I handled it. The notebook was nearly full except for a few empty lines and blank places that I was saving in case something important happened. I wanted to be sure I had a place to write it all down.

When I pulled the notebook from between the rocks to show Doris how dry the cave stayed all the time, loose pages fell from my hand and scattered across the dirt floor. She picked them up and stepped toward the light.

"It's my diary," I said quickly, and moved to take them from her hands.

She looked up from the paper she was reading and said, "Oh, but it's about this cave. Only you make it sound like Ali Baba's cave and not just a hollow place in the hill, like it really is."

I dropped my hands and stepped back. I was half angry—and so ashamed I couldn't look at her. Now she would know that I not only told stories, I even wrote them down to keep like some treasure. I wished with all my heart the floor would crack open and swallow me from sight.

"Tomorrow," I promised myself, "I'll tear it all in tiny pieces and throw it in Lick Crick where no one else can ever read it."

Then Doris spoke again. "Seely, I won't read anymore if you don't want me to; and I won't tell your secret to a soul. Cross my heart and hope to die. My mama thinks I'm lazy and selfish because I like to be by myself and draw pictures. I don't have any place to keep my pictures and Mama throws them away. She says I'm wasting my time. But I've got lots of time. I just start all over again on another piece of paper."

Suddenly, I felt all right again. "My mom says it's a disgrace the way I tell lies," I told Doris. "But it's not really lying. It's just seeing things the way you want them to be or telling the story different from the way it really happened to make it funny and happy."

I dug along the wall beside Jamie's rock ledge and cleared the dirt away, leaving a clean, smooth surface.

"You can have this end for your stuff if you want to share our hideaway," I said. "Jamie won't care. He likes you, too."

The next day Doris had her schoolbag loaded with brown wrapping paper and big black marking pencils from her papa's mill. After we finished cleaning the school, we stopped by the cave again and stored her belongings before going on to her house.

Doris asked me one night if I had hair under my arms or between my legs.

I said, "No. Why should I have hair under my arms or anywhere else?"

"I don't either," she replied. "But we've got to be real careful once hair starts growing there."

She walked a little farther, kicking at the dead leaves and twigs lying in the path. She stopped and waited for me to catch up to her. "You tell me if you see any hair growing on your body any place, and I'll be sure to tell you. I don't know why we get all hairy, but when we do, we can have babies real easy if we aren't careful."

I thought about what she had told me all the way home. I couldn't understand how one thing could have anything to do with the other. But I was sure going to watch for signs of hair.

Instead of Doris having the answers to the questions that were puzzling me, she had given me another problem to fret over.

It was raining when Doris came to my house for the first time on a Saturday. We had to stay indoors all day. Mom didn't like it, but she never said a word about it. Instead she went about the house tight-lipped and banging cabinet doors and pots and pans, as if they were at fault and the cause of the rain.

The rain didn't let up until late in the evening. We were eating supper when Carney knocked on the kitchen door and said his mama had sent him over to get Doris and walk home with her. Mom didn't ask him to sit down, nor did she ask them to come back again when they left.

After they had gone and Mom knew they couldn't hear her, she started to preach at me. "You don't need to think for one minute, young lady, that you're going to start running around with Doris Collier. I don't want her in this house, or to ever hear tell of you going over there."

"Why ever not? I like Doris. Her mama says I can stay all night with her anytime I want to. And I want to Monday night. I've already promised."

"Don't you sass me, Missy! You heard what I said. That girl will turn out to be just like her sister, Della. Fat with a big belly, and more than likely, she don't even know who it was that got her that way. Now, you shut up about it."

I shut up, but I didn't stop thinking about what she had said. Doris was as skinny as a broom. She would never be as fat as Della.

chapter thirteen

*M*onday night I sent a note home with Jamie to say I was going home with Doris to stay all night. He took the slip of yellow paper, folded it, and put it in his pocket.

"Does Mom know you're going to stay with Doris tonight?"

I crossed my fingers behind my back. "Yes. She knows it."

I knew it was a far cry from Mom knowing I wanted to go and her saying I could, but I was ready to risk her anger this once. I wanted to see what it was like to sleep away from home. I never had, and Julie got to all the time.

Doris and I took our own sweet time cleaning the school room. We used the last of the water to wash and scrub the brown scum from the inside walls of the big water crock. We filled the jug with fresh water every day, but it looked like no one had ever cleaned it. When we had finished, it took both of us to carry the jug outside to dump the dirty water and to lift it back on to the table when we were done with it.

It was after dusk when we locked the door and started down the path to her house. Doris took my hand and held tight as we approached the dark woods. She kept glancing back over her shoulder as if she expected something to creep up behind and grab her.

"I'm not really afraid of these woods when you're walking with me. But sometimes, when I'm alone, I think I hear footsteps like someone following me. Then, when I stop and look back, there isn't a soul on the path. One time, I thought I saw Simmy Walters hiding behind some trees. But maybe he was just going by here on his way to town."

I said, "Simmy Walters? Frieda's uncle? What on earth would he be doing on the path to your house? He doesn't live around here."

Simmy wasn't as old as my dad or Mr. Thompson, but I'd bet he was thirty. I couldn't imagine what he would be doing in our part of the woods. He hardly ever went to Frieda's. She told me he only came by once in awhile for a good meal and a place to sleep. I didn't know Doris had ever seen or heard tell of Simmy. I'd only seen him once.

Doris said, "He used to hang around with Della. But lately, he's sure made himself scarce around our house."

She peered into the darkening woods as if she expected Simmy to jump out in front of her. "Papa says he'll shoot his backside off if he ever dares to show his face at our house again."

I giggled, and the sober expression fled from Doris's face. She laughed and the scar on the left side of her face deepened into a wide dimple. I had asked her once how she had got the scar, and she said, "It was my uncle Mac's fault. He left his razor on the table and I tried to shave and cut my face."

That was the only time I ever heard Doris mention any family except the ones she lived with. I had thought she was like me and didn't have any relatives, just dead ancestors.

Doris and I went directly upstairs when we got to her house. There were four bedrooms up there, with doors opening off a wide hall. She and her mama had the two rooms on one side of the hall, and her papa and Carney slept on the other side. Della had the big room which had been built on downstairs. Even before we moved to Greene County, we never had that many rooms.

Doris couldn't believe it when I told her my mom and dad slept together in the same room, and I had shared a bed with Julie all my life.

After she had changed from her school skirt to a cotton dress, we went down to the living room. I told Doris I bet we could've set our whole house into that one room. She laughed and said she bet I would bet on anything. I said, "Well, I'll bet you've got the biggest house in the county."

111

We looked through the books that were shelved along one wall and took down a heavy encyclopedia. We carried it to a table in the middle of the room and began to turn the pages. Then it dawned on me. They didn't have a stove! Everybody we knew had a stove in the middle of their front room. But the Colliers didn't.

"Hey, where's the heating stove? How do you keep it warm in here?"

Doris said, "There's a furnace in the cellar under the house. It heats all the rooms, except Della's. She has a stove in there. Papa built it after we moved here and it doesn't have a cellar."

Della's room had been built of rough lumber and stained a deep walnut on the outside. It had a shake shingle roof that joined the eaves of the kitchen and came down to the ground on the far end. There was a wide plank door opening onto a porch, which ran the full length of the room, and a boardwalk leading to the privy.

Ben had built the privy, too. A sizable three-holer that set downhill from their well and downwind from the house. Doris and I were perched over the high seats when we heard her mama calling us to supper. We ran up hill all the way to the house and didn't get our breath until we were seated at the round oak table.

I sat next to Doris and faced Carney across the table. I bowed my head waiting for someone to give thanks. When no one spoke, I looked up. Carney winked at me and made a face. His mama said, "Carney," quietly. And I bent my head, again.

Carney's voice rolled out like he was calling hogs from

forty miles downstream. "Good food, good meat, good Lord, let's eat."

I forgot to keep my eyes closed and my head down. I stared at him until he finished speaking, then he winked again and stuck out his tongue at me.

Ben laughed and passed the meat platter to Carney. I kept my eyes on my plate and didn't look at him once all during supper.

Della left the table while the rest of us were still eating. When she stood to leave the table, she smiled shyly at me, and I thought how beautiful she was with her wide dark eyes and all that shining black hair framing her small, pale face.

She was fatter than she had been the last time I had seen her. Her stomach was bulging out where her legs met at her straddle and lay in her lap like a large, hard pumpkin when she sat down. She walked funny, too, like a woman carrying a heavy basket of wet wash out to the clothes line. As I watched her walk from the room, I thought, "Why, she looks just like Mom did before Robert came, like she's expecting a baby!" But how could that be? Della didn't have a husband.

Mrs. Collier left the table right after Della and followed her to her room and shut the door.

Doris and I did the dishes. She washed, I wiped, and we both put them away. Each dish had its place in the cabinet, and the shelves had clean white paper on them. Mom saved newspaper to line our cabinet drawers and shelves. I just supposed everyone did. But the white paper did look cleaner and prettier.

113

Mrs. Collier came out of Della's room and told us to take a lamp and go upstairs. We could do our homework up there. She said Della wasn't feeling well and our talking and giggling were disturbing her.

I had been sound asleep when the screaming woke me. I was still curled to Doris's back, the way we had gone to sleep.

Her hands were over her ears, and she was trembling and shaking, trying to muffle the sound of her crying.

I whispered, "Sh-sh-sh, it's only the hoot owls. A hoot owl nearly scared me to death, the first time I ever heard one scream. But they won't hurt you."

The next scream sounded nearer, like it was right in this house with us. I wondered if hoot owls could get in our room and what I could do if they did.

Doris turned to me and put her wet face against my shoulder. I smoothed her hair with one hand and patted her back with the other, just the way I did Jamie when he had one of his fits. I patted her and talked to her until she quieted her crying. I could tell by her breathing that she had gone back to sleep.

I couldn't go to sleep, but I didn't hear any more screaming. I heard footsteps in the kitchen, though, and the sound of metal touching metal with a soft clanging together. It reminded me of the ghost stories Jamie told. There was always a skeleton dragging a chain across the floor or up and down the stairs, in all of them.

I moved closer to Doris and listened to the creaking boards in the floor downstairs. Once, I heard a door open and close and someone walking on Della's porch. As I was drifting off to sleep, someone came upstairs, footsteps passed in the hall, and a door closed at the far end.

My last thought was that Carney had been trying to scare Doris and me with all those weird noises.

Mrs. Collier shook me awake. "You girls are late for school. Get up, and be quiet getting dressed. There's no time for breakfast. Now, you both hurry!"

My arms were numb where Doris had slept on them. My fingers tingled and I had trouble tying my shoes. I broke a shoestring, but we both broke all records getting dressed and ready for school. Carney was nowhere around as we grabbed our books and left the house, running for the woods and the short cut to school. We were in the clearing when the first bell rang and walked through the door as class was called to order.

I didn't learn much in school that day. My mind was on the night just passed and the one coming on. I would have to face up to Mom for going against her word. I hoped for a switching. It wouldn't last as long as a tongue-lashing nor hurt half as much. I wished with all my heart I hadn't gone near the Colliers. I wished it was tomorrow. Lord, I wished I was dead!

Doris left as soon as the dismissal bell rang. She was the first one out the door and walking fast, as if she couldn't wait to get home. I cleaned up half-heartedly and then I just poked along home. I could wait.

I sat at the supper table, my eyes glued to the plate of cold bacon and pancakes, my dry mouth chewing up food I couldn't swallow. Mom was giving me old billy-hell for going home with Doris. Every word she spoke was worse than a hickory stick across my back, and I knew I had it coming for disobeying her.

"I'll swear I don't know what I'm going to do with you, Seely. You won't mind a word I say to you. I'll let your daddy take care of you when he gets home."

I thought, "It's nearly over, thank God."

Whenever Mom said she would let Dad handle something or other, it meant she had washed her hands of the whole kit and caboodle. More than likely this would be the last I ever heard of it. She would never mention it to Dad. If he knew, it would be like stirring up a hornet's nest with a fiery stick.

The next morning I met Doris where the rail fence marked the boundary of the playground. She linked her arm through mine, and we walked together to the door. We both talked at once, hearing but not listening to what the other one was saying.

"Papa hadn't left for the mill, yet. Usually, when he and Mama are fussing, he gets up early and leaves for work. But not today. Mama got testy about Papa's tools on the kitchen table last night. Papa said she shouldn't be so touchy about where he left the tools of his trade. A man's trade was his woman's living. Then Mama told him to get her living off the table, she didn't want to look at it."

I laughed. Doris went on with her story.

"I don't think it's the tools they're fighting about. Mama's using them as an excuse to cover something else. Papa said, 'You were plenty pleased to see me dump them there last night.' Mama looked up and saw me and said, 'Shush, we'll not talk about it now.' I'll bet they could hardly wait for me to get out of earshot."

The last bell rang as we hurried to our seats.

chapter fourteen

*T*he dried brown corn-
stalks were higher than my head. Dead leaves rattled and
cracked in the cold wind, like skeleton bones, as I followed the path I had made last summer through the
green corn. This was the first time I'd been in the cornfield since the corn had been husked. I felt as if I was
walking through a forest of cornstalks. Wherever I
looked, all I could see were the tall brown stalks and gold
leaves waving in the cold wind. I thought how easy it
would be to get lost in this skeleton forest. I would just
let my feet wander in any row they happened to stumble
onto and not even look at the path. I had tried once to get
lost in the fog on the way to school, but somehow my
feet had found the way to the schoolhouse door.

The only sound was the crackling corn leaves above
my head. I was cold and wishing I had never promised

Clara to go with her today. I thought of all the other things I could be doing as I zigzagged my way down the narrow path.

The path ended behind the Brent barn, near the woodpile. I could see George cutting hickory bark for stove kindling and hear Clara calling from the house. He didn't seem to hear her, and I know he didn't hear me. He was talking to himself.

"Guess if I was dead and in hell with my back broke, I'd still hear that damn fool woman hollering, 'More bark, George. Come and put a stick of wood in the stove, George!' Helpless damn fool woman."

He must have seen my shadow fall across the woodpile. He stopped talking to himself and turned around.

"Hi there, little one. You want to see Clara? She's in the kitchen. Go right on in, she'll be right glad to see you."

I walked toward the back door, kicking at a few wood chips and looking at the worn, scuffed toes of my shoes. I hoped Clara would be "right glad" to see me. Maybe she had changed her mind or forgotten she'd asked me to go to the city with her.

I was uncomfortable about going to the county seat with Clara. When she asked Mom if I could keep her company on the drive, Mom said it would be good for me. I was always a little leery of anything Mom said was good for me. They were usually things like castor oil, spinach, and turnip greens.

Clara Brent was drying the breakfast dishes and putting them in the glass-front cabinet when I knocked on the door and then walked in without waiting. Most of the women didn't like it when the kids did that, but Clara didn't mind one whit. She said it saved her the trouble of walking to the door. I could see why she wouldn't want to walk any more than she had to. Her tiny feet and ankles didn't look hardly strong enough to carry all the weight she piled on them.

She said she was glad for my company on the trip to the county seat. George wasn't any fit companion on a drive of any kind, she told me. She told me a lot of things that George wasn't.

Clara drove right down the middle of the road, swerving to one side when we met another car, then back to the middle again. She chatted and asked questions all the while about everybody I knew. Usually, she just kept on talking and didn't give me a chance to answer her. But when she asked me if Della Collier's baby was a boy or a girl, she paused and didn't go on, waiting for me to tell her.

I must have resembled a tongue-tied imbecile, because Clara said, "You mean you don't know? Or ain't she had it yet? It was due ten days or two weeks ago."

So that was the reason why Della was so fat. She *was* going to have a baby. "But she doesn't have a husband!" I'd blurted my thoughts out loud.

Clara turned her head to look at me and ran off the edge of the gravel road. She got the car back in the middle of the road before she said, "Didn't anyone ever tell you, Seely, that a husband isn't necessary for a girl to have a baby?"

We didn't talk about having babies at our house. Babies came, they were there, and we accepted them. It seemed to me, they grew overnight. One day, a family wouldn't have a baby, then the very next day there was a baby in the house. But there was always a husband there first.

Clara gave me an odd look from the corner of her eye and didn't say anything more about Della. We were coming into the city limits, and I guess she had to pay attention to her driving. It was just a little after ten, but already the streets were packed with people who had come to town to do their Saturday trading. Clara dodged the oncoming traffic and the cars parked along the street, until she came to the courthouse. She parked haphazardly in two spaces on the town square, took me by the hand, and struck off catty-cornered across the street.

"You've been so good to help me all summer," she said, "and then with the canning this fall. I'd like to get you a few things. I don't know what you kids hanker for nowadays, so you come along with me and pick out what you want."

I told her I hadn't done anything. It was the truth. I had been at her house when she was canning, but I just watched her and listened to her stories, the same as I had been doing all summer long.

She said it was time I learned to pick out my clothes and buy wisely. A girl was never too young to learn how to spend money. She chuckled and pulled me into a store.

I was taken by the soft lavender color of a skirt and blouse in the window. But Clara rummaged through a load of dresses on a long iron rack and pulled a horrible mustard-colored one with long sleeves from a hanger and held it up to me. I slumped so it would hang long. She put it back on the rack and picked out another. I stood there shaking my head at every dress she showed me.

Finally, she said, "Seely, what do you think?" I pointed to the lavender skirt and blouse in the window. Clara liked them, too, and she bought them. She bought me three pairs of cotton-knit panties, as well, which made a change for every school day, if I counted the two pairs Mom had made me from feed sacks. I always had one pair on and one pair drying.

I tried on one pair of shoes after the other to find a pair that didn't squeeze my feet. Dad always bought my shoes, and they would pinch and burn my toes till they fell off my feet. One year, I had worn the shoes he bought for Jamie. They were wide, square-toed, and thick-soled and didn't touch my feet any place. The kids at school had laughed at me for wearing a boy's shoes, but I had worn them anyway and pretended I didn't know what they were laughing about.

When we'd finished shopping, Clara headed for the café whose rusty sign screeched and whined in the wind. Inside, steam covered the windows and soaked the fly-specked menu pasted on the inside glass. The smell of coffee and bacon frying made my mouth water.

Clara headed for a booth at the back of the room. With the high sides around us, we couldn't see the other people, and no one could watch us eat.

She slid her tiny feet out of her high-heeled pumps

and rubbed her ankles together while we studied the grease-spotted menu propped against the wall.

Clara ordered for both of us. When the food came, I ate greedily. I was too hungry to be polite and wait for her. Peanut butter on cold biscuits would have tasted good to me right then, and I hated peanut butter above all things on earth.

"Honey, how old are you, now?" Mrs. Brent asked while we were eating.

I swallowed my mouthful of food. "I'll be twelve in December. Ten days from today, on Tuesday."

She cocked her head to one side and peered at me from under the folds of her eyelids. I wondered if she could see the two stubby horns beginning to show on my chest. She was staring in that direction.

I wore my shirts as loose as possible and slumped my shoulders when I thought of it to keep the bumps from showing. But the blouses were old, and I was outgrowing them before they wore out. Slumping didn't hide as much as I hoped it would.

"It's not going to be long, now, till you'll be needing some brassieres. I guess your mom hasn't noticed, but you're getting to be a young lady."

Clara took a bite of roll and chewed thoughtfully. "Have you started your periods yet?" she whispered.

I was squirming and trying to slump my shirt loose in front. My face was hot and I knew it must be red. The only periods I knew of came at the end of a sentence. I had never heard of having one. But just from the way she asked, I figured it had something to do with the bumps on my chest and the soft downy fuzz growing in my arm pits, but I wasn't sure. And until I could ask Doris about it, I wouldn't say anything. Not even to Clara.

She leaned across the table and patted my hand. "Well, never mind that now. It's late and we'd better be getting along toward home."

I slid out of the booth and gathered up my packages.

"My, what a lot of brought-on pretties you'll have to show off tonight."

Mom wasn't going to like it, I knew. She wouldn't allow us kids to take anything that had a tinge of charity, and these things would smack to high heaven of charity to her. I could just hear her now. "You'll not keep a stitch of that stuff, Missy. Don't need to harbor the thought for one second. If your daddy can't buy for you, you'll do without!" I hugged my packages closer to my chest.

Maybe Mom wouldn't notice me tonight, but wait till she saw me in these things tomorrow morning. That thought wiped the smile off my face in a hurry, and I walked a little slower down the street behind Clara.

chapter fifteen

*F*loyd worked at the sawmill for Ben from daylight to dark. He didn't have much time for fooling around, he told Julie, but sometimes he borrowed the teacher's car and took her in to McVille for a soda.

Mom watched them like a hawk. I could come and go as I pleased, like going to town with Clara, but Julie had to account for every minute she was out of Mom's sight. I would hear Mom questioning Julie when she came home from a ride in the car with Floyd, and Julie's irate answers.

Mom told her once she was going to end up just like Della Collier if she wasn't careful. Julie had answered angrily, "If I do, you'll have drove me to it!"

She never should have mentioned driving anywhere. Mom started in about the car again.

I wasn't sure I was going to like being a grown-up woman. But so far, I hadn't figured out how to keep from it. I would much rather stay the way I was and be eleven all the time.

Julie was grown-up, and there was one rule for the things she could do, and a lot of others on what she didn't dare do. If she didn't abide by them, Mom said she was courting hell's fire or, worse yet, an end like Della Collier's.

I got up early the Sunday morning after I'd been to town with Clara and put on the new lavender blouse and skirt and blue shoes before I went downstairs to breakfast. Mom took one look and nearly dropped the pan of biscuits she was taking from the oven. "Where on earth did you get that outlandish outfit?"

I started to tell her. "Mrs. Brent gave . . ."

"Well, you can give it back! There's no call for that woman to be buying your clothes."

"Here it comes," I thought. I could recite it word for word.

"If your daddy can't buy your dresses, you can do without. Now, change your clothes and call your brothers to breakfast."

I yelled from the foot of the stairs. "Jamie! Robert! Come and eat!" I didn't change my clothes.

Mom said, "I told you to wake your brothers, not the folks who live a mile down crick."

I ate with one eye on the clock and the other on the

back door. I wanted to be ready to grab my coat and leave for church the minute Doris and Frieda walked in the door.

Doris didn't have anything new for church, so we swapped blouses. I pulled her sailor middie over my head while she buttoned into my lavender one. Doris had stubby horns growing on her chest, also. I wondered if she hated them the way I did. She didn't slump or try to hide them. She acted as if she didn't know they were there. I hadn't thought about it before, but Frieda's blouse had always been full across the chest. Especially when she was wearing a sweater, like today.

In church that morning, Carney Collier sat behind us on the hard wooden bench saved for the latecomers. He poked Frieda in the back with his hymnbook and tried to talk to her when we stood for prayer. Finally, he slipped her a note written on a flyleaf torn from the hymnal.

The note said, "You're as pretty as a speckled pup. Will you walk home with me after church?"

We giggled when we read it, and a woman seated in front of us turned around and frowned and shook her head.

Carney walked with us to the dirt lane that angled off toward the mill. Frieda walked a few steps up the lane, talked for a moment, then came back to where Doris and I were waiting for her.

She said, "Carney's going to meet me here next Sunday and walk to church with us."

Big deal! Who would want to walk to church with

Carney? I hadn't forgotten how he had behaved the night I stayed at their house.

We teased Frieda about getting a beau in church. We said we bet the only reason she ever went was to see the boys.

She blushed and said, "Well, I'm not getting any younger, and I don't want to be an old maid."

"I'll probably be an old maid," Doris said. "I'd get skinned alive if I ever so much as looked at a boy."

"It's a sure bet that I'll die an old maid. I'd have to be skinned before a boy would ever look at me. Not that I'd want one to," I added.

Doris smiled and touched my face. "You'll be a pretty woman, Seely, when you grow up. You've got good bones."

I didn't want to have to go that far to be pretty. Doris was just trying to make me feel good. It was what grown-ups often said about people when they couldn't find anything else good to say. If I had to grow up, it was going to be for a better reason than that one.

But I did think God had slighted me, and I had told Him so in church. I had prayed and asked Him to please make my hair turn dark chestnut, like my mother's, and fall in deep waves to my shoulders, like Julie's; but it never changed. It still hung white and straight as a string, like the girl's hair on the Dutch cleanser can.

I was about ready to give up on prayers and wishes. It was just like Mom said, "Wish in one hand and blow in the other, you'll get the same thing."

Doris and I slipped quietly into Mom's bedroom to

change our blouses again and closed the door. I had my arms over my head, struggling to get out of the middie blouse, when I heard the door open. I turned my back as the footsteps came toward me, then I felt Mom's hands at the buttons, loosening the sleeves, and lifting the middie over my head. She turned it right side out, handed it to Doris, and passed the lavender blouse to me.

"If you're bound and determined to keep that outfit, you'd best take care of it. You know I don't hold with you loaning your things."

Doris was tugging at my hand, wanting to get out of the house. So did I, but Mom had a fold of my skirt in her hand, rubbing it between her thumb and finger.

"This feels like good material, soft to the touch but tight-woven." She dropped the skirt and stepped back. "Well, what are you girls standing around in here for? Go and play outside."

We raced out of the house, past the barn, across the footlog and into the woods. Laughing and breathless, we dropped on to the big, flat, overhanging rock to rest. During the past year, Jamie and I and the wind had worn the huge rock smooth and clean.

From up there, we could see the high banks where Lick Crick ran into the wide, muddy water of White River and far off, the sandy bottom land where watermelons grew round and juicy in the summertime.

The big rock was warm on the side where the sun had touched it, and the cold wind didn't strike us there. We sat close together on the warm stone and imagined we were flying the Atlantic with Amelia Earhart; we were well known public figures, dressed up in red satin and patent leather spike heels, having dinner at the White House. The President was at one end of the long table and Mrs. Roosevelt was at the other. Doris and I were seated right next to the President.

Then Doris said, "What are you eating tonight?"

I thought the play acting was finished. I said, "It's Sunday. Chicken and dumplings, for sure."

She rolled around on the rock, screaming with laughter. "I can just see President and Mrs. Roosevelt eating stewed chicken and dumplings for supper."

She was still laughing and wiping her eyes.

I turned away from her. "I don't care what they eat for supper. I was through playing that stupid old game, anyway."

The silence stretched between us. I felt chilled to the bone and wanted to move closer to Doris, but I hated to be the one to give in. I got up, walked around the top of the rock, and sat down as near as I could get to her. "Let's talk about Someday, Doris. All the things we're going to do Someday."

"You mean, when we grow up? I'm going to paint this hill country in every color of the rainbow. I'll be a very famous artist and probably die a tragic death before my time."

I said, "People don't die before their time. I know. Whenever somebody dies, Mom always says, 'Well, it was their time to go.' "

Another long, heavy silence settled around us. This time it was Doris who spoke first. "Oh, Seely, you're just being ornery. You know it was just pretend. I draw pictures because there's nothing else to do back here in the hills. It's all make-believe, like your fancy stories. We'll probably both end up like all the other hill women, with a pot of beans on the stove and ten kids underfoot."

We giggled and moved close together again on the big flat rock.

"Let's go to Frieda's house and see what she's doing. Maybe she has some scrap paper we can use. We've got all day for our drawing and writing, and here we sit, doing nothing."

Every time we went to see Frieda, Doris stayed in the yard and drew pictures of the dilapidated barn. I had thought at first she used her drawing as an excuse to keep from going into the house, but she truly thought the old falling down barn was beautiful.

She had stacks and stacks of sketches of the faded gray barn in the cave. She made drawings of the footlog on Lick Crick, too, with the weeping willows drooping along the bank, their branches trailing to the water's edge. Lately, she had been drawing the bare skeleton trees that stood on the hillside, the animal tracks winding down them like blood vessels on the back of a man's hand. In her pictures, the tracks all led to the river, and the river ran out of the hills.

Doris liked to draw pictures of me, too. While I sat quietly writing or reading, she would make pencil drawings of my long hands and solemn face. She would say, "Smile, Seely. You look so sad and stern when you're not smiling. No wonder the kids think you're mad all the time."

When Jamie tagged along with us, Doris would put our

two faces close together on the same piece of paper. Jamie always had a small, shy smile; and sometimes she would catch the soft, dreamy look in his eyes. Doris said we were like the two sides of a man's life. Jamie was the dreamer and planner of beautiful things and I the stern discipliner. In the pictures Doris gave to Mom, I could see a strong resemblance between my dad and me. I decided to look more closely at him the next time he came home.

I thought Jamie favored Mom. But I held my tongue. We had to keep him in good humor with us so we could use his school paper. Or borrow for us when we used all he had. If I told him he looked like a girl, he would refuse to help us.

We used the bare, blank spaces in my history workbook and the reverse side of class assignments for our drawing and story-writing. When we had exhausted all other resources, we borrowed from the teacher.

Every time Dad came home, I had to ask him for money to buy more paper.

"Good diddlely damn! Seely, what do you do with all the paper you buy? Supply the whole school? Damn it, you got a big yellow Golden Rod tablet the last time I was home!"

He'd swear, then he would give me the dime I needed to buy more paper.

Dad never stinted when it came to buying school books and supplies. He said an education was better than owning your own piece of ground. That was one thing nobody could take away from you, once you had it.

132

Doris and I would walk to Bud Watson's general store and buy the thickest pad of paper he had.

"Seely, maybe we should have chosen a trade where the training didn't cost so much," Doris said.

But we continued to waste our paper, week after week.

chapter sixteen

*F*rieda and I were coming back from Old Man Bishop's well, the buckets bumping our legs and slopping over into our shoes with every step. We hadn't said a word since we lifted the heavy buckets and started down the road to the schoolhouse.

"A penny for your thoughts, Seely."

I said, "Show me first your penny."

We laughed and set the buckets down to rest and rubbed the red marks where the wire bucket bails had cut dents in the palms of our hands. Then we stuck our hands inside our coat sleeves to warm them.

"It's my birthday. I'm twelve years old today."

"My little water-bucket buddy is growing up. Pretty soon, you'll think you're too big to carry water with old Frieda."

She smiled and the tuck in her upper lip pulled the smile to one side of her face. "I'm too big now, Seely. I'm almost eighteen. If I didn't have my heart set on getting a school diploma, I'd quit and go to Kentucky and marry Clarence."

Clarence Bridgeman had quit school soon after the term had begun in the fall and joined the regular army. I knew Frieda had been writing to him, but I didn't think she liked him well enough to marry him. I didn't know how anyone could like him that much.

I said, "Do you really like him that much? Pretty as you are, Frieda, you could marry anybody you wanted to. Why do you want to marry Clarence?"

"After awhile, a body gives up expecting anything better, and they settle for what they can get." She gave me another crooked smile. "And I can get Clarence. He don't mind that I can't speak plain for spluttering."

I laughed with her and picked up the bucket and went on down the lane to the schoolhouse. She didn't say anything more about marriage or her leaving school. I hoped she would forget about both and let everything stay just the way it was now.

But the next day, as soon as the schoolhouse door closed behind us, Frieda started talking about Clarence.

"I feel like a fool every time I get up to leave the room," she said. "When Clarence was here, I didn't feel so bad about being so big and still in school. He was older than me, and we'd been here together since the second grade. You know what, Seely? I think the teacher picked on Clarence just to get rid of him."

I said I didn't know if the teacher picked on him or if Clarence baited the teacher just to rile him. But they sure didn't get along very well.

The last day Clarence had been to school, he and the teacher had been at odds about one thing or another from the minute the bell rang. We had been in the middle of our Health and Hygiene class when Mr. Thompson asked Clarence to tell him what a hangnail was.

Clarence had snickered and said, "Ain't that something you hang your coat on, teacher?" Then he laughed out loud.

The teacher's face was as red as a beet and the veins stood out on his neck like fat fishing worms. I thought he was going to bust a blood vessel, he was so angry. He screamed at Clarence and threw the health book with all his might and hit him between the shoulder blades. Clarence stumbled when the book struck him and nearly fell, but he caught himself just in time and slouched on down the aisle to his seat.

Mr. Thompson continued to yell at Clarence. He told him to get out and never come back. "Take your stuff with you. I want no excuse to ever see you here again," he said.

Clarence cleaned the junk from his desk and shuffled out the door, shoulders bent and shamefaced. His hair had grown long and shaggy again, and red curls fell over his ears and turned up around his collar. I could feel his hurt and shame, and I was sorry for Clarence.

Clarence never looked back, and we never saw him again.

Later on, Frieda got a letter from him. He had joined the army and was somewhere in Kentucky.

Frieda was still talking about him. "His dad went all the way to Kentucky on a Greyhound bus to see him. And once he got there, he just stayed. That's what I'd like to do," she said. "Right now, I've got a big hankering to walk to the hard road, catch one of them big buses, and keep right on going."

Frieda was still at school when we drew names for the Christmas gift exchange. I got her name and wondered all the way home what I could give her. There wasn't anything at Bud Watson's store good enough for her.

I wondered who had my name. I had a horror of going to school on the day when the Christmas gifts were given out. Maybe I'd be left out. It happened nearly every year. When the presents were all gone from under the tree, there was usually one person whose name hadn't been called. The other kids would clutch their presents close to their chests and stare wide-eyed at the one who didn't get anything. I couldn't bear to think of that ever happening to me.

Mom gave me a string of red beads that she'd had for a long time to give Frieda for Christmas. She said they were far better than anything we could buy. After we had polished the beads and put them in a box, they looked almost brand new.

The gifts at school were given out on Friday before Christmas. Frieda liked the red beads and smiled as she fastened them around her neck so everyone could see her present. Carney Collier had my name, and I wouldn't show my gift or thank him for it. He had given me a bare naked celluloid doll in a brown paper sack and tied it with a twine string. But for once, no one was left out, and Mr. Thompson gave us each one a bag of candy and an orange.

A thump-pause, thump-pause woke me on Christmas morning. When I couldn't stand the uncertainty of waiting for the next thud, I got up, dressed hurriedly in the cold room, and ran downstairs. As I pushed the door open, a blunt-pointed arrow thudded into the attic door behind me. Robert was playing with a long wooden crossbow gun. A rawhide string was pulled tight from each end of the bow and hooked over the hammer of the gun. Just as I reached the foot of the steps, Robert pulled the trigger again.

"Where did you get that thing?" I screamed at him. "You might have killed me!" I started toward him, and he began to yell for Mom.

"Mommy! Mommy!" I mocked him, and stuck out my tongue at him.

Mom came in from the kitchen, and I asked, "Who armed that little bandit?"

"Now, Seely, don't start a fuss. Rob made that and brought it for him last night."

So that was why the attic door was closed this morning. Dad was home. While he was away, our door swung wide open, and Mom left the one to her room ajar, in case we needed her during the night. Also, it allowed a little bit of heat from the stove in the front room to filter up the steps and spread through the bitter cold of the attic. Dad liked to keep all the rooms closed off and save on fuel. We were surrounded by forests and fallen trees, but he wouldn't hear of wasting a stick of stove wood to heat the attic.

It was just before Christmas that Ben Collier had told Jamie he would give him a quarter if he would haul away all the short ends and scrap lumber that were piled in a heap near the big circle-saw. Jamie and Ben shook hands on the deal, and Jamie ran home to get a bushel basket from the barn to carry the wood. I followed him back to the mill.

Floyd Perry helped us fill the basket, placing the pieces snugly to the top then running a broken slat through the wire handles so I could help Jamie carry it. We toted enough wood to fill the box behind Mom's cookstove and still the pile loomed high beside Ben's circle-saw. For three days we lugged the loaded basket home from the mill and racked the wood outside the back door.

Mom had questioned our right to the wood, but Jamie told her that Ben Collier was paying him to haul it off. Ben wanted the wood moved away from the mill, so we moved it to our house.

On the fourth evening, Ben handed Jamie a quarter and thanked him for cleaning away the scrap wood. As we hurried along the path to get home before dark, I puzzled over Jamie's good luck. It seemed to me there had to be something wrong. I knew it wasn't stealing, but I couldn't quite figure out how it was possible for us to profit twice from the same piece of work. It seemed almost dishonest.

Now, on Christmas morning, Jamie sat perched on the

step stool seemingly unaware of my shouting at Robert, eating an orange and dropping the seeds and peels on to the floor by his bare feet. He had a new navy blue sweater pulled on over his faded pajama pants, and a navy stocking cap rolled to fit the back of his head. His dark tangled curls fell from beneath the cap and over his ears, making him look like one of the paper angels that dangled from the tree beside him. He smiled at me, and orange juice dribbled from the corner of his mouth.

I said, "Jamie, you're making a mess!" And wiped his chin.

I looked around the room, but I didn't see anything for me or Julie. Maybe Mom and Dad thought we were too old for Christmas. Or it could be that Dad just didn't like us anymore and hadn't brought us a gift. He didn't act like he knew we were on the place. Maybe he had forgotten we were.

I had asked Frieda one time if she knew why it was we never got to sit on our dad's lap or get hugged like the little kids.

She'd said, "I don't think anybody likes big kids. They don't pay no attention to you after you're old enough to go to school."

"Then why do people have babies if they don't like kids?"

"Oh, they like babies all right," Frieda answered. "It's just us big kids they can't stand."

Every thought and feeling I ever had reflected plain as a mirror on my face. The hurt and disappointment I felt at being left out on Christmas must have shown truly and clearly for Mom to see.

"Rob brought something for you girls, too. Surely you don't think your daddy would bring presents for one and not the other."

By this time, I didn't know what to think of my dad. After the way he had acted during the summer and last fall, I wouldn't put anything past him.

"There's something for each of you under the tree."

I knelt to reach the largest box, and Mom stopped me.

"Seely, the red box is for you. That one wrapped in hollyberry paper is for Julie."

I grabbed my package and ran upstairs to show Julie and tell her she had a Christmas present, too.

She sat on the edge of our bed, dressed and shivering, her arms hugging herself to keep warm.

"Come on," I urged her. "There's another box bigger than mine for you to open."

She smiled and reached for my present. "First, let's see what you've got here. Then we'll go look at mine."

I ripped at the box. Torn paper and string lay unnoticed where it fell. I could feel my heart hammering as we pulled away the top layer of paper, and I saw the creamy buff and cocoa sweater lying in the box. I couldn't believe it was for me. Julie slipped the sweater around my shoulders and framed my face with the wide shawl collar.

I hoped with all my heart that Julie's gift would be as beautiful as mine. If it wasn't, I would give my Christmas sweater to her, and I would wear my old one.

Mom called us to breakfast. Julie held back, then reluctantly followed me down to the kitchen. She nearly balked when she saw Dad seated like God at the head of the table, but then she stepped quietly into the room and took her seat.

Robert had brought the crossbow to the table and laid it by his place. It took up one whole end and threatened to knock the dishes off the table every time he touched it.

I said, "Mom, does he have to bring that contraption to breakfast? I don't have room to eat!"

Julie took the gun in her hands and examined it closely. "It's no wonder Robert is so proud of this gun," she said softly. "This is the most beautiful thing I've ever seen."

She put the crossbow down carefully beside his plate and hugged him to her. "Take good care of it, honey. There's an awful lot of somebody's time and patience tied up in that."

Dad cleared his throat a couple of times, then he said, "The nights can get to be almighty long when you're away from your home and family. It's then a man has time on his hands and a chance to do some whittling, if he can lay claim to a piece of wood. Finding the right-sized piece of hickory to whittle on held me up there for awhile."

A smile played tag from his eyes to the corner of his mouth, and he chuckled deep inside to give us to understand he was joking with us. When we didn't laugh or say anything, his big rough hands moved to his coffee cup and played a soft tap, tap, tap, with the spoon on his saucer.

"I've hankered for one of them crossbows ever since I was a boy no higher than my daddy's belt buckle, like

Robert there. But my daddy never had the time given to him to make me one. During the long evenings, I got to thinking about that. Him working from daylight to dark every day of his life and no time left to call his own." Dad paused and rubbed his eyes.

"I had the time and a boy who had never heard tell of a crossbow gun and wouldn't know one if he seen it. I made up my mind then, by God, I'd make him one if it took me the rest of my life to do it. Well, it didn't take quite that long, and when it was done, I told your mother if Robert don't want it I'll keep it for myself."

The boys roared with laughter at the idea of a man Dad's size, who had to duck his head to go through doorways, playing with a toy gun.

I studied Dad's face as he laughed and joked with the boys. It was hard for me to believe he had ever been a boy. I couldn't picture him wishing for things he couldn't have, wanting them so much he could still remember what it had been like not to get them. I looked from Dad's face to Robert's and I could see the same dark-honey hair, serious blue eyes, and the sober expression as they passed the crossbow back and forth between them. I thought to myself, "Robert is the living image of Dad. It's no wonder he loves him best."

Julie looked across the table at Mom, and when their eyes met, Mom nodded and Julie glanced quickly away. She slipped quietly from the room and returned shortly carrying the holly-wrapped package.

Dad and the boys weren't paying any attention to her or to what she was doing. They didn't seem to see the box or hear the rustling paper as Julie opened it. Robert and Jamie were begging Dad to tell them how he had made the crossbow. What part did he make first? How did he get the bow to curve like a half moon? And where did he get wooden nails? They said they had never seen wooden nails before.

Dad said he made the wooden pegs, too. Then he laughed aloud at their big-eyed look of disbelief. From her place at the table, Julie gave a smothered gasp, and half-laughing, half-crying, she lifted a cloud of pale blue wool and buried her face in its softness.

When she raised her head, her eyes were wet and shining as bright as the first star over Bethlehem. She seemed to glow with the joy and wonder of her Christmas gift; more like a little girl of seven, than a grown-up seventeen.

Dad didn't see the look of love and happiness on her face as she turned toward him, started to speak, then burst out crying. For just a moment she seemed rooted to the spot, then she hugged the soft blue wool to her chest and ran from the room.

Dad seemed stunned. He spoke quietly, disbelieving. "I thought she would like it."

He turned to Mom. "Zel?"

"She liked it fine, Rob. You don't understand. . . ."

Dad shoved his chair back and got to his feet. "I'll be damned," he said. "I'll never understand that girl, Zel. Not if I live to be a hundred years old."

He closed the kitchen door gently behind him and walked into the snow flurries, bareheaded and in his shirt sleeves. Mom clucked her tongue on the roof of her mouth, shook her head, and swore he would catch his death of cold, but she made no move to take him a coat or interrupt his walk in any way.

But Julie did. She came back to the kitchen, soon after he left it, wearing her new blue sweater. When she saw Dad walking in the snow, she grabbed his old sheepskin coat off the back of the door and carried it out to him. I don't know what Dad and Julie talked about while they walked in the snow, but when they came back to the house, they were both smiling.

chapter seventeen

When we started back to school, it was fifteen degrees. The snow squeaked under our feet. It seemed like the cold stillness of January would never end.

But it did. After the first week of February, the weather turned off warm and stayed warm, more like spring than a lull in winter. The days were getting longer, and we didn't have to hurry to get home before dark. Jamie went by the sawmill on his way home from school, and Doris and I dawdled along the path to her house and played under the bare sugar maple trees. In some of them, the little spouts were still plugged in for maple sugar sap, and rusty tin cups dangled on wire hooks from the last running.

The late winter sun slanted through the tree tops,

shedding a pale yellow light around us and making weird patterns at our feet.

Doris said, "I'm glad it's daylight. Shadows like that would scare me if it was dark."

I laughed at her. "If it was dark, you couldn't see the shadows."

"Well, I could if the moon was shining!"

I said, "Doris, you're just a fraidycat. Scared of your own shadow."

Under one of the huge maples, where the roots had broken through the soft dirt and lay on top of the ground like long, knobby-knuckled fingers, the earth was scuffed and marred by large boot tracks. It looked as if a big man had paced restlessly back and forth under the tree while he waited for someone to meet him. Near the edge of the path in the soft black dirt, we saw a smaller footprint, a woman's shoe mark. The two sets of tracks left the tree close together and faded on the hard-packed trail.

Doris stepped into the woman's tracks and pressed first one foot and then the other down on them erasing all trace but her own from under the tree.

She said, "They could have belonged to anyone. But people know we come by here. They won't think anything of it if they see our tracks along the path."

When I got home, Mom had the doors wide open and the windows raised as far as they would go, while she cleaned the copper pans with ammonia and scrubbed the pine floors with lye water. She said it was too hot. It wasn't natural.

"This weather won't last. It's too early. Probably leading up to a tornado or cyclone before it breaks, and then we'll be swamped by another spring flood," she said.

We wore our coats to school and let them drag on the path behind us on our way home. I stayed and played with Doris every evening until her mama came and warned me it was nearly dark, and I would have to go home.

Late one evening as I was loping along with my eyes on the path, I nearly ran headlong into Della and Simmy Walters walking on the path just ahead of me. Della was so thin and tiny, Simmy's arm reached all the way around her waist, and her head barely touched his shoulder. They were talking so earnestly, they hadn't heard me come up behind them. I stepped off the path and waited under the trees until they turned down the lane leading to the sawmill.

I thought to myself, "Old Simmy ain't no coward. He's walking right into Ben's reach, and Della is the only thing he has in his hands."

Doris always had a funny look on her face and drew away whenever Della's name was mentioned, so I didn't tell her I had seen Della and Simmy walking together in the woods.

Saturday morning Mom moved the furniture back against the wall and took the carpet up and carried it to the clothesline to beat the red clay dust out of it. Mom was airing bedclothes on one side of the house and beating dust from the carpet on the line in the barnyard when Doris got to our house that morning.

Doris said her mama had sent her to my house to play,

so she could get some housecleaning done. I said if we stayed around where Mom could find us, she was sure to find something for us to do. We'd probably be called to hold the line steady while Mom and Julie beat dust out of the rug into our faces.

We walked over to the Brents' house and talked to Clara. I think having Doris with me hampered Clara's overflow of information and put a damper on her questions. Usually, she just opened her mouth and let the words roll off her tongue freely. But this morning she would start to say something, then stop in the middle and change the subject.

I wondered where she came by all her news. Clara never seemed to know anything good about anybody. She carried bad news like a disease that was catching and passed it on to whoever happened to pass by.

About noon, Clara gave us peanut butter and jelly on yeast bread and told us we would have to carry it with us. She and George were leaving, going into town to do some trading.

We dragged our feet and munched the hard brown crust on the bread. When we came to the lane leading to the Walters' house, Doris said, "Let's go to Frieda's. It's too early to go home. The cleaning won't be half done yet."

At Frieda's house we looked through the Sears Roebuck catalog. Frieda showed us the red dress she had picked out for Graduation Day, if she passed. Doris and I chose the one we wanted, just alike, and knew all the time we wouldn't get it. Not in a million years!

Doris was supposed to meet her papa at the mill and walk home with him. He shut the mill down early on Saturday so the men could get to the store to do their trading. We had plenty of time to get there, so we crossed the ridge and followed the deep hollow up to the mill.

Floyd Perry saw us and motioned us back away from the buzz saw. We wandered around a bit, then found a bench and sat down to wait. While we were waiting for Ben to quit work, Doris sketched the mill and the old shed on the hillside behind it. I watched the men run the big logs past the speeding saw and stack the boards as they came off the other end like freshly sliced bread. Sawdust scattered through the air like ground cornmeal and settled like snow on the men's heads and clothes. Even their faces were covered with the fine tan dust.

I caught a glimpse of Ben sauntering over toward the big circle-saw, carrying a brand new toolbox. I wondered what he had done with the old one after he had dumped the tools out on the kitchen table that time. I don't know why it should, but the sight of Ben with a new toolbox made me think of the night I had stayed overnight with Doris. Somehow, there seemed to be some relation between the old toolbox, the screaming owls, and Della's talked-about baby.

I guess I was thinking out loud again when I said, "I wish you would draw a picture of Della's baby so I could see it. Everybody talks about Della and her baby, but I've never seen it."

I could hear the words echoing through my head and

hanging in the air between us. I wanted to call them back, swallow them, but they were already out and there was nothing I could do about it.

Doris stared at me as if I had hit her. Tears filled her eyes. She jumped up and started to run away, but then she stopped and walked slowly back to face me.

"You know Della doesn't have a baby! She and Simmy Walters got married last week, and maybe she'll have a baby, sometime. But she ain't got one now!"

Her voice rose, "You're just like everyone else, and I hate you!" As she finished speaking, tears streamed down her face, and she ran away from me to hide in the old shack on the hillside.

I didn't try to stop her. I sat on the bench and watched her go. I didn't know what to do. Mom had said if I wasn't careful, one of these days my mouth was going to get me in trouble for talking without thinking. Just this morning, when I told her I was going to Clara's, she said, "Seely, you've been around that woman so much you're getting to be just like her. I'll swear Clara's tongue is tied in the middle and flaps loose on both ends."

I guess she was right about it. Only Clara's loose tongue gave other people trouble, and mine made trouble for me. I wished I had bitten the hateful thing in two before it had hurt Doris.

I saw Ben Collier looking at me, so I got up and started to mosey along toward home. I wanted to go to the shack and tell Doris I was sorry. But I didn't think it was the time to say anything. Sometimes it's best not to say a word when a person is crying hurt.

I moped around the house until after supper.

"What's bothering Seely?" Mom asked Julie. "Is she sick? It's about time, I reckon."

I thought, "For Pete's sake! Can't I even think without being sick? And what does she mean, 'It's about time'? Don't tell me that now I even have to have a time to be sick!"

I slammed the door behind me and left the dishes wet and draining, to be dried later.

I met Doris just after I had crossed the footlog on Lick Crick. I was going to her house, she was coming to mine. We ran into each other's arms. She was crying, and I said over and over, "I'm sorry, Doris, I'm sorry."

She sat on the edge of the footlog, sobbed a couple of times, and wiped her nose on her loose shirttail.

"It's dirty, already," she said.

I sat down beside her and dangled my feet over the water. "Mom said I wasn't to come to your house, but I was coming anyway. She didn't say I couldn't play with you and be best friends."

She put her hand on my arm, then quickly took it away. "Maybe you won't want to be best friends when you hear what Mama said. She says no one wants to neighbor with a family whose girl has got in trouble and had a baby before she was married. Even if the baby died and the girl didn't show her face out of the house till the day she got married, they still won't let her forget it."

We sat quietly in the dark, swinging our legs over Lick Crick. Across the night sky, lightning flashed briefly, but it was too far away for us to hear the thunder.

The only sounds were the frogs singing and diving into the water from the creek bank. Far off in the night, we heard a hoot owl calling to his mate, and another owl answering him from the woods behind us.

"It wasn't a hoot owl we heard screaming the night you stayed with me. It was Della. Today at the mill, I thought you knew it was her."

I shook my head. No, I didn't know it. In the darkness, I answered her silently.

"Della's baby was dead when Mama went in to her. She called Papa and they fixed up his old tool chest with a piece of blanket to bury the baby. Mama said a girl knows when she is ready to grow up and leave home. She should have let Della marry Simmy Walters when she wanted to, then none of this would have happened."

"How do you know all this happened? You were in bed with me that night. I didn't know about it."

"I asked Mama when I got home today. I told her that people were talking about it. They thought we had a baby hidden away in our house. She said, 'No, not in the house, buried out in the apple orchard. Then she commenced to cry. She said it wasn't anybody's business. Let them say what they would. If folks didn't have somebody to talk about, they'd be sick."

I said, "Mom thought I was sick. She said it was about time."

Doris laughed softly. "Don't it beat all how nosey a girl's mama gets when it comes that time?"

"What time are you talking about now?"

"Hasn't your mama told you? Pretty soon now, every month for the rest of our lives, I guess, we'll have periods of bleeding. All girls have them. If we don't, we'll have a baby."

Well, for Pete's sake! Wasn't there anything good to look forward to when we grew up? This was the most revolting thing I had heard of yet.

I said, "I won't grow up then. I didn't want to be a girl in the first place, and I certainly don't want that to happen to me."

I could hear Mom calling, "Seely. Seely, come here this minute. Se-e-ely, you hear me!"

We sat and listened to the echoes of her voice die away. Doris took my hand and held it palm first to her face. "It will happen whether you want it to or not, Seely. You've got to grow up sometime. We can't stay children all our lives, you know that."

Lightning flashed a jagged streak across the sky, and we could hear the thunder now, rumbling through the hills and hollows.

"Doris, I've got to go in, now. Want to go with me? There's a storm coming up. Jamie and I will walk you home later."

"No, I'm not afraid anymore," she said, and then she hurriedly added, "nothing can happen so bad you can't live over it or forget it happened. Della says they can kill you, but they can't eat you. It's against the law!"

I knew that in spite of what she said, Doris was still afraid in the woods at night.

"Wait, Doris, wait for Jamie. He'll take you home." We touched hands and I started running toward the house.

chapter eighteen

*L*ong spikes of lightning split the sky and thunder rumbled and growled like an empty stomach. With every streak of lightning, the thunder reverberated through the hills, shook the house, and rattled the dishes in the corner cabinet. The storm clouds were black and rolling. The high whistling wind kept them moving on a level with the treetops like giant kites on a short string, hulking and hovering in the dark sky.

Mom was polishing the glass lamp globes with newspaper while I put the supper dishes away. We were both making more noise than necessary, trying to drown out the sounds of the approaching storm.

"Jamie should have been back from walking Doris home by now," I said. "He'll be caught in the dark woods when the storm hits, and he's scared to death of thunder storms."

"The rain is a long way off yet," Mom answered. "He'll be home and in bed long before it hits here."

But immediately following her words, making them a lie and taking away their small comfort, we were blinded by a fiery flash of light and shaken by the loud clap of thunder that came with it. Rain pounded its fists on the tin roof and beat against the windows. Mom had put Robert to bed and he'd gone to sleep. I thought the sound of the rain would surely wake him, but he slept right through it. Once I said to Mom that I hoped Floyd and Julie had made it to Nancy Ann's house before the rain started. She said there was no reason to worry about them and cupped her hands around her eyes to peer through the rain-swept glass, striving for the sight of Jamie coming home.

We had a regular gully-washer. The rain overflowed the eaves' trough and poured down the water spouts, splashing into the rain barrels and running over in a stream. Mom paced the floor from one window to the other, trying to see through the blowing rain.

At last, she said, "Lands' sakes, Seely, go to bed. You give me the shivers, sitting there with your big eyes staring at nothing."

"I'm not doing anything. I'm just waiting for Jamie."

She touched my hair as she walked by me. "I know," she said gently. "Go to bed now. Jamie probably stayed over at the Colliers'. If he'd started home and got caught in the storm, he would stop at the Walters'. He wouldn't try to come on home through a storm like this one."

I sat in the dark by the upstairs window watching the storm. When the lightning flashed, I could see the trees bent double like giants with the bellyache. For the first time in my life I wished Dad was home. He should be here. He would go right out in this storm and find Jamie and bring him home.

Once Dad had walked all over the county, stopping at every house looking for Julie and me. We had gone to Nancy Ann's house without telling anyone where we were going. We had stayed there until dark, and then we had been afraid to walk home through the woods. When night came and we weren't home, Mom grew frantic. She was sure we had been carried away by the gypsies. Dad said the gypsies weren't that damn desperate for girls, but he'd go look for us.

It had been about ten o'clock that night and sprinkling rain when Dad knocked on the Arthurs' back door. "Tell my girls to get their things. I've come to take them home."

He had switched our legs when our steps lagged, and with every swish of the willow stick, he told us what a damn fool he had made of himself hunting all over the damn county for two half-wit girls, who didn't have the sense to come home by themselves.

Dad had switched us good, but he had brought us home. If he were here now, he would go out and bring Jamie home, too.

I awoke in the morning, cold and cramped, on the floor by the window. The storm had blown itself out, and water stood ankle deep where last summer's garden had been.

White River would be out of its banks and the bottom land flooded with back water. Lick Crick would be running wild and bank full, the footlog slick or underwater, so we couldn't use it to cut through the woods. I thought the rivers were a beautiful sight to see, until they became flooded and overran their banks. Then I was afraid of them. Mom said they were a dangerous nuisance to everyone living in the hills and hollows, and something ought to be done about them. She never said what could be done, but like everything else in Greene County, she hated them.

When I went downstairs, Mom was drinking coffee at the kitchen table. She didn't look like she had been to bed all night. Her eyes, brown like Jamie's, were dull now, and her eyelids red and swollen.

She said, "I wish your daddy was here. One of us should go bring Jamie home. A body tends to forget he's just a little boy. Ten years old ain't grown up yet, not by a long sight."

"I'll go. You stay here with Robert. He'd have a conniption fit if he woke up and you weren't here."

I dodged the puddles in the gravel road, then waded into mud over my shoetops to get to the Walters' place.

Mr. Walters said they hadn't seen Jamie last night or this morning and offered to go to the Collier place for me.

I said, "No. I have to go for Jamie. I told Mom I'd bring him home."

I took the path through the woods and over the rain-slick ridge to the Collier house. I was almost there when I met Ben on his way to the sawmill.

He said, "Hey, what are you doing out so early on a day like this? I wouldn't have stepped a foot out of the house, but I wanted to see if last night's windstorm had left any of my mill standing."

"I'm on my way to your house to walk home with Jamie. I didn't have anything else to do."

Ben looked puzzled and scratched his head under his hat. He didn't look at me when he said, "The boy Jamie left our place right after he brought Doris home last night. Said he wanted to get home before the storm broke."

He hesitated a moment. "Guess he didn't make it, hey?"

"No. He didn't," I answered, and turned back toward home.

I figured Jamie would have been in a hurry and taken the shortest way home. I cut through the woods, following the path he would have taken after he had left Doris at her house. I spread the bare sucker limbs spaced like a picket fence around the tree-stump playhouses and looked inside. I stopped beneath the hanging cliff rock where we had watched the ground squirrels and chipmunks at play to see if he was there. It was warm and dry under the rock, but there was not one sign of Jamie. I searched every place where he could have found shelter from the storm until I came to the footlog on Lick Crick.

The footlog had been under water, but the creek had gone down, leaving the log wet and slick under my feet. Carefully testing each step, I crossed over Lick Crick and followed the path to the barn.

Mom was in the barn looking for Jamie. "I thought he

might have made it this far and took shelter in the hay-loft." She spoke wearily, as if the watching and waiting had worn her out.

I had been so sure he was on the path just ahead of me and I would find him safe and sound when I got home.

Mom said, "George went up the hollow toward the sawmill. He said he'd get the men to help him look for Jamie. I can't for the life of me figure where that boy can be."

She shook her head and started toward the house. I turned back to the woods and the path to the footlog. He wouldn't have tried to cross the creek above the foot-log. There was no fit place to ford the creek up that way. I thought maybe he had slipped on the wet makeshift bridge and fallen into the water. If he was hurt, I would find him down crick from the footlog. I turned my mud-caked feet downstream, my eyes never leaving the creek bank, searching for some sign that Jamie had come this way.

The river was still swift and rolling, but the flood-water had gone down until Lick Crick was about to its usual size. I marveled that in just one day I had seen Lick Crick change from a roaring, thundering river, which had threatened to ruin everything in its path, to a swift, swollen stream. "By this time tomorrow," I thought, "all the backwater will be drained into White River, and it will be as if we had never had a flood down here."

I had not found one trace of Jamie along the creek banks. I scraped the mud off my shoes and sat down to rest under the willow tree that had shaded our swimming hole in summer. I tried to think of some other place where he might have gone to get out of the storm. Ben, George, and Floyd Perry were searching the gullies and hollows back in the hills. There seemed to be no place left for me to hunt for Jamie.

A piece of dark blue cloth lapping in the waves of muddy water at the base of the tree caught my eye. Hanging onto the tree with one hand, I slid down the bank and grasped the piece of overall jacket with the other hand. The blue jacket was snagged in the river and I couldn't budge it. I pulled and tugged, and with the next hard tug the sleeve fell free, leaving a bare arm floating just beneath the surface of the murky water.

I knew then my search for Jamie was over. He was caught and held tight in the roots of our willow tree.

My hands were frozen on the soggy jacket. I couldn't drag Jamie from the muddy waves that tugged and pulled at him, but I wouldn't turn him loose. I knew I had to hold on to this last part of Jamie. I couldn't let it go free.

Ben Collier found me crouched on the creek bank and dragged me from the water's edge. I couldn't speak to him. I knew Jamie was dead, but if I didn't say it out loud, it wouldn't be true. I told myself he was playing. He would be home for supper and sleep in his bed tonight as usual.

But I couldn't tell myself it wasn't my fault. I knew I was to blame. If I had gone with him, this would never have happened. I knew he was afraid of the dark woods and thunderstorms, but I had sent him out alone, anyway. I had urged him to go.

"Hurry, Jamie," I told him. "Run to the woods. Doris is waiting for you."

If I had done as Mom had told me, Jamie would be alive. How many times had Mom said to me, "Seely, stay with Jamie and look after him." Or she would caution me, "Seely, take care of your brother."

But instead of blaming me, Mom tried to comfort me. "You have to understand, Seely. It wasn't anyone's fault."

She took my hands and pulled me close to her. "He had one of his spells and fell into the flood water. A sudden flash of lightning or just the noise of the storm could have brought it on him. We never knew what caused those spells. But we do know Jamie never suffered. He never once complained of any pain after he woke up."

"I promised I'd care for him." I sobbed. "I said I'd help, but I wasn't there to help him."

"Hush now, you've always cared for Jamie. Ever since you were knee-high to a grasshopper, you two were together. We couldn't separate you."

I guess she must have realized we were separated now. She wiped my face on her aprontail and took me on her lap as if I was a baby. She rocked back and forth, patting and soothing me as she spoke. "I won't have you blaming yourself for something that couldn't be helped. I've made up my mind, there'll be no more laying the blame on anyone in this family." She spoke so softly, I could barely hear her words. "I have faulted your daddy every day for moving us to these godforsaken hills. I've hardly given him a kind word from the first minute I set foot on this place. It's no wonder he's been so harsh and unkind at times. There were few times that I can recall any kindness to him."

She rocked quietly for a moment, the soft creak of the rockers lulling me. "Once I felt I could never forgive him for it, but there has been too much bitterness and unforgiving around here. Now, we'll not use Jamie's death as a base for building more misery."

Clara Brent came and carried the marble-topped stand table home with her. To make room for the coffin, I supposed. Mom helped her carry the table out to the car. While they were tucking spread rugs to protect the finish, Mom said, "I do appreciate this, Clara. It's real kind of you. I'd always pictured Grandma's table staying in the family, but I reckon she'd understand if she knew why I'm parting with it."

Clara's face seemed to crumble and cave in. She turned away and busied herself with the rugs. After awhile she touched Mom's arm and said, "George and me are glad to do whatever we can, Zel."

Neighbors who had never been in our house came out of the hills and hollows to bring baskets of cooked food and track mud into the front room. They stood awkwardly ill at ease and stared at Jamie. Mom cried and Dad shook hands silently. I ran and hid in the storeroom under the stairs. Julie fixed meals, which no one felt like eating, and took care of Robert, while I wandered around like a lost soul or sat quietly in the dark storeroom, away from everyone.

On the last evening, Doris and Frieda came to see Jamie. I saw them as they approached the house, walking slowly and holding hands as if drawing courage from each other to come inside.

From my hiding place, I heard Mom call my name. Then she said, "I don't know where that girl gets to. She was here a moment ago."

I heard their steps falter as they tiptoed to the place where Jamie lay. There was a long silence, then the front door closed gently behind them. The sound of their running feet as they fled our house was the last thing I heard. I fell asleep and slept all night in the dark space under the stair steps.

At the funeral, I couldn't look at Jamie. I didn't like it, and I knew he wouldn't like it, either. They had dressed him in stiff new corduroy pants with a jacket to match and folded his arms across his chest. He looked so uncomfortable, dressed up with his shoes on, lying on the puckered white satin pillows. I thought, "God must feel the same way about little boys that Dad said Mom did about little new potatoes; He just couldn't keep His hands off and let Jamie grow up."

Someone had borrowed two saw horses from Ben Collier's mill and set the wooden box across them. And now Jamie lay before the altar rail like a holy sacrifice for all the people who had come to hear Mom's sobbing and touch Dad's hand.

I sat beside Julie and counted the homemade bunches of flowers placed near the coffin. The women had made them by cutting tin cans into narrow strips and tying red and white crepe paper flowers to the metal stems. There were nine tin can baskets and three crepe paper flowers to each stem. I guess they couldn't find any green paper, there wasn't a leaf on any of them.

There was one store-bought bunch of fresh yellow flowers and green ferns spread across the casket. "From George and Clara," it said in wide gold letters on the ribbon.

I heard the preacher say, "Then in His mercy, may He grant you a safe lodging, and a holy rest and peace at last. Amen."

It was then I cried for Jamie. The flowers blurred into one long splash of color. I was blind to the time and the people's faces, until at last it was over, and we could return to a cold, empty house.

We left the flowers, the homemade and the store-bought ones, on the muddy red clay mound in the Flat Hollow churchyard.

chapter nineteen

*M*arch came to the hills like a wild animal, spitting snow and sleet and growling with the cold north wind that swept down the dark hollows. Doris and I huddled deep in our coats and let the strong gusts of wind push us to school. Then we walked backwards so we wouldn't have to face the bite and sting going home.

I had never been so cold. Even the red-hot potbellied stove in the front room at home failed to warm me. There didn't seem to be any warmth anywhere in the quiet house. I wondered if it was harder to heat an empty, quiet house than a noisy one filled with kids. I thought, "For a little boy, Jamie sure took up a lot of room."

Julie was gone, too. She had left home soon after the funeral and moved in with Nancy Ann and her mother.

Julie said if she stayed with them she could work after school each day and make enough money to pay for her graduation things. She said she thought Mom and Dad had enough to pay for right now. She was just trying to make things easier for us all.

She smiled at Mom and said, "I spend most of my time at Nancy's house. I might as well take my clothes and live there."

Mom had said, "Go ahead, Julie, have it your own way. But your daddy will bring you home."

But he hadn't.

I slept on my side of the attic room, and Robert slept in the bed he had shared with Jamie. At first, he had begged to sleep with me. Then it seemed as though every night he would wake me up crawling into my bed or cuddling behind me, his feet like icicles on the back of my legs.

I would chase him back to his own bed where he would curl himself around a pillow for bed company and close his eyes. When I was sure he was sleeping and not just playing possum, I would tuck the covers tight to him so he wouldn't sleep cold and go back to bed.

I knew that sometime we would get used to the empty places beside us where Julie and Jamie had always been, but it would take a lot of night time.

The long, cold winter had finally blown itself out, and now we had a warm, gentle breeze coming up from the south, bringing the smell of spring to the hills. The ice had broken loose from the river banks and had been washed downstream by the early spring rains.

167

I guess my dreams of staying a child forever had been washed away with the winter ice, because they were gone now. I had grown up during the last two months.

Mom said, "Don't worry about it, Seely. It's a natural thing. I knew it was about time, but . . ."

"If you knew, why didn't you tell me?"

I don't know where I found the courage to speak. Before I knew it, the words were out.

"Seely, if a body was told everything to expect from living, there would be no joy in their blessings. And I doubt that they'd be able to bear the trouble and sorrow if they knew about it beforehand."

I suspected that everyone could tell it just by looking at me. I searched my face in the washstand mirror for signs of a change. I thought surely there would be something different, but I was just the same as I had always been.

Other things changed during this time, but it was so bit-by-bit that I didn't notice until it had become a set pattern. It used to be Dad would get home late on Saturday night once a month, sleep while we were at church, and leave for Crowe right after Sunday dinner. But lately, he had been coming home early every Friday evening and leaving just before daylight on Monday morning.

If he and Mom weren't so old and hadn't been married for so long, I would have sworn he was courting her. He acted like it.

He followed her to the well, drew the water, then carried it back to the kitchen. On Sundays, he got up and went to church with Mom. And while she cooked dinner, he sat in the kitchen, smoked his pipe, and played checkers with Robert. Robert usually won the game because Dad was watching Mom instead of the checkerboard.

Dad seemed surprised when I brought home an eighth-grade report card for him to sign. He said I was pretty young to be thinking about high school, wasn't I? But he seemed pleased with me for once.

I found myself walking close to Dad's chair or brushing his arm in passing, wanting to share some of the attention he gave so generously to Robert. At times I wondered when I had stopped being afraid of Dad and started liking him again. I guess it must have been when he and Mom began to like each other again.

One evening after supper, Dad took out his pipe, carefully measured in the tobacco, and tamped it tight with his thumb. He fired a long splinter from the live coals in the cookstove and lit it, puffing long and hard, and sending small gray clouds to the ceiling.

When he had the pipe drawing to his liking, he looked at me and said, "Your mother will be needing a lot of help for the next week or so, packing and sorting the things she'll want to move to Lawrence County. It's a good house, big enough to stretch in, and not an hour's drive from my work. You come straight home from school and do as she tells you. We want to have things ready to go as soon as school is out for the summer."

I said, "Moving? But why . . .?"

Mom said, "Hush, and listen to your dad."

He frowned and said, "Let her speak her piece, Zel. She's getting old enough to have some say about what she does and where she's going from now on."

"There's people here," I began. "Julie and Jamie, we can't leave them. And there's others, too."

Dad puffed on his pipe and blew a smoke screen between us. "There will be people where we're going, Seely."

The smoke cleared, and I could see the deep lines around his eyes and mouth. "There ain't nothing we can do about Jamie. Not anymore. And Julie made her own choice. We don't need to worry about her. That girl has spunk and grit enough for two her size. She'll get along just fine. You'll see, when she comes home."

I listened to the tone of his voice more than the words he spoke. I thought, "Why, he's proud of Julie. He is truly proud of her!"

It was a good feeling to know he hadn't just thrown Julie away as if she didn't belong to us any longer. He hadn't tried to hold her or make her stay. He had let her go as if he didn't care. But now, he was looking forward to her homecoming.

Dad said, "Floyd Perry is a good boy. Make a fine man someday. And I'll say this for him, he ain't afraid of work. When they're married, he'll see to it that Julie never wants for a thing."

"But she ain't marrying Floyd."

"Ah, but she will. Whenever she is ready to settle down, Floyd will be there waiting for her."

Dad knocked the doddle out of his pipe and slid his

chair back from the table as if to say he would hear no more about it. The matter was closed as far as he was concerned.

I rid up the table, and Mom started washing the dishes.

"It will be a load off my mind to get out of these hills. We've had nothing but trouble and hard times down here. Jase dead by his own hand, and Dicie gone away to where none can reach her; friends I've known all my life taken by these infernal hills."

Mom dried her hands on her apron, then brushed the damp strands of hair from her face. "And Jamie, what chance of a life of any kind did he ever have down here?" She moved between the table and cabinets putting away the dishes I had wiped. "Well, times are better now, all over. There'll be no more hand-to-mouth living for you and Robert, once we're settled in this new place."

I didn't say anything. I'd had my say with Dad, and it hadn't done a lick of good.

She said, "There's nothing here for us, Seely. There never was. No future, nothing to look forward to; just these dark hollows and everlasting hills closing in and squeezing the life out of a body." She stood with her hands empty, looking out into the night. "There were times when I thought I'd lose all my children to them shadowy woods and dark hollows." She spoke quietly. "Lord knows, I've lost enough here."

I thought to myself, "There's a kind of light in the woods when you know where to look for it. They are not all shadows and darkness. If you stand back and look at the woods, you can always find a path through them.

I've roamed these hills and hollows from one end to the other, and the dark didn't get me."

Pretty soon now, I thought, the white dogwood blossoms would be spreading across the hills and the flowers from the redbud would mingle among them, brightening up the woods and hillsides. Streaks of warm sunshine on the floor of the forest would bring out the creamy kitten britches and the purple violets, too, but I wouldn't know when; I wouldn't be here to see them.

I rushed home every afternoon to help Mom pack and crate the things she wanted to take with her. We dragged the old barrel-topped trunk out of the storage space for Mom to pack her memory box in. The trunk used to set against the wall in the front room with Mom's yellow and white wedding ring quilt folded over its humped lid, but after she traded the quilt to Clara, she said the trunk was an ugly old thing and moved it under the attic steps and closed the door.

It was Mom's trunk to keep her treasures in, and she wouldn't allow us kids to rummage through it. But we knew all the things it held and the musty odor of age and sandalwood that escaped when we lifted the lid.

Mom's memory box held all of Jamie's things. There wasn't much. Just a few clothes, his Indian arrow heads, some bright marbles, and the old harmonica Floyd had given him. He had finally learned to play one song on it —"Oh, where, oh, where has my little dog gone? Oh, where, oh, where can he be?" and he had played it from daylight till dark.

Mom put her wedding dress with the lacy veil and the

other stuff that had been in the trunk back on top of Jamie's things and locked the lid.

By the end of the week, the house was bare of everything but what we needed to get by until school was out.

Clara brought Great-grandmother Curry's marble-topped table back to Mom and took a crate of chickens home with her in the trunk of the car. Later that same day, George came and led the cow away. He waved and called back over his shoulder, "Clara will be over in the morning for the rest of them chickens."

Mom ran her hand over the table and caressed the cool marble top. "I guess that just about takes care of everything. I'm rid of the livestock, and I've got Grandma's table back home where it belongs. Now we're all ready to go as soon as school is out."

Everything seemed to hinge on the last day of school. Everyone was ready to go but me.

I would walk through the kitchen, wander around the front room, go up to the attic, turn around, and go back to the kitchen. Sometimes, I'd roam about the yard, but never farther than the empty barn and not ever out of earshot, in case Mom needed me. Only once I ventured out of the yard. I ran to the cave and carried all our pretty junk back to the gully behind Lick Crick. I stood on the rim and pitched it away piece by piece and watched the bright amber bottles shatter into a million pieces when they hit the rocks.

I rolled my notebooks into a tight roll and tied a string around them. I didn't know what to do with them, so I kept them. I didn't want to use them. I couldn't seem to settle down in one place and be quiet long enough to write. Even when I wasn't up and about, I felt like I was racing against time.

Dad didn't seem to mind the bare floors and stacked boxes all over the house. He came home in a good humor and didn't appear to be in any great hurry to leave and go back to Crowe. It was as if a weight had been lifted from his shoulders or something he couldn't bear to face had been removed from his sight.

Where he had once found fault, he now found favor. He didn't even cuss and raise Cain when Robert left the washbasin on a chair and I sat down in it with my school dress on.

He laughed at me. "Don't fuss at him, Seely. There's no school tomorrow, and it will dry before Monday."

We only had another week of school. Doris and I would be the only ones graduating from the eighth grade. As hard as Frieda had tried and as long as she had waited to get a diploma, she had left home one day and never come back.

No one seemed to know where she had gone. I figured she had finally caught one of the big buses she talked about so much and gone to Kentucky.

Doris and I would be the last pupils to graduate from McVille grade school. The one-room schoolhouse had served its purpose in Greene County, and now it would be torn down. Next year all the kids would go by bus to the schools at the county seat.

"It's a shame it wasn't closed down last year." I told

Doris, as I slipped and skidded through the red clay mud. "If it had been, I'd be riding instead of sliding to finish this last week of school."

Every night I fussed and fumed while I cleaned the mud off my shoes. I told Mom it was like doing dishes; there was no end to it. You did it today, and tomorrow it was all to do over again.

She said, "Don't complain, Seely. Next year you won't have to wade red clay mud to get to school every day. Soon this will all be outgrown like them shoes you're cleaning."

Dad gave me the money to get a new dress for my graduation day. I went to the county seat with Clara Brent and bought three yards of orange, brown, and yellow voile to make a dress, and a pair of high-heeled slippers to wear with it. Clara said she used to be quite a hand at sewing. She would be glad to make up the piece of goods for me.

She made it up and used every scrap of the material to do it. The dress had a full gathered skirt with a wide flounce, long sleeves with ruffles at the cuffs, and high neck. I tried it on and practiced walking in the high heels, but the heels caught in the hem of the skirt and my ankles turned with every other step.

I had to learn to walk in them before Friday. I was afraid I'd trip and fall flat on my face when I wore them to get my diploma.

Mom said it wasn't proper for a twelve-year-old girl to wear spike heels, and I shouldn't have been allowed to buy them. She added that if she'd been along, the money wouldn't have been wasted on such foolishness. She thought I'd made a big mistake buying them.

Dad said, "Oh, leave her be, Zel. She'll outgrow the wonder of new high heels and early spring soon enough."

He laughed and waggled his pipe stem at me. "Mark my words, Zel. That girl will make bigger mistakes in her life than the proper kind of shoes to wear. Don't spoil it for her. Let her find that out for herself."

This was the first I knew that I could make a mistake and not be burned in hellfire and brimstone for it. I thought maybe making allowances for mistakes was one of the benefits given to grown-ups, but denied to children.

chapter twenty

On graduation day, I carried the new shoes and walked barefoot until I was in sight of the schoolhouse. Then I wiped the mud off my feet on the wet grass and put on the shoes. My feet slipped into my shoes easier wet than they had dry. The flounce caught on my shoe heel, so I held the skirt above my knees while I crossed the playground to the door.

A new dress and shoes without mud on them was enough to turn everyone's head, but I hadn't expected the way they turned to look when I stepped into the school room. It was packed to the walls with parents, children, and crying babies when I marched down the aisle between the crowded desks to the one I had claimed for the past eight months.

Snickers and giggles followed me to my seat. I felt my face flush hot and red. I wished with all my heart for the old faded lavender skirt and blouse I had worn to school all winter. No one would have noticed me in my old dress.

I scanned the faces for Doris and found her sitting across the room with her folks. She was smiling and motioning for me to come sit with her. But I shook my head and turned away.

She probably just wanted to talk about Indianapolis, I thought. That was all I had heard since the day her mama had promised her she could stay with Della and Simmy and go to high school up there.

"They have art schools in Indianapolis, and I can attend one of them if I'm eligible for enrollment."

Doris had been learning a lot of new big words and using them every chance she got. She said she didn't want her friends in Indianapolis to think she was an ignorant hillbilly.

I said, "What friends? You don't have any friends up there, yet. Besides, if they don't like you the way you are, they're not very good friends."

Her blue eyes had a devilish look when she replied, "Seely, are you insinuating I'm an ignorant hillbilly?"

We had both laughed. But I knew that was all she ever thought about.

I didn't hear the end-of-the-year program the children gave for their parents at the close of every school year. I was too busy telling myself, "You can stand anything for an hour. Just one more hour and this will all be behind you. Then no more school, no more mud to wade; and what's more important, you will have a diploma from common school."

The hour was over and Mr. Thompson was calling my name. "Caroline Cecilia Robinson!"

I sat still and quiet at my desk. I wasn't ready or eager to call attention to myself again.

"Seely," he called softly.

He held a rolled paper tied with a blue ribbon. I could see the man with the axe and oxen on the official seal of Indiana stamped on the paper. Mr. Thompson tapped the rolled diploma lightly against his hand and held it out to me.

"Like offering a carrot to a jackass," I thought, as I got to my feet.

I didn't look at the crowd. I felt as though I was walking a high, narrow footlog with Lick Crick roaring far below me. If I didn't look down, I'd be home safe; look down or hesitate, and I would be lost forever. I closed my mind to every thought but one. "It's over and I've made it! Just a few steps more. . . ."

Then my heel caught in my flounce, my ankle turned, and I stumbled the rest of the way to the raised platform.

Mr. Thompson took my hand to steady me and turned me to face the noisy, crowded room.

"I'm proud and happy to be the one to present this diploma to Cecilia Robinson. She is my first straight A student and has a perfect attendance record, also."

Mom and Dad should be getting this commendation, I thought. If they hadn't forced me into the rain and cold every day with threats of "a licking at school, two at home," I would never have done it.

Mr. Thompson said the same thing every year, but I made myself listen to the end of his prepared speech.

"With her thirst for knowledge and her determination to learn, I'm sure she won't disappoint me. Seely, this is yours. You've earned it."

I mumbled my thanks and accepted the precious piece of paper I had run the gauntlet to receive.

Everyone was clapping their hands, shouting, and stomping their feet as I fled from the room for the last time. As I crossed the worn threshold, I thought, "Someone else besides me will sweep up the dried mud and dust stomped off their heavy shoes here today."

I wasn't sure whether I was happy or sorry to see the last of this one-room schoolhouse. It was the end to a way of living that I had grown used to, and I dreaded to leave it for a new school somewhere else.

The small, unfriendly faces, which had once seemed so strange to me, were now as familiar as my own. We had shared our lunch sacks and we drank from the same tin cup. I would miss them. They were my friends.

I would have to make new friends where I was going, grown-up friends that would last awhile. And to do that, I would have to act like a grown-up. I wasn't a child, but I had a long way to go before I would be a grown-up woman. I felt as though I had passed the first barrier and hurdled the first obstacle to growing up. Now I wanted to be a woman.

Childhood had lost its appeal for me. Without Jamie,

it didn't seem so wonderful that I'd want to stay there forever. I would be leaving Jamie behind. He belonged to my childhood. And Teddy had been a part of it, too.

"But they would always be children," I thought. "Beautiful, carefree children to whom these hills had been a lovely place for a short stay." Tomorrow I'll start acting grown-up, I told myself, first thing tomorrow morning. But right now, I have to be getting home.

I kicked off the high-heeled shoes and threw them over the hill into the buckbrush. Holding my skirt above my knees, away from the mud and wet weeds, I walked home the same way I had come to school—skirt hiked above my knees and barefoot.

Two days later, I stood beside the borrowed truck and pretended I was glad we were moving out of the hills. If I hadn't been laughing and talking, I would have been wiping tears like Doris or holding my breath like Julie, to keep from crying.

Dad slid behind the steering wheel, and Mom helped Robert up into the seat beside Dad. With her hand on the cab door, she said, "Seely, you'd better tell Julie good-bye now and get on the truck. We're ready to go."

Julie was dry-eyed and quiet, but Doris unashamedly wiped tears away with her hand, leaving wet streaks on her face. For the first time, we didn't have a word to say to each other. And this would be the last chance we had to speak.

Dad started the truck and raced the motor. I climbed aboard and settled myself in a tight pocket between the rolled carpet and bedding. That cold November day when Julie, Jamie, and I had ridden to Greene County on the back of Jase Perry's old rattletrap truck seemed like a hundred years ago.

There would be no one to share the cookies or the warm sunshine on this trip out of the hills. Jamie, Julie, and Jase were staying in Greene County. Jase and Jamie would remain throughout eternity, but Julie, only for a little while. Then like the swift clear rivers, she and Floyd would move out of the hills and make their way into the world.

As the truck pulled away in high gear, I rested my knees on the rolled carpet and waved to Julie and Doris.

Doris ran after the fast moving truck, crying, "Come back, Seely! Come back! Come back!"

I ducked my head to miss the tree limbs swinging low over the road. When I raised my head and looked back, they were gone from sight.

W9-BXU-722

FAIR AND TENDER LADIES

FAIR AND TENDER LADIES

A Richard Nottingham Novel

Chris Nickson

This first world edition published 2013
in Great Britain and 2014 in the USA by
Crème de la Crime, an imprint of
SEVERN HOUSE PUBLISHERS LTD of
19 Cedar Road, Sutton, Surrey, England, SM2 5DA.

British Library Cataloguing in Publication Data

Nickson, Chris author.
  Fair and tender ladies. – (A Richard Nottingham mystery; 6)
  1. Nottingham, Richard (Fictitious character)–Fiction.
  2. Murder–Investigation–Fiction. 3. Leeds (England)–
  History–18th century–Fiction. 4. Detective and mystery
  stories.
  I. Title II. Series
  823.9'2-dc23

ISBN-13: 978-1-78029-055-3 (cased)

All Severn House titles are printed on acid-free paper.

Severn House Publishers support the Forest Stewardship Council™ [FSC™],
the leading international forest certification organisation. All our titles that
are printed on FSC certified paper carry the FSC logo.

MIX
Paper from
responsible sources
FSC® C013056

Typeset by Palimpsest Book Production Ltd.,
Falkirk, Stirlingshire, Scotland.
Printed and bound in Great Britain by
TJ International, Padstow, Cornwall.

For Lynne Patrick
With gratitude

But I'm not a little sparrow
I have no wing with which to fly
So I sit here in grief and sorrow,
To weep and pass my troubles by.

If I had known before I courted
That love was such a killing thing
I'd have locked my heart in a box of golden
And fastened it up with a silver pin.

Come All You Fair And Tender Ladies: traditional song

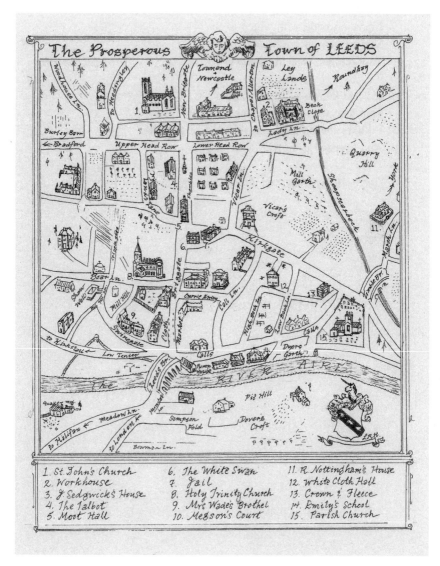

The Prosperous Town of LEEDS

1. St. John's Church
2. Workhouse
3. J. Sedgwick's House
4. The Talbot
5. Moot Hall
6. The White Swan
7. Jail
8. Holy Trinity Church
9. Mrs Wade's Brothel
10. Messon's Court
11. R. Nottingham's House
12. White Cloth Hall
13. Crown & Fleece
14. Emily's School
15. Parish Church

ONE

T he rain fell gently at first, a whisper that slowly grew louder as thick clouds rolled in from the west. By midnight it was a storm, the sound loud enough to fill the world. He watched it from the window, wind rattling the panes so hard it seemed they might shatter. He closed his eyes, welcoming the noise that drowned out his sadness.

The darkness was when he missed her the most. The ache for her hadn't gone; it felt stronger than ever, still filling his mind every day. Finally he lay on the bed to let the thunder and lightning take him away.

Before dawn it had all passed, the air clean and calm, with a soft breeze from the south and the puddles in the roads already beginning to dry up. In the half-light of a Saturday morning, Richard Nottingham, Constable of Leeds, stood in the graveyard outside St John's church, deep mud clinging to his boots.

'Rob,' he said, 'you go round the other side to the vestry door. Be ready in case he comes out.'

Rob Lister, in charge of the night crew, ran off and disappeared around the building. A crowd had gathered outside the lych gate, their voices angry and busy, kept back by two of the Constable's men.

Nottingham checked the load in his pistol and unsheathed his sword. 'Are you ready?' he asked, and John Sedgwick, the deputy constable, nodded as he swung his blade in the air.

At the church door, the Constable took a deep breath and turned the handle. 'Right,' he said.

The man was inside; they knew that. A carter had spotted him climbing over the wall and passed the word. They were ready to take him for murder, stabbing someone in the night for no reason. Nottingham had been pulled from his bed to lead the hunt, and for the last hour folk had pursued the man around Leeds, down by the Bridge, along Boar Lane, all the way up to Burley Bar then through the dark, stinking courts behind Briggate until they'd ended up here.

Pale light came through the church windows, catching dust motes in the air. The Constable took three paces; his footsteps boomed and echoed through the high building. Too many shadows, he thought, too many places to hide. He gestured to the deputy, then began to walk slowly to the aisle on the far side, alert for any sound or movement.

He felt the sweat on his palms as he gripped the hilt of the sword, and fear prickled at the base of his spine. He breathed softly and looked around, moving then stopping again, gazing and waiting. He heard the sharp click of the deputy's heels on the flagstones.

Something at the corner of his sight made him spin to his right. A dark blur rose from one of the box pews on the other side of the church, the man's voice a growl that became a scream.

'John!'

They brought him out between them. He was battered, bruises rising, the blood still flowing heavily from a cut on his face. The Constable let him fall to the ground, gesturing for two of the men to take him off to the cells.

He watched them leave, the mob following close behind, their voices strident and angry.

'No damage?' he asked.

'Didn't even cut me. It was a good thing you shouted, though, boss.' Sedgwick sheathed the sword and grinned. 'I'll tell you what, that's left me parched. I could use something to drink.'

'There's a jug back at the jail.' He waved Rob over as he emerged from the far side of the church. 'It's all over, lad, you missed it.'

Then, from somewhere down Briggate the Constable heard a roar. Without even glancing at the others he took off at a run, hearing their boots clatter behind him. By the time they reached the bodies on the ground the people had already dispersed, not a soul to be seen on the street.

He knelt, checking his men first. One was slowly coming

to, moaning, while the other was dazed, clutching his stomach. Sedgwick held his hand against the prisoner's neck.

'Boss,' he said. 'He's dead.'

A blade had found the man's heart. In the cold cell the Constable ran his fingertips over a thin line of blood under the ribs. Old bruises blotched his skin and he was so thin that his bones protruded. Whoever he was, it had been a long time since he'd eaten well. None of them knew his face and there was nothing in his clothes to show who he'd been or what name he'd carried. The only thing to mark him out was a large patch of deep red flesh, the colour of a ripe raspberry, on his neck. There'd be little chance of finding his killer. Every question they asked would bring a denial. Nottingham sighed, wiped his hands on an old piece of linen and went back to the desk.

'How are the men?' he asked.

'They'll be fine,' the deputy told him. 'I gave them a rollicking.'

'I doubt there was much they could do. How many were in that crowd? Twenty?'

'More, probably, boss.'

'Go and see the undertaker later, John. We'll get this one in the ground today.'

TWO

In the first light of a spring Monday in 1734, Richard Nottingham, Constable of the City of Leeds, walked down Marsh Lane towards Timble Bridge. Over in the fields the sheep were bleating, mothers and lambs together, the first calls of the shepherds in the distance and the faint lowing of cattle up on the hills.

He stopped and leaned over the parapet, gazing down at the water burbling through Sheepscar Beck. From the corner of his eye he saw something move and for a fleeting moment he thought it was Mary. He turned, drawing in his breath. But it

was nothing more than a bird rising from a tree into the pale
sky.

Rob Lister sat at the desk in the jail, writing up the night
report. Since he'd become a Constable's man, working under
Nottingham and his deputy, John Sedgwick, the elegant hand
he'd been taught at school had grown cramped, the letters
uneven and quickly scrawled across the paper. But as long as
it was legible that barely mattered; few would read the words
anyway. He dipped the quill back into the ink and glanced up
as the door opened.

'Morning, boss.'

'Anything overnight?'

'We pulled a body from the river not long after two. The
coroner's seen him. I put him in the cold cell.'

'I'll wager Coroner Brogden wasn't too happy to be dragged
from his bed at that hour. Who was it? Anyone we know?'

Rob chuckled softly. 'Tom Hardwell, so you can be certain
it was the drink. Not a mark on him.'

The Constable nodded. Every year a few fell into the Aire
when they were deep in their cups, to be found an hour or a
day later, washed up against the bank.

'What about the prisoner we took Saturday? Has anyone
managed to find out his name yet?'

Lister shook his head.

'You might as well go, then.'

Rob stood and stretched. 'Yes, boss.'

The lad had been courting Emily, Nottingham's daughter,
for almost two years, and since Christmas he'd lodged at the
Constable's house. It was an arrangement to satisfy everyone:
respectable enough for the city, yet still allowing the young
lovers to be together under a responsible eye. But once the
candles were blown out at night, Nottingham's gaze turned
wilfully blind.

With Mary's death everything had fallen into a time of
change. Emily had quietly given up her teaching position at
the dame school. Two years earlier she'd been left money, and
she'd used some of it to start her own establishment, renting
a building down on the Calls to teach the young daughters of
the poor their letters and numbers, fighting to give the lasses

a chance of something better than the poverty and the daily grind of desperation as they grew. Within weeks the class had been full, and many more were eager to come, ready to eat up knowledge. Her success made him proud. She'd taken well to the responsibility, prepared to work hard, long hours. But one thing about her hadn't changed; all too often she had to hare her way through the early morning, dashing up to the door of the school while the mothers waited outside with their girls.

'You're miles away there, boss.'

Lost deep in his thoughts, Nottingham hadn't even noticed the deputy arrive. He smiled. 'Just thinking, John, that's all.'

Sedgwick sat down, poured himself a mug of ale and downed it in a long, single swallow before smacking his lips together. 'Grand, that is. Going to be a good day again today.' He brought a heel of bread from the large pocket of his long waistcoat, the elegant design long since faded to small smudges of irregular colour. He ate, washing the food down with more drink and gave a contented sigh.

'Doesn't your Lizzie feed you any more?'

Sedgwick laughed. 'I'm still a growing lad, boss. Didn't you know that? I need my food.'

It was true, with his tousled hair, long legs and eager lope he often looked like an overgrown boy, always hungry for something to fill his lanky frame. He was fiercely proud of his family, his son James, doing well at the boys' charity school, his daughter Isabell, over a year old now, toddling and curious about everything in the world.

'Tom Hardwell drowned in the night.'

The deputy snorted. 'That was bound to happen sooner or later.'

'You'd better go and see his widow, ask what she wants to do about the funeral.'

'Yes, boss.' He stood, and crammed the last of the bread into his mouth before leaving.

Nottingham wrote up the daily report and walked over to the Moot Hall to leave it on the clerk's desk outside the mayor's office. At least the wound he received in his belly the year before had finally stopped troubling him. There was no more need to walk with a stick, and the twinges of pain rarely bothered him. Only the hurt in his heart still nagged.

As he turned the corner back on to Kirkgate, he saw a man standing outside the jail with a fretful expression, moving from foot to foot nervously. He was thin as wire, raggedly dressed, with a face caught on the cusp of age.

'Can I help you? I'm Richard Nottingham, the Constable of Leeds.'

'My brother,' the man said, raising dark, hopeless eyes. 'I'm looking for my brother.'

There was so much pain in the words that it made the Constable stop and look at him again.

'You'd best come in, Mr . . .?'

'Johnson.' The man gave a small bow, a strangely formal gesture for a man dressed like a scare-the-crow in a tattered coat and holed breeches, the soles of his shoes held to the upper by twine. He carried a small sack over his shoulder. 'Simon Johnson, sir.'

Inside, the Constable gave the man ale and sat back in his chair.

'Your brother's a grown man, Mr Johnson?'

'He is.' The man hesitated. 'That is, he's . . .' he began, then completed the sentence in a rush: 'Andrew isn't right in his head. I look after him.'

'Look after him?' Nottingham wondered. 'How?'

'He can't speak,' Johnson explained. 'And he doesn't think properly. Not like you and me. So we travel together. I protect him.' He gave a wan smile. 'We never stay anywhere long. People don't like him. He gets angry.'

'What happened to your brother?'

'At night I tie his ankle to mine, so he can't wander away while I sleep. When I woke up on Friday he'd gone. I've been looking for him since then.'

'There are plenty of people in Leeds, Mr Johnson.'

'He's easy to spot, Constable.' The man leaned forward and rubbed the back of his neck. 'He had dark red skin here. Would you look for him, please? I don't want him to be hurt.'

There was no gentle way to tell him, nothing to say that could lessen the pain.

'Mr Johnson,' he said quietly, 'I'm afraid your brother's dead.'

'But—' the man began, then, 'It's Andrew? Are you sure?'

'He had a mark on his neck like your brother. He killed

someone and then he tried to attack my deputy. I'm sorry.' At least he could spare him the worst of the truth.

For a long moment Johnson remained silent, all the sorrow, the anger and the loss playing across his face.

'Can I see him?' he asked finally.

'We buried him on Saturday. We didn't know who he was and no one came to claim him . . .' His words trailed away. He couldn't give Johnson any consolation.

The man stood slowly, shoulders stooped, looking older than when he'd entered.

'Constable,' he said, his voice achingly dignified, 'I'm sure you had no choice in what you did. You didn't know my brother. But I hope you'll understand if I say I hate Leeds and the men who did this to Andrew.'

THREE

The young man entered the jail warily, glancing around as if he wasn't certain he should be there. The Constable looked up from the papers in front of him as the candle guttered and threw dark shadows around the room.

It was still before dawn. When he'd walked up Kirkgate there'd been only the faintest glimmer of blue on the horizon. He'd found little to report from the night, and sent Rob off early to spend time with Emily before school.

'Can I help you?' he asked. How often had he said those words over the years? The man moved forward into the light. He looked no more than nineteen or twenty, with honest eyes, a tangle of thick, pale hair and soft down on his cheeks, his face creased by worry and fear. Dust covered his old, heavy boots, and he wore a coat that was threadbare at the elbows and cuffs, his tan breeches thin at the knee. The best clothes of a country lad, Nottingham decided. Someone lost, perhaps.

'I'm looking for my sister,' the man answered nervously. 'She's run off and I think she's in Leeds.'

Not lost, he thought. Searching.

'What's your name?' Nottingham asked. 'I'm the Constable.'

'Jem Carter, sir.'

'You'd better sit down and tell me about her, Mr Carter.'

He offered the man ale, and waited as he drank and wiped his mouth.

'What's your sister called?' he asked kindly.

'Jenny, sir.'

'And how old is she, Mr Carter?'

'Sixteen. Just last month.'

The Constable sat back and stroked his chin.

'Where do you live?'

'Ilkley, sir.'

He'd heard of the place, no more than that, a village some dozen or so miles away to the northwest. The man had either walked all night or slept in a wood somewhere. Carter was staring at him, eyes full of hope.

'What makes you think Jenny might be here?' he asked, although he'd heard every possible answer so many times he could have recited them all himself. The country girls arrived in their dozens each year, heads turned by tales of rich, handsome men seeking a pretty young bride, or the fortunes to be made in the city. But they were nothing more than stories. There was no gold on the streets of Leeds, only the empty tinkle of coins they earned on their backs. At the end of a week they'd be lucky to have two thin pennies left. How many ever made their way home again?

'She allus wanted to be somewhere else. Somewhere big.' Carter blushed. 'Our Jenny's one of them girls who's been full of dreams since she was a bairn. Me da said he'd find her a husband but she told him no, she wa'nt ready yet.'

'What does your family do?'

'We're farmers, sir,' he said with pride, sitting a little straighter on the chair. Nottingham nodded and pushed the fringe off his forehead.

'When did Jenny leave?'

'Saturday morning.' Carter sat forward, elbows on his knees. 'She said she were going to take some food to one o' t' old women down the other end of t' village. She does that,' he explained. 'She's a good lass at heart. When she hadn't come back by dark we went looking. She'd never even been there.'

And now it was Tuesday. Walking, the girl would likely

have arrived on Saturday afternoon. More than two days ago, but with a little luck she might not have disappeared completely yet.

'What does she look like?'

'She's nobbut a little 'un, a tiddler.' Carter smiled for a moment at the thought of his sister. 'Look at her and you'd reckon she were younger, mebbe thirteen. I used to tease her about it.'

'Does she have fair hair like you?'

'Aye, that's reet. But it's long, down her back, the way lasses have it.'

'What was she wearing, Mr Carter? Did she take anything with her?'

'Just an old blue dress, an apron and a cap. She had some food in a basket.'

'And money? Did she have any with her?'

He shrugged, not really knowing. 'A few pennies, mebbe. I'm sure she din't have more than that.'

Nottingham paused, thinking. 'Are you the oldest in the family?'

'Aye, sir, I am. I've two younger brothers and another sister besides Jenny. And there's me da. Me mam died where I were little.' He held up the middle finger of his left hand. 'Jenny wears a ring there that used to belong to our mam. It has a shape like a rose on it.'

'We'll look for her,' he said. The man's face brightened, but the Constable knew he had to add more. He didn't want Carter to believe he'd see his sister again in an hour or two. 'You have to understand, I can't make you any promises. We may not find her. We don't find everyone who comes here. She may not even be in Leeds, have you thought of that, Mr Carter? She could have decided to try her luck in London.'

'She'll be here,' the young man said firmly, as if he was trying to convince himself. It was what he needed to believe, Nottingham realized. 'Find her, mister, please.'

'We'll do everything we can,' he promised. 'What about you? Are you staying to search for her?'

'I am. Me da give me some money and told me to keep looking until I bring her home.' He hesitated. 'Do you know any good lodgings, sir?'

'Try Mrs Lumley on Call Lane,' the Constable advised. 'Ask anyone down there, they'll show you. She keeps a clean house and her prices are fair. Tell her I sent you and she'll treat you well. If I find your sister I can send word to you there.'

'Thank you.' Carter rose, standing as if a weight had been lifted off his shoulders.

He glanced at the man as he left, knowing that eventually he'd likely walk home alone and empty-hearted and no one would ever hear of Jenny again. Nottingham worked for a few more minutes, hearing the bustle of Leeds coming alive outside the window, the cries of the early hawkers, the trundle of carts along Kirkgate and the shouts of their drivers. As the clock of the Parish Church struck half past six he wearily put down the quill and set off down Briggate, seeing men set up trestles for the cloth market, dodging between the folks who thronged the pavements and a drover leading cattle up to the Shambles.

He looked for Four-Finger Jane at her usual spot by the opening to a court just up from the Rose and Crown. She wasn't there so, he walked on, crossing the street as he spied Little Sal standing close to the entrance of the Old King's Head.

'Hello, Sal.'

'Mr Nottingham.' Her eyes twinkled. 'Come to spend some of that money the city pays you?' She stood no more than four feet in her shoes, always ready with a smile. She'd been a fixture on Briggate for at least five years, suddenly appearing one morning with her grin and ready patter. The novelty of her size made her popular with the men and he'd heard tales about some of the things she was willing to do.

He smiled at her. 'If I was looking for that you know you'd be the first I'd come to see.'

'Aye, I know, love,' she answered with a wink, the lines of age showing through the white lead and powder around her eyes. 'That's what they all say. So what is it?' she asked wearily. 'I know you're not here to pass the time of day with me.'

'A girl, came to town on Saturday. Called Jenny.'

She shook her head in exasperation. 'Jenny? They're all

called Jenny these days. Or Sophie or Sarah or whatever sounds young or elegant.'

'This one really is a Jenny, Sal. She's blonde, small, sixteen but looks younger. Her brother's looking for her.'

'You know how many like that I've seen, Mr Nottingham?' she asked with a sigh. 'Dozens. Hundreds, mebbe. All of them hopeful for a week until they've no more money or food in their bellies.'

'I know,' he replied. What she said was the simple truth. 'Just ask around anyway, will you? I'll pay if you find something.'

'I will,' Sal agreed and stared at him, her eyes serious 'But I daresay you'll be keeping your money. You know the odds as well as I do. If she dun't want to be found, she won't be. And I'll tell you this, if she's a good reason for leaving home I'll not give her up.'

He nodded. 'Just do your best. Please.'

The Constable left her to her work, seeing her pull down her bodice a little to display more of her small breasts. He set off on his rounds of Leeds, walking the streets he knew so well, eyes alert, feeling the simple pleasure of the sun on his face.

By seven he was in the White Swan, a mug of ale and half a pie in front of him. He'd barely begun to eat when the deputy slid on to the bench opposite.

'Hardwell's widow is going to talk to the undertaker. They'll collect the body later today.'

'How did she take the news?' Nottingham asked.

'She knows what a feckless bugger he was. I heard something interesting while I was out, though. There's a new brothel opening tonight on Swinegate.'

'Tonight?' he asked in astonishment, wondering why they'd heard nothing of it before. 'When did this get out?'

'I don't know, boss. This morning was the first I'd heard.'

'Who's running it?' Nottingham asked. It worried him that there'd been no rumours about this, that no one had said anything to him. He should have known long ago.

'A widow called Mrs Wade, apparently.'

'I don't know the name.'

'Aye,' the deputy agreed, 'it's a new one on me, too.'

'Better see what you can find out about her, John.'

Sedgwick grinned. 'Already did, boss. Seems she came here about three months back with her son and a pair of daughters.'

'Three months?' he said in surprise. 'She's taken her time, then. Kept it quiet, too.' It seemed strange, wrong; most would have been eager to talk the place up and open as quickly as possible. 'Where's she from?'

'No one seems to know. From all I hear she's been busy pouring money into the house. That's why it's taken so long.'

The Constable raised his eyebrows in disbelief. 'It ought to be a bloody palace after all that time.'

Sedgwick laughed. 'Couldn't happen, boss; she took Amos Worthy's old house.'

Amos Worthy. Nottingham shook his head. The man was dead but he'd never be rid of him. 'I'm surprised she's opening in less than a year, then.' He smiled. 'Half that place should have been torn down long ago. And I doubt an army could ever get the rest properly clean.'

'They say she's been making friends with some of the aldermen, too,' Sedgwick told him.

'Has she now?' He sat back, thinking. Whoever she was, the woman seemed to have taken care to set everything up well. 'Maybe I'd better go and see her, before she starts believing she's above the law. What about the rest of her family?'

'Tom Farraday said the daughters are a pretty pair.'

'There's a son, you said?'

'A big lad, according to Tom.'

'Could be useful in a place like that,' Nottingham mused. 'While I think on it, someone was in this morning. His sister's run off and he thinks she's in Leeds. Probably got here Saturday night. Small, blonde, looks younger than sixteen.'

The deputy rolled his eyes. 'Sounds like half of them who end up here. And the other half have dark hair.'

'I know.' The Constable smiled sadly. 'I asked Little Sal to keep her eyes open.'

Sedgwick nodded his acknowledgement as the serving girl brought his stew and ale. Nottingham drained the last of his drink.

'Enjoy your food, John. I'll pay this Mrs Wade a visit after the cloth market.'

All along Briggate, from Boar Lane down to the bridge over the Aire, the weavers were ready. Every Tuesday and Saturday morning they travelled in from villages all around Leeds to display their cloth. As soon as the market bell rang, the merchants would move between the trestles that lined both sides of the street, examining the fabric and making their bargains in whispers. It had been going on for more years than anyone knew, back through the generations. Thousands of pounds would change hands in an hour, with barely a loud word spoken. The wool business was the soul of Leeds. It put money in the city's coffers and made those who traded in it rich.

The Constable walked around slowly, nodding greetings here and there, his eyes watching carefully for cutpurses. Trouble was rare, but he always came himself or sent the deputy. Even after a lifetime of seeing it the quiet magic of the cloth market still gripped him.

When it was all done and the merchants began to drift away before the closing bell, he walked down to Swinegate. It was a cramped street, tradesmen working busily in their shops, the tapping of hammers from the cobbler, goods artfully displayed outside the chandler to tempt people into buying. Puddles of stinking piss dotted the road, thrown out from windows at first light. He moved around mistresses and their servants and dodged between small groups of men making their bargains until he stood in front of the small wooden door.

It had been repainted, now a deep, shining black, coat after coat to give a heavy lustre. He raised his hand and knocked loudly, remembering how often he used to walk in unannounced, along the passage and through to the kitchen where Amos spent much of his day.

Until the cancer took him Worthy had been a pimp, and one of the most dangerous men in Leeds, with the aldermen deep in his pocket. His girls serviced them, he lent them money, and the men of the Corporation protected him. But there'd been a curious bond between the criminal and Nottingham, deepened when he discovered that Worthy had been his mother's lover years before. The Constable might have wanted to see the man swing, but he valued his company, too. And it was Worthy who'd spited Nottingham by leaving Emily money in his will, promising it would give her freedom. In the end he'd been right about that, too.

'Can I help you, sir?'

The girl looking up at him wasn't a servant, he decided immediately. She was dressed too well, in a rustling gown made to fit and flatter, her dark hair carefully curled where it peeked from her cap. Her looks stopped shy of beauty but there was an allure about her that men would remember and desire.

'I'd like to see Mrs Wade,' he told her. 'I'm Richard Nottingham, the Constable here.'

She dipped her head. 'Of course. Come in, sir, and I'll fetch Mama.'

The girl showed him through to the parlour and closed the door quietly behind him. He remembered the room as it had been in the Worthy's time, dirty, dingy, filled with cobwebs that were never cleared from one year to the next. Now it had come alive, the walls bright with flocked paper in the new style, a colourful Turkey rug over the gleaming boards on the floor. The windows, once so grimed that they kept out most of the light, sparkled. A long clock stood against the wall keeping quiet time. In spite of himself, he was impressed.

He'd barely been there two minutes, just enough to take in the strangeness of the place, when the woman bustled in. She was short and heavyset but carried herself regally, the silk of her dress swishing gently as she crossed the floor, her eyes bright and calculating, an aloof smile on her face.

'Mrs Wade.' He bowed his head slightly.

'Constable.' She smiled at his greeting. 'I've heard your name, of course. But I'm surprised to see you here. Is something wrong?'

'I've been told you're planning to open a brothel here.'

'I'm opening an establishment,' she agreed with a cautious smile. 'Tonight. But I prefer to think of it as somewhere gentlemen of standing can enjoy a glass of wine and some company,' she corrected him carefully.

'That's just a brothel by another name.' He smiled at her.

Mrs Wade inclined her head. 'If that's what you care to call it. I prefer a different title.' She kept her gaze full and direct. 'But it's hardly the only place of its kind in Leeds, is it?'

'True enough,' he acknowledged. 'I hear you've been living here for a few months now.'

'We have. I thought it made sense to get to know Leeds a little first, to meet the right people and make sure this was the proper place for us.' She waved a hand at the room. 'And it's taken a while to decorate the house, of course.'

'More than decoration, I think,' he said admiringly. The woman had taste as well as money. 'It certainly looks different.'

'Thank you. Of course, I understand you were a regular visitor when Mr Worthy was alive.'

He glanced at her sharply to see if her words held a deeper meaning but her face was impassive.

'Often enough,' he agreed mildly. 'If you've heard about Amos then you'll know why.'

'People have told me stories about him.'

'I daresay they have,' he replied wryly. 'Most of them are probably true.'

'Yet he was never convicted of anything?'

'No. Amos had powerful friends.' He paused. 'You've been making a few of your own, I hear.'

'I find that gentlemen of influence usually have money to spend.' She offered a bland smile.

'And you brought your family with you?'

'I did. My son and my daughters. That was Sarah who showed you in. My other daughter is Anne, and my son is Mark.'

'Might I ask where you lived before, Mrs Wade?'

'Here and there. We've been in so many places over the years.' She smiled again and he noted the way she skipped around his question. 'But I hope we'll be here for a long time.' She glanced at the wallpaper and frowned. 'After all, I've invested enough in it.'

'Then I wish you well,' Nottingham said. 'As long as you keep an orderly house we won't have any problems.'

'I trust you'll come to the opening tonight, Constable,' she offered.

'No, but thank you,' he replied. 'I doubt many of the other

guests would welcome me here. I hope it's a success for you, though.' He started to open the door, then turned as a thought struck him. 'Tell me, do you have a girl named Jenny here?'

'Jenny?' She pursed her lips then shook her head. 'No.'

'She'd have arrived in the last few days. Blonde, looks very young.'

'No, there's no one like that.'

'If she comes looking for work, would you let me know? Her brother's searching for her.'

'Of course, I'll be glad to do that,' she agreed quickly. 'I'm pleased to have had the honour to meet you, sir.'

Come evening, on the way home, Nottingham stopped at the churchyard, as he did so often, standing by the graves of his older daughter Rose and his wife Mary. There was space for him, too, when his time came. And there'd been many occasions in the last six months when he'd wished it would come soon, nights when the longing lapped at his neck and the loneliness sighed in his ears. His mind knew full well that Mary was no more than bones and rotting flesh under the earth but here, in his heart, he could believe she was still with him, listening, laughing, smiling, loving him. Since the murder he'd fallen out of love with the world, as if it had moved away and left him standing still.

He stayed for a few quiet minutes, then crossed Timble Bridge, home to the house on Marsh Lane. Inside, Rob and Emily sat at the table in eager discussion. She looked up, smiled, then came to greet him with a small kiss to his cheek.

'Busy day?' he asked, although he already knew the answer. For her, every day was filled with work from the moment she arrived at the school on the Calls, and she often sat late into the evening, planning and writing, tired but happier than he'd ever seen her. She'd even considered taking on an older girl to help her in the classroom.

'What I really need are books for them all,' she told him. 'Do you know most of them have never even opened one in their lives? But I just don't see how we can afford them.' The families of the girls paid what they could, but that was hardly anything; most could barely scratch together enough for their rooms, and food for their tables was often scarce. Emily stood most of the costs of the school from the money she'd been left, fretting over every penny to be spent. 'Do you think any of the merchants might donate?' she asked hopefully.

'Try Tom Williamson,' he suggested. 'He claims he's making money now and he has a good heart. Two girls of his own, as well.'

She beamed. 'Thank you, Papa.' He knew she'd do it, too, present herself at Williamson's warehouse and persuade him with her passion.

He went through to the kitchen for ale. Lucy, the serving girl he'd taken on shortly before Mary's death, was starting to ladle out the stew.

'I hope you're hungry,' she said. 'I made plenty.'

The lass always prepared ample and it had always vanished by the end of the meal. Rob and Emily both had the appetites of the young, as hungry as the devil himself by evening, and he was certain Lucy often finished a second plate when no one was watching. He didn't begrudge them the food; he was happy to be able to provide it.

'I can eat,' he told her.

She'd been a child from the streets, used to starvation and fending for herself. In the time when grief numbed him to the world she'd kept the house going, forcing him into routine, putting a full plate before him every night and coaxing him into swallowing one bite, then another and another, like a mother with her infant. It was impossible to imagine the place without Lucy now. She'd helped to ease the guilt off him with quiet words and silence when he needed it. But it still weighed him down; if he hadn't been so determined to catch a pair of killers Mary would still be alive.

They all talked over the meal, the servant sitting with them, as loud as anyone, and Nottingham wondered if he was the only one who missed another voice in the hubbub around the table. When they were done, Lucy vanished into the kitchen again and Emily followed her. She was teaching the girl to read, write and do her sums, determined to give her the same chance as every lass at the school. And Lucy responded with swift intelligence, gobbling down the knowledge then craving more.

'Anything I should know for tonight, boss?' Rob asked.

Beyond the missing girl and keeping an eye on the new brothel there was little. By now Lister knew what to do. The son of the city's newspaper owner had seemed like an unlikely Constable's man at first, a lad who'd left every job he'd taken, but he'd stayed with this one. Now he was almost as valuable as the deputy.

After Rob left to take charge of the night men Emily sat at the table to prepare her lessons for the next day. Nottingham heard grunts beyond the door as Lucy kneaded the bread dough, pushing down hard on it with her small fists before leaving it to rise overnight.

Finally he took himself to bed, opening the window to draw in the warm air and soft sounds that filled the darkness. He lay under the old sheet, his eyes closed but still wide awake. This was the time he would have held Mary as they drifted away into sleep with the quiet, loving intimacy of touch and scent.

He felt the hand against his shoulder and the comfort of the dream vanished like papers thrown into the wind.

'Boss!' Rob hissed and he sat up.

'What?' he asked, wiping at the puffiness around his eyes. The room was black; he couldn't make out any shapes.

'We found a body. You'd better come. It's a murder.'

'Aye, all right.' Already he was climbing out of bed, reaching without thinking for his hose and breeches. 'Where?' He pushed his arms into the long waistcoat, the fabric shapeless now, its pattern long since worn to nothing.

'Megson's Court, just below the Rose and Crown. Throat cut.'

He knew it well: old buildings half tumbled down and pushed one against the other, filled with all the stink of life and death.

At the front door he pulled on his threadbare work coat.

'Right, lad, show me.'

'Is it a man or woman?' Nottingham asked as they walked briskly up Kirkgate, the scuff of their boots the only sound in the night air.

'Man. I didn't recognize his face.'

Stars shone in a clear sky and the moon was bright enough to guide them along the road.

'What time is it?'

'The church clock rang three a while ago,' Rob answered. 'I thought I'd better come and fetch you. I sent one of the men for the coroner.'

'You did right,' he said thoughtfully. God knew that death was common enough; poverty and hunger demanded their toll every week. Murder came more rarely. An argument, a husband who imagined a grievance against his wife, a fight that blossomed out of hand when men had been drinking. He'd wager this had started in an inn or a beershop.

They passed the jail and turned down Briggate. The Constable led the way through the passage to Megson's Court, his shoulders rubbing on either side of the opening, the stench of piss and shit and death strong and sickly in his nostrils as he emerged into the square of ground.

Two men stood in one corner holding flaming torches, and he walked over to them. In the light he made out the body of a man lying on the ground.

'Hold the light so I can see his face,' he ordered, squatting beside it.

'Do you know him, boss?' Rob asked.

'I do. His name's Jem Carter. He came to see me this morning. He's the one who thought his sister had run off to Leeds.'

FOUR

The Constable rose stiffly, his knees aching, still staring at the body. He turned at the sound of footsteps, and nodded to the coroner as he approached. Brogden halted, wrinkling his face at the stink of the place before he even approached the corpse. For once he hadn't taken time over his appearance; there was a hole in his hose, and he had left his wig at home and pulled a hat down firmly on his head.

'Bring that damned torch closer,' he barked, bending a little to glance at the corpse before straightening again. 'Dead,' he announced, then walked away hurriedly without a backward glance.

'Take him to the jail,' Nottingham told the men. Once Carter was in the cold cell he'd be able to look at him properly. He glanced around the court. No candles glimmered behind any of the windows but this was a place where they kept clear of the law. 'Wait. Hold that flame up again,' he said suddenly.

The Constable rolled the body a little, studying the ground beneath.

'There's hardly any blood. Someone brought him here.' He glanced up at Rob. 'Start knocking on doors. Someone must have seen something.'

'Yes, boss.'

'I'll send Mr Sedgwick down when he comes in.'

He walked slowly back up Briggate. All around him the city was waking, the sky lighter, thin spirals of smoke beginning to rise from chimneys. Why would anyone kill Jem Carter? The man was only looking for his sister. What had he found instead?

By the time the deputy arrived Nottingham had already examined the body laid out on the bench in the cell they used as a mortuary. Carter's face was bruised into ugliness; someone had beaten him fiercely; his teeth were knocked out, cheekbones broken, jaw at an angle, marks all over his body. Whoever did this had been brutal, the Constable thought. There were grazes across the man's knuckles where he'd tried to defend himself. But it was the single deep slash across the throat that had killed him.

'Boss?'

'In here, John.'

The deputy joined him, glancing down at the corpse. 'Poor bastard took a battering. Who was he?'

'Jem Carter. The one with the missing sister.'

'He only arrived yesterday, didn't he? Where did they find him?'

'Megson's Court. But he was killed somewhere else; there was next to no blood around the body. I told him to lodge with Mrs Lumley. Go down there and see if she knows anything.'

'Yes, boss. Anything in his pockets?'

'Empty. Turned out. Not too surprising given where he was. Rob's talking to the people there.'

Sedgwick shook his head. 'He'll not have much luck. You know what they're like – see nowt, hear nowt and say bugger all.'

'True enough,' he agreed with a short sigh. All he could hope was that murder might loosen a tongue or two. 'Go and join him when you're done.' He paused. 'Whoever did it must have been strong; Carter's big.' He turned the man's hand over, feeling the thick calluses on the palm and fingers. 'He was a farmer, he'd be strong enough, too.'

'Doesn't mean he can fight,' Sedgwick pointed out.

'Or maybe he found his sister and someone didn't want him to take her,' he said thoughtfully. 'See what you can discover.'

The deputy knew the rooming house on Call Lane. Ma Lumley took pride in her home, kept the windows washed, and the step scrubbed clean each morning. She changed the linen regularly and never allowed more than three to a bed.

She answered at the first knock, wiping her hands on an old rag, eyes lively under her cap, her gown plain but clean. The woman had to be close to fifty, but she didn't seem to have aged since he'd first met her five years before.

'Mr Sedgwick,' she said, her mouth breaking into a wide smile. 'I don't often see you these days. How are those bairns of yours?'

'Doing grand. James is near the top of his class at the charity school.' He laughed. 'Give him another year and he'll be writing better than me. Isabell's charging round, trying to get into everything. My Lizzie swears that trying to keep up will be the death of her.'

'You've got a good lass there, right enough. Just make sure you hold on to her.'

'Don't you worry, I'm going to.'

She eyed him speculatively. 'What brings you here, any road? Must be work, you're not one for idle chitter-chatter.'

'Do you have Jem Carter stopping here?'

'I do; Mr Nottingham sent him down yesterday. A very nice lad, good country manners.' She clicked her tongue then looked at him suspiciously. 'Why, what's he saying, I didn't charge him fair?'

'Nothing like that.' He paused for a moment. 'We found him during the night. Someone killed him.'

'Killed him?' She echoed the words in disbelief, her hand rising to cover her mouth, all the colour suddenly vanishing from her face. 'Oh, my Lord. But. .?'

'We don't know yet.' He answered the question she hadn't asked. 'That's why I'm here, to see what you can tell us.'

She nodded, a helpless look in her eyes, biting her lip.

'Did he tell you why he'd come here?'

'His sister, you mean? Yes. It's so sad, is that.' She glanced at the deputy. 'Do you think . . .?'

He let her question lie and continued. 'What time did he go out last night?'

She remembered slowly. 'It must have been close to seven. Her next door was shouting for her youngest and she always does that then. Mr Carter said he was going out to see if he could spy the lass.'

'Did he say where?'

She shook her head. 'I doubt he'd know where to start in Leeds, Mr Sedgwick. He didn't know the place at all. Just walk around and hope to spot her, I suppose.' She thought of something and lifted her head. 'His pack's still in his room. I saw it when I was cleaning this morning. Do you want to take a look at it?'

'Yes, please.' He followed her into the house and up the stairs. There wasn't a speck of dirt to be seen anywhere. 'Didn't you notice he hadn't come back last night?'

'I thought he must have gone out early this morning,' she answered.

The room smelt of sweat and sour breath, and the window stood wide to draw in a little air. She'd made up the bed, the sheet tucked carefully over a pallet of packed straw. She pointed into the corner at a leather satchel.

'There it is. You'd better take it, I suppose. Happen his family will want it.'

It weighed next to nothing in his hands. He lifted the flap and pushed a hand inside, feeling a shirt and a pair of soft woollen hose. No papers, and no man would be fool enough to leave his coins there. He hoisted it on his shoulder.

'Was there anything else he said? Anything at all?'

'No.' She pursed her mouth, scraping at her memory, then shook her head. 'No, nothing. He was quiet. A lovely, polite lad.' Her voice trailed away, then she said. 'You find whoever did it, Mr Sedgwick. He deserves that.'

'We'll do our best. You know that.'

At Megson's Court he found Rob still knocking on doors and learning precious little for his time. A few allowed that they might have heard something in the middle of the night but none of them would admit to looking.

'Go home, lad,' he said. 'You look like you need some sleep. I doubt the folk in here would give us the warmth off their piss, let alone something we can use.'

'You're right about that,' Lister admitted, frustration showing on his face. He took a slow breath and walked away, raising his arm in a weary farewell.

The deputy looked at the houses. He'd had dealings with one or two men from this court, letting them off small charges when he could easily have taken them to the jail. Murder seemed like a good reason to call in favours. He strode over to a squat stone building in the corner, letting his fist fall against the old, rotten wood of the door.

'Morning, Roger,' he said. The old man who answered was buttoning up his breeches, and a long grey beard spilled over his chest in a wiry tangle. He looked fragile, as if he might keel over at any moment, but the deputy knew his eyes and hands were sharp; he could still cut a purse with the best of them. 'You've had some goings on during the night.'

'Have we, Mr Sedgwick? I were sleeping.'

'Were you buggery. I know you, you wake if a fly beats its wings.' The man lowered his eyes. 'What did you see? We found a body.'

'Nothing.'

The deputy stared at him. 'Right, you've done your duty and said nowt. Now you can tell me the truth.'

'I couldn't make out much,' Roger said hastily.

'With that moon? It was bright as day.'

'He stayed in the shadows. All I could see was that he was pulling summat that looked like a man.'

'What did he look like?'

'Nay, Mr Sedgwick, I don't know. Just a man. Nowt special.'

'Tall? Short? Fat? Thin?'

Roger looked up pleadingly. 'I don't know. Honest, I don't.'

'How long was he here?'

'Just dropped the body and left. No more than a few moments.'

'What time was this?' the deputy pressed.

'Two, mebbe. I'm not sure.' The man shifted uneasily. 'Really, I'm not.'

'And who came out after?'

'A couple of them,' the old man admitted reluctantly. 'I saw them go through the pockets.'

Aye, they'd do that here, Sedgwick thought. 'Who was it?' he asked. Roger didn't reply. 'Who?' he repeated.

'Dick Chapman. I couldn't see the other one properly.'

The name was no surprise. Chapman was someone who'd take his grandmother's last pennies from her pocket along with the food she'd bought to eat.

'Anything else I should know, Roger?'

The old man shook his head.

He tried Chapman's door, a room up two flights of stairs in a building where the wood seemed to crumble under his touch. He pounded loud and long enough to make the neighbours shout out in complaint, but no one answered. No matter, he thought, he'd find him later.

Rob felt the sun on his back as he crossed Timble Bridge and strolled up Marsh Lane. He was drained, the weariness of a long night spreading through him. He unlocked the door and walked through to the kitchen, pouring himself ale before listening to Lucy read as she took a break from her cleaning. She still stumbled over many of the words, pausing and trying them out in her mind first, but in six months she'd come a long way.

He loved living in this house. Not only because he was with Emily; here he felt part of a family, more than he'd ever known with his own parents. Even with the sadness, and the ghost of the Constable's wife who hovered over the place, there was life and warmth here. It seemed like home.

Lucy finished the passage and for a few minutes he went through it with her, explaining the words she didn't know before letting her speak the piece twice more until it came fluently off her tongue.

Finally he stood, more than ready for bed. But after he lay down, rest wouldn't come so easily. The picture of the body they'd found kept slipping into his mind, the face beaten to a mess. Even when he found sleep it was broken by shards of dreams that stirred him. By early afternoon he was awake, restless and hot in the bed but still tired. He wondered if John had been able to find something at Megson's Court. They hadn't talked to him, closed their doors in his face before he'd said five words, or heard him out then shook their heads quietly and went back to their lives.

Sometimes he wondered if he was made to be a Constable's man, whether life mightn't be better if he did something else. He was still only nineteen, there were years ahead of him. But he loved the work more than anything he'd ever done, the way it was always different, especially all the long nights that might spark into flame in moments, when the blood surged through his body.

The Constable found Little Sal easily enough, in the same spot as the previous morning. Now she looked exhausted, barely raising a smile as she approached him.

'Tuesdays, Mr Nottingham,' she complained. 'As soon as the market's over and they have money in their pockets, all they want to do is spend it. They fair wore me out yesterday.'

'There's a few more coins if you have any word for me,' he offered.

She shook her head. 'You save it, love. I asked some of the others. There are a couple of new lasses, right enough, but none of them sound like the one you're after.' She hesitated, then said, 'Mind you, now I think about it, I've not seen so many fresh faces this last week or two.' She smiled ruefully. 'Maybe they're learning, eh?'

'They never learn, Sal. Not lads and not lasses.' He dug into the pocket of his breeches, feeling for a coin and passed it over. 'That's for trying.'

'You're a grand man, Mr Nottingham.' She stared at him pointedly. 'And if you ever feel the urge again . . .'

'I'll know who to see.' He gave her a small bow then left.

It was too easy to disappear in a place like Leeds, especially for someone without money. The poor simply vanished; they became unseen, ghosts at the fringe of life. If she'd really come to Leeds, the likelihood was that Jenny was already a whore somewhere, trying to keep body and soul together. But if she wasn't . . . He'd have Rob go to the camp by the river and talk to Bessie. The girl could be there, down among those who'd come to the ends of dreams and gathered together at night for safety and company, with no home except the grass by the river.

By late afternoon the Constable was back at the jail, completing another report when the deputy arrived.

'Did you find anything?'

'Not too much.' He recounted what he'd discovered. 'The rest of them were all blind and deaf, slept through the whole thing. You know what they're like, a bunch of crows. The only surprise is that they weren't all out stripping the corpse.'

'Have you seen Dick Chapman yet?'

'He wasn't home. I went back later but there was still no answer.'

'Make sure you find him,' the Constable ordered. 'I want Dick to feel the fear of God.'

'Yes, boss,' Sedgwick answered with a grin. 'I'll enjoy that.'

'After that, go on home. I'll finish things here.'

In truth there was little more to do. He completed the reports and walked up Briggate to the Moot Hall. Around the building, the butchers in the Shambles were closing their shutters for the day; packs of dogs roamed from one door to another, ready to fight for the last of the scraps thrown out on the cobbles.

The Moot Hall stood in the middle of Briggate, the street parting around it, and he climbed the polished stairs then walked along the thick Turkey carpet in the long hallway. A desk stood at the end, the young clerk scribbling quickly, his head down, concentrating on his work. Nottingham placed the papers in front of him and the man looked up in surprise.

'Constable,' he said. 'I'm sorry, I . . .' He raised an ink-stained hand in apology.

'No matter, Mr Cobb. Just pass these to the mayor. I'm sure he has no wish to see me.'

Cobb frowned. The Constable had clashed with Mayor Fenton the year before and come close to losing his post. In the end he'd won, humiliating the mayor, and bad blood had flowed between them ever since. Fenton's term would run until September and Nottingham doubted he'd see the man again before then.

The clerk took the papers and added them to a pile on the corner of his desk before picking up the quill pen once more. But Nottingham didn't leave immediately.

'By the way, Mr Cobb,' he said softly, 'I think his Worship would dismiss you if he knew you were selling information to criminals.'

'What?' The man's head jerked up and the blood left his face.

'We've known it for months. Did you really think we wouldn't?' Cobb's eyes darted everywhere, as if he was seeking an escape route. It had been luck that they'd even discovered it, a stray word from a crook with knowledge that could only have come from Cobb. Nottingham had let it lie for a long time; now seemed a good time to press the advantage.

'I . . .' the man began, then couldn't find more words.

'Don't worry, I've not said anything.' The Constable paused. 'And I won't.' He waited, seeing relief pass across the clerk's lips. 'But it stops now.'

'Yes, sir, of course,' Cobb said, eager to comply.

'And you start giving me the information instead.'

The man nodded, knowing he was in no position to bargain.

'Then I wish you good day.'

FIVE

The air had cooled slightly and the first sketchings of dusk were in the sky when the deputy banged on the door again. This time he heard footsteps shuffling across the floor, and the handle turned.

Dick Chapman was short, with a sly cast to his eyes and the sharp face of a weasel. Before he could say a word, Sedgwick reached out and pushed him back into the room, following and closing the door.

'You've been robbing the dead.' The deputy towered over the man, standing close enough to smell the ale on his breath.

'Not me, sir. Never.' He shook his head for emphasis.

'How much did you get from him?'

'Nowt, Mr Sedgwick. I didn't do owt.'

The deputy grabbed him by the stained, discoloured stock and lifted him.

'Maybe you'd like a night in the cells, Dick. Happen that would help your memory. What do you think?' He dragged Chapman higher until his feet left the floor, then let him drop.

'It were just a few coins.' He snuffled the answer, careful not to meet the deputy's gaze. 'He didn't have much. It were only enough for a pie and a drink.'

'And what else was in there?'

'Nothing,' Chapman answered eventually. As the deputy took a step closer, he added, 'A piece of paper. I threw it away, it wun't owt.'

Sedgwick turned in disgust. At the door he said, 'I'd better not hear your name for a long, long time or I'll put you in the jail and forget where I put the key.'

Finally he was home, in the small house on Lands Lane. Isabell tottered across the floor to him, arms out for a cuddle, a broad smile on her face, He swung her up, nuzzling his nose against her and leaned across the table to kiss Lizzie. This was what made it worthwhile, to come back to his family, leaving death and desperation on the other side of the door.

'You look worn out,' Lizzie told him.

'Long day,' he said, lowering Isabell gently then tickling her until she giggled. 'And a dead man to start it.'

'I heard. Anyone you know?'

'Not a local.' He poured himself a mug of ale from the jug. 'He'd come looking for his sister. She'd run off from home on Saturday to look for her fortune.'

Lizzie said nothing, but folded her arms and gazed down.

'Is James upstairs?' he asked.

'He's done his homework and settled down in his bed.'

Sedgwick slipped up the stairs to kiss the sleeping child on the cheek. When he returned Lizzie had cheese and ale set out on the table for him.

'That lass, the one who came here, have you found her?'

He shook his head. 'Mebbe she'll find her way home again. Some do.'

'Do they?' She raised sad eyes. 'Not many I ever saw.'

'Or we'll find her.'

'How many do you find, John?' Lizzie asked. 'Honestly, how many?'

'Only a few,' he admitted.

She was silent for a long time. 'I've never told you how I started as a whore, have I?'

She hadn't and he'd never asked, never wanted to press her. He'd been willing to wait; if the story ever came he wanted it to be in her own good time. He poured more ale and looked at her.

'I was thirteen when I started to grow.' She put her hands over her breasts to show what she meant. 'Men started looking at me. My da ran a beershop in Harrogate and he was always busy with that. My mam had died so I looked after everything in the house.' She went quiet for a few moments, the pain of memory on her face. 'I had an older brother. He thought I were there for his pleasure. When I told my da he wouldn't believe me. Just clouted me across the room for a liar. So I left and came down here.'

He reached across the table and tenderly stroked the tears from her cheeks.

'The carter who gave me a ride to Leeds wanted paying. I didn't have any money, so . . . I thought, I have summat men want, I might as well make some money from it.' She straightened her shoulders and gave a wan smile. 'Now you know.'

'I'm sorry, love,' he told her.

She brightened a little, but the sadness remained behind her eyes. 'It's all in the past, John Sedgwick. I've got you, I've got Isabell and James. I'm happy now.'

Rob started by asking in all the inns and alehouses if Jem Carter had been there before he died. He began close to the

Rose and Crown, next to Megson's Court, knowing full well it was likely to be a fool's errand; the chances of anyone remembering the man were small. By ten his tongue had grown thick from repeating the man's description.

Each landlord he asked shook his head slowly, unable to recall anyone tall and blond whose clothes marked him out as a country boy. At the Old King's Head he settled back with a mug of ale, and Landlord Taylor leaned on the trestle, stroking his chin.

'I'd have remembered if he'd been in. I don't forget a new face. Can't in this business, you never know when they'll be back or cause trouble.'

Rob drank, the liquid like balm on his throat.

'Better to be prepared?' he asked.

The man nodded wisely. 'When you've seen as much as I have you'll know how true that is, lad.'

'I'll take your word.' He drained the mug and stood. 'More work to do. I needed that, thank you.'

There was a faint chill in the night air, but also the sense of summer drawing close with its promise of long days and shaded evenings. He made his way slowly up Briggate, asking his questions and receiving the same answers. Finally he came to the Talbot and took a deep breath before opening the door.

He knew many of the faces, men he'd hauled off to the jail for fighting and drunkenness. It was a place for those who lingered on the wrong side of the law. And he knew Bell, the landlord who stood staring at him. One of the doors behind the man led upstairs to the rooms the whores used. The other went through to the pit where he held cockfights every week.

'What's tha want?'

'Just a few questions for you, Mr Bell.' He tried to sound pleasant but it was nigh on impossible with this man.

'Nowt to say.' He turned his back and began talking to a customer.

Empty mugs stood on the trestle. Rob drew out his cudgel and casually swept it along the wood, sending the cups spinning and shattering on the floor. Bell turned sharply, his face dark as winter.

'What do you think you're doing, boy?'

'Getting your attention, Mr Bell. I said I wanted to ask you something.'

The landlord rubbed his large fists slowly but Rob stood his ground.

'I'll be sending your master the bill for them.'

'You do that.' Lister paused. 'Now, did you have any strangers in here last night?'

'Mebbe. Mebbe not.'

'Which is it?' He tapped out a soft, slow rhythm on the trestle with the cudgel.

'Aye, there was one,' Bell admitted after a while.

'What did he look like?'

'Fair hair, sounded like he were just up from the country. Talked to Tom Finer a while and left.'

Rob smiled. 'That wasn't too hard, was it, Mr Bell?'

The landlord took a step forward. 'Better not get too cocky, lad,' he warned. 'I might not be feeling so helpful next time.'

Tom Finer, he thought as he walked back down Briggate. Bell had spoken the name as if it should be familiar but he'd never heard it before. Still, John or the boss would know the man; between them they seemed to know everyone in Leeds, high or low.

He made his way down to the bridge, then took the old stone stairs to the riverbank. A few hundred yards upstream small fires burned in the night and he followed the path towards them. As he approached a figure came out of the darkness.

'Hello, Bessie,' he said.

'Mr Lister.' In the glow he could see her broad smile, hair neatly caught under a cap, a shawl gathered around her shoulders, fleshy arms showing. She stood in front of him, protective of those gathered round the blazes, the ones with nothing, no roof, no food, no hope, coming each night to the only place they could call home. Bessie looked after her poor like family, tending and caring. 'What brings you here?'

'Work,' he admitted. He did what he could, gave them food sometimes. It was little enough, he knew that.

'How's that girl of yours?'

'The school's keeping her busy.'

She nodded over towards the flames. 'Sophia's little one

goes there and she comes back so happy.' She pursed her lips. 'Now, what can I do for you?'

'I'm looking for someone who might have found her way here. Her name's Jenny. She arrived in Leeds on Saturday. A blonde girl, small. She's sixteen but she looks younger.'

'I've no one like that,' Bessie answered. 'I'm sorry. If she wanders in I'll send word.'

'Thank you.' He began to turn away.

'You know what they're like, Mr Lister. Plenty that think there's money to be made here. They learn the truth soon enough.'

The night passed quietly. The sky was light in the east, and the prospect of another sunny day lay ahead. Rob finished his last round not long after five. Servants were stirring in the grand houses, making everything ready and comfortable for when their masters woke.

By the time he reached the jail the Constable was already there, glancing through the papers on the desk.

'Did you find anything on our man?'

'He was talking with Tom Finer at the Talbot.'

'Tom Finer?' He said the name in disbelief. 'You're sure that was the name?'

'I'm certain, boss. Why, who is he?'

Nottingham sighed, surprise still on his face, 'Someone I haven't heard of in years. He vanished when I wasn't much older than you.' He paused and ran a hand over his chin. 'Who gave you the name?'

'Landlord Bell.'

'Really? You got something out of him? I'm impressed.'

'He said he'd send you the bill for the mugs I smashed,' Rob told him with a smile.

Nottingham grinned. 'You're learning to speak his language, eh? Tom Finer,' he repeated quietly. 'I can see I'm going to have to find him later.'

'I went down to see Bessie, too. The girl hasn't been there.'

'You go on home, lad. If you're lucky you'll catch Emily before she leaves for school.'

Tom Finer. It had to be almost twenty years since he'd gone, so long that he'd slipped out of mind. If he was back it couldn't be good news. Especially if he'd been talking to a man who was dead a few hours later. When Nottingham had just been a Constable's man Finer had been around, a power with his finger in half the crime in Leeds. Then he'd vanished, no word and no trace. There were rumours that Amos Worthy had murdered him but they'd never managed to find proof. The man had simply disappeared.

He was still considering the news when the deputy loped through the door and poured himself some ale.

'Morning, boss.'

'Tom Finer. Does the name mean anything?'

'No.' He shook his head. 'Should it?'

Nottingham leaned back, hands laced behind his head. 'Some history that seems to have returned, that's all. Seems he was talking to Jem Carter in the Talbot last night. I'll ask around and see if I can find out where he's living. You keep looking to see if anyone remembers talking to Carter yesterday.'

SIX

Who would remember Tom Finer, the Constable thought? Most of those around now had come since his time. If they knew his name at all it would only be from tales. He sat at his desk and thought for a while then walked out into the spring air.

On Briggate folk were smiling. Even the carters who normally cursed everyone had been caught up by the good weather. He passed the Moot Hall and ducked into the Talbot. Sunlight strained through the grimy windows and picked out the dirt on the tables. The place was almost empty, just two old men huddled around the dead hearth and landlord Bell leaning on the trestle smoking a clay pipe, mugs lined up in front of him.

'I wondered how long it'd be before you came in.'

'You know why I'm here, Mr Bell.'

'You owe me for eight mugs.' The landlord stood up slowly, facing the Constable.

'Send a bill to the aldermen.'

'Aye, and wait a year for me money, if I ever get it.'

'Tom Finer,' Nottingham said.

'I thought that name would catch your ear if the boy remembered it,' Bell answered with a slow, mocking smile.

'How long's he been back?'

Bell raised an eyebrow. 'Why should I tell you? What's in it for me?'

The Constable said calmly, 'Fighting, murder, selling stolen goods.' He counted them off on his fingers. 'Half the bad things in this city come out of here, Mr Bell. Maybe it's time I saw about having this inn closed. There are a few on the Corporation who'd listen if I planted the idea, too.' He stopped. 'You know me by now, I don't make idle threats. Is that clear enough for you?'

'He's been in Leeds a fortnight or so,' the landlord answered grudgingly.

'And where's he staying?'

'He has rooms on the Head Row, next to Garraway's Coffee House.' He stared at Nottingham. 'And that's all I've got to tell you.'

'It's enough for now. I'll bid you good day, Mr Bell.'

It was no more than a few yards to the top of Briggate, then he turned up the Head Row and followed the road along the hill. For decades this had been as far as Leeds extended, but now many of the rich folk were moving and building their new mansions farther out, away from the smoke and dirt and people. Already Town End was filling with grand houses, and some were appearing on the road out to Woodhouse. Another few years and the Leeds he knew would be hard to find for all the stone walls and gardens.

Steam filled the windows at Garraway's but he could make out the merchants seated at the tables inside, discussing business or reading the London papers that had come north. He passed the place and stopped at the building beyond it, close to Burley Bar at the edge of the city, a neatly-kept house with three storeys, the wood of the front door carefully polished to a deep shine.

A maid answered his knock, offering a small curtsey.

'I believe Mr Finer lives here.'

'Yes, sir. He has the top floor, sir,' she said with a bob of her head.

'Would you tell him Constable Richard Nottingham would like to see him, please?'

'Yes, sir.' She gave one more nervous curtsey and scurried up the stairs. He waited in the hallway, the only sounds the muted passing of people and carts outside.

'He says to go up, sir,' the girl told him when she returned. 'It's right at the top, you can't miss it.'

'Thank you,' he told her with a small bow that made her blush.

The door was open. He tapped on it lightly.

'Come in,' a voice said.

The Constable entered a well-appointed parlour, the paper on the walls a design of pale stripes, a pair of chairs gathered by the hearth, a table under a window that looked north to the moor where sheep grazed in the sun.

The man standing before him wasn't the Tom Finer that he recalled. The one in his memory had thick, dark hair that curled down to the nape of his neck and a heavy, powerful body. This one was still big, but most of the hair had gone; what remained above the ears was wispy and white.

'Not what you expected, am I, Mr Nottingham?' he said with a smile. At least the voice was still the same, an easy warmth that he knew could turn to ice in a moment. 'They made you Constable after Arkwright went, did they?'

'Yes.'

'Sit down,' Finer said, gesturing at one of the chairs. 'Some wine? Ale?'

'Not for me,' Nottingham said, settling on to the seat.

'How did you hear I was back?'

'Landlord Bell. He said you were talking to a young man there two nights ago.'

'Two nights ago?' The man frowned, then placed it in his mind. 'You mean the one looking for his sister?'

'He was dead before morning. Someone slit his throat.'

Finer raised his eyebrows. 'I'm sorry to hear that. I knew someone had been killed; I'd no idea it was him. And you wondered if I had something to do with it?'

'You can understand why. I know your past.'

Finer put his hands in his lap. The flesh was pale as parchment and mottled with brown spots. An old man's hands, the Constable thought.

'I bought him a few drinks and we talked for a while. That's all.' He smiled. 'He talked, mostly. I listened. But I did suggest he could look for his sister at that new brothel everyone was talking about.' He shrugged. 'I thought it might be worth a minute or two of his time.'

'Did he go?'

'I don't know.' He reached for the decanter on the small table and poured himself a glass of wine, drinking deeply then setting it aside. 'But I can tell you I had nothing to do with his death.'

'Did he mention anyone he'd met?'

'I think I was probably the first soul he'd had a real conversation with in Leeds. He seemed a pleasant enough lad. None too sharp but devoted to his sister.' He took another drink, finishing the wine, and sat back.

'What happened to you all those years ago?' Nottingham asked. The question had been preying on him since he'd heard the name.

'Seventeen years, Constable, if you want to be exact.' He glanced at the decanter and poured himself another glass, sipped and sighed slowly. 'Amos Worthy wanted to kill me and it wasn't just an idle threat.' He shrugged. 'I had plenty of money so I left while I still could. Not a word to anyone. And now Amos is dead.'

'Cancer.'

'I went down to the churchyard and walked on his grave.' He laughed, a small, hollow bark. 'I know, it's childish, but it gave me some satisfaction to outlive the bastard. Did he ever tell you . . .?'

'That he and my mother were lovers?'

Finer nodded. 'Obviously he did. I was sorry to hear about your wife, by the way.'

'Thank you.' He paused, not wanting to pursue that subject. Not with this man. Not with anyone. 'What's made you come back after all this time?'

'Seventeen years in London and I still missed Leeds.' He smiled wryly. 'You wouldn't credit it, would you? It's true, though. I made plenty down there, but I'd had enough of the place.' Nottingham could hear the capital in his voice with its veneer of sophistication and drawn-out vowels. 'Always noisy, people everywhere. It was time. Look at me. I'm an old man now, Mr Nottingham. I decided to spend the last of my days here.'

'Quietly?' the Constable asked pointedly.

'Very quietly,' Finer agreed. 'These rooms are comfortable, they'll serve me well.'

He had no doubt that the man was paying handsomely for somewhere like this. But he was equally certain that Finer had prospered down in London; he was ruthless enough to do well anywhere. His coat and breeches showed expensive tailoring, and the buckles on his shoes shone like real gold.

Nottingham stood. 'I'd best move on,' he said.

'I wish you well in finding the murderer, Constable.'

'No doubt we'll be running into each other, Mr Finer.'

'Perhaps we will, laddie, perhaps we will.' He raised his glass in a toast as Nottingham left the room.

Walking back to jail, he considered what Finer had told him. He didn't believe that the man had really returned to Leeds simply to wither and die. The person he recalled was subtle, and never did anything without a host of reasons, each one nesting inside another to hide the truth. There was more going on, that was Finer's way. He didn't know what yet, but he'd need to stay alert to find out. But did he believe what the man had said about Jem Carter? There didn't seem to be any reason for him to kill the lad, but the Tom Finer he recalled had always seemed so plausible that he could explain away the devil.

The problem was that it was hard for him to be sure of anything any more. Since his decision, his risk, had cost Mary her life, every decision, every step, every breath had become fragile. He'd become cautious, wary, a man without certainty or compass.

SEVEN

S tanding on Briggate, the deputy paused to think. Where would Jem Carter have gone? Tuesday had been a market day; he'd have looked around there in the hope of spotting his sister. But most of the traders wouldn't be back until the next market on Saturday, and by then their memories would be dim.

One or two were local, though, selling their goods most days of the week up by the market cross. Martha Whittaker and her daughters baked their pies every night, then she carried them from her home on the other side of the river each morning. She'd been doing it for years; he could remember his da buying him one when he was a nipper. By nine she'd be done, everything sold to the customers who loved the food that was heavy on the meat and fair on price, and she'd go back to her bed for a few hours' rest before starting again.

She was sitting on a small old stool at the side of Briggate, the few remaining pies laid out on a tattered cloth in front of her. She looked up as his shadow fell over her, her eyes rheumy and squinting, her hair close to silver in the sunlight.

'Mr Sedgwick, isn't it?'

'Aye, Martha, it is. Business good?'

'Fair to middling, fair to middling. If you're looking, the beef's tasty today, it cooked up a treat.' She leant forward and whispered, 'The lamb's a bit stringy.'

He dug out some coins, paid her and put a beef pie into the deep pocket of his coat. She slid the money away carefully and sat back, looking at him. Although she dressed plainly enough in an old gown that had seen many better years, he knew she made good money from her business, enough to support three daughters and a son, her man long since gone.

'Were you busy during the market?'

'Always busy then,' she replied. 'Always.'

'Did you have someone around asking questions, looking for a girl?'

She thought for a long time and then shook her head slowly. 'No one like that, love. I'm sure of it.'

He thanked her and moved on, seeing Sad Luke sitting on the steps of the cross. He lived somewhere beyond Cavalier Hill, and went out early in the morning to gather the wild onions, garlic and herbs that grew out there, collecting berries and fruit into summer and autumn. He was no older than the deputy, but no one had ever seen a shred of happiness on his face. No matter how good the weather or how much money he made, Luke's mouth was always set in a quizzical frown.

'Mr Sedgwick,' he said with a small bob of his head.

'Morning, Luke.' He took off the battered tricorn hat and wiped his forehead. 'Grand day.'

'Aye, fair.' The man squinted disappointedly at the sky. 'Too hot later, mebbe. And too dry this summer if it stays this way.'

The deputy smiled to himself. Luke would never change, forever gloomy and seeking out the bad in everything.

'Were you at the market yesterday?'

'Allus am.'

'Did you have a stranger asking about his sister?'

'Him?' Luke ran his tongue across his thin lips. 'Aye, he was here. Tried to tell me my onions weren't no good.' He sounded affronted at the small memory.

'What else did he say?'

'Nowt, really.' He rubbed a finger along his nose. 'I told him he'd do best to go looking for the whores. That's where half the lasses end up anyway.'

'How did he take that?'

'Walked off,' Luke replied flatly. 'Daft bugger.' He looked up at the deputy with wide eyes. 'And them onions were right good, too.'

He needed to ask in the brothels, Sedgwick decided; Jenny might have found work there. But two of them had heard nothing of her, shaking their heads when he asked about new girls. Finally he walked down to Vicar Lane and rapped lightly on the door of a well-tended house, as ordinary as all its neighbours. Only the shutters closed tight against the daylight marked it out as anything different.

He waited a while then tried again, knowing that anything

before mid-afternoon was early here. Finally a bleary-eyed maid let him in and shuffled off for the mistress.

Fanny Hardcastle had dressed quickly, her face still puffed with sleep and her hair loose, hanging grey and drab to her shoulders. She saw him and her mouth turned down at the corners.

'I hope you know what time it is, Mr Sedgwick. Some of us are not long to our beds.'

Her brothel was long-established, opened decades before by Fanny's mother. It was almost an institution on the city, catering to many of the merchants and aldermen in town, making them feel comfortable and cared-for in a house that was sometimes better than home, with good seats, warm fires and excellent company.

He gave her his best smile, trying to charm her into a good temper.

'How's your mam?'

'Not doing so well. She gets her attacks and whatever the apothecary gives her doesn't help.' The woman pulled a shawl tight around her shoulders. 'You'd better not be here just to ask after her.'

'It's to do with a murder.'

'A murder?' Her eyes narrowed. 'You mean that man they found yesterday?' She straightened her back and raised her head. 'It's nothing to do with us, I'll tell you that right now.'

'I know, love. Don't go fretting yourself.' He smiled again. 'I'm looking for a girl who might have been here. Small, fair hair, name of Jenny.'

'Country girl? Tiny little thing?'

'The sounds like her.'

'I know her, right enough,' Fanny told him with a curt nod. 'She came by on Sunday, looking for work.' He was suddenly alert, staring at her. 'But I told her, we're full of lasses. You know what it's like here. Mam and me treat them well and they don't leave. Except Sophie, of course, she went off to wed Mr Marcham back in January. Most of them stay for years. I had to send that one on her way.'

'Do you know where she went?'

Fanny shook her head. 'I've no idea, Mr Sedgwick. She

looked that sad when I turned her down I thought she was going to burst into tears.'

'You've not seen her since?'

'Neither hide nor hair. I felt so sorry for her that I gave her sixpence.' He was impressed; Fanny Hardcastle was usually so tight with her money she could make a coin squeak. 'To tell you the truth, I hoped she'd see sense. She'd have been better off going back home and marrying a farmer's lad. I can tell the ones who are cut out for this, they've got a brass front. Your Lizzie had it. Not this one, though.' She looked at him appraisingly. 'So who was this man to her, then?'

'Her brother.'

She grimaced. 'That's a bad business, Mr Sedgwick.'

'I know, love.'

'I hope you find whoever did it.'

'You and me both, Fanny.' He stood. 'Give my best to your mam. I hope she feels better soon.'

The Constable had just finished his dinner, a pie bought from a seller down by the bridge. He brushed the crumbs from his old coat and looked at the river. Too many things were gnawing at him: Jem Carter's murder, the missing girl, the return of Tom Finer. Could Finer have killed? He still wasn't sure, even though something inside said no.

A voice next to him said, 'Penny for them, Richard.'

He turned and saw Tom Williamson, one of the few wool merchants who treated him as an equal. He was dressed in a coat and breeches of pale yellow silk, his stock sparkling white, a full, dark periwig on his head: a peacock in his gaudy.

'Not worth your money,' Nottingham told him. 'You're looking prosperous.'

Williamson had inherited his company from his father. As soon as he'd taken charge he'd started to bring in new ideas, sought out fresh markets, and in just a few years it had paid off handsomely.

'Not my idea,' he said, pulling at the coat as if he felt awkward in it. 'Hannah thought the material would be in the London style. I told her it'd be filthy up here after half a day. Look at that.' He pointed to the marks on the sleeve and the knee. 'You can't run a business and dress like the gentry.'

'You can employ a factor and spend your days at leisure.'

'Never,' Williamson laughed. 'I enjoy it too much. Some people are called to the church, I was called to the wool trade. You know me, Richard.'

It was true enough. The merchant never seemed happier than when he was at the cloth market or working in his warehouse.

'Mind you,' Williamson continued slowly, 'they've asked me to become an alderman.'

Nottingham had heard the rumours for a few weeks. They'd been little more than whispers, but they'd had the ring of truth.

'Congratulations,' he said warmly. Williamson sighed, but there was pride in his small smile.

'Old Petty's retiring.' He glanced around and leaned closer. 'They say it's because he's nearly dead, but the truth is he's such a contrary bugger the rest of them can't take it any more. I was going to say no but Hannah won't let me. She wants to be an alderman's wife.'

The Constable smiled. 'You'll do well. They need some fresh blood.'

'They do,' Williamson agreed, then added drily, 'just not mine. I've little enough time as it is. But when a wife insists . . .' He shrugged helplessly. 'By the way, your daughter came to see me this morning.'

'That's my fault, I'm afraid,' Nottingham admitted. 'I suggested she try you for funds.'

'It was a good idea, Richard. She's passionate about that school, isn't she?'

'Very,' the Constable said.

'Persuasive, too,' he said with a chuckle. 'I gave her money to pay for her books. I might even suggest Hannah becomes involved. Now our two are being schooled she's been looking for good works.' He paused. 'Mind you, I'm not sure I'd fancy her chances against your Emily.'

Nottingham laughed. 'She's always had her own mind. Once it's made up no one's going to change it.'

'Is she still walking out with James Lister's boy?'

'She is. They've been courting a while now.'

The two of them stood silently for a minute, watching the water flow.

'Charles Waterson went to the opening of that new brothel the other night,' Williamson said. 'He says it's quite the place.'

'As long as there's no trouble there I wish them well.' The Constable stirred. 'I'd best be on my way. Congratulations again.'

EIGHT

I t was a pale, tender morning as the Constable walked down Marsh Lane and into Leeds. There was the scent of dog roses in the hedgerows, the air full of hope and promise for many. By the time he reached the jail on Kirkgate he was smiling; today might be a good day.

'Morning, Rob. How was the night?'

'You'd better look in the cold cell, boss,' Lister said, his expression pained.

Nottingham strode through. The body on the slab was covered with an old blanket. He drew it back and saw a girl's face, the blue eyes staring at nothing.

'We pulled her from the river about an hour back. She was caught in some bushes downstream from the warehouses. No one saw her until first light.'

The Constable nodded, removing the covering from the girl. Twigs and moss were caught in her fair, wet hair. She was small, not even five feet tall, and her face was so young. He rubbed her hands, feeling rough calluses on the palms, and an old, worn ring with a design like a rose on her middle finger. The clothes clung to her thin body, the pattern of her dress so faded and blurred, the boots worn.

'I think we've just found Jenny Carter,' he told Rob quietly. 'Her brother said she had a ring like that.'

'She can't have come too far. The river's not flowing fast.'

'I'll take a good look at her. Maybe that'll tell us something.' He paused.

By the time the deputy arrived he'd had time to examine her. There were no wounds he could see, and the only bruises looked to have come from the water. He stood back and sighed softly. She looked as though she'd drowned. But why, when she'd come looking for her fortune? Why would she end up in the Aire after just a few days?

'That's Jenny Carter, John. Her brother told me about the ring she was wearing.' He stroked the dead hand. 'Both of them dead within a day of each other. Strange, isn't it?'

'What are you thinking, boss?'

Nottingham shook his head. 'I don't know, John. But it's a coincidence. You know I don't like those.'

'They happen,' Sedgwick countered.

'Maybe.' He shook his head and blew out a long breath. 'Maybe you're right.'

'She tried for work at Fanny Hardcastle's. I asked this morning. Fanny turned her away.'

'What about the other places?' the Constable asked. 'Did you go there?'

'I did. She hadn't tried any of them.' He hesitated. 'There's something else, boss. I heard when I was asking about Jenny. You remember that man the mob killed?'

'I do. Andrew Johnson.' He recalled his brother's face and his words. 'What about him?'

'One of the young whores down near the bridge told me she saw something.'

The Constable looked up with interest. 'Go on.'

'She said two men attacked him. He was trying to sleep in a doorway down on Briggate. All he did was defend himself.'

'Christ.' He let out a long sigh and ran a hand through his hair. 'So he put a knife into one of them. What happened to the other man?'

'He ran off. She'd been scared to say anything.'

'It was Wilcock Simms who died, wasn't it?'

'That's right. A real troublemaker. Loved to drink. I don't even know how many times we had him in for fighting.'

'I remember him. Worked at the tannery.'

'That's the one.'

'Did the girl recognize the other man?'

'King Davy.' The deputy gave a dark smile. They both knew the man's reputation. David King was a man who lived on the knife edge of temper. A few drinks could tip him over, and he'd start a brawl for no reason. He liked to call himself King Davy and there were few brave enough to gainsay him.

'Did he see her?'

'She says not. And she hasn't told anyone else. You know what they say, you don't peach on the King.'

If Davy knew or found out, the girl would be risking a hard beating, probably worse. 'Let's have Mr King in.'

'Yes, boss.'

'You'd better take two of the men with you, just in case.'

'I can handle him.'

'Take them, John,' he ordered. 'No chances. You know what he's like.'

The deputy left, and Nottingham wrote up the daily report and carried it over to the Moot Hall. He handed it to Cobb the clerk, who looked up at him shamefacedly.

'Mr Nottingham,' he said nervously as the Constable started to turn away.

'Yes?'

'You wanted . . . to know things that were happening.'

'I'm listening, Mr Cobb.'

'Mr Williamson's going to be an alderman.'

Nottingham smiled. 'I thought you had news. He told me himself yesterday. You'll need to do better than that.' He stared at the man until the clerk began to blush.

'I'm sorry, sir.'

King sat back in the chair, long legs extended, looking around as if he owned the place. The Constable watched him carefully. He was young, no more than twenty-five, dark hair hanging lank to his shoulders, with a cocky glint in his eyes, mouth curled in a mocking smile. It was the type of face women might enjoy, Nottingham thought, at least until they came close; the man carried the stench of the tannery with him, and the mix of raw leather, piss and shit filled the jail. A long knife in its old sheath hung down his leg.

'Thank you for coming, Mr King,' he said.

'Our King Davy's a good Leeds man. He's happy to help,' the deputy observed dryly. He was leaning against the wall, ready to move in case the man's temper took hold. 'No trouble at all,' he said pointedly. Davy grinned and bobbed his head in a bow.

'You were a friend of Wilcock Simms,' the Constable began.

'Aye,' King replied slowly. 'He were a good man. Worked wi' 'im three year. I went to his funeral, an' all. Plenty of us did.'

'What happened to him was unfortunate.' He'd chosen the word carefully, watching for any change or anger on Davy's face. King clenched his fists.

'I'd have killed the bastard who did it meself,' he said coldly. 'He were lucky that mob got him or he'd have had to deal with me.'

'Were you with Mr Simms the night he died?'

'Aye,' Davy admitted. 'We were in a few places.'

'What did you do later?'

He shrugged. 'Walked. Found some little whore on Briggate.' King laughed. 'Stupid bitch thought there were just one of us.'

From the corner of his eye the Constable saw Sedgwick stiffen.

'How long were you with her?' Nottingham asked calmly. King might be telling the truth; whether he was or not, he was using the tale to taunt them.

'Don't know.' King grinned. 'We weren't listening for the clock or owt. Just having our fun.' He glanced towards the deputy. 'Thought your woman might be out there. She's a whore, in't she? Worth a penny, mebbe.'

The Constable flashed the deputy a warning with his eyes, and sat back in his chair. 'What did you do when that was over?'

'Went home. I'd had my fill for t' night.'

'Was anyone waiting for you at home, Mr King?'

'Only the old cow as runs the rooming house. She's always after me for her money.' He turned and spat on the floor. It was a challenge; Nottingham chose to ignore it.

'Did she see you arrive?'

'Course not.' He drew out the words. 'Late home, early out, that's me. Good way to avoid her.'

'And what about Mr Simms? What did he do when you'd finished?'

King shrugged. 'Don't know. Last time I saw him he were still in the whore.'

The Constable glanced at Sedgwick. The deputy was staring hard at Davy, his face tight with anger. King had answered too readily, he thought. He'd been prepared, right down to the story about the prostitute.

'And you've no idea what happened to Mr Simms?'

'No. Course not.'

'Then I thank you for coming here, Mr King. My condolences on the loss of your friend.'

The man stood lazily and stretched. 'You want me, you know where I am.'

'What do you think, John?' Nottingham asked when they were alone.

'I think I'm going to break King Davy's crown,' he replied with quiet fury.

'I daresay you'll have your chance sooner or later. He was just trying to get to you.'

'He did that, right enough.'

'Our Davy was there when Simms was killed, I'm sure of it. They likely thought they'd found an easy mark.'

'Aye.'

'It's too late to make a difference now,' the Constable said sadly.

'We couldn't have done anything else, boss. You know that.'

'We could have protected him better than we did. Then he might still be alive for the truth to come out.'

The White Swan was crowded with sweating men drinking down their ale to cool off. Nottingham sat on the bench across from the deputy.

'Anything?' he asked.

'Nothing more on Jem Carter yet,' Sedgwick said. 'I was thinking about his sister, though. Maybe she heard what happened to him and then killed herself.'

The Constable pursed his mouth. It made as much sense as any other explanation he could imagine. Grief or guilt could have taken her into the water. It had happened before; he could understand it well enough. But something about the two of them dying so close together niggled at him.

'It's possible,' he acknowledged. 'Tom Finer told Jem to go down to the Wades for the brothel opening. Maybe I'll go down and ask.'

'Plenty of people went to that, boss,' the deputy said with a shrug. 'Doesn't mean anything. If the meat in that stew's fresh I'm having some.'

The sun was at its peak as he made his way along Swinegate, sliding between the people, the clamour of trade loud all around him. Maybe Mrs Wade would recall Jem Carter. It would be one more pace along the path; God knew there were few enough of those. At the black door he knocked, and heard footsteps bustle down the hall.

'Good day, Miss Wade. I'd like to speak to your mother, if I may.'

The girl led him through and once again he was waiting in the parlour with its thick Turkey rug and slowly ticking long clock. The minutes passed. He looked at the paintings, sat and stood up again, then Mrs Wade entered, expensively dressed in dark blue silk and crisp white lace, her eyes inquisitive.

'Constable, forgive me,' she said in a rush. 'I hadn't expected to see you again. Is something wrong?'

'Not at all,' he answered with a smile. 'It's just a question. Did your opening go well?'

She laughed. 'Very much so, Constable. There must have been half a hundred gentlemen here. I could hardly move through them all.'

'That's a good start for you.'

'All I could have hoped,' she agreed with satisfaction. 'Did you come here just to ask me that?'

'Do you remember if any of them was a country lad, quite young?'

She shook her head. 'I honestly couldn't say. There were so many I didn't know. So many I didn't even see. I'm sorry, Constable, but I can't help you. Who is he, anyway?'

'Someone killed him Tuesday night.'

'I heard about that,' she said with a frown. 'It's truly terrible. But I couldn't tell you if he'd been here.'

'Thank you anyway. Has your business stayed good?'

'Excellent. The gentlemen of Leeds seem to like us.' She

looked around the room, smiling. 'I think I made the right decision moving here.'

'Then I hope it stays that way. The last time I was here I asked you about a girl.'

'I remember.' She cocked her head. 'What was her name again?'

'Jenny. Small, fair hair. I wonder if she came looking for employment after we talked.'

She bit her lip, thinking. 'I've had a dozen girls looking for work. I saw them all myself. We have four here and I've been thinking of taking on another since we're so busy. But no, there was no one calling herself Jenny.' Mrs Wade eyed him. 'Do you always take this much trouble over a missing girl?'

'We found her body in the river. The murdered man was her brother.'

'That's a terrible thing,' she answered after a little while. 'I'm sorry if I seemed short with you. I only wish I could help.'

On the way out he saw a young man climbing the stair, hands pushed into the pockets of his breeches. He had wide shoulders and dark hair. The son, Nottingham thought. What was his name? Mark? Then he disappeared from view without glancing back.

NINE

On Saturday morning Nottingham stood in the doorway of the house on Marsh Lane, waiting for Emily. She was making an early start, with plenty to do at the school before the pupils arrived. Finally she rushed down the stairs, a shawl pulled around her shoulders, eyes shining at the prospect of a day spent teaching.

There was a widening band of pale blue at the horizon as they crossed Timble Bridge, the girl hurrying to keep pace with her father.

'You'll be there before your pupils for once,' he teased.

'Papa!' she said, feigning outrage. 'I'm not as bad as that.'

He smiled, amused. 'If you say so.'

'I didn't have time to talk to you last night, Papa,' she said. 'You came home late.'

'Aye, I know.' Work had kept him busy until well after dark then he'd sat in the White Swan for a hour, quietly sipping a a mug of ale.

'I wanted to tell you, Mr Williamson's wife came to the school yesterday,' she said excitedly. 'She's very grand, isn't she?'

'Is she now?' He thought back to his conversation with the merchant. 'What did she think?'

'She wants to help us.'

'Help?' he asked. 'How?'

'She's going to talk to some of the other merchants' wives and raise money for us. We'll be their charity.' She smiled widely and clutched his arm happily. 'It's good news, Papa.'

'It's wonderful news,' he agreed.

'It means we'll be able to afford more books. Maybe even somewhere larger . . .'

'I hope you can, love, but don't go making plans before the money's there.'

'Oh, I won't,' she promised, but he knew she was already thinking ahead. It was her way; since she'd left the cradle she'd been a dreamer.

They turned from Kirkgate on to the Calls; he'd escort her all the way to the school. His mind was elsewhere when she cried out, 'No!'

Someone had smashed half the mullions on the street window of the school. This was deliberate, he thought immediately, not children throwing stones. Glass glittered in the street. He put his arm around her, drawing her close.

'Let me look inside,' he said. He saw her hand was shaking as she gave him the key. But there was no one within and the closed shutters had kept most of the damage out of the room. He made sure the back door was secure then brought her in.

'You sweep it up,' he told her. 'I'll have Thompson the glazier come by this morning.'

She looked up at him uncomprehendingly. All the earlier joy had vanished from her face. 'Why, Papa? Why would anyone want to do this?'

'I don't know,' he told her. There could be so many reasons; he'd have Sedgwick ask people if there were any rumours flying around. 'You go on,' he said gently.

Rob was at the jail, yawning wide as the Constable entered.

'Get yourself to the school,' Nottingham ordered.

'Why? What's happened?' Lister asked urgently, standing up and reaching for his coat. 'Is Emily all right?

'She'll be fine, she's just shaken. Someone broke the windows there. See Thompson on the way. Tell him I asked if he could look to the job this morning.'

'Yes, boss.'

'You could give her a hand down there, there's glass to clean up.'

'I've got a job for you, John,' he told Sedgwick once the deputy had arrived and downed a mug of ale. 'Go down to the Calls. Ask if anyone saw or heard anything last night. Someone smashed the windows at Emily's school.'

'What?' he asked in alarm. 'How is she?'

'She's not hurt. Rob's down there now. I want to know what happened. It was probably drunks, but . . .'

'Aye, boss, of course. I'll find out what I can.'

The Constable paced the room, wanting to do something yet knowing there was nothing more he could do; Sedgwick and Rob would look after everything. But Emily was his daughter. He needed to look after her, to protect her.

After the clock struck seven he took the report to the Moot Hall and left it on the clerk's desk, then strode back down Briggate for the cloth market. The weavers already had their cloth laid out, talking to each other as they enjoyed their Brigg End Shot breakfasts of beef and beer. At the top of the streets the merchants gathered in small knots, gossiping, heads nodding quietly.

He waited impatiently until the bell rang the half hour and the market began, then walked up and down a few times, alert for cutpurses, nodding to the whores who stood entranced by the business, the bargains made in whispers.

For once he couldn't settle to watch it all happen. Instead he stalked off, turning along the Calls to stand where he could see the school and the sharp glass of the broken windows waiting for the glazier. There were other things, more urgent things he needed to think about – Jem Carter's murder, Jenny, even Tom Finer – but this pushed them all out of his head. It was probably nothing more than drunks looking for destruction and noise, but what if there was more? What if someone hated the idea of poor girls being educated? What if someone wanted to hurt Emily?

Finally he tore himself away, his mind still blazing, and strode to the Saturday market at the top of Briggate. He wandered around, squeezing his way through the press of people. Vendors shouted out their wares, voices competing against each other, trying to draw people in to buy. He'd come out of habit; two of his men would be here, ready to respond if someone yelled that they'd been robbed. He just needed to be somewhere familiar, a place to give him some order. His gaze moved across the faces, barely noticing them until one on the far side of the street made him stop. It was Simon Johnson, the brother of the man killed by the mob, bargaining for something from one of the stalls. The sight came as a shock; from the way he'd cursed Leeds and its people he'd have expected the man to be long gone. He was about to go over to the man when a voice cut into his thoughts.

'Constable, we meet again.' He turned and found Tom Finer at his shoulder. In spite of the weather, the man was dressed warmly in a coat and breeches of heavy wool, a tricorn hat pulled down on his head. Outside his rooms he looked smaller, almost frail, his hand resting on a polished stick. The Constable looked across the street again; Johnson had gone. Yet one more thing to add to the turmoil.

'Enjoying the market?' Nottingham asked and tried to smile.

'They say the sun's good for old bones.' Finer gazed around the crowd with a broad grin. 'But this is good for the soul.'

'I'm sure there were markets in London.' He began to move away but Finer wasn't ready to let him leave yet.

'More than you could imagine. It's all different down there.'

'Even the crime?'

'Even that, laddie, even that,' the man agreed with a grin. 'You have to be ruthless to succeed down there.'

The Constable gave up; Finer wanted to talk.

'And were you a success?' Nottingham asked.

'I got by. I made money if that's what you mean.' He paused, considering his words. 'But I'll tell you something. Up here, when a competitor . . . left, shall we say, there'd be one or two more eager to take his place. Down in London it was forty or fifty, each one ready to prove he was harder than the last.' He sighed. 'I'm glad to be away from it, laddie, and that's the truth. It wears a man down.'

'Leeds has changed since you lived here.'

'I can see that.' He raised the stick and pointed to the new houses at Town End, on the far side of the Head Row. 'There's all those, for a start. But enough of it's still the same for me to feel comfortable. And murder never changes much, eh, Constable?'

'What would you know about murder, Mr Finer?' Nottingham asked. 'Or are you thinking of one in particular?'

The man looked him directly in the eye. 'Just what I hear, laddie. Nothing more, if that's what you're thinking. I told you, I barely talked to the man.' He paused. 'I gather you pulled his sister from the river, too.'

'You listen to the gossip.'

'There's enough of it around,' the man pointed out. 'There have never been that many secrets in Leeds if you know where to listen. You should know that by now. I even know what happened at your daughter's school last night.'

'What have you heard about that?' Nottingham asked, suddenly serious.

'Nothing that's not common knowledge,' Finer said with a small shake of his head. 'If there's any word I'll gladly pass it on to you.' He hesitated. 'You don't understand why I've come back, do you?'

'No, Mr Finer, I don't,' the Constable answered truthfully. 'And I don't trust you, either. Do you blame me?'

'I suppose not,' the man acknowledged. 'But time will tell. I know you've been asking some questions about me.' He tapped a thin finger against his nose. 'You can keep your eye on me all you like, you'll see I wasn't lying.'

'I'll do that, don't worry. And I'll be glad to be proved wrong.'

'I'll bid you good day.' Finer shuffled off into the throng.

If the old crook had become an honest man it would be one thing less to think about. But Nottingham doubted it. People never truly changed who they were. Sooner or later he'd be at his scheming again. He left, worries flooding back into his head. There were too many questions he needed to ask.

At noon he settled on a bench at the White Swan, ordering ale and a chop. He'd almost finished the meal when the deputy slid along the bench to sit across from him.

'What have you managed to find out, John?'

'There's plenty down that way who heard the glass break, but by the time they looked out there was no one to be seen.'

'What do you think?'

Sedgwick considered his answer. 'If you want my guess, I'd say it was drunks. You know how they get on a Friday night. Ran off as soon as they'd done it.'

'I'll have Rob check regularly tonight. Just in case.'

The deputy chuckled. 'Knowing him, the lad'll go down there a few times, anyway.'

He wandered down to the Calls again, stopping across from the school. He felt the need to be here, to keep a watch on her. The glazier had done a good job; the panes all fitted, and the newer ones sparkled in the bright afternoon sun. He could hear Emily talking and the higher voices of the girls repeating her words. He listened a while longer then forced himself to turn away. A woman was staring at him.

'That's your lass doing that, in't it?' She was probably close to thirty but looked older, wearing an ancient, patched dress, her face worn, cheeks sunken, her hands rough and red.

'It is.'

'We're right glad she's here.' She looked directly at him, her eyes hard as stone. 'Makes a change for someone in this city to care about us.' The woman nodded towards the building. 'I've got two in there. Happen they'll be able to do more than fetch and carry or keep pushing out bairns of their own when Miss Emily's done with them.' She paused. 'I'll tell you summat, love, we're going to make sure last night dun't happen again. My man's going to be out here while dawn. He dun't know it yet, but he will be, same as half the others round here.'

'If they find someone, call one of my men,' he told her.

'We'll do that once we're finished.' Her mouth was firmly set.

'Just make sure you don't kill him.'

She gave a short laugh. 'We're not fools, love. We're not going to hang for nowt. But we're not going to have someone buggering about without teaching them a lesson.'

He smiled at her. 'I daresay Mr Lister might come by at times, too. Just to keep an eye on things.'

The woman nodded. 'He'll be welcome enough as long as he dun't get in the way. We've needed a school like this here and we're going to look after Miss Emily.'

'I'm sure she'll be glad of that,' he told her, pride in his heart.

There was ample warmth remaining in the afternoon when Rob returned to the school. The girls had gone for the day but he knew Emily would still be there, tidying and preparing her lessons for Monday.

He knew how much she believed in this. They'd spent hours discussing it, and he'd helped her find the building and make it ready. When they were alone it was what she talked about, her plans and dreams for the place. It filled her days and her nights, but he didn't resent that, even if she was always tired.

He opened the door and walked in. She was sitting at the desk and raised her head quickly, her eyes fearful.

'You scared me for a moment,' she said, sitting back and beginning to smile.

'I thought I'd see if there was anything more I could do.'

'You can walk me home.' Her voice was weary. 'I've finished.' She stood and looked around the room, at the tables and benches. 'Some of the girls were terrified when they saw the broken windows. Susanna was close to tears for a while.' Emily closed her eyes for a moment. 'I'm just worried that something else will happen.'

'I talked to some of the women on the way here. They're scared you'll leave if there's anything else.' He sat on one of the tables, his legs dangling.

'I'd never do that,' she protested.

'That's what I told them,' he said with a nod. 'But they're going to have their men out tonight to keep watch.'

'Really?' Emily's eyes widened in surprise and gratitude.

He reached out and took her hand. 'They want you to stay here. You're giving the girls a chance.'

Her face reddened. 'I'm just doing what I can.' She gathered her books into a small pile and handed them to him. 'If you want to help, you can carry these home for me.'

He waited as she closed and barred the shutters and locked the door, checking twice that it was secure. Then she put her arm through his and they headed down towards the Parish Church, nodding greetings to the folk they passed on the way.

'Do you think it might happen again?' she asked as they crossed Timble Bridge, Sheepscar beck burbling under their feet.

'No,' he told her. 'It was probably just drunks causing mischief.' He'd thought about it before sleep that morning and again as soon as he woke. There would be people who thought it was wrong to give some learning to poor girls, he knew that. For now, though, he'd choose the simple, likeliest explanation. He stopped to kiss her. 'Everything will be fine,' he assured her.

'I hope so,' she said as she held him close. 'I really hope so.'

As soon as they were in the house on Marsh Lane, Lucy bustled through from the kitchen, concern on her face.

'Are you all right?' she asked. 'I heard what happened.'

'I'm fine.' Emily smiled gently and put her hand on the girl's arm. 'Don't worry.'

Rob left them to chatter and went to pour himself ale. Lucy had never said what she'd endured when she lived wild but he could guess at some of it. When he'd first met her she'd been wild and wary of trusting anyone. Living in the Constable's house had changed that; she'd softened. She was a part of the family now, just like he was, willing to face the world to defend the boss and Emily.

A meal was bubbling in the pot, the rich smell filling the place, making his stomach rumble as he realized he hadn't eaten since the night before. He picked up a spoon and was about to dip it into the stew when Lucy came through.

'You can put that down right now,' she told him sternly. 'Wait until Mr Nottingham's home and we all eat.' She folded her arms and stared at him. 'Don't go giving me that smile, either. It might work on Miss Emily but it won't on me.'

He left, feeling her watchful eye on him.

By the time the Constable returned, Rob had paged through the *Mercury*, the paper his father published. There was little to catch his attention; he had no interest in politics or stories culled from the London papers, full of names he didn't know or care about. Emily sat at the table and worked diligently, underlining passages in a book, the scrape of her quill the only sound in the room.

They ate quickly, every one of them hungry, exchanging quick snatches of conversation between mouthfuls, all carefully avoiding what had happened that morning. Rob reached for more of the stew.

'It's good,' he said, and Lucy beamed at the praise.

'The books Mr Williamson paid for should arrive from Harrogate next week,' Emily said, her eyes glistening with anticipation. 'I'm looking forward to seeing the girls when they have real books to read.'

'You'll do them proud, love,' Nottingham said and pushed the plate away. 'That was grand, Lucy. I couldn't eat another mouthful. I'm off to my bed.'

It was his way to give the young couple some time together before Rob had to leave for work.

'Anything special for tonight, boss?'

The Constable shook his head. 'You know what do to, lad.'

On a warm Saturday night Rob was kept busy enough. Drunken arguments quickly dissolved into fights with cudgels and knives, and blood drawn; often he had to wade in with his men, cracking heads and hauling men off to the jail. He still found moments to wander down to the Calls and talk to the husbands keeping watch there. They'd seen no one suspicious; some of them grumbled at missing a night's drinking, but he knew they'd never dare say that to their wives.

On Sunday morning he dressed in his good clothes, strolling next to Emily as they went to the Parish Church. Nottingham walked ahead of them, Lucy at his side. It was the same every week; the Constable would doze during the sermon, only coming awake for the final prayer.

Once the service was over, Nottingham went to stand by Rose and Mary's graves. The others waited outside the church porch. Tom Williamson's wife, Hannah, drew Emily away for a few moments and talked to her quickly before pressing something into her hand.

Rob watched her return, her eyes wide in astonishment, her fist clenched tight.

'What did she want?' he asked.

Without saying a word, Emily opened her hand and showed the two guinea coins that filled her palm. He heard Lucy draw in her breath loudly.

'She'd heard about the windows so she went to some of the merchants' wives and collected money for us.' He voice was quiet with astonishment. 'Two guineas.' She shook her head in astonishment. 'That'll pay for so much.'

'That's a fortune,' Lucy said reverently, watching as Emily slid the money into the pocket inside her dress.

'Mr Williamson's an alderman now,' Rob told her with a wink. 'You're making some powerful friends.'

TEN

Five days had passed since they'd found Jem Carter's body, four since they'd pulled his sister from the river. The Constable had watched the bodies start the journey back to Ilkley for their funerals, and he still knew nothing about their deaths. No idea as to a killer or why the girl had apparently committed suicide.

He leaned on the parapet of Leeds Bridge, watching faint clouds high in a pale blue sky. Seven o'clock on a Monday morning and it was already teasingly warm with the promise of aching heat later. He'd set off early on his rounds and ended up here, watching the sluggish water and thinking, with no answers at all.

Finally Nottingham pushed himself away and began to walk

back up Briggate. The inns were alive with the sound of servants and early customers in need of their morning ale, and shops along the street had their shutters flung wide, displaying all the goods for sale. He spotted Sedgwick loping down the street towards him, half a head taller than many of the others.

'I'm sorry I'm late, boss,' he said breathlessly. 'James's teacher wanted to see me.'

'Is something wrong?' the Constable asked.

The deputy grinned with pride. 'He says James is doing so well he wants to give him more work.'

'That's grand, John.'

'Aye. Lizzie'll be happy when I tell her, too. My lad, eh?' He shook his head in disbelief. 'I did find something interesting yesterday. I was in Sam Hart's dramshop back off Kirkgate and we started talking about King Davy. Seems he was in there Tuesday night.' The Constable looked at him expectantly. 'He was talking to someone who sounds a lot like Jem Carter, and they left together.'

'Is Sam sure it was Tuesday?'

'You know what he's like – right even when he's wrong. But I believe him this time; people don't forget when Davy's been in.'

'What time was this?'

'After dark is all he remembers, so it couldn't be too early. What do you think, should we have the king in again?'

'Yes.' He thought for a moment. 'Make it after dinner. Take Holden and one of the others with you. Ask around this morning, see if anyone else saw Davy with someone that night.'

At the jail he spent an hour working on reports and requests, scribbling until his fingers ached and the ink in the pot had almost run dry. It was the part of the job he'd never liked. Words on paper had never come easily to him. Years of doing it hadn't helped.

Finally he was done, the last note, a letter to London asking about Tom Finer, folded and sealed. His fingers were blue from the ink, as cramped as any clerk's. He wiped them on a piece of linen from his breeches pocket then took the finished work over to the Moot Hall.

'Reports and letters, Mr Cobb,' he told the mayor's clerk. 'See them on their way, please.'

'Yes, sir.' The young man looked around cautiously then beckoned the Constable close. 'The Corporation's thinking of re-opening the workhouse,' he said very quietly.

'Are they now?'

The workhouse had closed back in 1728 after being open for just three years, a place to hide the poor out of sight and make them work for their food and beds. It had been a failure then; why would anyone want the place open again?

'Someone's offered to put up the money to get the building in order and find contracts for work,' Cobb confided.

'Who?'

The clerk searched for the paper on his desk and read the name.

'Someone called Mr Finer.' He looked up at the Constable. 'I don't know the name, sir. Who is he?'

'Someone who used to live in Leeds, lad. Who's going to handle it for the Corporation?'

'Mr Williamson. They thought it would be a good start for him.'

'Thank you, Mr Cobb. That's all good to know. You've done well.'

Outside, he stood in the sun for a minute, feeling it warm his face, then made his way out along Vicar Lane. The old workhouse building was there, at the corner of Lady Lane, the stone worn and blackened, the windows all gone. It had been built before he was born, brooding, fearful and dark, the place folk went when there was nothing else left. Then it had become a charity school for twenty years before the Corporation made it a workhouse once again in 1725.

As Constable he'd had to attend the opening, parading next to the new master, Robert Milnor, and wheezing old Shubaal Speight, there with his two sons and his wife, so desperate to run the place. But three years later it had shut once more, and Speight and Milnor were dismissed in disgrace. For all he knew, Leeds was still paying the debts the workhouse had quickly run up. Speight had found few contracts and been so harsh in charge that the inmates had refused to work for him.

Now they were going to try again. More stupidity. He

shook his head and turned away, walking back towards the river. The warehouses along the towpath had their windows and doors open wide. Outside one of them a group of workers, stripped to their shirts and breeches, passed around a jug of ale.

Tom Williamson sat in his office, coat neatly draped over the back of his chair. He looked up as Nottingham entered, smiling and throwing down his quill.

'Richard. For God's sake come in and save me from these letters. Do you want some ale?'

'Thank you,' he said, and took the cup and drank.

'No more trouble at the school?' the merchant asked worriedly.

'Nothing else, thankfully.'

'Your daughter must be relieved.'

'Even more so when she received the money from your wife. She's very grateful.'

Williamson smiled. 'Between you and me, it made Hannah very happy. She has her charity now and she can persuade the other wives to part with the money their husbands have earned.' He drained the mug and started to pour another.

'The workhouse,' Nottingham said.

'You've already heard about that?' he asked in surprise.

'You know what it's like in Leeds. Just lean into the wind and you can hear what's going on.' He paused. 'What does Tom Finer have to do with it?'

'He's offered to pay for repairs to the building and find contracts once it's open. Do you know him, Richard? Most of the older aldermen seem on good terms with him.'

'He's been gone for nigh on twenty years.' The Constable recounted the facts quickly. 'He left because Amos Worthy was going to kill him. He was a whoremaster, a crook and very likely a murderer, everything you can imagine. I don't suppose the aldermen mentioned that.'

'No,' Williamson answered slowly and seriously.

'You need to be very careful with Tom Finer,' Nottingham warned.

'I will,' the merchant mused. 'When I met him he seemed friendly enough. He said he wanted to give something back to the city.'

'Tom Finer wouldn't put money into something unless he had a way to make a good profit out of it.'

'He said he did business with my father back when I was a boy.'

'He may well have done,' Nottingham said carefully. 'He knew everyone who mattered in the city back them. And he took care of the people in power so he could carry on with all his schemes.'

'I didn't know any of this, Richard.'

The Constable leaned forward, elbows on his knees, his voice earnest. 'There's something else to think about – if anything goes wrong with this, you're the one they'll blame.' He watched Williamson sit back and frown. 'You're the new man on the Corporation. They'll find it easy enough to dismiss you in disgrace.'

The merchant sipped slowly at his ale. 'He could have changed.'

Nottingham shook his head. 'Men like him don't change.' He saw Williamson look at him doubtfully. 'Believe me. He'll want you to think he's come back here for his final years.'

'He did say that.'

'I doubt Tom Finer ever did anything unless money was involved. I've sent a letter to London to ask about him.'

'Can you let me know when you receive a reply?'

'I will. But if I were you I wouldn't commit the city to anything yet. And make sure a good lawyer looks at any documents Finer gives you.'

'Thank you,' Williamson told him. 'Though after the way the mayor treated you last year, I'm surprised you said anything.'

'For all I care, Finer can dupe the city,' the Constable answered with a smile. 'I just don't want them making a fool of you.' He stood.

'I appreciate that, Richard.'

'Just carry a very long spoon if you're supping with Tom Finer. That's my advice.'

Strolling up Briggate in the full, hot sun, he felt a quiet sense of satisfaction. He knew Finer's plans now and he'd been able to do something to delay them, at least. Nottingham had no doubt that the reply he eventually received from London would contain a litany of allegations, none of them proved. Finer was smart enough to profit from his crimes and too clever to pay for them himself. A quiet word about someone's dark indiscretions, a little money changing hands or someone sacrificed to the law was all it took to keep him free and living well.

At the White Swan he ordered bread and cheese, and downed half a mug of ale in a single swallow. The deputy arrived, placing a full tankard on the table.

'Thirsty weather,' he said. 'I've been walking and talking all morning.'

'You do that every day,' Nottingham reminded him with a grin. 'Did you find anything more on Davy?'

A harried serving girl placed his bowl of stew on the table and the deputy began to eat hungrily. 'Nothing on him, but a little more about Jenny. You know Catherine Robinson, runs the rooming house on the other side of the river?'

The Constable nodded. She had a small place tucked away in one of the small streets behind the grand merchant palaces of Meadow Lane. 'What about her?'

'She had a girl come on Saturday night who sounds just like Jenny Carter. A little thing, looking lost and hoping for a bed.'

'Did she stay there?'

He shook his head. 'Didn't have the money.'

'And she went to Fanny's brothel on Sunday?' Nottingham rubbed his chin thoughtfully.

'That's right, boss. Catherine told her to go to Mrs Lee's.'

A farthing a night at Mrs Lee's. Two beds, one for men, one for women, everyone packed in together with the fleas and the lice. It was better than sleeping in the open air, but only barely.

'Have you been to see her?'

'Right before I came here,' Sedgwick answered. 'The girl was there right enough, spent her last coin to do it. She had a little food with her. Catherine said she was talking with Molly the Mudlark.'

They all knew Molly, a cheerful lass who scraped her living wading in the Aire and pulling out whatever she could find. Mostly the items were worthless and useless but sometimes she'd find something to sell for a few pennies.

'Go and see Molly once we've talked to Davy,' Nottingham ordered. He watched the deputy finish the stew, rubbing a heel of bread around the bowl to sop up the last of the juices. 'Enjoy that, did you?'

'It'll see me through.' He finished his ale and stood. 'Right, I'll go and drag our friend back to the jail.'

'Just be sure to take two of the others with you.'

King looked less comfortable this time. He tried to stretch out his legs but the Constable had deliberately placed the chair too close to the desk, forcing him to sit upright. Sedgwick stood by the door, a brooding presence behind the man's shoulder, and Nottingham waited, sorting through papers for a few minutes. Let the man wait, he thought, and let him feel wary and hunted.

Eventually he pushed the pile aside and stared at Davy. There was no smirk on the man's face this time, no air of brash confidence.

'Thank you for coming, Mr King,' he said.

King tried to shrug, but it came across as a nervous gesture. 'What do you want, any road?' he said. 'I'm losing pay being hauled off here, and he wouldn't say nowt.' He gestured over his shoulder at the deputy.

'Just a few more questions, that's all.' He brushed the hair out of his eyes. 'Tell me, where were you Tuesday night?'

'Tuesday?' The question was unexpected, Nottingham could see that, and it took King aback. 'I don't remember.'

'In the dramshops, maybe?'

'Mebbe,' he agreed cautiously. 'Why?'

The Constable smiled. 'We know you were, Mr King.'

'Then what's tha' asking me for? And what if I were?'

'You talked to someone while you were drinking.'

''Appen. I talk to plenty of folk.' He shifted on the chair, trying to make himself more comfortable.

'Someone called Jem Carter, maybe?'

'Who?' Davy blinked at the name.

'Jem Carter,' Nottingham repeated. 'Big, fair hair, from the country.'

King shook his head. 'Never heard of him.' His expression brightened. 'I saw Peter Cross. He's blond.'

The Constable glanced at Sedgwick. The deputy nodded and slipped out.

'What did you and Mr Cross do?'

'I saw him out on Kirkgate and we went to Sam Hart's. Had a drop of gin, then we went on to a few other places.'

'Who else did you meet?' Nottingham knew he was simply filling time now, asking questions until the deputy returned. But he felt sure that King was telling him the truth. The man hadn't had time to prepare a lie, and he wouldn't have given a name they could check otherwise.

'A few, here and there.'

'Who, Mr King?' he pressed.

Davy concentrated, trying to remember. 'There were Tom Harper and Will Thompson.' He opened his eyes wide and started to grin. 'And we saw that lad who works for you, too. What's his name?'

'Mr Lister?'

'Aye, that's the one. We were having a bit of a song and he told us not to be so loud. That do you, Constable?'

'Very good, Mr King.' It was over, he knew that. The man realized he was on safe ground. 'You may go, and I thank you for your help.'

King stood, smirking now. 'Any time you want. All you have to do is ask.'

The afternoon felt more like August than the beginning of June. The sky was a soft, pale blue, not a breath of wind stirring, the sun so warm that the deputy took off his coat and unbuttoned the long waistcoat as he walked out along the riverbank.

He'd found Peter Cross easily enough, working up at the Shambles, hefting sides of beef, the stink of old blood making Sedgwick stand well away. Cross had unwashed pale hair and an accent that wasn't local; it would be easy to mistake him for a country lad if you didn't know him. But he remembered being out with King Davy, each place they'd gone and who they'd seen. The King was innocent. No matter; sooner or later he'd find a way to make the man pay for his remark about Lizzie.

His mood brightened as the afternoon passed. He knew he'd find Molly in her usual place, downstream from the

warehouses and above the dye works where liquid flowed out
and turned the river red and black and green. There'd be one
or two others with her, working from first light until dusk,
pulling all she found on to the bank and hoping for something
she could sell.

He could see the girl in the distance, her ragged old dress
pulled high and clouted between spindly legs as she waded in
the shallow water, bending and scooping up handfuls of mud,
sifting through for treasure. A boy and a girl lay on the riverbank in the sun.

The deputy walked heavily as he came close, giving them
all a chance to hear him. The two on the grass scuttled away
as soon as they saw his face and he stifled a smile. Molly
waved and moved towards the bank, extending a hand so he
could haul her out of the water.

'I've not seen you in a long time, Mr Sedgwick,' she said
cheerily, keeping her legs bare to dry in the heat.

'You've been a good lass, Molly, no need to go chasing you
down. Anything interesting today?' he asked, nodding at a
small collection by her feet.

'Nowt special. Just a few bits of metal.' She smiled
happily, showing a mouth with both front teeth missing,
giving her face a strangely childish look. Thick red hair
cascaded down her back and the freckles on her bare flesh
appeared dark against her pale skin. She claimed to be fifteen
but could easily have passed for eleven, and she'd been a
mudlark as long as he'd been a Constable's man. 'I found
a ring yesterday, I were that excited. It were only brass, but
still . . .' She shrugged. 'One day happen I'll find a gold
one.'

'You never know, you might,' he told her. 'I hear you were
at Mrs Lee's on Saturday.'

'Aye. I found a farthing last thing in the day and I thought
I'd treat meself. Right comfy it were, too.'

'You met a lass called Jenny there.'

'Jenny?' She grinned. 'Oh, I liked her, Mr Sedgwick. She'd
only just come to Leeds. And she give me some of the food
she had in her basket. She were nice, she were. I told her she
could come down here with me if she liked.'

'She didn't want to?'

'She thought she could make money in Leeds.' She cocked her head. 'Why are you asking about her, any road?'

'She's dead, love.'

For a moment Molly's face fell, her mouth collapsing at the corners. She said softly, 'Aye, well.'

How many had she known who'd died, he wondered. 'Did she say where she was going on Sunday?'

'Just that someone had told her about a place where she could get rich.'

'Where was that? Did she say?'

'No, Mr Sedgwick. I din't bother asking, neither. I knew it were all words, it'd never happen. The likes of us never get rich, do we?'

'True enough, love.' He dug in the pocket of his breeches and put two pennies in her hand, enjoying the way her eyes widened in joy and surprise.

'You look after yourself, Molly lass,' he said.

ELEVEN

'You look far away, laddie.'

People seemed to be saying that to him too often these days, the Constable thought. But it was true, his mind kept drifting back to happier, loving times. He looked up and saw Finer watching him, amusement flickering across his mouth.

In the shank of an afternoon that felt too hot and too long he'd found a quiet, cool corner in the Old King's Head. A stream ran under the cellar to chill the ale. He took a sip before answering.

'I was just thinking.'

'Well, here is as good a place as any for it.'

'I thought you'd be enjoying the sun, Mr Finer.'

'There's a time for that and a time for this.' He raised the mug in his hand and gestured at the empty bench across the table. 'Room for one more?'

'If you like.' He didn't relish company but the man intrigued him. Finer settled with a slow sigh.

'That's better,' he said. 'Twenty years back I'd have stayed standing. Now I'm happy for a rest.'

'Are you settling back into Leeds?' Nottingham asked.

'I am.' He drank, savouring the liquid in his mouth, then swallowed and smiled.

'No thoughts about what you might do?'

'Do? I'm not going to do anything.'

The Constable raised his eyebrows. 'Really? I thought you might have had plans, Mr Finer.'

'Been hearing things, have you, laddie?' He laughed.

'Words are like wildfire here, you ought to remember that.'

Finer lifted his hands and spread them in surrender. 'I'd like to give something to this place. Is that so bad?'

'Not at all,' Nottingham agreed. 'But I have my doubts that you're just doing it out of charity.'

Finer shook his head slowly. 'I've told you, I'm not the man I was, Constable.'

'So you say.'

'I've no reason to lie.'

'No?' Nottingham asked.

'No,' Finer answered flatly. 'I've walked around enough since I came back. I've seen all the poor here. There's that camp down by the river.'

'Bessie looks after those folk well.'

'I'm sure she does, but we both know they'd be better off with a roof over their heads. What'll they do in winter? I have more money than I need and no one else to spend it on. I might as well use to help those who need it.'

'And make a profit along the way?'

Finer chuckled. 'Not quite what you think, laddie. I'm not so daft that I wouldn't want my investment back. I didn't grow up here for nothing. But after that, all the money will go back into the workhouse to keep it running.'

'So it's not charity at all?' Nottingham asked.

'It's my money that'll pay to make the workhouse liveable again. Have you been in there lately?'

The Constable shook his head.

'It's going to need hundreds spent on it.' He listed the points on his fingers. 'Then there's finding contracts, a good master for the place. Do you have any idea how much they paid the last one?'

'No.'

'Fifty pounds a year and his lodgings.' He sounded outraged. 'And he still let the whole bloody thing get out of hand. That's why they closed.' He stared at Nottingham. 'It's going to cost me at least five hundred to have the place ready.'

'A very tidy sum.' More than many merchants cleared in a year, he knew that.

'I have it and I'll pay it.'

'What if you don't get it back?' The Constable drained his cup, his eyes firmly on the man.

Finer shrugged. 'Then I don't. I won't be starving without it. But I'm sure if it's done right, the workhouse can pay for itself. You know what the problem's been before?'

'What?' He wanted to hear the man's opinion.

'The people in charge of everything were clerks. How much do they really know about business?'

'Certainly not business like yours.'

'I've spent my life turning one penny into two, laddie,' Finer countered.

'And how many have you hurt doing that?'

The man frowned, then replied, 'I keep telling you, all that's in the past now. The Corporation's in favour of my plans.'

'I've no doubt they are. They'll love anything that sweeps the poor off the streets and doesn't cost them a penny.'

'Where the poor will be fed and have beds to sleep in,' Finer said pointedly.

'Out of sight and doing something useful.'

'You're never going to believe me, are you, Constable?'

'Prove me wrong, Mr Finer,' Nottingham challenged. 'Do that and I'll give you my apology.' He stood. 'I'll tell you this, though – I'll be watching you carefully all along the way.'

'You do that, Mr Nottingham. And when you see I've been telling you the truth I'll happily accept that apology of yours.'

The Constable meandered home along Kirkgate, his heels clattering quickly over the wood of Timble Bridge. He thought about the conversation with Finer. The man sounded persuasive enough, but when hadn't he? He'd always been the type to try charm first, and violence if words didn't work. Yet what if he was wrong, and Finer really had turned into a man of good works?

If. That small word. He shook his head to clear it. More doubts to fill his mind. For every two steps forwards he took, his mind would drag him back one.

'When she's old enough I thought we could send Isabell to Emily Nottingham's school,' Lizzie said. The girl was settled on her lap, constantly leaning forward to reach for everything on the table.

'That's a long way off yet.' Sedgwick was spooning pottage into his mouth, a mug of ale in his other hand to wash down the food.

'She's a girl so she can't go to my school,' James pointed out smugly.

'We know that, clever boots. But you want your sister to be able to learn, don't you?' He reached across and tousled the boy's hair.

'I suppose so,' James answered reluctantly. 'But George says girls aren't as clever as boys.'

'If George says that to his mam he'll be getting a clout around the ear,' Lizzie told him. 'He'll deserve it, too.'

The boy lowered his head and nodded but Sedgwick could see him smirking.

'I'd better never hear you saying something like that.'

'No, Da.'

'What homework do you have tonight?'

'Sums again.'

'Right. You've finished your supper so go upstairs and do it.'

He waited until the lad had scrambled up the stairs.

'I think sending her to school is a grand idea.'

Lizzie put the girl on the floor, watching as she pushed herself on to her feet and started to totter about the room.

'Away from there,' she warned, then, 'I want her to have the same chance as James.' The boy was learning so quickly at the charity school, dutiful in his work and starting to develop a good, clear hand for his writing.

'So do I.' He extended his arm, waving his fingers until

Isabell saw them, and began to walk unsteadily towards him. 'If she has her letters and her numbers she'll never go hungry.' Only two years had passed since he'd learned to read himself. Back then he'd had dreams of becoming Constable after the boss retired. Now he knew better. He didn't have a face that fitted with what the Corporation wanted. He'd done the job for six months when Nottingham recovered from a wound and he'd been barely tolerated by those who held the power and the purse strings.

The boss might have spent much of his childhood as a waif while his mother had to whore for pennies, but he'd started life as a merchant's son. Underneath it all the ones who ran things believed he was one of them, something Sedgwick could never be.

Rob stood a better chance of being the next Constable than he did. His father was publisher of the *Leeds Mercury;* he knew the right people, could speak the right way.

'John!' Lizzie's voice pulled him from his thoughts. She pointed and he scooped up Isabell before she could fall, tickling her to make her giggle wildly and kick against him with her short, stubby legs.

'You're going to be a smart one, you are,' he told her. 'There'll be better than this for you and your brother.'

Rob paced anxiously around the office in the jail. He'd completed the night report and looked in on the three drunks asleep in the cells. Outside there was the slow rumble of wheels as a cart made its early way down Kirkgate towards the Parish Church.

He chewed on his lower lip, starting at every noise and hoping it was the Constable arriving. In the distance he heard the bell at the Parish Church ring once for the quarter hour. Finally the door handle turned and he stood straighter.

'Morning, lad,' Nottingham said. 'Going to be another lovely day.'

'Boss, there's something you need to see.' He picked up a piece of slate from the desk and passed it over. 'This.'

TWELVE

t was a crude drawing, no more than a few lines scrawled with a stone. A stick figure in a dress with a noose around her neck, hanging from a gibbet. Nottingham examined it. 'Where was it?'

'At the school.'

The Constable looked at him sharply. 'Whereabouts?'

'I was down by there a little after three,' Rob explained. 'The gate at the end of the back yard was open and someone had forced the door. It was on Emily's desk.'

Nottingham held up the slate, studying the picture again. There was no mistake about its meaning. 'Anything else you could see? Any other damage?'

'Just this.' Lister hesitated. 'What do I do? Should I tell her?'

Nottingham stood by the desk, trying to untangle his thoughts. His chest was so tight he could barely breathe. He gripped the slate to try to hide the shaking in his hands. He was going to punish whoever had done this.

'Go ahead,' he said eventually. 'She needs to know. And make sure you walk her to school and back every day. I mean *every* day.'

'Yes, boss.'

The Constable's mind raced as he imagined everything that could happen. 'I want you to check inside the place each morning before she goes in. I'll tell John to have his men keep an eye on it during the day.'

'I'll have one of the night men stay on watch, too. The husbands have stopped staying out.'

The Constable nodded his approval. 'I'll have a word with the locksmith and see those doors are fixed and that gate's made secure,' he said. 'There's a wall at the back of the property, isn't there?'

'Yes, about as tall as me.'

'And the gate goes all the way up?'

'Yes, boss.'

Nottingham thought for a moment. 'Did you put the incident in your report?'

'I did.'

'Write me a new one and leave it out,' he said. 'I don't want everyone knowing about this. Do that, then take yourself off.'

The Constable was studying the slate once more when the deputy came in. No one was going to hurt his daughter. No one.

'Take a look at this, John.' His voice was calmer than he felt.

'A drawing?' Sedgwick asked in confusion. 'Where did you find it?'

'Rob did. Someone broke into the school during the night and left it on Emily's desk.'

'Christ.' The deputy exhaled slowly.

'It wasn't drunks the other night. Someone doesn't want her there.'

'I'll keep Holden on the back of the place.'

'Good. But I want all this to stay quiet for now.'

'Why, boss?' Sedgwick asked. 'If the women down there know they'll have their men out on guard again.'

'And if they do that, they'll scare off whoever's behind this. I want to catch the bastard, John.'

'We will, boss.'

'I'm not going to have anyone do this to her.' He tossed the slate on to the desk, his gaze fixed on the picture. 'Did Molly tell you much yesterday?'

'She saw Jenny, but the girl didn't tell her anything useful. What about the Wades?'

'Mrs Wade doesn't remember Jem Carter, and Jenny never went there. A waste of good time.'

'You don't need to walk me to school,' Emily insisted. 'I'll be fine by myself. You look like you need to sleep.'

'I want to,' Rob said. 'Besides . . .'

'What?' she asked with a flash of irritation. He took hold of her hand. 'What is it? I'm going to be late.'

'Someone broke into the school last night, through the back door.'

'Broke in?' She stopped abruptly, looking at him in disbelief. 'But you said it was just drunks,' she began. 'Did they damage anything?' She started to move away, ready to rush to the school, but he kept hold of her.

'There's something else.'

'What?' She looked at him. 'What, Rob?' she said, fear in her eyes, then shouted, 'What?'

'There was a drawing on a slate,' he told her, keeping his voice low. 'A girl, hanging.'

Emily stayed silent for a few moments, scarcely breathing.

'Where is it?' Her face began to flush with anger. 'I want to see it.'

'I took it to the jail.'

'And what did Papa say?'

'He's the one who told me to escort you to and from school and check the room every day. He wants to keep you safe.'

'I'm not going to let them scare me.' She tried to keep her voice firm, the words more for herself than for him. 'I'm not,' she repeated, staring at Rob.

'I know,' he said gently. He could feel her fingers gripping his tightly, squeezing against him. 'Come on,' he said, keeping his voice low. 'We're nearly there.'

For once they arrived at the school before the pupils. He waited as she unlocked the door with the heavy key, her hands fumbling with the lock.

'Let me go in first,' Rob said.

'No,' she said, and the vehemence of her reply surprised him. 'This is my school.' He opened his mouth, but she continued, 'I don't care what Papa told you. I have to do it this way. I *have* to.'

Rob nodded and followed her inside. He pulled back the shutters and let light into the room. It was exactly as he'd seen it when he'd come during the night, everything still in place, the lock hanging from the back door where it had been forced open.

Emily put her books on the table that served as her desk.

'Why?' she asked him. 'Why do they want to do this?'

'I don't know.'

'We're helping people. We're not hurting anyone.' She looked around the room, her eyes bleak. 'You know, I'd actually started to believe the other night was nothing.'

'People round here want you,' he reminded her. 'You saw the way the women had their husbands out before.'

'Someone doesn't.'

'We'll find him,' Rob promised. 'We're going to have someone watching the place all the time.'

'A school that someone has to guard . . .' She let the words tail away.

'And we'll have someone fit a new lock here and on the back gate.'

Emily walked around the room, her fingertips sliding across the wood of the tables and benches.

'The girls will be here soon. I'm not going to let anything happen to them.'

'They'll be safe,' he assured her gently, and added, 'So will you.'

'How do I tell them? How do I tell them that someone hates them so much he wants to destroy all this?'

'Don't,' he said, seeing the astonishment on her face. 'Please. Your father doesn't want anyone else to know.'

'But—' she began.

'There's no need to scare them.'

She pushed her lips together. Her eyes glistened but he knew Emily wouldn't let the tears fall.

'We want to catch whoever's doing this,' Rob continued. 'Think about it. If the women here send their men out again we won't be able to do that. Please.'

He waited as she weighed her answer.

'I won't say a word,' she agreed reluctantly.

'Thank you.' He kissed her. 'I'll come back this afternoon to walk you home.'

He walked across Timble Bridge in the sunlight, feeling bitter at his impotence, unable to do anything to ease her fears. He smelt the honeysuckle and the heady scent of the roses climbing in the hedgerows but for once they didn't bring a smile.

As he entered the house on Marsh Lane he could feel exhaustion creeping through his body. Lucy came through from the kitchen, wiping her hands on her apron, and stared hard at him.

'Tell me what's happened,' she said. 'And don't say it's nothing, I can see it on your face.'

He explained it to her, seeing her cheeks flush with anger.

'I'll go and spend nights there meself,' she offered when he'd finished.

'There's no need. We're going to have someone watching the place all the time.'

She snorted. 'Aye, and I know how good that is.'

'Do you really think Mr Nottingham would let anything happen to her?' Rob asked. 'Do you think I would?'

'It already has, though, hasn't it?' She shook her head. 'Words don't mean owt.'

'We'll find whoever's done it.'

'Mebbe,' Her voice was filled with doubt. 'That lass is going to be scared.' She pulled the knife from the pocket in her dress. He knew she kept the blade sharp and ready; those years of living wild had left her cautious. Even the months in this house, safe and secure, with a home, hadn't managed to remove that.

'We'll look after her.'

'All of us,' she said, staring at him.

'Yes,' he agreed. 'All of us. I'm off to my bed now, but I'll go back to the school this afternoon.'

The Constable sat staring at the slate for a long time. He'd sent a note to the locksmith, asking him to secure the gate at the school and go back later to repair the back door and fit a solid bar to it.

Who? Who would want to do this? Who would hate the idea of girls being educated so much?

He heard the bell ring for the cloth market but he didn't move; for once they could look after themselves. The minutes passed as he stared at nothing; finally he roused himself, scribbled out his daily report, and left it at the Moot Hall before making his way to the Tuesday market at the top of Briggate.

Crowds packed the street, cries of 'What do you need? What do you lack?' coming from the stalls, the patter of the sellers entertaining the women, making them laugh and shriek in delight.

He smiled and nodded at the faces he knew, stopping to talk to a few, asking a single question: who did they know who didn't want girls educated? He moved again, seeing someone he knew and working through the press of people for a few more words.

Finally Nottingham pushed his way out, able to breathe more easily away from the rank smell of unwashed bodies. He walked down to the Calls, standing out of sight, close enough to the school to hear Emily's voice through the open windows. After a few minutes he cut round to Call Brows, counting off the houses until he found the right one, checking that the workman had done a good job on the gate. The wall was a head taller than him but nothing a young man couldn't scale. Later he'd have someone put a layer of mortar at the top and push broken glass into it, hating himself for making the place into a fortress yet knowing he'd do anything to keep his daughter and everything she loved safe.

By the time he reached the White Swan for his dinner the deputy was already there. The Constable raised his eyebrows questioningly and saw Sedgwick give a brief shake of his head. He sat wearily on the bench.

'I've been asking round a little,' Nottingham told him. 'No one seems to know who'd want to do ruin to the school.'

'So what do we do now, boss?'

The Constable took a long drink of his ale. 'You know,' he said thoughtfully, 'I saw Simon Johnson up at the market last Saturday.'

'Who?'

'The brother of that man killed by the mob. The one who cursed us all.'

'He's still here? What do you think? He's behind this?'

'I'm not sure,' the Constable admitted. 'But if he hates Leeds so much I wonder why he's still here.'

'Do you want me to look for him?'

'No, leave it with me. I know what he looks like.'

'I checked earlier. The only people who've been at the back of the school today are the locksmith and you.'

'Whoever it is, he'll be back,' Nottingham warned grimly. 'Folk like that can't keep away once they've started.'

'We'll have him when he returns,' the deputy said. 'How's Emily?'

'I haven't seen her yet.' The Constable stroked his chin. 'I left that to Rob. She knows she can always talk to me.'

'I know what I'd like to do when we find him.'

'It's not just you,' the Constable said darkly. 'But we'll make sure he faces justice. Like everyone else, John,'

'Not if the people who live round there catch him first.' If that happened, there'd be another man murdered by the mob.

'Something else you should know about,' Nottingham told him. He explained about Tom Finer, his history and his plan for the workhouse.

'He could make good money there,' Sedgwick surmised.

'I know. And as long as they're not having to pay, the Corporation won't care how he does it.'

'Do you think he could have changed, boss?'

The Constable shook his head. 'No. Maybe he really did come back here for his old age. I can believe that. But I know what he's like – if he sees a chance, he's going to take it. That's his way. He's sly, John, he always was. He's the only one I've ever seen who could get the better of Amos Worthy. And he still knows secrets about some important people here.'

'What are you going to do about it?'

'I've warned Tom Williamson.' He sighed. 'I really don't know what else I can do. I've written to London to try and find out what he did down there. But it's the folk in the Moot Hall who'll be making the decision.'

'And the poor who'll pay the price.'

'Isn't it always?' Nottingham asked drily.

'We should tell Bessie so she can warn all those down by the river.'

'I'm going down there. I want to ask her about Simon Johnson, anyway.'

'What do you want me doing this afternoon, boss?'

'See if you can find anything about the school,' he replied without even thinking. 'And Carter and his sister,' he added.

THIRTEEN

A cart had lost a wheel just up from the bridge and tipped its load out across the road. The driver was holding the horse, calming it with gentle words and watching as two apprentices from the blacksmith sweated to work the rim back on to the axle and secure it.

The road was blocked, the traffic at a standstill. A small crowd had gathered, and one or two of the men loudly offered advice; small boys darted in and out among the people. One of the barrels had cracked, spilling salt, and women scooped it quickly into their bags.

Nottingham saw one of his men standing on the other side of the road. He nodded and walked on; another ten minutes and everything would be moving again. He clattered down the old stone steps besides Leeds Bridge and strolled out along the bank.

The river moved lazily, its sound barely more than a whisper in the still air. A pair of willows hung out over the water as if they were leaning in to drink. The grass was flattened and he saw rings of stones and charred patches where the fires burned at night. There was a small shelter up in the treeline, and he crossed the open space.

As he approached Bessie came out, standing with a knife in her hand until she recognized him and grinned.

'Mr Nottingham,' she said warmly. 'I can't remember the last time you were down here. It's usually Mr Lister.'

She seemed to have grown even stouter in the months since he'd seen her last, more flesh on her arms, her waist thicker. But the smile was the same, and she carried herself with the same regal neatness, her clothes old, but always neat and clean.

He pushed the fringe off his forehead and asked, 'Are they behaving for you, Bessie?'

'Good and bad, same as ever,' she replied with a small shrug. 'At least with this weather there aren't as many of them.

Some have gone off to the farms looking for work. How are you?' She looked pointedly at him and he understood her meaning.

'I miss her,' he said simply. There was no need for more. 'I'm looking for a man called Simon Johnson.'

'I know who you mean, he's been here. Eyes as sad as the world, the one whose brother . . .?'

'That's him,' the Constable nodded. 'Where is he now?'

'I've not seen him in a little while. He spent a few days down here. Always kept himself to himself, didn't want to talk much. Has he done something?'

'I don't know. There's been some trouble at my daughter's school. I just wanted to ask him about it.'

'What's happened?' she asked. 'Come on, sit down and tell your Aunt Bessie about it.'

She listened attentively, pouring them ale from a jug in her shelter and asking questions when he was done.

'You think Simon might be doing it?' she asked.

'I've no idea, Bessie,' he said with a frustrated sigh. 'I was just surprised to see him still in Leeds. I wondered if he had a reason.'

'I don't know what to tell you, Mr Nottingham. I'll send word if he comes back and I'll keep my ears open. We need that school. And you need to keep her safe.'

'I do.' He tried to smile but it was a weak, wan effort. 'You ought to know, there's talk about re-opening the workhouse.'

'I'd not heard anything about that.' Her voice rose sharply.

'They're keeping it quiet for now.'

She frowned, knowing full well what it meant. There'd be no more camp; men, woman and children would all be pushed away into the large old building. 'I can see it in your eyes, though. You think it'll happen.'

'Maybe,' he said. 'I hope not.'

'Do you know when?'

'Not yet. As soon as I find something out, I'll tell you.'

'What do you think we should do?' Bessie asked.

'I'm not sure there's anything you can do. The wheels are already in motion.'

She reached out, taking his hand between both of hers. He felt the calluses on her palms and the warmth of her skin.

'Thank you,' she said. 'I'll tell everyone.'

Rob waited with Emily in the school room while the locksmith finished the door. He lowered the bar into place and handed her the key.

'There'll not be anyone coming in through there now.'

'Thank you,' she said. 'How much do I owe you?'

'Nay, lass,' the workman told her with a smile. 'No charge. I owe Mr Nottingham a basket full of favours.' He gathered up his tools and left.

'That's saved you money, anyway,' Rob said.

'I'd sooner have paid him myself,' she answered, a bristly edge to her voice.

'But you asked Mr Williamson for money for books, and you took the money his wife offered,' he pointed out, confused.

'They're not family,' she told him. 'I don't want to be Papa's girl.' She looked around. 'This is *mine*. Do you understand?'

He nodded. To him, help was help, but it was better to say nothing; he knew her pride.

She took the books from her desk and handed them to him.

'I'm worried someone will destroy it all,' she said.

'We'll make sure they don't.'

Emily closed the shutters and locked the door, pushing against the wood to test it, then slid her arm through his as they walked towards the Parish Church.

'I'm proud of you,' he said, turning to kiss her; but she pulled away.

'I'm not,' she answered him softly. 'I don't want to feel this way.'

'Well, John?'

The afternoon had passed, heat still clinging to the ground. The Constable had propped the door to the jail open, trying to draw in some cool air. He'd spent a fruitless time asking questions and chasing Simon Johnson. If the man was still in Leeds, no one seemed to know where; he'd turned into a wraith.

'Bugger all, boss.' He slumped into the chair and poured a

mug of ale, draining it in a single swallow. 'About the only thing I learned today is that the Wades come from Whitby.'

'Whitby?' Nottingham echoed. 'How did you hear that?'

'Will Landry. I saw him in the Talbot. He did a lot of the work on that house of theirs. He overheard one of the daughters and the son talking.'

'I wonder why Mrs Wade didn't want anyone to know.' He shrugged. 'Anyway, it doesn't matter. We've got too much to worry about without her. I want whoever's behind this at the school. Somebody knows.'

'Yes, boss.'

'I want the names of everyone who's against girls or the poor being educated.'

'Christ, boss,' the deputy protested. 'There could be hundreds of them.'

'I don't care if we have to talk to every single person in Leeds. I want whoever did this.'

Sedgwick found Holden in a small hollow on Call Brows. He was squatting on his haunches, a jug in front of him, looking for all the world like a drunkard awaiting his dreams as the sun began to dip. But the deputy knew his man was keeping a keen eye on the back gate of the school. He sat down on the grass.

'Anything?'

'Folk passing by, but no one's stopped, no one looking suspicious.'

'What do you think?'

Holden considered his words before answering, staring down at the ground for a long moment. 'If you ask me, it'd be a fool who tried anything in the daytime.'

'Aye,' he agreed. He understood why the Constable wanted someone keeping watch; he'd have done the same. But there was no sense having one of the men here in the daylight when nothing would happen.

The deputy lifted the jug and took a drink. The ale was warm but it still slid easily down his throat.

'If there's nothing by the time you leave, tomorrow just go back to what you were doing before.'

'Yes, Mr Sedgwick.' Holden took the jug back with a grin. 'Leaves you dry, all this keeping still.'

'That's what they say. Not that I have the chance to find out.'

The Constable lay on his bed. The window was open and the faintest of breezes stirred. Somewhere off in the distance an owl hooted, and an answering call came a moment later. Not every crime was solved, he thought, not even every murder. There were three he could recall where he'd never found the killer. Every one of them was still clear in his head. Sometimes, when the nights were long and sleep wouldn't come, he'd go over them, poring over each detail, still worried that he'd missed something, made some mistake that let a man go free.

He wondered if Jem Carter could become number four. They'd looked, they'd scoured the city and still found absolutely nothing, no reason at all for him to die. Then there was Jenny . . . he pictured her face, the blonde hair wet from the river and clinging to her skin, the ring on her finger. There was nothing to suggest she hadn't taken her own life. Perhaps the deputy had been right, and she'd heard about her brother's death then filled with guilt or grief she'd jumped into the water.

But those words weren't true. He knew that. They were excuses. The truth was that only one thing filled his heart – finding whoever was doing the damage at the school. Nothing else mattered, not even murder. Even if he found this murderer, there'd be another, and another. He was going to protect Emily and make sure no one tore her dreams apart.

But who could he talk to? Who was there to listen to his worries and his fears? He closed his eyes and waited for sleep, reaching out across the sheet, holding on for the moments he could almost believe Mary was with him.

FOURTEEN

'I've taken Holden off Call Brows, boss,' the deputy said.
'Why?' Nottingham asked sharply.
'He's just wasting his time. There won't be any trouble

during the day. If there's a problem it'll come after dark, and Rob has men out then.'

The Constable nodded. Sedgwick was right. He'd allowed his fierce desire to protect Emily to push ahead of good sense. There were other jobs Holden could be doing.

'I'll still go by and check a few times,' Nottingham said.

'No harm in that, boss.' The deputy grinned. 'I might drop by a time or two myself.'

'Today we'll find out who doesn't want girls to have an education.'

The deputy poured a measure of ale and took a sip, his face troubled.

'I've been thinking, boss,' he began slowly. 'Jenny Carter.'

'What about her?'

'She went to those brothels.'

'Yes.'

'But Mrs Wade said she'd never asked for work there.'

'That's right.'

'It just seems odd to me. It makes sense she'd go there, too.'

'Why would the woman lie about it?' Nottingham asked. 'If Jenny had gone there she could have just said so.'

'I don't know,' the deputy admitted. 'And didn't you say Tom Finer told Jem to go down there?'

'I asked Mrs Wade if she'd seen him. They were so busy that first night she doesn't recall.'

'Happen she's telling the truth. But whether she is or not, someone killed Jem Carter, boss, that's a fact.' He hesitated, then rushed on. 'I want to find whoever did that to the school, but we can't ignore everything else.'

'What do you suggest, then, John?' Nottingham asked in exasperation. 'We've all been out asking questions and we've found nothing. What else can we do?'

'I want to keep trying. Someone knows.'

'Of course.' He should be out there himself, too. He wasn't doing his job. 'Thank you,' he added.

'We'll get the bastard, boss.'

'He's going to wish he'd never started.'

At the end of a long day he'd stopped at the Rose and Crown to wet his throat, and now he had a little time to follow an idea. It might come to nothing, but even if the boss seemed to have time for little but the school, he wasn't going to forget a murder. He'd follow every piece of information that came his way. He crossed the bridge and disappeared into the small streets that spread behind the large merchant mansions on Meadow Lane until he found the house he was seeking and knocked on the door.

The woman who answered had a harried look and strands of grey hair coming out from her cap. Behind her he heard the squall of children. Before he could say a word she turned and bellowed, 'Shut up! If I have to come back there you're going to regret it.'

Silence followed and she faced him with a long sigh.

'Can't keep the little buggers quiet for more than five minutes. What can I do for you, Mr Sedgwick?'

'Is Ezekiel at home?'

'He's off in York. He'll have stopped in Sherburn. He's got a lass there he thinks I don't know about, the daft bugger.' She shook her head. 'Any road, he should be back tomorrow. Is it important?'

'Just wondering about something, that's all.'

Ezekiel Fadden had a carting business, travelling to York and beyond. He'd heard the man talk about his visits to the coast.

'Do you want me to have him look for you once he's home?' the woman asked. Voices rose back in the house. 'I told you, be quiet,' she shouted to them. 'Sorry, Mr Sedgwick.'

'Aye, that would be good. Do you know if he goes to Whitby?'

'Five or six times a year. He likes it up there. Why?'

'I have a few questions about the place, that's all.'

'Thinking of moving, are you?' she laughed.

'No, love. Take me out of Leeds and I wouldn't know what to do.'

'Knowing him he'll be back in good time to go drinking in the evening.' A child started to scream and she rolled her eyes. 'I'll tell him.'

Rob stood in a patch of sunlight on the Calls, watching the girls leave the school. They seemed to explode out of the door, full of laughter, shouting and running. For a brief moment there was nothing but noise, then they disappeared into the distance and the street was almost silent.

He entered the room, seeing Emily move around, straightening the tables and benches and picking up small pieces of rubbish the children had dropped. He kissed her lightly on the back of the neck then took the broom from the corner and began to sweep the floor.

'Thank you,' she said. He could see the strain and exhaustion on her face.

'Sit down for a minute. You've earned a rest.'

She slumped on the chair, gathering the books off the table. 'Is all this worth it?' she asked wearily.

'Worth it?' He didn't understand what she meant.

'This.' She raised her head and looked around the room. 'The school. What I'm doing here.'

He put up the besom and looked at her. 'Of course it is. You know it is,' he said softly. 'You're giving all these girls a future. The women round here all admire you.'

'But someone doesn't.' She sighed.

'We'll catch him.'

'You keep saying that, Rob. But will you? What if he . . .?' She looked down at the table.

'What?'

'What if he does something to one of the girls?' she said, her voice empty. 'That's what I keep thinking. That's what scares me, what he'll do next.'

He put his hand on hers, gripping it tightly.

'We won't let him.'

Her eyes glistened as she raised her head and she wiped at them angrily.

'You can't stop him, can you? Not really. Not you, not Papa.'

He couldn't reply; she was right. If someone was determined, clever and ruthless enough, he'd succeed. They couldn't look after every child, or have men at the front and back of the school all hours of the day and night.

'Come on,' he said. 'Let's go home.'

He closed the shutters, dropping the bars behind them. When he turned she was still sitting at the desk and hadn't moved.

He took her arm, helping her to rise. Her mouth was set in grim defiance.

'I'm not going to lose this,' she said with determination. 'I'm not. I'm not going to let him win.'

'He won't. I promise.'

She stayed silent, her arm through his, but he knew her thoughts were elsewhere as she walked beside him. He let her be, simply staying quiet and enjoying her presence. At Timble Bridge she stopped, and rested her elbows on the parapet to stare down at the water as it eddied over the rocks and pebbles with a soft, sweet sound.

'Don't you ever wonder where all the water goes?' she asked after a long time.

'The sea,' he answered. 'That's what they told me at school, anyway.'

'I know. But if all this water goes there, what happens to all the water already in the sea?'

'I don't know.' None of that had ever interested him. He'd gone to school and learned what he needed to know. Most of it had simply bored him. Thrashings from the master had done nothing to change his mind.

'Have you ever seen it?' Emily wondered. 'The sea?'

'No.' He'd thought about it at times and tried to imagine it.

'I haven't, either.' She smiled. 'Maybe we should go there some day.'

He smiled. 'When we have the time and the money.'

'Dreams don't cost anything. That's what one of the girls said today.' She sloughed off the dark mood like a coat and took hold of his hand. 'Come on, let's go home.'

The sun was low when the Constable finished work at the jail. It had been another fruitless day. How many people had he talked to? Thirty? Forty? He'd lost count. And out of them all there hadn't been a single one he believed responsible for the damage at the school. The only useful thing he'd done was to catch a cutpurse as he came up behind a man with his knife out, trying to steal his money. Disarming him had been simple enough, and the man had come to the jail without a fight. Now he was sitting in the cell, cringing in terror, knowing full well what waited for him.

In the morning the Constable would escort him to the prison in the cellar of the Moot Hall, and the man would wait for the Quarter Session. There was no doubt about his guilt. If the judge was lenient it would be transportation to America for seven years. If he wasn't it would be the hangman's dance up on Chapeltown Moor.

Finally the Constable locked up and walked out into the late warmth. The evening shadows were beginning to gather, the warmth like velvet against his skin. He stretched slowly, his muscles aching from a long day, and just the faintest ache from last year's knife wound. He wasn't ready to return to Marsh Lane yet. He needed time to himself. He'd seen the looks Emily and Lucy gave him; they could be too attentive, rather than letting him alone with his thoughts and memories.

The White Swan was busy with men slaking their thirst after hours of work, voices loud and merry. He ordered a mug of ale and glanced around to find Tom Finer staring at him. Everywhere he turned these days he seemed to see the man. Finer raised his cup in greeting and waved him over.

'Finished for the day, Mr Nottingham?'

The Constable sat on the bench. 'Unless something happens.'

Finer smiled. 'I doubt that's too often.'

Nottingham shrugged. 'Once is more than enough.'

'Has it been quieter since Amos died?'

The Constable smiled at the question. 'Not so as you'd notice. Why, Mr Finer, do you intend on keeping me busier with your workhouse plans?'

The older man smiled, but it was strained. 'Everything I do is legal these days, Constable. I told you that.'

Nottingham raised his mug in a toast. 'I'll hope that's true.'

Finer took a drink of his ale and made a face. 'Not the best in Leeds here, is it?'

'Better than the Talbot.'

The man nodded slowly. 'True enough, Mr Nottingham. But the gossip's more interesting there.'

'If it's so good, what brings you down here?'

Finer stroked a chin covered in thin white bristles. 'Old

haunts. I remember getting roaring drunk in here one night with Arkwright, back when he was the Constable. He challenged me to a bare knuckle fight out on Kirkgate.'

'I never heard about that. Who won?'

'We'd had so much ale that neither of us landed a punch,' he laughed. 'Amos stood and cheered us on. He won ten pounds that night by betting there wouldn't be a winner.'

'I might have put money on that myself.'

'You'd just be a young 'un then, you'd probably not even started working as a Constable's man yet. A long time ago. I remember when you started out with him. You looked like you'd nothing about you. I'd seen more fat on a worm than you had back then.'

In spite of himself, Nottingham grinned. 'A lifetime,' he agreed.

'Two or three, perhaps. For me, anyway.' He drank a little more and pushed the cup away. 'I remember the ale as better than that.' He paused. 'I know you think I've come back to Leeds to cause trouble, but I haven't.'

'So you keep saying. Time will tell.'

'It will,' Finer agreed. 'You'll see.' He eased himself to his feet. 'I think I'll go to the Talbot and hear what's been happening. And then home for my supper.'

'I wish you well.'

'I doubt you do, Mr Nottingham, but thank you anyway.' He nodded and left.

The Constable drained his ale. Was he wrong about Finer? Lately it was so hard to be certain, but deep inside a small knot told him he was right. He remembered something Amos Worthy had told him once – repeat a lie often enough and it'll become the truth. The more that Tom Finer said he'd put crime behind him, the more folk would believe it. Being doubtful might be no bad thing.

FIFTEEN

'**M**r Sedgwick.'
The deputy heard the small voice and felt a hand
tugging at his sleeve. Looking down, he saw Ezekiel
Fadden's oldest boy staring up at him.

'What is it?' he asked, trying to remember the lad's name.
He looked to be about the same age as James, his own son,
with a grubby face and hands, and shoes far too big for his
small feet.

'Me ma said to tell you me da's back if you want to talk
to him.'

'Aye, thank you. Will,' he added as it came to him.' He
pulled a farthing from the pocket of his breeches and placed
it between the small fingers. 'Is he at home?'

'He's wetting his whistle at the Old King's Head,' the boy
said carefully. 'That's what she said to tell you.'

Sedgwick laughed and tousled the boy's hair. 'Right, off
you go, then. You've done your job.' He watched the boy run.

The doors of the Old King's Head were wedged open to
let in the fresh air and the light. A man swept the floor, and
the serving girl leaned against the trestle talking idly to the
landlord.

Fadden was standing by the window, gazing out at Briggate.
The deputy bought himself a mug of the cold ale and joined
him.

'Maggie said you'd been looking for me,' the carter said
warily. 'Have I done anything wrong?'

'Not that I know of,' Sedgwick answered and saw the man
ease a little. Faddon had done something, he thought, and
wondered if he'd been found out. Sometime he'd discover exactly
what. Information was always useful. 'You go to Whitby.'

'Not that often any more,' he shrugged. 'It's mostly York
or Hull these days, that's where the business is. Gives me
chance to stop over in Sherburn. There's a little lass there
who's sweet on me.' He winked. 'As long as Maggie doesn't

find out I'll be fine.' He drained the mug and gave it a long glance.

'Another?' the deputy asked.

'Aye, go on. You need a good wet, driving a team all day.' Sedgwick held up a pair of fingers for the serving girl.

'When were you in Whitby last?' he asked.

'Must be close to three months ago,' Fadden answered after a while. 'Once the road over the moors was clear after winter.'

'Did you hear of anything out there?'

'Like what?' The man picked up the fresh ale and drank.

'Any crime folk might be talking about?'

'Nowt as I recall,' Fadden answered with a thoughtful frown. He hesitated. 'Well, there was summat odd. Some shopkeeper who'd died. He'd given his servant the night off. When he came back the master was dead in his chair with a rug tucked all around him. That what you mean?'

'It could be. Any word of people leaving the town suddenly?'

The carter laughed. 'Nay, who cares about that? There are always people flitting, you should know that, Mr Sedgwick.'

The deputy nodded. He hadn't expected much, but it was worth asking. 'The merchant, was there much stolen?'

'Like as not. I didn't pay too much attention. Why, summat to do with Leeds, is it?'

'Probably not.' He saw the interest die in the man's eyes. Another hour and a few more drinks and he'd have forgotten the conversation. Sedgwick drained his mug.

'Enjoy your ale.'

'I'll do that,' Fadden said with a broad grin.

'And that Sherburn lass? Don't be too sure your wife doesn't know.' He left the carter looking worried.

Back at the jail, Sedgwick sat at the desk and slowly wrote out a note, taking his time over the shape of each letter and thinking how to phrase what he needed. Finally he sat back and read it through. It wasn't as elegant as Rob or the boss could manage, perhaps, but it would serve.

He sealed and addressed the note then carried it to the Moot Hall, leaving it on Cobb's desk to be sent.

Sedgwick strolled back down Briggate, his eyes alert for anything and everything. There was still time to ask a few more questions. Sooner or later there'd be a word, a hint, something to pry it all open, he felt sure of that; it had happened often enough before.

He started to grin. It was his lucky day. Twenty yards ahead of him, parading as if he owned the street, was King Davy. The deputy lengthened his stride. Just as they reached the entrance to Queen's Court, he caught up with Davy and pushed him hard into the opening, catching the man off balance and pinning him against the wall with a forearm against his throat.

He reached down to pull King's knife from its sheath and tossed it away. Davy was struggling, trying to free himself. Sedgwick raised his knee and began to grind it into the man's bollocks, taking pleasure as his face began to turn red with pain.

'Still got something to say about whores, have you, Davy?'

King's eyes were beginning to bulge and he tried to claw the arm off his neck. The deputy pressed harder, lowered his knee and brought it back up sharply.

'Well,' he asked again. 'Have you? Still got words to say about my Lizzie?' King had his eyes closed, trying to shake his head. 'You're going to be very polite to all the girls in future, Davy.' He waited. 'Understand?' The man gave a tiny nod and Sedgwick stood back, watching as Davy collapsed on the ground, gasping for air, hands clutched around the agony between his legs. 'I'm going to be asking. If I hear anything bad I'm going to come looking for you. And next time it'll be a lot worse than this.'

He strode off, leaving the man in the dirt. Smiling, he continued on his way.

The sun was as hot as full summer, blazing down and leaving spring no more than a memory. The Constable was sweating in his coat, the shirt damp against his back. He marched out along the riverbank to Williamson's warehouse, still weighing whether to tell the man about the threats at the school. Best not; after all, they'd given Emily money and promised more. He didn't want their hearts turning faint now.

A clerk motioned him through. The merchant was in his office, stripped to his shirt with the windows wide to catch the thin breeze that lifted off the Aire.

'You look drawn, Richard,' the merchant said. 'Sit yourself down and have something to drink.'

He downed a cup of ale gratefully. 'It's nothing more than usual,' he explained. 'Too many questions to ask and too few answers. I thought I'd ask what progress there's been on the workhouse.'

'Straight to business?' Williamson smiled. 'There's not much to tell you. The Corporation's received Mr Finer's proposal and they've asked me to look at the figures. I have to tell you, everything I've seen in it makes sense.'

'He's out to make money somehow. I'm certain of that.'

Williamson exhaled slowly and answered with care, 'I've only had time to examine things quickly so far. But if he does what he says, the workhouse will pay for itself. He'll get his investment back and that's all he'll receive. It's very fair for the city. I'm sorry, Richard, but it all seems honest.'

'Look closer, please,' Nottingham said. 'There'll be something hidden away in there, I'm sure of it. I remember what he was like.'

'I will. It's my responsibility, after all. But I have to tell you, if I can't see any fault I'm going to recommend that the Corporation accepts his offer. You understand that, don't you?'

'Of course,' he said tightly, and stood up. 'I'll leave you to your work.'

The Constable walked along the Calls, feeling the heat trapped between the buildings and hearing his daughter's voice loud through the open windows, then the smaller, hesitant sound of the girls haltingly repeating the words back to her. For a minute he stood silently to listen. Mary would have been proud of her, he thought, and the idea made him smile.

He moved on, finding himself crossing Timble Bridge before he even realized it. The house on Marsh Lane was in sight and he felt suddenly weary. All work had served to do was bring the same answers over and over. He wanted to rest.

He closed the door quietly and turned to find himself facing Lucy, her knife in her hand.

'I didn't know who it was,' she told him, returning the blade to the pocket of her dress.

'I'm sorry,' he said.

'Why are you home so early, anyway?' Lucy asked suspiciously. 'Mr Rob's still asleep upstairs.'

'I'd had enough,' was all he said, going through to the kitchen and pouring ale.

She followed him, and stood with her thin arms folded. 'Have you found out who did all that at the school yet?'

'No.' The word came out clipped, abrupt, showing his frustration. He looked at her apologetically but her gaze was stony.

'When I was in town this morning for some errands, people were talking about the workhouse opening,' Lucy continued.

'It might,' he allowed.

'What's going to happen to all those children?' she asked angrily. She'd been one of them, with no home, scavenging for food where she could, staying hidden from sight to keep alive another day. Then he'd taken her on as a servant and she'd blossomed. But part of her would never quite leave the past behind.

'The city will want them in there,' he said. 'The same with the folk by the river.'

'It's not right.' She was on the edge of tears.

'I know that.' He rubbed his face and shook his head. 'Believe me. But it's not my decision.'

'You're the Constable,' she accused him. 'Can't you do something about it?'

'It's up to the Corporation,' he explained. He knew how weak his reply sounded.

'You can try!' she blazed and went out into the garden, letting the door slam behind her. He sighed and ran a hand through his hair. Over his head he heard footsteps on the floorboards; Rob was awake and dressing. A few minutes later he appeared, yawning as he tore off some bread and cut a piece of cheese.

'You're back early, boss.'

'We're not getting anywhere. No one knows anything.'

'Something will break soon,' Rob said confidently. 'It has to.'

'Maybe.' He didn't feel so certain.

'I'm going to meet Emily.'

Rob pushed the last of the cheese into his mouth and left. The Constable stood for a few moments, then went into the garden. Lucy was on her knees, pulling furiously at weeds around the onions.

'I'm doing what I can to stop the workhouse,' he told her.

'Will you win?' she asked bluntly and he couldn't give her an answer, certainly not the one she wanted. She stood, brushing the dirt from the front of her dress. She'd grown in the months since she'd arrived at the house but she was still a head and a half smaller than him. 'Back when were young and lived out there, would you have gone into the workhouse?'

'No,' he replied without hesitation. However hard it was, he'd loved his freedom then. He'd seen people starve, lost to violence and desperation, but he couldn't have imagined it otherwise. 'Would you?'

'Maybe during that bad winter,' she allowed. 'But I'd have hated it. Please,' she urged, 'do what you can, Mr Nottingham.'

SIXTEEN

Rob stood in the kitchen, draining a mug of ale and wiping up the remaining crumbs of yesterday's bread with his finger. The night had seemed to drag on and on, with little trouble beyond a pair of drunks pulled from the river before they could drown. He'd walked by the school every hour, checking the place and the men he'd set to watch it now the husbands had stopped spending their nights out there. Now, back in the house on Marsh Lane, he was waiting for Emily, hearing the sound of her footsteps on the floorboards above. Late again, she was dashing around.

Lucy set the bread dough for its second rise, covered the bowl with a piece of linen, and pushed one of last year's apples over to him.

'If you're still hungry, eat that,' she said. 'There'll be nothing hot until later.'

He smiled and took a bite. The sweetness of the fruit was long gone, but it was something to put in his belly after work. Finally he heard Emily rush down the stairs.

'I thought you wanted to be early today.'

'We will be,' she told him. 'Don't worry, there's plenty of time.'

'The hour rang ten minutes ago,' he reminded her. At this rate the girls and their mothers would be milling around outside the place again when they arrived.

They hurried into Leeds, almost running over Timble Bridge then cutting through the churchyard to the Calls. Some of the women were already gathered by the school. He saw them clutching their daughters tight, the stiff, wary way they all stood and the looks of concern on their face.

'Wait here,' he said to Emily, and broke into a run. The women moved back as he approached.

'What's happened?' he asked.

'Someone's forced it,' one of them told him. He glanced and saw the broken lock, the wood splintered around it. 'Stay back,' he ordered, drawing his knife.

With one swift movement he pushed the door back all the way to the wall, letting it bang against the plaster. He entered carefully, glancing around the room. There was no one inside. The floor was covered in paper, torn, cut, a sea of it around his boots.

The women flooded in behind him, ignoring his instructions. Emily pushed through them to stand next to him. He heard her wordless cry, then she was on her knees, scrabbling in a box in the corner. It had arrived the afternoon before, filled with new books for the girls. Now all that remained inside were the empty covers. She sat back and looked up at him hopelessly. 'Why?' she asked. 'Why is someone doing this to us?'

The women and girls were kneeling, too, starting to gather the pages. Rob bent, picked up a leaf and stared at it, not seeing the words. How had this happened? Ericson had been across the street at three o'clock when he'd come by here and checked the handle himself. An hour later folk would have been up, ready to be off to their work. Anyone trying to get in should have been spotted. There'd be no putting these books back together; all they were good for now was the fire.

Slowly, Emily roused herself, saying nothing as she worked with the others, trying to restore order to the room. But he kept staring at her face as despair quickly turned to sad defiance then fury.

Finally the floor was clear. He stood, reaching out to help her to her feet.

'I'm not closing the school,' she announced to everyone, her face set, her voice firm. 'If that's what someone wants, I'm not going to do it.'

The women murmured their approval.

'We'll not let them, love, don't you worry,' a voice said from the back.

'Thank you.' Emily smiled, breathed slowly and turned to Rob. 'I'm going to send someone for the locksmith. I still have the money Mrs Williamson gave me, that'll pay for the repair.' She reached out and took his hand. 'We'll be fine now.'

'But they'll have their husbands out again,' he protested. 'Whoever did this might not come back.'

'Good,' she said, staring hard at him. 'I don't want him back. I don't want any more of this. I'm a teacher. I'm not here to fight battles.'

He nodded. Perhaps the people here could keep a closer watch than his men.

'In God's name, Rob, where was Ericson?' the Constable raged.

Lister looked down at the floor. 'He said he went off to sleep after he'd seen me go round.'

'Christ.' Nottingham banged his fist down on the desk.

'I told him he doesn't have a job any more.'

'If you hadn't I bloody well would have! What about the one on Call Brows? Was he sleeping, too?'

'He didn't see or hear anything, boss.'

The Constable shook his head, beyond words. 'How's Emily?' he asked finally.

'She's angry,' Rob replied. 'Scared, too, but you know what she's like: she's never going to admit that.'

'It's all out in the open now,' Nottingham said with a sigh. 'Everyone knows there's trouble at the school. We'll have to use that to find out who did this.'

'How?' Sedgwick asked. He leaned against the wall, sipping at a mug of ale as he listened. 'We've already been asking. What else can we do?'

'Ask again,' Nottingham ordered, his voice tight with

frustration. 'Press them. Someone will know what's happened. Get them to peach every name they can. Spend the morning on it.'

The deputy nodded. 'Yes, boss.' He put down the cup and left.

'You go home and sleep,' the Constable told Rob.

'I'm going to talk to some people first. This is my fault. Ericson.'

Nottingham softened a little. 'I've hired worthless folk before, too. Don't blame yourself for someone else's failings. Now,' he said through clenched teeth, 'let's find this bugger and make him pay.'

Before the Saturday cloth market Nottingham was on Briggate, moving among the weavers and the merchants. The sky was clear and pale, the sun already warm on his neck. He'd walked along the Calls, stopping to listen to Emily talking to her class, her voice tired and hoarse. The locksmith was already repairing the door, and gave him a quick nod as he passed.

He listened to the noise and laughter around him that ended abruptly with the ringing of the bell. Business began in earnest, the quick whispers and bargaining and the handshakes to finish each deal. He saw it but he paid no attention.

Who? Who had enough hate in them to do something like this? Nottingham glanced at the faces all around, each one absorbed in business. Someone in Leeds had done it, someone had taken his chances. And he had to catch them; he had to protect Emily and the girls in the school. She might have grown into a woman with a man of her own, but she'd always remain his daughter, whose tears he'd wiped away, who'd taken his hand to walk her first few, faltering steps. These days more than ever, he needed to watch over her. But so far he hadn't even managed that properly. Since Mary's death, it seemed, little had gone well for him.

The night before, after Rob left for work, Nottingham had climbed the stairs and tapped lightly on the door of Emily's room. She was sitting at the table, the tallow candle guttering and filling the air with its sour smell. The window was open and the shutters pulled back. In the distance, through the dusk, he could see lights from a few houses and farms. Emily turned and smiled at him. He sat on the bed, running his tongue around inside his mouth.

'You know, Mama would have been so proud of you,' he said after a while.

'I hope so.' Her fingers stroked the feather of the quill pen. 'I think of her up in heaven looking down on us all.'

'She liked Rob,' he continued. 'She always felt you two were a good match.' He watched her blush slightly and took a breath. 'We need to talk about the school.'

'What about the school?' She looked at him quizzically. 'I'm not going to close it.'

'I don't want you to,' Nottingham said gently, reaching out and placing his hand over hers. 'I'm proud of you, too.'

'Thank you, Papa.'

'But it's my job to make sure people are safe. Everyone in Leeds. You know that. But you especially. You're my family, I don't want anything to happen to you.'

'I know.' She sighed. 'At first, when they left the slate, I was scared. Now I'm angry.' She raised her head, then paused. 'And it makes me sad. I can't understand why someone would want to do something like that.'

'I don't either, love,' he said softly. 'But something I learned a long time ago was that people are strange. You can never really know what's in their minds. I just don't want you or any of the girls hurt.'

She squeezed his hand. 'He won't make me leave,' she said again.

'I know that.' He squeezed back lightly. 'And I'll look after you. Rob, too.'

'Do you think he's mad, whoever's doing this?' Emily asked.

He shook his head. 'We'll find out when we catch him.'

'Do you have any idea . . .?'

'Who's behind it?' He completed her question. 'I wish I did.'

'Papa,' she said slowly, as if the words had been weighing on her mind. 'I know you meant to help when you sent down the glazier and the locksmith.'

'I was being a father. And the Constable.'

'I know.' She bit her lip for a moment. 'But *I* need to be the one who looks after things at the school. People need to see it's *me*. Not my papa, not the Constable.' She smiled, trying to pull the sting from her words. 'I'm glad you did it. Honestly, I am. But please, from now on will you let me send for workmen?'

'Of course,' he promised.

She smiled her gratitude. 'I know you'll find whoever's doing this.'

He tried to grin but it wouldn't reach his eyes. He closed the door, seeing her turn back to the books. In the bedroom he took off his boots and lay back, forcing his eyes to close. Her words had hurt, a pain around his heart. All he'd wanted to do was help, to see things done swiftly and honestly.

He could never look at her without seeing all the people she'd been, the little one who used to charge around the house laughing, the lass who could lose all time in a book, the wilful and the silent. But the world had changed. She'd grown into a woman. A woman who'd always refuse to rely on anyone else. He had to learn that afresh each day, to remember it.

And now there was this.

The hour of the market seemed to pass in a few heartbeats and the bell tolled again. Voices rose, weavers heaving lengths of cloth on to their shoulders to take to the warehouses while workers dismantled the trestles to carry them to the other market at the top of the street.

'Thinking, Richard?' Tom Williamson said.

'I am,' he answered with a frown. 'A good profit this morning?'

'If I'm lucky I might make a little money,' he answered cautiously. It was an understatement; Nottingham knew full well that the merchant had become one of the most successful in Leeds, forward-thinking and starting to bring in good money from the American colonies.

'Someone broke into the school last night,' the Constable told him.

Shock spread over Williamson's face. 'Good God. Was there much damage?'

'Enough. All those books you paid for were all destroyed.'

'What?' he asked in horror, and the only reply Nottingham could offer was a shake of his head. 'I'll send Hannah a note; maybe she can help. Do you have any idea at all who's doing it?'

'I've been asking. Have you heard anyone saying anything against the place?'

'The school? No one.'

'How about people objecting to educating the poor?'

'It's not something they really talk about.' Williamson said, and the Constable knew he was right. 'Mind you, I did hear Walter Mitchell, you know him, Larkin's factor, say something,' the merchant continued. 'He didn't think there was any need, all they'd ever do was work as drudges, anyway.' He shrugged. 'But a few of us had shared some bottles of wine. I doubt he meant anything.'

'Mitchell?' Nottingham was struggling to bring the man's face to mind. 'Is he young, brawny?'

'That's the one. He's always loud after a few drinks. But I know him, Richard,' the merchant protested. 'There's no real harm in the man. He wouldn't do anything.'

'Someone did,' the Constable pointed out. 'I think I'll talk to Mr Mitchell.'

Williamson raised his hands. 'It's your business. But you'll be wasting your time.'

'We'll see,' Nottingham said. 'Any more word on the workhouse?'

'I'm still going through the figures Mr Finer gave me.' He hesitated for a moment. 'It's exactly as I told you, so far everything he's proposing makes sense.'

'Keep looking. You have to keep looking.'

'I will, I promise,' the merchant agreed. 'But I have to keep my mind open.'

The Constable nodded. 'Of course. Thank you.'

'And Richard, please don't tell Walter Mitchell you heard anything from me.'

Larkin's warehouse was behind his house on Briggate, a large, old stone building. The heat hit the Constable as he walked in, the heavy smell of wool tickling his throat.

Mitchell had rolled out a length of cloth he'd bought at the market to inspect it closely for flaws. He'd thrown his coat over a table and unbuttoned his elaborate waistcoat. His breeches were covered with dust from the fabric. He glanced up and waved Nottingham over to a desk to wait.

The factor took his time, picking here and there at the wool until he was satisfied and nodded to the workers to roll it up again. He rubbed at his clothes, poured himself a mug of ale and came over to the Constable.

'You chose a bad time,' he said bluntly. 'You ought to know Tuesdays and Saturdays are always busy.'

'My apologies.' Nottingham kept his voice genial. Mitchell was an imposing figure, fully six feet tall with broad shoulders and heavy arms. He'd taken off his periwig to show hair cropped close against the skull. A thin scar ran from his mouth to his chin, leaving his face with a twisted, sinister look.

'What do you need, Constable? I've got too much to do here.'

'Where were you last night, Mr Mitchell?'

The factor's eyed narrowed. 'Last night? I was at home, in my bed. Where the hell do you think I'd be?'

'Can anyone attest to that?' Nottingham asked calmly.

'Of course they can. My wife was right there next to me and the servant saw me out this morning,' he replied brusquely. 'What's this about, anyway?'

'There was damage at my daughter's school last night.'

The factor looked at him uncomprehendingly then began to laugh loud enough for the workers to stop and stare. 'You think I was responsible?'

'Were you?' The Constable asked evenly.

'For God's sake, don't be a bloody fool.' He dismissed the idea in a moment. 'Why would I want to do something like that?'

'I hear you don't feel the poor should be educated.'

'Of course I don't. Waste of time.' His face cleared as he understood. 'Tom Williamson been peaching on me, has he? I knew you two were close.' He leaned forward, spreading his large hands on the desk. 'Let me tell you something, Mr Nottingham, and I'm not going to repeat it. You're right, I don't think there's any sense in giving education to the poor. They won't use it. But that's as far as I go. Is that clear enough for you?'

'Perfectly, Mr Mitchell.'

'Then some of us have work to do. You don't need to come back here.' He strode away, yelling an order to one of the men who scurried to obey.

Outside, the Constable drew in a breath, the warm air welcome. He believed the factor; there was nothing false about his outrage. He walked down Briggate, ignoring all the clamour of the market, crossed the bridge and slipped through the streets to a neat house that stood out from its neighbours, the windows shining, the paint on the door bright and glossy.

The big man who answered his knock had skin so black it almost seemed blue in the sunlight. He smiled, displaying a full set of white teeth.

'Mr Nottingham. Good to see thee,' he said, his Leeds accent as broad as any the Constable had ever heard. 'Come on in. He's in the parlour.'

'Thank you, Henry. You look well.'

'Aye, grand weather always brings out the best in me.'

Joe Buck was seated at his desk working through his accounts, dressed as elegantly as ever in a coat and breeches of the best silk with silver buckles on his shoes. Fine enough for royalty if they should ever drop by, the Constable thought, and a reminder of the good money the man made fencing stolen goods.

'You look like a man with a hundred cares and nowhere to put them,' Buck told him.

'Maybe I am, Joe. I feel that way,' Nottingham admitted wearily. 'You know my daughter runs a school.'

'Of course I do. I've heard nothing but good things about it.'

'In the last few days the windows have been broken, she's been threatened and last night someone destroyed all the books there.' He counted the incidents out on his fingers and looked at Buck. 'What do you make of that?'

'I'd say someone doesn't like the place,' the fence said slowly.

'I need your help.'

'I haven't heard a whisper. But I'll put the word out for you.'

'Thank you.'

'Your lass, how is she?'

'She's angry,' he replied. 'So am I, Joe. I want whoever's doing this.'

'I'll see what I can find out,' Buck promised. 'I'm glad you came, though, I was going to send you a note.'

'Oh?'

'I hear Tom Finer's back in Leeds.'

'You heard right.'

'He used to be a nasty piece of work, by all accounts.'

'More than you'd want to know. He and Amos, they made a real pair.'

'I hope you're keeping an eye on him, Mr Nottingham.'

'I'm doing that, Joe. Why, are you worried he might want to go back into the stolen goods business?'

'From what folk have been telling me, I wouldn't trust him as far as I could throw him.'

'I wouldn't either. But you know me, Joe. I don't trust anyone. Whatever you hear about the school, I want to know. I'd be grateful.'

'You will, Mr Nottingham. I promise.'

SEVENTEEN

R ob wandered through the inns and alehouses along Briggate. The weavers were enjoying a final drink before putting goods on their packhorses and starting back to their villages. Some were happy, with a better price than they'd expected weighing down their pockets. Others sat sullen, jingling fewer coins than they'd hoped, or left with a length of unsold cloth.

Most of the faces he knew in Leeds were the ones who came out at night, and there weren't many of those around at this hour. Finally he spotted Matthew, tucked in a corner at the Turk's Head, an empty cup on the table in front of him. He worked moving cloth to warehouses after the market, a few coins to keep him going until something else came along.

Rob bought a mug of ale and carried it over.

'You look like a man with a thirst,' he said, seeing the hunger for drink in the man's eye as he glanced up.

'Aye, thank you, Mr Lister, I could reet do with that.' His

hand snaked out for the mug and he took a long sip. He was perhaps thirty, his beard and hair stringy, most of his teeth gone, dressed in clothes that were more holes and hope than material.

'You know about the school on the Calls?'

'Aye,' Matthew replied, his eyes unfocused, fist tight around the ale.

'Do you know anyone who wants it gone?'

The man turned his head slowly. 'Gone? What's tha' mean?'

'Someone's been damaging the place at night.'

Matthew pursed thin lips and shook his head. 'Nowt I know.'

As Lister made to stand up, the man added quietly, 'Get thisen to Leviticus Holt. Seen him creeping round all hours of dark.'

Rob knew Holt, a small, vicious man who took strange ideas into his head. It was possible, he thought.

'Where's he staying now?'

'Don't know,' Matthew answered. 'I keep out of his road.'

It was the sensible way; there was no knowing when Holt would turn on someone. Most kept their distance, wary of his odd, unpredictable ways.

He tried other places along the street, but heard nothing of use in the answers or the gossip. Finally he gave up, leaning wearily against a wall, the sun hot on his face.

'You'll get no work done like that.'

He opened his eyes and saw the deputy loping towards him.

'If I stay here much longer I'll be asleep.'

'Go on home, then. Found anything?'

'Someone suggested Leviticus Holt.'

'Aye,' Sedgwick nodded his agreement. 'I wouldn't put it past him if he has it in his mind. I'll find him.'

'Good luck.'

'Catch him early enough and he'll be sober. He's harmless then.'

Lister pushed himself upright. 'I'll leave him to you.' He waved an arm lazily and walked away.

Leviticus Holt, the deputy mused. It made more sense than any other name else he'd heard. There was a streak of madness in the man. He hoarded his grievances the way a miser held his coins. The last he knew, Holt had a room at the bottom of the Head Row in one of the old houses the city kept threatening to tear down.

He brought the cudgel from his coat as he entered the place, looping the thong around his wrist. The stairs felt fragile under his boots as he went down to the cellar, one hand against the wall to steady himself.

The door was unlocked and he pushed it open, letting in a few glimmers of light. Holt was asleep on an old pallet. The room stank of stale sweat and the old piss that overflowed from a bucket in the corner. There was nothing else, no table or chair, no clothes hanging from nails on the wall.

Sedgwick tightened his grip on the stick and pushed his boot against Holt's leg.

'Wake up, you bugger,' he said loudly.

For a moment there was nothing more than the thick rasp of breathing, then Holt sprang up quickly, one hand going for the knife in his belt, a snarl on his lips. The deputy brought the wood down hard on the man's thick wrist, making him cry out.

'You didn't ought to have done that,' Holt said, doubling over and cradling his arm.

'Try that again, I'll break the bloody bone,' Sedgwick warned him. 'And then I'll haul you off to the jail. Is that what you want, Leviticus?'

The man glared, rubbing his bruised arm. 'I think you already broke it.'

'Don't be so daft, that was nothing more than a love tap. You'd know if I meant it.'

'What you want?' the man demanded.

'Where were you last night?'

Holt chuckled. 'Drinking, where else?'

'Where?'

'Talbot, Old King's Head.' He shrugged. 'I don't remember.'

'And after?'

'Came back here. I was sleeping until some bastard woke me,' he complained.

'What about the damage you did to the school on the Calls?'

'What school?' Holt asked in confusion.

'The one Emily Nottingham runs.'

The man shook his head. 'Don't know it.'

'I don't believe you.'

'Honest.' Holt's eyes were wide, his breath full of ale. 'I don't know no school.'

The deputy stared at him then stepped back slowly. The man was telling the truth. He'd probably never even heard of the place, let alone done anything to it.

'Go back to sleep,' he said.

Nothing. He blew out a long breath when he was back in the sunlight, tucked the cudgel away and inhaled deeply to clear away the heady stench of the cellar. Whoever had done all this was staying very quiet.

By the time he reached the Calls he'd stripped off the coat, carrying it over his shoulder. Even then he could feel the sweat under his arms and damp on the back of his shirt.

A knot of women had gathered across from the school. As he tried to pass one of them recognized him.

'You're the Constable's deputy,' she said, the words coming out as an accusation.

'Aye, that's me, love,' he said with a smile and a wink.

'What are you doing about that?' she asked, glancing to where the locksmith was finishing work on the door.

'Everything we can.'

'Not enough, though, is it?' another woman pointed out accusingly. 'You let that happen last night.'

'If you know who did it, tell me,' Sedgwick told her.

'If we knew that we'd string the bastard up ourselves,' the woman answered, staring directly at him. 'You should be out looking, not coming by here. You'd think the Constable would want to look after his own daughter.'

'We can't watch everywhere night and day,' he pointed out.

'Aye, well, you won't have to,' she said. 'We're going to have our men out here again and God help anyone they find.'

'If they catch anyone, make sure they hand him over to us,' the deputy warned her.

'We'll see. If you can't do your job, we'll do it for you,' she said.

'No, love, you won't,' he answered firmly. 'I don't want to

have to drag your man off for murder. You find anyone, bring them to the jail and let us take care of it.'

'Why should we?' another voice objected. 'You've done bugger all so far.'

He looked at her, a young woman barely turned twenty, hands defiantly on her hips, long, dark hair to her shoulders.

'I mean it. You want to see your man swinging up on Chapeltown Moor?'

'No,' she answered finally.

'Have your men out if you want,' he told them. 'Mr Lister will come around. But no drinking and no trouble, you understand?' He waited until they'd agreed, then added, 'If you hear any whispers as to who it might be, anything at all, you come and see us.'

It was dark by the time the deputy returned to the house on Lands Lane. As he walked in, Lizzie put a finger to her lips and pointed to the cradle where Isabell lay sleeping.

'She's just gone down, I don't want her awake again.'

He trod lightly across the floor and sat at the table, waiting as she put pottage in a bowl for him.

'Is James finishing his homework?'

'He's asleep, too,' she said. 'Went to his bed as soon as he'd eaten.'

'Is anything wrong?' he asked.

'He's just growing, John. They have times like that.'

'What about this one?'

She smiled. 'She's been full of this and that all day. Slept a little earlier on, then she wore herself out again.'

'Aye, I know that feeling,' he laughed. 'Except for the sleep. I could use some of that myself.'

It had been dinnertime before he'd been able to give any attention to finding Jem Carter's killer. Throughout the afternoon the deputy had gone from thief to thief, from men to women, the bold and the furtive. By the end of it he was no wiser. None of them had seen the man on his final night.

He'd finished with a welcome drink in the White Swan, wondering if the boss would come by. The place was full of workmen enjoying the end of their week, ready to cool themselves with a mug or two of ale before going home.

Talking led to a second cup, then a third, and a conversation with a diffident man seated in a corner away from the door. Sedgwick knew him by sight, a night watchman at the water engine down by Leeds Bridge, about to leave for his work.

He might have seen something on the Tuesday, he allowed.

'Big man, you said, fair hair?' he asked.

'That's the one.'

'The one I saw were big enough, fair hair on him, but he must have been drunk. The one he were with was bigger. He were holding him up.'

'How late was this?' the deputy asked, keeping his voice under control, trying not to sound too eager.

'After two. I were out having a piss and a walk.' He packed the clay pipe away in the pocket of his coat and stood. 'I'll be late if I don't get a move on. You want more I'll be done at eight in the morning.'

After that Sedgwick had drunk up and gone back to the house on Lands Lane.

'The day's over, John,' Lizzie said now, rubbing the back of his hand. He'd eaten the food she'd made, his belly was full and he had his family around him. 'You can stop thinking about it for a while.'

'Aye,' he agreed with a sigh. 'Let it go until tomorrow.' He looked down at the little girl, her head to one side, eyelids moving as she dreamed. 'How long before she wakes?'

'Hours, I hope.'

'And James is asleep?'

'Yes.'

'Been too long since we had time to ourselves.'

Her lips curled into a smile. 'What did you have in mind, John Sedgwick?'

'Just something to ease our minds a little.'

'I've no idea what you mean, sir,' she said coyly.

'Happen I'd better show you, then,' he winked.

EIGHTEEN

He woke early, the way he always did, sliding out of bed without waking Lizzie or disturbing James on his pallet. He found bread and the remains of some cheese, and scraped away the mould with his knife. That and some ale, it was a breakfast for a king.

The morning air was warm, another hot day in the making, and he left his stock loose as he walked to the jail. Rob was there, sitting back in the chair, the night report complete and waiting on the desk.

'Nothing more at the school?' Sedgwick asked.

'Everything's quiet. I checked every hour.' Lister stood and stretched.

'How's Emily?'

'Quiet,' he said after a moment. 'She's terrified, but she'd never admit it.'

'If I were a lass and someone was doing that to me, I'd be scared, too. What about the rest of it? Busy night?'

Lister shrugged. 'Saturday night, hot weather.' He lifted his hand to show the cuts on his knuckles. 'You know what it's like. Always some who want to show what they can do.'

'Many in the cells?'

'Just five, the worst of them. It's all written down ready for the Petty Sessions tomorrow.'

'I'm worried about the boss,' the deputy said. 'This business at the school's all he can think about now.'

'Do you blame him? It's his own daughter.'

'Aye, true,' he said doubtfully. The Constable hadn't been himself since his wife had died. Only to be expected, but there were still crimes that had to be solved. 'Anyway, I might have something on Jem Carter's murder.'

'Oh? What's that?'

'Someone I was talking to yesterday. I'm seeing him again this morning. If it's anything I'll tell you. You'd best get yourself home and all prettied up for church.' He looked at the lad's strained, careworn face and grinned. 'Mind you, from the look of you there might never be enough time for that.'

He checked on the men still sleeping off their ale and bruises in the cells, then started on his rounds. The clock struck six, already full light. Another two hours and maybe he'd have something useful from the night watchman. Then the boss would have to pay attention.

The deputy walked along Vicar Lane, then up the hill of the Head Row before returning down Briggate. A few folk were out, those who had jobs even on the Sabbath, trudging along wearily. He felt a spring in his step, the warmth and joy of the weather as he slipped into Currie Entry.

The blow exploded against the back of his head and sent him sprawling to his knees. Before he could move he was being kicked hard. Sedgwick struggled to open his eyes, but they wouldn't do what he wanted. As he started to reach for his knife a heel came down hard on his hand and he felt searing pain as the bones broke.

The deputy tried to curl into a ball, but the boots were relentless, on his body and his face. He tasted blood in his mouth and felt it gushing from his nose. He tried to push himself away, across the ground, but the boots and blows followed, each kick hard and vicious, never letting up until the blackness came and he knew nothing more.

People fade from memory, Nottingham thought as he lay in the darkness. The shutters were open wide to let in some sweet, cool night air and he breathed deeply, thinking of those he had loved and lost, trying to summon their images in his mind. Mary, Rose, his mother, even Amos Worthy, as much friend as foe.

Mary's face was fixed clear; he still saw it every day in quiet corners, still talked to her. But the others . . . now, when he tried to imagine them, their features were like old ink on paper, faded, hard to make out, the details gone, edges blurred.

He stretched out his arm across the bed and his fingers sketched out the shape her body would have made. Finally sleep claimed him, taking him into dreams that vanished with the morning, leaving only the sense of loss that came with every day.

* * *

The Constable walked down Marsh Lane with Lucy on his arm, Emily and Rob a few yards behind. The bell at the Parish Church was pealing for morning service as they crossed Timble Bridge. The sound of running footsteps made him glance up and he saw Bob Holden pounding down Kirkgate towards them.

'You'd better come quick, boss. It's Mr Sedgwick.'

The Constable looked at Emily and Lucy. 'Go in by yourselves,' he said, and began to race up the street with Rob close behind.

'What happened?' Nottingham asked.

'I don't know,' Holden answered, breathing hard. 'One of the men saw him on the rounds but he didn't come to the jail and tell us what to do. I sent them out looking for him.'

'Where is he?'

'Currie Entry. He looks bad, boss.'

Most of the day men were gathered around, muttering and trying to avoid looking. The Constable pushed through them, knelt by Sedgwick and put his fingertips against the man's neck. There was a pulse; he was alive. But there was plenty of blood on the flagstones around his head, his eyes were swollen shut, and the man's right hand was a mass of crumpled bone and flesh.

'Get the stretcher and send for the apothecary,' he ordered quickly.

'Already done it, boss,' Holden said quietly.

Nottingham stared down at the face, feeling the man barely breathing. Christ, he thought. 'I want everyone out. Rouse the night men, too, Rob. Ask questions. I need to know who saw him this morning. Anything at all. Understood?'

He pushed himself upright and turned to Holden. 'Have him carried home. I'll go and see Lizzie now.'

'Yes, boss.'

'He was supposed to meet someone who had information on Jem Carter's murder,' Rob said.

'Who?'

'He didn't tell me the name.'

'Find him.' He raised his voice. 'You're in charge for now. I'll be at the jail in a while.' He raised his voice. 'I want whoever did this and I want him today. There's a guinea for whoever brings him in.' And he strode away quickly, his face set and hard.

He could hear voices inside, Lizzie's and James's, playing a game of some kind. He knocked and there was sudden silence. Then Lizzie opened the door.

'Mr Nottingham,' she began, a question in her voice, wondering why he'd come. Then she understood and her face began to crumple, hand rising to cover her mouth, the other going to her belly as if she'd just been struck. She began to moan and he moved forward, holding her tightly as she started to shake.

'He's alive, Lizzie,' he said gently. 'He's alive.'

She pulled away from him, tears pouring down her cheeks, and her hand reached out for James. The boy looked up at him without a word.

'They're bringing him back here,' the Constable continued, keeping his voice calm.

She was gulping for air and he helped her on to the bench. Isabell was still asleep in her crib. Nottingham knelt down in front of Lizzie.

'I don't know how bad it is,' he told her. 'The apothecary will be here and he's going to do everything he can.'

'How?' she asked, barely able to speak the word. 'What happened?'

'I don't know yet.' He took her hand again. 'He's going to need plenty of care. A bed down here.' Nottingham stared at her until she nodded, then he turned to James. 'You'll need to be very grown up while your da's sick.'

'Yes, sir,' the boy answered. His eyes were wide.

'Do everything your mam tells you, understand?'

'I will, sir.' He could tell that the lad didn't understand what was going on, that he was scared and trying to be brave.

'Good.' Nottingham smiled and tousled James's hair. 'Lizzie,' he said, and repeated her name to pull her out of her thoughts. 'We're going to find whoever did this. I promise. And we'll have John back on his feet before you know it.'

He prayed it was true, that the injuries were no worse than they appeared. He'd seen men look as bad as that before and be back to work within a month. But there was no saying what else might be wrong.

'I'll come back later,' he told her. 'If there's anything you need, anything at all, let me know and I'll make sure you have it.'

She nodded numbly. She'd heard the words. Whether she'd taken them in was another matter. He pressed her hand lightly then left to walk quickly back to the jail.

He found Lucy waiting outside. 'Where's Emily?' he asked her.

'She stayed for the service with a friend of hers. I heard what happened to Mr Sedgwick.'

He unlocked the door and she followed him in.

'Is it all over town?' he asked.

'Must be by now. Is he going to live?'

'I don't know,' Nottingham answered bleakly. 'I hope so.'

'Where have they taken him?'

'Home.' He didn't need these questions now, not when he was trying to think, to start the hunt for John's attacker.

'Who's going to look after those little ones?' Lucy persisted. He hadn't even considered it; his thoughts hadn't gone that far.

'Mr Nottingham.' She stood directly in front of him as he tried to pace, making him pay attention. 'If he's as bad as that, she's going to have her hands full. She won't be able to take care of the bairns as well.'

It was true, he realized. The deputy was going to need all Lizzie's care and time.

'I'm going over there,' Lucy decided.

He nodded. It was exactly what Mary would have done: given help where she could.

'Stay as long as she needs you,' he said. 'Rob and I won't be seeing much of home until we find who did this.' He paused, then added, 'When the apothecary's examined Mr Sedgwick, will you ask him to come here?'

'Yes. Keep someone watching the school, too,' she said. 'Please.'

And she was gone.

He sat at the desk, trying to think who'd attack the deputy. The list was long, men he'd arrested, men he'd questioned and pushed for information. But he'd go through every one of them and more to find who'd done it, and he'd make sure the culprit swung from the gallows.

Outside people were passing, the cheery talk of families making their way back from the churches, but he paid them little mind. All he could do was wait for some word, anything, from someone.

When the door opened, the Constable looked up expectantly. It was the apothecary, Leadhall, a youthful man who'd taken over when the old one died three months before.

'How is he?' Nottingham asked. His mouth was dry and he gripped the chair tightly.

'Bad.' The man put his heavy leather bag on the desk and sighed. 'Very bad. He could die.'

'Die?' The word seemed to fill the room.

John couldn't die.

NINETEEN

'He hasn't woken yet. I don't know what damage there is inside his body.' Leadhall began to list the injuries. 'His nose has been smashed hard, his jaw's broken, several ribs gone. His right hand's ruined. Even if he lives, I doubt he'll ever use it properly again. He's bruised all over and it looks like his skull's cracked where he was hit with something.'

'What do you think?' Nottingham asked seriously.

'I don't know,' the apothecary answered finally. 'That was a brutal beating he took. Even if he lives he won't be the same person. He might not be able to walk again or do anything for himself.' He shrugged helplessly. 'Maybe dying would be a blessing.'

The Constable ran a hand through his hair.

'I'll go back and see him this evening,' Leadhall continued. 'I've told them to send word if he wakes.'

'Thank you.'

He felt empty, the numbness rising inside. He knew it had

been severe, but he'd never expected this. Nottingham looked around the room, not sure he could imagine the place without the deputy as part of it. People died, God alone knew how he wore that pain, but John . . . it didn't seem possible.

He was still thinking when Rob bustled in.

'Everyone's out and looking, boss. A few remember hearing someone running early on but no one saw anything.'

'I'll be out with you soon,' he said bleakly.

'How's John? What did Leadhall say?'

'He could die.'

'Die?' The word seemed to halt him. 'But—'

'At the very least he might never work again.'

'Jesus.' Rob hissed the word.

'For right now you're my deputy. Put your best man in charge of the nights.' The Constable could feel his heart beating fast, his palms were slick and damp.

'Yes, boss.'

'Who had John seen lately, who had he talked to?'

'I know he went to see Leviticus Holt yesterday.'

'I'll talk to him. Get every name you can, go and see them. Do whatever you have to do. I want answers on this.'

'Yes.'

'Lucy's gone to help Lizzie. I don't want Emily staying in the house on her own.'

Rob thought for a moment. 'What about the Williamsons?'

The Constable nodded. 'Good idea. I'll send Tom Williamson a note. I still want you escorting her to and from the school, and I want to keep someone on Call Brows at night. The women have their men out on the Calls.'

'Yes, boss.'

Nottingham pushed his way into the tumbling old house and down the stairs. Before he entered the room he pulled out the cudgel, then he stormed in and dragged Holt out of his bed on to the floor.

The man tried to rise but the Constable held him down, pressing a boot on his chest.

'Someone attacked Mr Sedgwick this morning,' he said.

'So?'

'He was talking to you yesterday.'

'Aye, the bastard.'

Nottingham put more weight behind his boot. 'Maybe you wanted some revenge.'

'Nay, not me.'

'Tell me why I should believe you, Leviticus?'

'I were here, sleeping, same as I were when you came.'

The man's eyes told the truth. Holt could be violent but he'd never been able to lie well.

Nottingham moved back. 'You hear anything about what happened, anything at all, you come and tell me.'

Back at the jail he read Williamson's reply to his note. The merchant and his wife would be pleased to have Emily to stay. Underneath, the man pledged his help to catch Sedgwick's attacker, anything he could do.

He strode out for home, hoping his daughter would agree to the idea readily. He didn't have the time to argue with her. Every minute mattered. When he unlocked the door he found her reading, a pile of books beside her chair. As soon as she saw him she stood, her face heavy with worry.

'Papa, how's Mr Sedgwick?'

'He's been badly hurt. We don't really know more than that yet. Lucy's gone to help Lizzie.' She nodded her understanding. 'I've asked Tom Williamson if you can stay there until this is all over.'

'Papa—' she began, but he cut her off.

'I don't want you staying here on your own,' he insisted. 'Not when someone's been damaging the school.' He could hear how anxious he sounded, the desperation in his tone. 'Please.'

'Yes, Papa.'

Five minutes later she was ready, everything she needed in a small bag. He hurried her along the way, grateful for one weight off his mind but needing to return to work, to catch whoever had done this.

The house had belonged to the merchant's father, and his grandfather before that; it wasn't so grand on the outside, but Hannah Williamson had spent good money on decorations, the thick Turkey carpet spread across the parlour, the delicate wooden chairs and the portraits on the walls. It was only

moments before Williamson came through, his wife behind
him, ready to take Emily off to her room.

'Nothing yet, Richard?' Williamson asked once they were
alone.

'No. We'll find him.' His voice sounded dead.

'I talked to some of the aldermen at church. If there's
anything you need, more men, more money, you only have to
ask. The city won't tolerate this.'

'Thank you.'

'And we'll look after Emily for you, don't worry.'

The Constable walked the length of Currie Entry from Briggate
to Call Lane. The sun had dried the blood into a dark patch,
almost black against the flagstones. A heavy branch lay on the
ground by the end of the street. He picked it up and examined
it, looking around to see if it had come from one of the trees
beyond the wall in Alderman Atkinson's garden. He saw the
colour at one end and sniffed it.

It was easy to imagine someone using the wood hard on
John's head, then beating him to oblivion. But the knowledge
didn't help at all. He stood, trying to picture it in his head.
Who? Who?

'Boss.' The word dragged him back into the warm sun. Rob
stood in front of him.

'What have you found?'

'Someone spotted a man running up Call Lane towards
Kirkgate.'

'Any description?'

'Nothing useful. Big, dark hair, dark coat. They weren't
really paying attention.'

'Have the men work along Kirkgate and Vicar Lane. See if
anyone else noticed him.'

'Yes, boss.'

'When you've done that, meet me at the jail.'

By the time Lister arrived, Nottingham had the swords out,
one lying on the desk, the other buckled around his waist.

'Where are we going?' Rob asked.

'To see King Davy. That description, it could be him,' the
Constable replied. 'He's worth a visit, anyway. We had him

in last week and he was insulting Lizzie.' He indicated the weapon. 'If he gives any problems don't be afraid to use that.'

King lodged in Mrs Crowther's house in Queen Charlotte's Court, as slovenly a place as the Constable had ever been in, dirt in the corners, the sheet on the bed rarely changed from one year to the next. They marched there side by side, neither of them speaking. As they passed the workhouse Nottingham noticed the piles of rubbish outside the building, as if men had already begun work there. It was something for another day; he had more urgent matters to deal with now.

Mrs Crowther was just as he remembered her. Heavier, perhaps, although it was hard to tell; she'd always been a big woman. As she spoke she rubbed the bruise on her cheek.

'He done this to me. Rushed in this morning, put what he had in a bag and hit me when I told him I wanted what he owed me.'

'Which room?' Nottingham asked, glancing quickly at Rob.

'Top of the stairs on the left. When you find him, I want that money,' she shouted at his back. 'It were three shilling and threepence.'

He kicked open the door. The room was empty, the shutters wide, letting in the sun. It stank of sweat and piss; the chamber pot in the corner was close to overflowing. A rat scuttled across the floor and disappeared into the wainscoting. King had gone.

'How long ago was he here?'

The woman shrugged, the flesh on her arms wobbling. 'Two hour. Three. I don't know.'

'How did he seem when he was here? Was there blood on him?'

'There was summat on his boots,' she answered after a moment. 'I don't know what it were.'

'Sounds like it's him, boss,' Rob said when they were back outside.

'It does,' Nottingham replied grimly.

'He could have run off by now.'

'Not Davy,' the Constable said with a certainty that surprised him. 'He wouldn't have a clue where to go. I doubt he's ever been outside Leeds in his whole life. Have the men talk to his drinking friends. And make sure they go in pairs. Davy's not going to come easily.'

He heard the lad run off and stood, thinking. King Davy. A beating was his way. But where would he hide? Where would he feel safe? Where would he run?

TWENTY

B y evening they'd visited everyone who knew King. None of them had seen him since the night before. He'd been out until late, drinking in the dram shops, spending his pay like he had a pocket full of money. After that he'd gone off by himself. The Constable would have the night men question the whores later; maybe he'd been with one of them.

Nottingham sat in the jail, sharing a jug and bread with Rob. Any minute he expected the deputy to walk in grinning, with his hunger and his thirst and his easy laugh. But that wouldn't happen. It might never happen again.

He couldn't stand to lose someone else. He relied on John; these last months, when his mind was so often fogged and distracted, he'd needed him more than ever. He wasn't just a deputy, he was a friend, someone he'd trusted with his life.

'I'll go over and see him in a minute,' the Constable said. He ran his hands down his cheeks, trying to rub away the exhaustion.

'I'll come with you.'

'Stay here. Someone has to look after things. You can go later. I daresay they won't be getting any sleep there, either.' He stood, feeling his bones ache. 'Keep the men out all the time. Any sign of Davy, I want them shouting. And I want to know.'

'Yes, boss.'

Dusk was close, darkness just beginning to hem in on the horizon, but the air felt thick and warm as he walked up Lands Lane to knock on the door. For the briefest moment he was surprised to be facing Lucy, then he remembered.

The deputy lay on a bed of straw that had been hastily pushed together, an old sheet thrown over the top. Lizzie sat on a stool by his side, clutching his left hand, the undamaged one.

Nottingham put a hand lightly on her shoulder and she looked up at him.

'Any change?' he asked and she shook her head. He saw the dried tracks of tears down her cheeks and knew she'd cried herself out. 'Has the apothecary been back?'

'A few minutes ago.' Lizzie's voice was dry and hoarse. He took a mug of ale from the table and handed it to her. 'He doesn't know when John will wake up,' she said emptily. 'Have you found who did it yet?'

'Everyone's out looking. It looks like it was King Davy,' he told her, wondering if she knew the name.

'Aye, John's talked about him before.'

There was nothing more he could do. He felt like an intruder, prowling on the edges of private grief.

'I'll come back in the morning,' he said into the silence. 'Rob will be by later.'

The Constable went up and down Briggate. It was Sunday evening, the inns all closed for the Sabbath, but he banged on the doors until the landlords answered. He passed the word: if King Davy came in the next day, he wanted to know immediately. At the Talbot Landlord Bell had seemed reluctant at first.

'I'll put it to you this way,' Nottingham hissed sharply. 'If I find out he's been here and you haven't let me know straight away, this place won't exist the next day. You understand that?' He waited, staring hard at the man until he finally nodded agreement.

On his way he spotted Tom Finer strolling up Briggate. The old man waved and came over to him.

'What is it, Mr Finer?' He didn't try to hide his irritation. 'I don't have time tonight.'

'I'm sorry about your deputy. I hear it's bad.'

'Bad enough. What is it you need?'

'It wouldn't have happened in the old days. I wouldn't have let someone like David King run wild. Neither would Amos.'

The Constable let out a long breath. The old days had gone. 'We'll have him soon.'

'Your men are all over the place, laddie.'

'Do you know where he is, Mr Finer?' That was the only thing that mattered now.

'A few minutes ago someone was telling me about a man they'd seen around the tannery.'

'Then why didn't you say so right away?' Nottingham yelled.

The man looked him in the eye. 'Because a moment or two isn't going to make any difference. Use your common sense, laddie. He'll be looking for somewhere to pass the night unseen.'

The Constable stormed away, back to the jail, anger roaring inside him.

'Gather up as many men as you can in the next quarter hour,' he ordered Rob.

'Do you know where he is?'

'Pray God I do.'

While Lister was gone he removed a pair of pistols from the drawer, loaded and primed them. He pulled the sword from its scabbard and left it fall back in softly. With luck they could take King Davy alive. If not . . . he wouldn't shed tears over the loss.

Rob managed to collect eight of the men. Enough, he thought.

'I've heard that Davy's down in the tannery,' he told them quickly. 'There are two doors. I want four of you round each one. Mr Lister and I will go in. If Davy makes it out, take him.' He paused. 'I don't care how you do it. Remember what he did to Mr Sedgwick.'

He sent them on their way and handed Rob the pistol.

'Use it if you need to.'

But before they could leave, the door opened and a man edged in, eyeing them with curiosity.

'I were supposed to meet that deputy of yours this morning. He here?'

'You can't have heard, Mr . . .?' the Constable asked, glancing at Rob.

'It's Mr Granger, boss,' Lister told him. 'He's the night watch down the water engine. We used to talk sometimes when I saw him.'

'Aye. I'm just on me way there now. He'd said he'd meet me.'

'I'm sorry,' Nottingham told him. 'He's been badly hurt.'

'You're the man with some information about a murder,' Lister interjected.

'Ee, I don't know about that, lad.' Granger removed his hat and scratched at a thinning scalp. 'I just saw summat, that's all. A big lad, looked like he'd had a skinful, being dragged along by another man. The neet that murder happened.'

'Mr Granger,' Rob said, 'we're on our way to arrest the man who attacked Mr Sedgwick.'

'Aye, well.' The night watchman didn't seem satisfied. 'I'll come down to the water engine in the morning and talk to you.'

'That's what he said, too.'

Rob smiled patiently. 'Mr Sedgwick would have come if he could. But one of us will be there in the morning, I promise you.'

'Alreet,' the man agreed reluctantly.

They waited until he'd gone.

'What do you think, boss?'

'I don't think he even took in what's happened to John,' the Constable said. 'Still, he might know something useful. But the morning's a long way off yet. We've plenty to do first.'

The men were assembled by the doors to the tannery. Nottingham spread them out, covered by the darkness, then set off around the building with its choking stink from the piss and shit they used to tan the hides. One of the windows had been forced and he eased himself inside, Rob close behind.

Normally he'd be quiet, try and take his man by surprise. Not this time, though. He wanted King to know he was being hunted. He wanted him full of fear and panic, bolting out where the men could grab him.

'Mr King,' the Constable shouted, hearing the boom of his voice as it echoed around the stone. 'I know you're here. I know you attacked Mr Sedgwick.' He paused, listening for any noise and hearing a faint scrape. He motioned Rob around towards the sound. 'I'll give you one minute.' He stepped forward three paces, his tread heavy and loud.

There was the sound of dashing feet in the distance, then the swift creak of a door and fresh air against his face. Then Nottingham heard a scream. He started to run, blundering his way out into the yard, moonlight showing the silhouettes of men. Someone was on the ground.

'Is it him?' he asked.

'It's Will Daley,' he heard a man answer. 'Davy knifed him.'

'Then get after him,' Nottingham yelled. 'He's not gone far. Find him.'

He put his hand against Daley's neck. Nothing. He turned to see Rob standing on the other side of the body.

'It's Will. You'd better get Mr Brogden down here,' the Constable said quietly. 'And the stretcher.'

'King?'

He nodded towards the trees in the distance. 'He's over there somewhere. The others are after him.'

They sat in the jail sipping ale as the candles threw large shadows around the room.

'I sent the day men home for some rest,' Rob said. 'They'll be back at six.'

The Constable nodded. Daley's body lay in the cold cell, ready for his widow to claim it in the morning. As they'd waited for Brogden the coroner to come and officially pronounce the man dead, Nottingham had gone over everything again and again in his mind. Had he done right to flush King from the building? Yes, he had. King worked at the tannery, he knew every corner, each place to hide. The only way to catch him was outside.

He'd heard the men searching the wood at the top of the hill. But it was so dark there that Davy could have hidden six feet away and they'd never have seen him. When it was light they'd start looking once more.

He pushed the fringe off his forehead and sipped a little more of the drink. They'd said little since returning; conversation seemed pointless. Another man was dead and they still didn't have Davy. And all the responsibility lay with him. He'd been in charge, he'd made the decisions. More guilt to add to the weight on his shoulders. Off in the distance the church bell rang six. Rob stood and opened the shutters, letting in the clear early daylight.

'I'll do the rounds, then take Emily to school,' he said.

'Take the pistol. If you run into King Davy you're going to need it. Then go and see Granger at eight.'

'Yes, boss.'

Alone, Nottingham returned to the cold cell and looked down at the body. Another good man gone, he thought, and prayed that the deputy would recover.

'How's Mr Sedgwick?' Emily asked.

'The same,' Rob answered sadly. 'I went last night.'

'Is there anything I can do to help?'

He shook his head. All they could do was wait and pray.

'What about the man who did it?'

'We haven't caught him yet.' He didn't want to say more. After the day and the night he needed talk that was light and amusing, anything to push the pictures of hurt and death out of his head. 'What's it like at the Williamsons'?'

'It's very grand,' she replied, but there was no awe or jealousy in her voice. 'Everything's so . . .' She searched for the word. 'Rich. The girls are lovely, though. So smart.'

'Do you think you'd like to live that way?'

'No.' She didn't even hesitate. 'I'd always feel afraid to touch things, like I'd make a mess.'

'I'm sure they have maids to clean everything up.'

'Oh, they do,' she assured him with a small, embarrassed laugh. 'As soon as I put a glass down, one of them was there.'

There was no one outside the school, but he knew the women had kept their husbands out during the night; he'd seen them as he passed, searching for King Davy. Even so he went in with her, a hand on his knife, ready. Nothing. Everything was as it should be. He smiled and kissed her.

'I'll be back this afternoon.'

Rob made his way to the bottom of Briggate and turned on to the small path below the bridge to wait for Granger. The man emerged from the water engine exactly as the clock struck eight. He patted a tricorn hat on to his head, glanced up at the sky with an approving nod and walked over to Rob.

'Tha's come, then.'

'I promised I would, Mr Granger. You said you had something to tell us.'

'Aye, well, happen it's summat and happen it's nowt.' He brought a clay pipe from his pocket and lit it, puffing until he was satisfied with the smoke. 'It's like I told you last night.'

'Someone who seemed to be dragging another man?'

'That's reet,' Granger agreed. 'Big lads, the pair of them. Looked like they'd had a long night on t' ale.'

'What time was this?' Lister asked. He was desperate to be back on the hunt for King but Granger was going to talk at his own pace. This might be the longest conversation he'd enjoyed in a week.

'Two,' Granger answered with slow certainty. 'I allus take a break then. Come out for a pipe if it's dry.'

'So this all happened by the water engine?'

'Nay.'

'Where, then?' he asked with an indulgent smile.

'I took a turn up Briggate there.' He pointed with the stem of the pipe. 'They were 'bout halfway up.'

That would fit with Megson Court, Rob thought, feeling a surge of hope.

'How well could you see them?'

'Moon came out while I were looking. T' one who looked in his cups, he had fair hair. I saw it shine, like. T' other were dark.'

'Did you know either of them?'

'I've seen the dark 'un before.'

'Where?' he asked urgently.

'Nay, lad, I can't remember,' Granger said mildly, as if it had no importance. 'Here or there.'

Rob tried to rub away the grittiness from his eyes and wondered if the man had anything more to offer. 'How long did you watch them?'

'Na more 'n a minute. I had to get back to my work. Any road, it weren't none of my business.'

The phrase caught Rob's ear. 'What do you mean, it wasn't any of your business?'

'Looked like they'd been fighting, that's all. Best to keep out o' t' way when it's like that.'

Rob took a deep breath and ran a hand through his hair, leaving it standing wildly. 'You said one of them was helping the other. Why would you think they'd been fighting?'

'When moon shone on 'em I could see blood on fair 'un's face.' He smiled with satisfaction.

'Was there anything else you noticed?'

'Tha's had it all now, lad.'

'If you remember where you've seen the man before, come and tell us, Mr Granger.'

'Aye, I'll do that. But you should see Matthew Wilson.'

'Why?' He knew Wilson, one of the figures who came alive during the night, walking the streets like a ghost and vanishing with the light.

'He were out walking, too. Din't I say that?' The man gave a brief nod and walked up the road. Rob stared after him for a moment, shook his head and strode back to the jail.

It was still early when the Constable entered the Moot Hall, before any of the clerks arrived to begin their day. The building smelt clean, of soap and wax, the windows sparkling in the early light. He left the report on Cobb's desk, the brief catalogue of injury and death and failure.

He knew he should be out at the woods by the tannery, leading the search for any sign of King. Instead he turned the other way, to Lands Lane, to see the deputy and hope for something, anything.

Why had Davy attacked him? What had happened? The King was violent but he wasn't stupid. He'd never go for a Constable's man without a reason.

He'd barely turned the corner when he saw the door open and Lizzie step out, looking around as if she'd never seen any of it before, as if the whole world was strange. He opened his mouth to speak, and then he saw her face.

TWENTY-ONE

Slowly she trudged towards him, as if placing one foot in front of the other took all her strength. When she was close enough he put his arms around her, and she began to shudder and shake, clinging tightly to him. The tears would come soon enough, he knew that, and it would be a long time before they stopped. Tenderly he stroked her back, the way he had with his daughters when they were young.

He had no comfort to give her. She'd loved John, she'd given him every piece, each moment of herself. Now there'd just be emptiness for the rest of her life. Folk started to come from their houses, leaving for work, glancing curiously as they passed. Let them look, he thought. It didn't matter. She needed this.

'Come on,' he said finally, and escorted her gently back to the house. The shutters were closed. He could hear Lucy upstairs, talking to James and Isabell. The deputy was on the pallet, covered with a sheet.

Nottingham poured two mugs of ale and handed one to Lizzie. She shook her head at first then took it, draining it quickly.

'He squeezed my hand,' she said. 'He squeezed it before . . .' Her voice was raw, and fragile as air. She gazed up at him, her eyes full of pain and hopelessness. 'What am I going to do, Mr Nottingham?'

'I'll take care of everything,' he promised her. It wasn't an answer to her question but it was all he could offer her. 'Lucy will look after things here.' He waited as she nodded. 'John was a good man.'

'He was the best I'll ever know.' She pushed her knuckles against her eyes.

He remembered the things John had done, his loyalty, his belief, the way he'd ensured that the men who killed Mary had vanished when Nottingham was lost in the law. Soon he'd feel his own pain. But that could wait.

He returned to the Moot Hall, striding angrily down the street. Cobb was at his desk, head bowed over the papers.

'The mayor wants to see you, sir,' he said.

'In an hour or two,' Nottingham said briskly. 'Tell me, what's Mayor Fenton involved in that he doesn't want anyone to know about?'

'Sir?' the clerk asked, confused.

'You heard me, Mr Cobb. What?'

The man bit his lip. 'He's bought an interest in a sawmill

across the river and they've received a contract for work from the city.'

'That'll do well for a start.' The Constable gave a dark grin. 'I'll see Mr Fenton a little later. For now, I haven't been here, you understand?'

'Yes, sir.'

Rob was dozing in the chair at the jail. He woke with a start as the door opened.

'John's dead,' Nottingham told him flatly.

'Fuck.' He opened his mouth but no more words would come.

'Go out to the woods, see what you can find there. I'm going to arrange the funeral.'

'Yes boss.'

The Constable went to the church and made his demands of the curate, then to the undertaker, and across to ask Joe Buck to pass the word. Tom Williamson was already at his warehouse. He listened carefully to everything Nottingham suggested, and gave his agreement without reservation. Out on Briggate Four-Finger Jane cried when he told her; she'd let the other whores know. For the next hour he moved around the town, talking to those who could spread the news. Only when he'd finished did he go back to the Moot Hall.

'Go through, sir,' Cobb said.

Mayor Fenton looked sleeker than before: a little weight gone, the clothes more expensive, his shave closer and shinier. An empty coffee dish stood on the edge of his desk and the air was perfumed by the tobacco from his pipe.

'You made mistakes, Nottingham,' he said, his eyes hard and heartless.

'Mr Sedgwick just died,' the Constable told him.

'I'm sorry to hear that.' He picked up the report and tossed it in front of the Constable. 'You made a pig's ear of it.'

'I did.' The responsibility was his; he'd admit it. 'And we'll have King for two murders. But two of my men have lost their lives. They were doing their duty. They deserve something.'

Fenton stared at him. 'What do you want?' he asked.

'A pension for their widows. The city to pay the rent of Mr Sedgwick's house.'

'No,' the mayor answered simply.

'The aldermen will vote for it. If you object, the *Mercury* will publish all the details about that sawmill you've invested in and the contract you gave it.'

'Don't threaten me, Nottingham.'

'I'm not threatening, Your Worship.' He didn't need to raise his voice. 'I'm promising.'

For long seconds the room was quiet, just the faint sounds of Briggate outside the windows. Finally the mayor gave a short nod.

'I'll draw up the papers,' he said. As the Constable turned away, he added, 'Don't ever believe you've won, Nottingham.'

Outside the air seemed cleaner. People came up to offer their condolences, and he told them about the service the next morning.

Rob walked through the woods, eyes on the ground where men had trodden down the grass and the bracken. He wasn't going to find anything useful here. He felt stunned, scarcely able to believe it. Only yesterday morning he'd talked to John, joked with him the way they always did. Now he was gone. The man who'd taught him everything in this job.

When they found King the man wouldn't last until trial, let alone survive to see the hangman. He'd make sure of that. Rob had seen death often enough in this job; he'd killed men himself. But this was the first time he knew he'd be happy to murder without care or remorse. His soul would sing as he did it.

He'd spread the men around Leeds, fanning them out through the city. Once word of the deputy's death spread no one would shelter King. They'd find him. The boss would want him alive, to face justice and the rope. But he knew what the man deserved.

Rob reached the jail to find the Constable pacing, his hands bunched into fists, his body tight and tense.

'Come with me,' he said. 'Do you still have the pistol?' Lister nodded. 'Someone's seen King.'

'Where?'

'Down in the Ley Lands, near Sheepscar Beck.'

'Do you want me to fetch some of the men?'

Nottingham shook his head. 'Not this time. Just the two of us.'

As they marched out along Vicar Lane, past the grand houses and the tumbledown, he told the boss what he'd learned from Granger. But they were simply sounds to fill the silence. There'd be time for Jem Carter when all this was done. For now, nothing else was important.

They stopped close to a small copse by the water, a stand of oak and ash and willow, thick enough to hide a man.

'He's in there,' the Constable said.

'What do you want to do, boss?'

'I'm going in. You stay here. If King comes out, shoot him.' He kept his eyes on the wood.

'Boss,' Lister objected, but Nottingham simply shook his head.

'Be ready, that's all.' He walked slowly ahead and vanished between the trees.

Rob waited. The gun was cocked and heavy in his hand. The sun beat down, burning his neck, but the sweat that ran along his spine felt cold. He could barely breathe, and strained to peer into the woods but saw nothing. Each moment seemed to stretch out. His heart was pounding. For the third time he checked the sword and knife in their sheaths.

Finally the crack of a pistol echoed through the valley, a report that sent birds scattering and squawking into the sky. Rob raised the gun, his arm steady. The seconds passed. He heard footsteps in the undergrowth and tensed his finger on the trigger.

The Constable emerged, the gun down by his side, his shoulders slumped.

'Fetch the coroner.' Nottingham stared at Rob, his eyes empty.

TWENTY-TWO

The Constable walked across the field to Lady Lane, wearier than he'd ever been in his life. It had only taken a moment to spot King as the man tried to hide behind a fallen tree trunk. From there, he'd only needed to wait, silent and unmoving, until he stood, ready to run. They'd looked at each other and the man began to raise his hands. Nottingham fired, watching the shot tear Davy's chest open. No mercy. Not this time.

The street was dusty and his throat was dry. People tried to talk to him but he brushed by. Soon enough they'd all know what had happened. Not that it mattered, not with John dead. An eye for an eye might be the old way but there was precious little satisfaction in it.

He paused at the top of the hill. Men were carrying rubbish out of the workhouse and piling it in front of the building. He could hear hammers and sawing inside. Two labourers stood in a patch of shade by the ale barrel while someone else pored over a drawing stretched out on a piece of wood.

'I didn't even know the plans had gone through yet,' Nottingham said and the man turned.

'Don't ask me,' he said with a tired shake of his head. 'I just do as I'm told. It's a reet bloody mess in there, too. Going to take the rest of the week to clean it all out properly. They didn't bother to tell me that before I hired this lot.' He spat on the dry ground.

'When do they want it finished?'

'End of the month. They'll be lucky. I doubt any of them's ever taken a look inside. Half of the rooms have rats' nests in them. We've been killing the buggers all morning.' The man glanced at Nottingham. 'You look like you could do a full day's work, you need a job?'

'Already have one,' the Constable answered, seeing the corners of the man's mouth turn down. 'For now, anyway. Good luck.'

'Luck? It's going to take bloody prayer, lad.'

All he wanted was to go home, to close his eyes and try to forget. He hadn't paid a debt; he never could. Instead he'd done the last thing he could manage for a friend who'd done everything for him.

He forced his feet along the street, not looking at anything, just concentrating on moving.

At the warehouse, Williamson was directing two men who were shifting lengths of cloth from the shelves to the large open doors that overlooked the Aire. He turned when Nottingham entered, said something to the workers and came over to him.

'What is it, Richard? We're busy here,' he said, annoyance in his voice until he saw the Constable's face. 'What's happened? You found him?'

'He's dead,' Nottingham answered shortly. Each word felt as heavy as a hundredweight. The merchant was staring at him curiously. 'Have you given your recommendation on the workhouse?' he asked.

'This morning,' Williamson answered in surprise. 'We're debating it at the meeting on Wednesday.'

'Come with me,' he said.

'Now?' Williamson asked in exasperation. 'I have a shipment to prepare.'

'Please.'

The merchant wavered for a moment, then nodded, passing the paper to a clerk and picking up his coat from the desk before following the Constable.

'It'd better be important, Richard,' he warned as they walked along Vicar Lane and out to the Ley Lands.

'It is.'

'What happened with . . .?'

The Constable shook his head and stayed silent until they reached the site. 'There.'

The Constable saw the amazement on Williamson's face. The merchant waved the foreman over.

'When did you start here?' he asked.

'This morning, sir,' the man answered.

'And when do you have to be finished?'

'I was told to have it all done by the end of the month.' He wiped some dust from his mouth. 'Won't be easy, either. There's more needed than anyone told me.'

'Who's paying you?'

'The Corporation of course,' the foreman replied, as if it was obvious.

'I don't know what to tell you, Richard,' Williamson said once the man had returned to his work. He was still staring at the building. 'We haven't . . .' He shook his head. They began to walk back slowly.

'I didn't know,' Williamson said finally. 'Truly, I didn't.'

Nottingham didn't respond.

'I feel like a fool.'

'Don't,' the Constable told him. 'Finer's probably been planning this since the moment he came back to Leeds.'

'But his figures make sense.'

'I'm sure they do. They were meant to.' His voice turned hard. 'I'll wager a week's pay that in a year they'll look very different and the Corporation won't even care. The poor will be off the streets. That's all that matters to them.'

'It's not what's important to me. I hope you believe that.'

'I do. They used you,' he explained gently.

'You warned me. I'm sorry, Richard.'

'It's not your fault. You were given a document and you went through it properly.'

'I'll still bring it up at the meeting.'

'It won't make a damn bit of difference. It's started now and they're not going to stop.'

Williamson nodded. He seemed bowed, betrayed, and there were lines on his face that Nottingham had never noticed before.

'We still need to send that order out today. I'll be at the service tomorrow. And that other matter's in hand.'

The Constable watched him go. He was tired to his bones, his eyes bulging from lack of sleep and pain starting to tighten around his heart. As he walked along Briggate he could hear Sedgwick's voice in his ear, suggesting a brief stop for a drink or a pie, talking about how well James was doing at the charity school or suggesting another way of looking at a case that troubled them.

Nottingham loosened his stock and wiped the sweat off his neck. He wanted his bed, to sleep without dreaming, but it would have to wait a while yet.

Lucy answered the door at the house on Lands Lane. Her eyes were still red where she'd been crying and she held a small piece of linen tight in her first. She looked up into his face and asked, 'Have you done it?'

He nodded. 'Where's Lizzie?' The body had gone, he saw; the pallet was cleared and all the straw swept away.

'She's upstairs with the children.'

The Constable felt as if he'd never reach the top, that his legs wouldn't carry him all that way. But finally he was there. She was feeding Isabell, spooning something into the girl's mouth while James played on the floor with a wooden animal.

'It's done,' he told her.

'Dead?' she asked.

'Yes.'

'Good.' She spat out the word. 'I hope he goes to hell.'

'Does that mean my da can come home now?' James stood up, his long face so much the image of his father.

'No.' Nottingham sighed, not even sure how to answer the question. 'I'm sorry, James. I wish it did.' He turned to Lizzie. 'I've arranged the funeral for eleven tomorrow.' She nodded, her eyes lost. 'I'll come for you and the children.'

'Thank you.' She tried to smile but couldn't.

He sat in the jail for hours; he didn't know how many had passed. Maybe he'd slept, he didn't know that either. Finally he roused himself and trudged down Briggate, then out along the riverbank to the camp. People were beginning to gather, to build their fires from branches and twigs they'd scavenged, ready to cook whatever scraps they might have. There was no hint of a breeze to stir the warm air. Bessie was sitting with one of the groups, talking with a woman who had a baby at her breast. Someone pointed and she turned, rising slowly to approach him, the way she did with everyone, keeping strangers away from her folk. She folded her arms under her bosom.

'I heard about Mr Sedgwick,' she said. 'I'm sorry.'

'So am I, Bessie. So am I.'

'I heard what you did, too. Good riddance to filth like that.'

He looked around the camp. 'Not so many here today.'

'There'll be more later. But some have gone off to look for work on the farms. It's that time of year.'

'And the others?'

'Trying their luck elsewhere rather than risk the workhouse,' she answered, looking him in the eye. 'Do you blame them?'

'No, I don't. They started work on the place today. It's supposed to be done by the end of this month.'

Her eyes widened. 'I didn't even know the Corporation had agreed yet.'

'They haven't,' he told her, and saw her mouth harden into a thin line.

'I see. Same as ever in this place, then,' she said with disgust. 'I remember what it was like, the way they made the inmates wear those metal discs on their coats.'

He recalled that, too. 'They're still cleaning the place out, all the rubbish is piled by the walls.'

'There'll be plenty of it to cart off, I'm sure of that.'

'There already is,' he said and glanced up at the cloudless sky. 'And the weather's very dry. I've seen fires start when it's like this.'

'You should have warned them, Mr Nottingham.'

'Not my job. I just wanted you to know.'

Bessie pursed her lips and nodded. 'Thank you.'

TWENTY-THREE

There could be no good day for a funeral, the Constable thought. The blue sky, the sun were a mockery. Lizzie was next to him in the church, cradling Isabell. He'd escorted her, Lucy holding James's hand as she walked behind from the house on Lands Lane. Emily had closed the school for the day, and sat on his other side with Rob, her face tight, hands clasped in her lap.

The air was hot and still; with so many filling the building, it hurt to breathe. He turned his head, glancing at the faces he knew, all here to pay their last respects. So many of them. But no more than John's due.

Later, outside, he held Isabell as Lizzie stooped to gather up a handful of dry earth and sprinkle it in the grave, her head bowed, shaking with the tears. Very gently Nottingham put his arm around her to help her back.

He waited until the others had filed past, each of them scooping up the dirt to tip it down on to the coffin, then added his own, saying farewell to the man he'd known so well. Molly the Mudlark threw in the earth from her small hand, reached into the pocket of her ragged dress and added a small lump of metal before she hurried on.

Then it was over, and the crowds moved away with a quiet word to Lizzie or a touch on her arm. Tom and Hannah Williamson remained standing in the church porch.

The merchant came over, sadness and embarrassment on his face, drawing a leather purse from the pocket of his expensive dark coat and holding it out to Lizzie. The Constable knew there was another, smaller one for Daley's woman. The alderman had done his men proud.

'We arranged a subscription,' he said, pressing the money into Lizzie's hand. 'It's not much, not for all Mr Sedgwick did.' He bowed briefly and returned to his wife. Nottingham drew out the two documents he'd collected from Cobb earlier that morning.

'The city's going to pay you a pension and the rent on the house,' he told her, seeing her eyes widen and the tears start falling again. 'You won't want for anything, I promise you that.'

She couldn't say anything, and he didn't need any words. She had a lifetime of loss ahead. That much he knew.

Finally he was alone in the churchyard. He walked over to stand by the graves, Rose and Mary, and the sun burned his neck as he stood, talking to his wife in his head.

Rob and Emily walked quietly along the Calls to the school, the sad, solemn air of the funeral hanging over them. She was ready to come home, he knew that; the Williamsons had been kind, but two nights there were enough for her.

First, though, she needed a few books to prepare the next day's lessons. He waited as she unlocked the door, knowing she was holding her breath and hoping no one had been in. He knew it was safe enough, at least for now. The women still had their husbands out, but there'd be fewer of them each night. Soon they'd need a night man front and back on the place again.

He threw back the shutters, letting light flood the room as she searched through a pile on the table.

'Got them,' she said.

She was interrupted by a tap on the door. Rob raised his eyebrows and she shook her head, not expecting anyone. Carefully, one hand close to his knife, he opened up.

'Mr Williamson,' he said in surprise. 'Mrs Williamson. Come in, please. We were just about to leave.'

'I hope it's not a bad time,' the merchant said. 'A sad enough day.'

Lister nodded, standing aside as they entered.

'I'm sorry, there's only the benches to sit on,' Emily apologized.

Williamson turned to his wife. 'This is Mr Lister,' he said. 'He's James Lister's son. From the *Mercury*.'

Rob offered a small bow and Hannah Williamson smiled.

'Emily told us you two have been courting,' she said. 'You work for Mr Nottingham, don't you?'

'Yes, ma'am.'

'He keeps us all safe,' Williamson said.

'Forgive me,' Emily interrupted. 'I hadn't expected anyone.'

'We were talking on the way back from the . . . service.' Williamson placed his hand over his wife's. 'We've enjoyed your company the last few days. We agreed that we'd like to pay to replace the books that were destroyed.'

'All of them?' Emily's voice rose in disbelief.

'It would be our honour.'

'Thank you.' She looked from one of them to the other, her eyes wide, close to speechless. 'Thank you.'

'Your dedication has impressed me,' Mrs Williamson told her, and looked at her husband expectantly.

'We'd also like to cover the expenses of the school,' he said.

'But—' Emily started, then closed her mouth.

'You run it exactly as you want, just the way you have been,' the merchant continued. 'We don't want a say in any of that. It's your school. The only thing you need to do is send the bills to us.'

Rob stared at Emily. Joyful tears ran down her face; she reached into the pocket of her dress for a handkerchief and wiped hurriedly at her face.

'I don't know what to say,' she told them.

'All you have to do is say yes,' Hannah Williamson prompted kindly.

'And you truly don't want anything at all in return?'

'Nothing,' Williamson assured her, his wife nodding in agreement.

'Then I . . . Yes.' She looked from one of them to the other then blurted, 'Yes, of course. Yes. Thank you.'

Rob sat quietly and watched, the first time he'd known her lost for words, the expression on her face caught somewhere between laughter and tears.

'We met your mother a few times at church,' the merchant said. 'I think she'd have been so happy to see what you're doing here.' He stood, helping his wife to rise from the low bench. 'If there's anything you need here, just ask us. Anything at all. We'll do whatever we can.' He bowed, first to Emily, then to Lister, and led his wife out.

They listened to the footsteps fading and the sound of the street. Then she turned and ran to him, holding him tight as if she couldn't believe the last few minutes had really happened.

'They want to pay for it all!'

'You deserve it,' Rob said, kissing her lightly on the lips. 'You've earned it. Everything they said was true.'

She pulled back for a moment, her eyes suddenly doubtful.

'Do you think Papa had something to do with this?' she asked suddenly.

'No,' he said with certainty. They'd been too busy finding John's killer to think of anything else.

'I can't believe it,' she said, clutching him again, her smile wider than the river, and for a moment he saw the little girl she must have been. Her joy filled the room and the words flooded out of her.

'Come on, I want to go home and tell Lucy. And Papa, when he comes. Tomorrow I'll tell the girls and we can all write a letter of thanks.'

It was evening when Lucy returned to the house on Marsh Lane, subdued for once, not wanting to talk, quickly settling in the kitchen to begin baking bread for the morning. The Constable understood.

He listened with pride as Emily poured out her news, eyes

glowing with pleasure. He embraced her and congratulated her, but today her words couldn't touch his heart.

How would he go on without John? He'd trusted him completely. He'd never even needed to think about it. He'd known the deputy would be there, doing whatever he demanded. People had liked him. People talked to him, he knew how to draw them out, he was one of them. And Lizzie had loved him.

Now they'd all have to manage without him. Rob was good; he'd learned so much and come so far in the last two years. He was dogged and eager to learn. But he'd never possess John's easy manner or be able to coax words and secrets from people with a smile or a drink.

The night slowly settled around him. Emily and Rob went to their bed and Lucy made up her pallet in the kitchen. The Constable kept the window open, catching the smallest hint of a breeze in the leaves and the distant song of the night birds. He sat in his chair by the empty hearth.

Maybe his time had passed. Maybe he should finally see the sense in all those things Mary told him before she died. He'd done what he could in Leeds – he had the scars on his body to show that. But the ones in his mind and across his heart ran deeper.

For every killing he solved there'd be another, from now until the end of time. For every runaway he found there'd be two more he'd never see. Each day he grew more weary. He'd always done his job with everything in his power. He'd cared, he'd hoped. But since Mary died nothing had been the same. And now . . . he felt as if a door had closed.

He'd find Jem Carter's murderer and whoever had been damaging the school. But when those were done he'd write his letter of resignation and try to discover what peace remained in his heart.

The thoughts and memories swirled as he lay down to sleep. Tomorrow they'd to begin finding answers to all their questions.

The pounding on the door woke him immediately. He pulled on his breeches and took the cudgel from the table before answering. It was Drinkwell, one of the night men, breathless from running, soot smeared across his face.

'Fire, boss.'

'Where?'

'The workhouse. Spotted it a few minutes ago. They've got a bucket chain going.'

'Go on back. I'll be there as soon as I can.'

He turned and saw Rob near the top of the stair.

'Get yourself dressed, lad, we've got a blaze to deal with.'

By the time they arrived the fire had taken full hold, cinders and sparks rising high in the air. It had broken through the roof, and flames were licking at the sky and lighting up the whole area. The men were working hard with their buckets but the Constable could see they'd never win. If the wind rose a little everything could leap to Queen Charlotte's Court; it was little more than ten yards away.

'Stop it spreading over there,' he ordered.

More folk began to arrive, curious, drawn by the light and the flames. Nottingham and Rob worked with them, sweating, aching, keeping the houses damp enough so no fire could take hold. Finally, just as the sky started to lighten, a low creak like a moan came from the workhouse. Everyone stopped and turned to watch as the building began to topple in on itself, charred timbers falling so heavily that the ground shook.

It was over. The fire was still burning but there was little more damage it could do.

'See Emily to school then do the morning rounds,' he told Rob. 'I'll keep my eye on this.'

With the excitement done, folk began to drift away to work or their beds. The sun appeared, making the heat of the blaze shimmer as it rose into the air. The workhouse was gone. It would need to be completely rebuilt and he knew the Corporation wouldn't spend the money for that.

The Constable saw the foreman, standing off to the side as the labourers clamoured around him, wondering if they'd be paid for the day. He waited until the argument had ended.

'No more work for you here,' Nottingham said.

'Just to haul away whatever's left when it's cooled down,' the man replied sadly. He nodded over at the others. 'No wages for them, neither. Would have been a few weeks' work, too.' He wandered off, shaking his head.

'What do you think started it, Mr Nottingham?' He turned

at the sound of Finer's voice. The man was staring intently at the ruins, the burned wood and broken stones, as if he could will them back into shape.

'There were piles of rubbish all around yesterday. If someone set a fire in them . . .' He didn't need to say more.

'And do you think you'll find out who did it?'

The Constable sighed. 'I don't know. I'll try.'

'But not too hard, I suspect.' Finer gave a fragile smile. 'And not so easy with your deputy dead.'

'I didn't see you at the funeral.'

'I'd never met the man. I'm sorry for your loss but I had no business there.' He paused. 'You being here, this is where you should be. This is your business.'

'I always do my job,' Nottingham chided him, then pointed out, 'It's odd, though – I understood that the Corporation wasn't even going to debate your proposal until today.'

'This afternoon, at their weekly session,' the man agreed.

'But the work had already started.'

'And I thought you understood the way of the world, Mr Nottingham.' Finer's tone hardened. 'Come on, you know better than that, laddie. Or if you don't, you're not the man I thought.'

'You might be surprised at some of the things I know.'

The man gave a roar of a laugh. 'That's better. Perhaps I misjudged you, Constable. Perhaps Amos really did teach you more than I'd imagined.' He gave a small bow and walked away, his head still held high but his steps slow, feet shuffling against the ground.

Nottingham stayed a little longer, walking around the wreck of the place, not smiling, not frowning. At least no one had been hurt or killed and there was no damage to the court. And it meant no one would suggest another workhouse for several years. Unless someone peached there'd be little likelihood of ever finding the person responsible. And he didn't really care.

He broke his fast with wild strawberries from a seller yelling her wares as she walked up and down Briggate. They were small, gathered from the woods, the juices sweet in his mouth, and he licked the red stains from his hands, savouring the last taste of them on his skin.

A breeze came, catching his hair and lifting the fringe off his forehead; without thinking he pushed it back down. He passed the Moot Hall, the tang of blood from the butcher's shops so strong he could taste it in his throat. Servants were lined up outside the baker's to take home loaves. A storyteller caressed a few onlookers with his words, then stopped, looked pointedly at his hat on the ground and only started up again when someone threw in a coin.

Another day. He'd send Rob to question Matthew Wilson, the man that Granger, the night watch at the water engine, had named. And he'd go hunting for Simon Johnson, to see if he had anything to say about the damage to the school.

TWENTY-FOUR

Where could he begin to look for Johnson, though? There was nothing to distinguish him, he was someone who faded easily out of sight and mind; no doubt he'd grown used to it, depended on it as he wandered the roads with his brother through the years.

He asked here and there, but all he received were shakes of the head and blank looks. There were so many places a man could disappear in Leeds. He knew that from his younger days, a time when disappearing could mean staying alive.

Nottingham walked through the courts and the yards that ran off Briggate, finding those he knew and asking them. But no one had even heard of the man. By dinner he was beginning to believe he'd imagined it, that Johnson had never been at the market at all. He wandered down by the school, hearing Emily's voice through the open window, confident and caring as she corrected one of the girls.

He cut through the ginnel and came out on Call Brows, his eyes alert for anyone hiding and waiting, but the street was empty. Finally he gave up, and settled in the Old King's Head for a pie and cold ale. Part of his mind expected Sedgwick to slide on to the bench across from him, ready to eat and pass on some snippet he'd learned during the morning. But never again. They'd never know why John had died, what had made King attack him. Another useless death.

Most of the people he cared about in the world were dead, and too soon, all of them too soon.

The Constable ate quickly, not really tasting the food. It was just something to fill his belly and keep him until evening. Outside, he felt the sun on his face and sighed.

Rob only knew Matthew Wilson from the nights, a man who shunned company and kept out of the light. He remembered the flush of surprise that had covered Wilson's face when he'd addressed him; he was a man used to being invisible.

Rumour was that he lived off the Bradford road, well beyond Burley Bar, with only animals for company. Lister set off, not sure quite where he was going, removing his stock and wiping the sweat from his face with it.

He was the deputy now. He knew he wasn't ready for it, he still had so much to learn. And he'd never be as good as John. The man had taught him everything about the job. In his life he'd been luckier than most; he'd never lost anyone close before. The killing of Emily's mother had torn at him, but nothing like this. All the questions he still wanted to ask, all the laughter he wanted to hear.

He looked around. Beyond the town the houses were farther apart, and there were sheep in the fields, and the sound of clacking looms from the open windows. He knocked at a door, smiling as he looked down at a small girl.

'Is your ma home?' he asked, and she moved aside, replaced by a woman with a suspicious look in her eyes.

'If you're selling owt we've not got the money to buy.'

'I'm looking for Matthew Wilson. Do you know where he lives?'

'Him.' She snorted. 'What do you want with him?'

'Just some business,' Rob replied mildly.

'Aye, well, if you have business with him you should know where he lives.' She nodded along the road. 'Third house down on the other side. But don't be surprised if the old bugger dun't answer.'

'Thank you,' he told her, and moved on. The place she'd indicated was set back down a rutted track. As he drew close he could hear barking. The house looked neglected, roof slates hanging askew, some missing, one window empty of its glass. At the door he took a breath and brought his fist down.

A chorus of dogs howled, four or five of them, he guessed. He tried again, then again, but no one answered. Finally he stood back and shouted, 'Mr Wilson, I need to speak to you.'

The words brought more barking and eventually the shuffle of footsteps inside. The heavy door opened a crack, just enough to show the man's face.

'Do you remember me?' Rob asked. 'I work for the Constable.' He didn't feel comfortable calling himself the deputy. Not yet.

Wilson nodded.

'I need to talk to you about something you might have seen,' Rob said.

For a moment he believed the man might turn his back and lock the door. Then he nodded briefly and Lister entered. There was little light in the room, and it stank of too many years without cleaning. The dogs clamoured around, snuffling at his hands with wet noses and rough tongues until they were satisfied he was a friend.

There was a simple table and a single chair, a straw pallet in the corner and bowls on the floor for the animals. A small life, Rob thought. Wilson was a ragged man with a thick beard that hung on to his chest, clothes mended far too many times to count. His eyes looked hunted, as if he'd spent years avoiding something. Maybe he had.

'You were out walking, a week ago Tuesday night. Mr Granger, the night watch at the water engine, saw you.'

'I remember.' It was the first time he'd heard the man speak and he was surprised by the richness of his voice, deep, warm and educated. 'I know Mr Granger. Another man who lives in the dark.'

'He saw a man helping another man that night, just after two. It was on Briggate, near Megson's Court.'

'Yes,' Wilson answered slowly, closing his eyes. 'The moon was bright.'

'How well could you see them?'

'Well enough.' He smiled, showing broken, stained teeth.

'What did they look like?'

'I should ask why it's so important that you know, Mr . . . Lister, you said?'

'Yes.'

'Are you related to the publisher of the *Mercury*?' Now he'd begun, Wilson's words came readily enough.

'He's my father. And one of the men you saw was probably a murderer.'

'The dark one, I'll wager.'

'Why would you think that?'

'Because he wasn't helping the other man. He was dragging him, swearing and cursing.'

'Can you recall what he looked like?'

'A big man. Broad.' Wilson put a hand against his bony chest to illustrate. 'He had long hair, his own, not a wig. Well dressed, very fashionable.'

'You have good eyes,' Rob told him.

The man smiled. 'Age doesn't ruin everything, young man. Don't ever believe it does.'

'Was there anything else about him?'

'His hands,' Wilson answered without hesitation.

'Hands?'

'I don't think I've ever seen hands that big on anyone before. I had to stare at them to believe it.'

Few would have hands large enough for people to notice. And those who saw wouldn't forget. Rob felt the sharp surge of excitement. Now they'd find him.

'Thank you,' he said and the man dipped his head in acknowledgement. At the door Lister paused; there was a question he'd wanted to ask for a long time. 'Tell me, what is it that takes you out at night, Mr Wilson?'

'Ask your father,' the man replied mysteriously. 'He can tell you.'

'We don't speak.'

'Then perhaps you should.' Wilson shook his head. 'Your father will know what I mean, Mr Lister. Maybe being reminded of the tale will make him think. I'll lock the door behind you.'

Walking back through the town he looked at every man he saw, gauging the size of their hands, watching for any that appeared particularly large. At the jail he wrote down the details he'd learned from Wilson, going through it again to add a little here and take away something there until he'd caught the heart of the conversation.

He poured a mug of ale and sipped it. Warm, but it took the edge off his thirst.

'What did you find?' Nottingham asked. Rob passed the paper across the desk and the Constable read quickly. 'Big hands?' he asked. 'A smith? A labourer?'

'That's what I wondered, boss. But well-dressed?'

'True,' he agreed with a nod. 'You're sure this man Wilson is right?'

'I believe him.'

'Then we'd better start looking more closely at people. If he has good clothes, he has money. That narrows it down. And dark hair.'

'That still leaves plenty.'

The Constable raised his eyebrows. 'But it's somewhere to start.'

Nottingham cut down through the tenting fields, where lengths of washed cloth were tied out in the sun to stretch on the frames, the air heavy with the winter scent of damp wool. But as he reached the riverbank he caught the first smell of something different on the wind and looked west to the horizon. Clouds. No more than a few yet, all light as fog, but there'd be rain behind them. A few more hours and it would arrive; he could almost taste it. Enough to please the farmers, he hoped, and to do more than damp down the dust.

Bessie was sitting at the entrance to the shelter she'd built, a raggle-taggle affair of worn canvas and old blankets between tree branches. Her hands held a pair of wooden needles and she seemed to move them without thinking, taking up yarn from a skein to knit.

'Now you see how I spend my time, Mr Nottingham.' She greeted him with a warm smile.

'Useful, I'm sure.'

'Aye, gloves, mufflers, there'll be plenty glad of them come winter. I heard about the workhouse. All gone, is it?'

'Destroyed,' he confirmed. 'I think that's the end of that scheme.'

'For now, anyway,' she cautioned, placing the knitting in her lap. Somewhere close by a sparrow was chirping its shrill song, answered by another farther away. 'I'll not say as I'm sorry. But you know what they're like. Sooner or later it'll be back.'

'Not until long after we're in the ground, Bessie. No one's said anything to you about starting it?'

'They wouldn't dare. They know what'd happen.' She looked directly at him, her voice firm, until he gave her the smallest of nods.

'I'll leave it at that. Just stay dry later.'

'Don't you worry about me, Constable. I'll be fine here.'

'Tell me you had nothing to do with it, Richard.'

His mind had drifted away again as he sat in the jail, thinking of a time when the people he cared about had all been alive. Then Tom Williamson had burst in, pulling him back to the present. He looked worried, careworn.

'The workhouse?' Nottingham guessed.

'I was just up there. It's gone. There's nothing left.'

'I know.' His voice sounded tired. 'I was called out in the middle of the night to help fight the blaze.'

'Do you know who started it?'

The Constable waved his hand at the window. 'It could be anyone. You saw all the rubbish piled outside yesterday. All it needed was a spark from someone's flint.' He shook his head hopelessly. 'The one thing I can tell you is that it wasn't me.'

'I'm sorry.' Williamson had the good grace to look embarrassed. 'But . . .' He didn't need to say more; they both understood.

'They can't blame you.'

'I hope not.'

'They won't,' Nottingham assured him. 'Your job was to look at the figures. Nothing more than that.' The merchant gave a small, tight smile. 'Even Tom Finer took it well.'

'You saw him?'

'As the fire was dying down.'

'I owe you an apology,' Williamson said.

'Not needed. In your shoes I'd have wondered the same thing.'

As the Constable locked the jail, the promise of rain was so heavy in the air Nottingham felt he could touch it. Even before he reached the Parish Church it began, a teasing summer shower, warm and gentle, tender on his face, that faded as quickly as it arrived.

But no sooner had it passed than another came, this one heavier and more violent, the drops bouncing up from the street to soak his hose and boots. He looked for shelter and ran to the church porch, hearing the noise of the downpour growing louder until it became a roar to fill the world. For a minute or two the rain was so heavy that he couldn't even see as far as Kirkgate. All he could do was wait and watch the tiny runnels of water growing wider and deeper, running like streams across the dry ground.

During the afternoon he'd spent time in the inns, looking and listening, asking questions about Simon Johnson, and about a man with dark hair and large hands. It had all been fruitless, frustrating. But he was familiar with the feeling; he'd had it all too often over the years. He wouldn't give up. These would be the two last things, and he'd take care of them both. It would only need one small piece of inform- ation, a name . . .

If John was here, he began to think, then shook his head. No more. No more.

The rain began to slacken. At first it seemed more promise than fact, then gradually it eased away until all that remained was a light drizzle, leaving the air fresh and clean. He glanced up at the sky; the clouds scudded away, blue over on the horizon, and a wind stirred the leaves.

The Constable walked out of the shelter and over the sodden ground to stop at the graves. His daughter, his wife. The words on Rose's headstone stood out, wet and dark. Mary lay next to her, the dirt settled to no more than a small hump of earth, the grass grown over it, glittering with raindrops, covering her like a Turkey rug.

In his head he talked to her every day, heard her laugh and

saw her smile. But standing here now he found that the words wouldn't come; for once, all he could summon up was a picture of her bones, pale and empty, her soul escaped.

He sighed and slowly made his way home. Sheepscar Beck was in full spate as he crossed Timble Bridge, the morning's trickle turned to an evening flood that licked at the banks and the willows hanging low over the water.

Marsh Lane was muddy, the dirt clinging to his boot heels, and he tried to scrape it away before he entered the house; if he didn't, Lucy would complain at him for tracking it over her clean floors, just the way Mary would have done. For a fleeting moment he could hear the comfort of his wife's voice in his ear, chiding him, and he smiled at the memory. Emily was sitting at the table, her pen scraping away on paper. The smell of cooking came from the kitchen, the scent of beef and cabbage filling the place.

'Were you caught in it, Papa?'

'I missed the worst of it. How was school?'

She beamed. 'The girls behaved all day.'

He raised his eyebrows in surprise. 'All of them?'

'Yes,' she laughed. 'Even Joanna Harris managed not to answer back.'

'That must be a first.'

'It feels like it. And the new books for them should be here next week, then they can really start to read and learn.'

He felt her excitement. 'We'll make sure nothing happens to them,' he promised her. 'Is Rob back yet?'

She shook her head. 'He's still out.'

Lucy came through, carrying plates brimming with food.

'He'll have to take his chances later, then,' she said. 'It's hot now.' As they ate the girl kept glancing at him. 'Have you been over to see Lizzie again?' she asked.

'Not yet,' Nottingham said. 'She needs a few days.'

'You should go.'

'I will.'

'Soon, please,' Lucy said, and something in her tone made him stare at her. In truth, he'd meant to go during the day but things had pulled him here and there, the fire, the snippet of information about Carter's killer. Tomorrow, he told himself. He'd make time then.

It was strange, he thought as he ate. Lucy was young but the head on those small shoulders was wiser than all of them. She'd been the one who gave him courage after Mary's death, who kept him steady. She'd pushed him, cajoled him, argued with him if he needed it. She might be a servant in name, but she was as much a part of his family as any of them. God help the man she ended up marrying; she'd be a grand wife but she'd expect a lot from her husband.

'The workhouse is gone then,' Lucy continued. 'That's no loss.'

'Only to those who've put money into it.'

She snorted her dismissal. 'But not for those who don't have anything.' She examined him. 'All those ashes have put holes in your coat. I'll sew it for you.'

Nottingham glanced across at Emily. Her head was carefully bowed over her plate, and he could tell she was attempting not to smile. They both knew Lucy's sewing. She tried hard but she had no skill for it, the stitches awkward, her repairs worse than the damage.

'Don't bother, it'll only get more.' He took the last mouthful, chewed slowly and lowered the fork. 'I'll—' he began, then the door crashed open.

TWENTY-FIVE

'Y ou'd better come, boss. We've found a body.' Rob looked bedraggled, clothes covered in mud and dirt, his hair dried wild from the rain.

Even before he'd finished speaking, the Constable was standing, ready.

'Where?' he asked as they hurried along Marsh Lane.

'The far side of Upper Tenters. Someone was out ratting and his dog started digging.'

'Have you sent someone for the coroner?'

'Already done, boss.'

'Who is it?'

'A girl. She's not been there more than a day or two by the look of it. The earth's still fresh.'

'Do you know her face?'

'No, boss.'

Rob led the way, through Low Tenters, steam rising from the wet cloth that was stretched out, then out beyond Upper Tenters and into the woods beyond, following a slim, slippery track through the trees to a clearing.

Two of the men stood with their shovels, a pile of dirt beside the grave, their faces covered with linen. As soon as he drew near Nottingham understood why. The stink from the body was putrid, enough to make him gag and pull a kerchief from the pocket of his breeches.

'Has the coroner been yet?' he asked.

'And gone,' one of the men answered, the cloth muffling his voice. 'Wouldn't even come close.'

Breathing through his mouth, the Constable knelt at the edge of the grave. There was still just enough light to make out her features. She was young, no more than sixteen or seventeen, long brown hair framing her face. He brushed the maggots away from her nostrils, lips and eyes. There were no marks on her face or neck that he could see and when he lifted her hands, no cuts of any kind. The skin of her palms and fingertips was hard. Whoever she'd been, she'd spent a few years working hard. The weather hadn't been kind to her corpse, heat quickly ripening her flesh and eating away at anything inside. The gown that covered her body was cheap, fourth- or fifth-hand most like, worn through at the elbow and fraying at the neck. Another dead body in the endless procession.

'Take her to the jail,' he ordered. There he'd be able to examine her properly, to find what had killed her. She'd been in the ground long enough to be missed but no one had reported her.

He walked back to the jail, Rob at his side.

'I've been thinking about the school, boss,' Rob said tentatively.

'Go on.'

'The men won't be able to keep their husbands on watch much longer, and we don't have enough men to cover the front and back.'

'I know.' He'd realized that himself.

'Why don't we have someone inside the school at night? I'm sure Emily would agree.'

Nottingham nodded. It was a striking idea. And they'd have surprise on their side if someone tried to break in. Someone like Simon Johnson.

'Who did you have in mind?'

'Thaddeus Todd,' Lister replied immediately. 'He's big and he thinks well.'

'Can you trust him?'

'I've never found him drunk or sleeping.'

'Use him, then. And start asking around about missing girls. You saw her, you know what to do.'

It made no sense. The Constable had examined every inch of her body but found no wounds, no cuts that could have killed her. Her neck was free of bruises; she hadn't been strangled. How had she died? And why had someone buried her out there?

He looked again, slowly checking every inch of flesh, worried he'd missed some small, vital thing, but there was nothing to see. Finally he opened her mouth and for the briefest moment the scent of something rose above the stench of death. He brought his face closer but it was gone.

He stood back, the candlelight in the cell flickering across the empty face. Who are you? he wondered. What happened to you? He dressed her again, giving her the decency of clothing, at least, now there was nothing left to learn from her body. In the morning the undertaker would collect her; if no one claimed her she'd vanish into a pauper's grave, all the dreams she might have had come to nothing.

Dead two days, he thought. Three at the most; it was difficult to be exact in the summer heat. But no longer than that, there'd be more of her gone otherwise.

At the desk he sipped ale to take the taste of death out of his mouth. Something had killed her. The only thing he could imagine was poison. He'd seen no sign of it on her lips or face, but that faint smell when he'd opened her mouth . . . it was nothing he recognized, but that meant little.

He needed information, a name to bury her with. Yet she'd been gone a few days and no one had reported it. There was little chance he'd ever know who she was.

The sun was shining, the sky a brilliant blue as he walked outside. Next door at the White Swan he had bread and cheese to fill the emptiness in his belly. He didn't taste the food; his mind worked as he ate and washed it down with a fresh mug.

Jem Carter, the damage to Emily's school, now the girl . . . At least he didn't have to worry about Tom Finer. The fire at the workhouse had ended his plans. For a little while, anyway. The man would doubtless plague him again.

He drained the cup, stood, and walked up Briggate, stopping at the Moot Hall to leave the daily report with Cobb the clerk, then on to the Rose and Crown. The inn was already bustling with travellers waiting, a wagon being unloaded in the yard.

In the stables, Hercules was brushing down one of the horses that had just arrived, long strokes on its mane, whispering soft words into its ear as it ate from a bag of oats. He was an old man, stooped now, with more love for animals than for people. He'd seemed ancient when Nottingham had first met him, years before. Since then he didn't seem to have aged a day. He tended the animals, made his home in one of the stalls, and in the evenings collected the pots and cups off the tables in the inn.

But Hercules saw and he listened. Few even realized he was there, a silent figure beneath the attention of most people.

'Sad about Mr Sedgwick,' he said, not even needing to turn and see who was there.

'I miss him.'

'Comes a time when a man's heart is filled with the dead.'

'Maybe,' he agreed, knowing how true the words were. 'I'm looking for someone.' He described the man as Hercules continued brushing the horse.

'Seen someone like that.'

'When?'

'Three day back,' the man answered without hesitation.

'Tell me about him.' The Constable leaned against the door of the stable, listening carefully.

'His hands were big, all right. Like a leg of beef.' He made a fist and shook his head. 'Dark hair down to his neck, good coat, clean linen.'

'How old?'

'Twenty-five, mebbe,' the man said after some consideration. 'Big all over, you'd notice him if you saw him. The kind of face lasses might like until they saw his eyes.'

'What about his eyes?'

Hercules stopped his work and turned to stare at the Constable. 'Cruel, Mr Nottingham. No caring in them at all.'

'What was he doing here?'

'With a lass, having their dinner. In one of the private parlours. They had the look of kin.'

'Kin?'

'Their faces,' Hercules replied as if it was obvious. 'The shape, you could see it. Brother and sister.'

'What was she like?'

'Not big like him.' He thought for a moment. 'Fair hair, pretty enough, happen a year or two younger than him.'

'Have you seen either of them before?'

The man shook his head.

'What were they talking about?' the Constable asked.

'Nowt when I was there. They kept quiet.'

'Did you hear a name at all?'

'No.'

Nottingham left two coins on the shelf.

A brother and sister. How did that information help him? Whoever the woman might be, she wasn't the dead girl in the cold cell; the corpse had brown hair and was no more than sixteen or seventeen.

They had money enough to dine at the Rose and Crown, and the sense to keep their mouths shut when someone else was around. Still, it was one more link to add to the chain, and enough to make Nottingham spend part of the morning going round the other inns on Briggate, asking after their guests. No brother and sister, and no one recollected any.

Out of habit he returned to the White Swan for his dinner, a cold game pie and a long cup of ale. He looked up, startled, as someone moved on to the bench across the table.

'Nothing on the girl, boss,' Rob said, wiping the sweat off his forehead with the back of his hand.

'I didn't expect there would be. Keep on trying. I know a little more about this man with the large hands.'

He explained it all, Lister attentive as he gulped down his food with the eager appetite of the young.

'Someone knows them,' Rob said when the Constable was done.

'Then we'd better find out who. Do what you can this afternoon. But make sure you take Emily home when she's finished at the school.'

'Yes, boss.'

Nottingham stared out of the window and suddenly stiffened. He moved quickly, dashing out of the inn and running down Kirkgate. Rob followed, unsure what was happening, knowing only that it had to be be important. He caught up with the Constable just as he gripped a man tightly by the arm, swinging him round.

'I'm surprised to see you still here, Mr Johnson.'

TWENTY-SIX

They took him back to the jail. The Constable pushed Johnson into a chair and sat on the other side of the desk, his palms flat on the wood.

'The last time I saw you, Mr Johnson, you were cursing Leeds and everyone who lived here.'

Rob stood close enough to see the man's face redden.

'I was angry,' he said, sorrow filling his voice.

'I'd have thought you'd want to leave this place far behind you.'

The man stayed silent for a long time.

'Well, Mr Johnson?' Nottingham asked, then pressed again, 'Well?'

'I found a job,' he answered softly.

'Doing what?'

'I help set up the trestles for the markets.'

Nottingham watched his face carefully for any sign of a lie. 'That's only two mornings a week, Mr Johnson. How do you fill the rest of your time?'

'I'm . . .' he started, then shook his head. 'I'm looking for more.' It came out almost as apology.

'What made you decide to look for work in Leeds?'

'I didn't have any money.' He shrugged. 'I needed some to move on.' He hesitated. 'I said things I didn't mean.'

Nottingham smiled gently, softening his tone to coax out more information. 'We all do that, Mr Johnson. Where are you living?'

'I lodge with Mrs Frame.'

He knew it, across the river, cheap beds in a dirty house.

'Tell me, what do you know about the schools in Leeds?'

'Schools?' The man looked confused. 'Nothing. Why?'

'My daughter runs a school.'

Johnson simply looked at him, baffled.

'Not long after you told me you hated Leeds and everyone in it, things began happening there. Broken windows, threats, books destroyed.'

The man's eyes widened. He began to rise and Rob placed a hand on his shoulder.

'You think that I . . .?'

'Give me a good reason to believe you didn't, Mr Johnson.'

'I didn't.' He sounded desperate, eyes wild and bulging. 'I didn't even know about it.'

In spite of himself, the Constable believed him. If the man was a liar he was one of the best. His expression, the way he held himself, everything spoke of his innocence. He doubted Johnson had paid attention to any school, let alone Emily's. All he was trying to do was get through this life without too much pain.

Nottingham nodded at Rob and the lad moved away.

'I'm sure you understand my concern, Mr Johnson.'

'Your daughter, of course.' He nodded eagerly, the sweat shiny on his face.

'And perhaps you'll see why I thought you were responsible.'

Johnson lowered his head slightly.

'I didn't do it.' He sounded close to tears.

'I know that now. My apologies for the way I cornered you.' He stood and extended his hand. 'You're free to go.'

'You're sure, boss?' Rob asked after the man had left.

'Certain.' He sighed loudly. 'So we're back where we started, with no idea who's been in the school.'

'What do we do now?'

Nottingham pushed the fringe off his forehead. 'I don't know. I wish I did.' He glanced over to the corner, imagining John there, leaning against the wall, a mug in his hand, thinking of the next step.

'We'll find him, boss.'

The Constable gave an empty smile. He'd been certain that Johnson was their man. Now he had no other ideas, nowhere to turn. Whoever did it would be back; they always came back. He just had to hope putting a man in the school at night would be enough.

'Carter's killer,' he said. 'We have work to do.'

The girls had already left the school when Rob entered. He'd wanted to be there earlier but he'd been following a tip to find someone with big hands. In the end the man had been old and bald. Large hands, yes, but definitely not who they were seeking.

'How were they?' he asked, sitting on one of the tables. He tried to remember when he'd slept properly. Days ago, it seemed. The ache of weariness filled his body, there was still dried mud on his hose and breeches and his skin felt slick with sweat.

'Unruly,' Emily answered, raising her eyebrows and counting off the reasons on her fingers. 'They're excited about the books coming, I think they're still scared about what might happen, and it's too hot. Do you know what I'd like to do?'

'What?'

'Jump into some cold water and stay there for an hour.' She laughed. 'Silly, isn't it?'

'It sounds perfect,' he told her. He could almost feel the coolness, washing away the dirt, every moment of the day.

'All we need is somewhere we can be alone.' And that was something they'd be hard pressed to find in Leeds, he thought. His day wasn't even done. After he'd walked Emily home there were more hours to go.

She was slow to gather her things, checking every shutter

and the bar on the back door before turning the key and checking the lock. Then she slipped her arm through his as they walked down towards the Parish Church.

'You haven't found him yet, have you?'

'No.'

She turned her wide eyes on him. 'I look at the girls every morning and hope he won't do something that hurts them.'

He wanted to assure her, but he couldn't lie to her about it.

'Having someone in the school at night will help,' he said and she nodded cautiously. She'd been reluctant, but he'd persuaded her in the end.

At the house on Marsh Lane he changed his shirt, the dry, clean linen delicious against his skin, and downed a long mug of ale before walking back into the city. He talked to the whores who'd come out along Briggate, asking about the missing girl, blushing as they teased him, but they all had the same answer: none of them knew her.

It was the same across the river, down along the dusty streets. Someone had possibly known her but she couldn't be sure. It wasn't enough. By dusk his throat was raw from talking and he slipped into an alehouse. Just one drink before going home.

He sat in the corner and listened to all the chatter around him. Names and faces he didn't know. John would have recognized some of them, started a conversation and learned something. He couldn't. He didn't have the gift for it and he probably never would. The boss might have named him deputy but a title didn't make the man.

As he was leaving, a man at one of the tables grabbed his arm.

'You the Constable's man?'

'I am.'

'That lad of yours who got himself killed. I knew him when he were small.' He was older, with a red, hearty face and eyes that seemed to smile. 'Allus in trouble, he were. Little things, like. Heard he'd got himself a woman and bairns.'

'Two of them. One's just a baby.'

The man shook his head. 'That's bad. He looked after folk, did Mr Sedgwick. Find a boy doing summat he shouldn't, give them a quick clout and that were it. Someone hitting his wife,

a word and a threat and it'd be reet as rain.' He took a sip
from the mug. 'You could do worse than be like him.'

'I know,' Rob said. 'Believe me, I know.'

The long shadows were forming as the Constable walked up
Lands Lane. The day had been too long, too hot for early
summer, but still not enough hours in the day and too little
achieved.

He knocked lightly on the wood, looking down at James as
he opened the door, his small face grave.

'Hello, sir,' he said.

'Hello, James. Is your mam here?'

'Come in, Mr Nottingham,' Lizzie called from inside. 'Don't
be keeping him on the step, James.'

The shutters were closed to help cool the house, leaving
the kitchen dim. Sorrow filled every corner of the room, so
strong he believed he could wrap his fingers around it. Lizzie
sat on the bench, a plate in front of her, the food untouched.
Isabell was asleep in her arms.

'Don't you still have some sums to do, James?' she asked.

'Yes, ma.'

'You go upstairs and finish them while I talk to Mr
Nottingham.' She waited as the boy slowly climbed the stairs
then looked at him. 'I don't know if he really understands
John won't ever be back.'

'How are you managing?'

She shrugged, a small gesture that said everything. 'I cry a
lot. How did you feel after Mary died?'

'Lost,' he answered after a while. 'Hopeless. I still do.'

'I want him back,' she said and he didn't know how to
reply. 'Do you even know why it happened?'

'No.'

A tear slipped down her cheek. She wiped it away with the
back of her hand and tried to smile. 'Look at me, I'm crying
again. He was the first decent man I'd known. The first who
didn't . . .' The words trailed away and she shook her head.
'The only one I ever loved.'

'He loved you, too,' the Constable told her.

'Aye, I know that.' She fixed her gaze on him. 'You arranged
all that, didn't you? The subscription, and the city paying the

rent.' Nottingham said nothing. 'I know you did. None of them would have cared otherwise. I'm grateful, really I am. We all are.'

'It's the very least they could do.'

'I'll bet they didn't think of it themselves, though. He loved that job, you know. He was so proud to be your deputy.'

Nottingham reached across the table and put his hand over hers. 'I couldn't have asked for anyone better. And he was a friend. A loyal one.'

'Make a friend of John and he'd never let you down.' The tears began again. 'I miss him. Every time I breathe. Every time I hear something and turn around and it's not him.'

'I know,' he said softly.

'Does it get better?'

Better? He wondered at the word. 'You learn to live with it. To get by.'

'Is that how you feel?'

'Yes.' There was so much more, but she didn't need to hear his troubles; she had enough of her own. 'If there's anything I can do to help you, just tell me.'

'You can't bring him back, can you?'

'I wish I could.'

She glanced down at Isabell. 'James will remember him. This one won't ever know what he was like. That's all I want, Mr Nottingham. For him to walk through that door with his grin and his appetite and for everything to be the way it was.' She stared at him. 'Honestly, you've done enough as it is. I've got to learn to do it by myself.'

'I mean it. If there's anything you need, if you want Lucy to help for a few days . . .'

'No.' She shook her head. 'It's very kind, but we'll . . . get by.'

The Constable stood. 'I do want to help.'

'I know,' Lizzie said. 'Thank you.'

By the time he reached home it was close to full darkness. Lucy brought him the plate she'd kept warm, sitting across from him at the table.

'You'd best be careful, that's hot,' she warned. He ate a mouthful and smiled.

'It's good.'

'Did you go and see her?'

'I did,' he answered, noticing the relief on the girl's face that he'd kept his promise.

'How is she?'

Nottingham chewed slowly, framing his answer. 'Like I was after Mary died.'

'I could visit her again,' Lucy offered.

'Leave her be for now.'

'Is that what she wants?'

'I think it's what she needs,' he answered eventually. 'All we do is remind her.'

She nodded, her mouth tight, waiting to take his dishes back to the kitchen.

'You helped,' he assured her. 'She needed someone to look after the children.'

'I'd have stayed if she'd let me.' Lucy glanced around the room, at Emily, her head over a book and Rob dozing in a chair. 'Look at you, you're fine here, all of you. Anyone could take care of this house.'

'No. You're family here,' the Constable told her simply.

'Am I?'

'You know you are.'

Finally she gave a quick nod and disappeared into the other room.

TWENTY-SEVEN

Nottingham woke early, and left the house well before the first band of daylight to walk into town. The night man had left a few scrawled lines: no problems at the school. He wrote up the daily report, hearing Leeds come to life through the open window, the clop of hooves and drag of wheels on the roads, the shouts and laughter of the people.

As the clock struck seven he went over to the Moot Hall. Outside in the Shambles the butchers were hacking at carcasses, blood running in the gutters, dogs barking and howling for meat. Inside everything seemed hushed, as if he'd stepped into another world, separate, richer.

He expected to find Cobb the clerk outside the mayor's office, but it was another man who was working there and greeted him with a sober nod.

'Good morning, Mr Nottingham.'

'Good morning.' He put the paper on the desk. He'd seen the man before, he was sure of that, but where? He was older, grey peppered throughout his hair, his face long and deeply serious. The clothes had seen better days but they were clean and presentable; he was washed and freshly shaved. 'Where's Mr Cobb?'

'I believe Mayor Fenton decided he'd prefer a different clerk, sir.'

So Cobb had paid the price for passing on the mayor's secrets to the Constable. For a moment he felt guilty. But only for a moment. Without the information he'd never have secured a pension or rent payment for Lizzie.

'I'm sure he's found a good one. What's your name?

'Roundell Jenkins, sir.' His face stayed impassive as he answered.

It wasn't familiar. Sooner or later, though, he'd place the man.

Back at the jail he'd scarcely seated himself when a boy ran in, a letter clutched tight in his hand, eyes wide in awe of seeing such a place.

'What is it, lad?'

'For the Constable, sir. Came in on the mail a few minutes back.'

He passed the lad a farthing and tore open the seal. It had taken less time than he'd expected; maybe everything moved faster down in London.

> Sir,
>
> I trust this finds you in good health. Your request was passed to me but I had no knowledge of Tom Finer, so I needed to ask others who might be familiar with him. He is, as you already suspected, a well-known figure to some in the law, although he has never been convicted of anything.

I endeavoured to make my inquiries on your behalf as extensive as possible, and I have learned that Mr Finer was active both here in the City and in Westminster. He was, I am reliably told, suspected of involvement in at least ten murders over the years, although there was never enough proof to bring him to court. The members of the watch in both areas are certain he sold stolen goods, but again, this was impossible to prove.

In the last several years Mr Finer is known to have invested in property in Covent Garden. There was speculation that he forced his way into some of the deals, and when the buildings were later sold that he amassed a goodly sum of money. According to my information he made many contacts, both in business and government. Some found him to be charming and good company but others have claimed they were afraid of him.

According to those who know, he left London with neither warning nor word to anyone. He simply dismissed the servants who worked for him, had his belongings packed and left, not even saying where he was going. One thing I can tell you is that there was no special investigation under way into him and no one wishes to recall him to the capital for any reason. Without your letter we would have been unaware of his whereabouts.

I wish you well of the man, sir, and hope that this is of assistance to you.

Your Servant,

Joseph Franklin

Assistant Clerk, Central Criminal Court

He read it again, paying as much attention to what was unstated as to the words on the page. Finer had left London with his fortune in his pockets. Just as it had been in Leeds, the authorities knew what he'd done but they'd never managed to catch him for it. Witnesses would have suddenly vanished, payments would have been made and he would never have seen the inside of a jail.

So what had made him leave London so suddenly? There was no mention of someone after him, and Nottingham knew it wasn't simply a rush of desire to spend his declining years quietly in Leeds; the man had already shown his colours in his dealings at the workhouse.

He'd hoped for more, for some reason to send Finer back to London in chains. That wasn't going to happen; as the clerk had gratefully pointed out, the Constable would have to look to the man himself. And there was little in the note that Finer hadn't said himself, either in fact or hints. Suddenly a connection fell into his mind, and he realized he'd seen Roundell Jenkins, the mayor's new clerk, drinking with Finer in the Talbot. So the man has his source in high places now. He'd need to be very careful about what he put in his daily report in future. He glanced at the letter a final time and tossed it aside on the pile before walking out. There was work to be done.

Rob had waited, ready to leave, impatient for Emily to dash down the stairs. As it was, the women were already waiting outside the school when they arrived, and he stood aside for them all to enter once the door was unlocked. Another night without damage.

He began to stroll up Briggate, then broke into a run as he heard the shouts of an argument, a man and a woman at the entrance to one of the courts. By the time he arrived, the man had his fist raised, ready to hit her a second time, his face flushed and twisted with anger. Lister pinned him against the wall, the cudgel ready in his hand.

'She told me it were free,' the man protested.

He knew the girl. Kate. She'd been a servant once, then let go when she couldn't hide the bulge of a baby any longer. Since then she'd been a whore, scraping by, never giving any trouble. She had a hand to her cheek, trying to cover the red mark where she'd been struck, tears in her eyes.

'He's a lying bastard, Mr Lister.' She spat at the man's feet. 'I told him a penny ha'penny and he said yes.'

Rob turned to the man, tightening his hold on the collar. 'Well?'

The man glared, then finally nodded, deflating, the fury still in his eyes.

'Then you can give her tuppence.'

'But—'

'The extra's for hitting her,' Rob said, raising the cudgel so the man could see it. 'Turn out your pockets.'

He waited as the man obeyed, spilling coins on the ground.

'Take your money,' Lister told the girl, and she scrambled around, picking up two coins then vanishing. 'And you, you'd better cause no more trouble.'

'For not paying a slut?' the man asked incredulously.

Rob pushed his face close enough to smell the fear on the man's breath.

'You'd better be glad you didn't end up in the jail.' He let go and watched the man slump.

Rob had barely gone ten yards along Briggate before Kate was at his side.

'Thank you, Mr Lister,' she said. 'I thought he were going to hurt me.'

He caught sight of her face; the mark was spreading. 'It looks as if he already did.'

She shrugged. 'I've had worse. There's some right buggers out there. At least he didn't break anything.'

'You need to watch yourself.'

'I will,' she promised. He expected her to leave. Instead she stood there, looking at him. 'It's terrible what happened to Mr Sedgwick.'

'Yes,' he agreed grimly.

'I feel sorry for his Lizzie with those bairns. He were allus good to us out here, allus fair.'

'I'll try to be the same.'

'Nay, I'm not saying you wouldn't.' She smiled and touched his arm lightly. 'That body you found. The one buried past Upper Tenters.'

'You know who she was?' He hoped as he waited for the answer.

The girl shook her head. 'But I think I saw summat,' she said.

'What?' he asked.

Kate took a breath. 'Well, it were late Sunday last. Middle of the night. I'd no money nor food so I thought I'd go out and see if anyone were looking.' She glanced at him and he nodded for her to continue. 'There's allus a few out late and some of them might be in the mood. I'd given my little one a tot of gin, so I knew she'd sleep. Anyway, there were no one with owt to spend.' He listened patiently, waiting for whatever she really had to tell him. 'I went out along Mill Hill, up toward Shaw Well and Boar Lane to see if there might be anyone there. You know where I mean?' He nodded, fixing it in his mind's eye. 'I saw someone taking the path down towards the woods there.'

'Was he carrying anything?' He could feel his heart beating faster.

'Summat.' She shrugged again. 'It were too dark to see much. But I'll tell you, he were a right big bugger. I could tell that.'

'Why didn't you say anything before?'

Kate looked at him as if he was simple. 'What was I going to say, Mr Lister? I didn't know who he were. It could have been nowt.'

'What time was this?'

'Two, three mebbe. I'd not even have thought about it again if there hadn't been talk about the lass who was found, and then seen you.'

'Did you see the man's hands at all?' Rob asked hopefully.

'His hands?' She stared at him blankly. 'No. Why?'

'It doesn't matter.' He fumbled in the pocket of his coat and passed her a coin, seeing the brief flash of gratitude on her face before she left.

'What do you think, boss?'

'It could be anything,' the Constable said carefully. 'But at that time of night I'd wager it was nothing legal. It's a pity that lass didn't see his hands.' He stroked his chin. 'One thing bothers me, though.'

'What's that?'

'I just wonder . . . Jem Carter was beaten, he'd had his throat cut. The girl we found had no marks on her at all. Whatever did for her, it wasn't violence. I think it was probably poison. People don't usually change the way they kill. It doesn't make sense.' He paused, thinking. 'Everyone who's seen him has said how big he is. If he's that large, why can't we find him?

'Maybe we're not looking in the right places.'

Nottingham sat back and looked at Lister. 'What do you mean?'

'He's somewhere in Leeds, we know that much,' Rob began. The Constable nodded, and he continued, 'Maybe he's keeping out of sight during the day.'

'I'd believe that, except old Hercules at the Rose and Crown saw the man eating with someone he thought was his sister.'

'Perhaps they're both killers. She's the poisoner and he was getting rid of the body.'

'It's possible,' Nottingham agreed reluctantly. He didn't know; it just felt too complicated. 'But why those two? Carter didn't have anything. Neither did the dead girl, from the look of her.'

'I don't know.'

The Constable steepled his fingers under his chin. 'Neither do I. There's no sense behind it.'

'And then there's Jenny Carter's suicide. Maybe there's more to that, too.'

'No,' Nottingham disagreed. 'There's nothing to show she didn't kill herself. Unless we learn something, we have to believe that.'

'Yes, boss.'

Rob spent much of the morning asking after a large man with big hands. Someone like that should stand out, especially if there was a sister. A few claimed to have noticed him but had paid no mind, nothing more than a pinprick in their memories.

And he wasn't going to forget about the school, either. Even if there was no more damage, the business wasn't over until the man was caught. Yet he felt he was going round and round, simply chasing himself. No one had any information.

Yet by late afternoon he knew no more about anything than he had first thing that morning. Another day of frustration. If John . . . he started to think, then stopped himself. That was history now. It was over. He was the deputy. He had to live up to everything Sedgwick had taught him.

Emily was pacing in the schoolroom, her face drawn, biting

her lip. As soon as she saw him, she gathered up her books, waiting as the closed the shutters and locked up.

'How were they?' Rob asked.

'Fine.' Her tone was sharp enough to make him stop.

'What is it?'

She shook her head and started off along the Calls, fast enough that he had to hurry to catch up, suddenly worried.

'What's wrong? What's happened? Tell me, please.' But she said nothing.

He followed her along the path by the river, beyond the warehouses, then up a track into a copse. She'd brought him here once before, to show him the secret place she'd shared with her sister, back when they were children, when Rose was still alive. Now, with the bushes and branches full and thick, the hollow was hidden, a place apart from the world where no one would interrupt them. Emily settled on a fallen log, smoothing down her dress. Rob sat beside her, anxious, trying not to press her, to let her air her troubles when she was ready.

She picked a thread from the skirt, fidgeting, her face set, anxious.

'I'm going to have a baby,' Emily said finally, staring straight ahead. There was no joy in her voice.

'What?' He'd been expecting something terrible, his mind racing through every bad thing that could have happened. But he'd never thought of this. 'Are you sure?'

The look she gave him was withering. 'Of course I'm sure. Mama taught me how to know.' She stood, walking around the clearing in quick circles. 'I don't want this,' she told him. 'Not now.'

'But . . .' he began, then didn't know what to say. He rose, ready to hold her, to comfort her, but she moved away.

'I've only just started the school.'

He let the silence grow for ten heartbeats, then asked,

'What are we going to do?' A woman became pregnant, her belly grew, she gave birth and then there was the baby; that was all he knew. Even with Emily, he'd never truly imagined himself a father. The two of them simply existed together. They were, and that was all. The thought of someone else, a child, had never been part of it. He hadn't looked that far ahead.

'I don't know,' she answered emptily, slumping next to him,
then putting her head against his chest and sighing. 'I've been
trying to think of that since I first realized.'

'How long have you known?'

'Long enough. Lucy guessed.'

In the world where he'd grown up, the rules were unwritten
but perfectly clear. No wife would work. She was there to
keep a home, to provide an heir or daughters to marry off.
But Emily had made her own world, so different from everything he'd known before.

'We'll need to marry,' Rob said, and she nodded glumly.
She'd always said she'd never wed, never be the property of
a man, and he'd accepted that. But this changed everything.
She knew that as well as he did. She was the Constable's
daughter. Folk might turn a blind eye to Rob lodging in the
house, but for Emily to be pregnant and unmarried was out
of the question; it would never be tolerated.

'I know.' She sounded so small, lost, hopeless. He'd never
seen her like this before. Even after her mother's death, in the
long silences of grieving, there'd been a sense of iron about
her. Now everything she'd believed in was falling away around
her. 'Can I trust you enough?' she asked, looking straight into
his eyes.

'Yes.' He didn't hesitate. If she was his wife, all she owned
would become his; that was the law. The money she'd inherited
and used to start the school would belong to him. He could
spend it however he chose and she had no recourse. 'I don't
want your money. You know that.' He paused. 'I love you.'

She tried to smile. 'I'm scared, Rob. I'm terrified. This, the
school . . .' Her voice trailed away.

'We'll manage,' he told her. 'Your father—'

Emily shook her head quickly. 'I don't want him to know.
Not yet. Please.'

He nodded. In the past he'd dreamed she'd turn to him with
the desire to get married, but never like this, drifting into it
because there was no other choice. He reached out and took
her hand, squeezing it lightly. She didn't pull away this time.

'I'm not going to give up teaching,' she said after a while.
'I can't. Not now. The girls need me.'

'But you'll have to,' he told her.

'Why?' she asked. 'Why? Tell me that. I'll still be the same person. I can teach just as well when I'm carrying a child or after it's born.'

He couldn't answer. All he knew was the way he'd been taught, what was acceptable.

'Those girls in school,' she continued, her voice rising, 'do you think they'll be able to stop working once they've had a baby? Half their mothers have to take in laundry to help make ends meet. They won't be shocked if I'm in school. They're the ones I care about.'

'I just want you to be happy,' Rob said, but his words seemed feeble, not strong enough for all this.

'Then find whoever's trying to harm the school,' she snapped. 'That would be a start.'

'We're trying.'

Emily took a long breath. 'We'd better go home,' she said. 'Lucy will be wondering what's happened to us.'

TWENTY-EIGHT

B y Saturday there had been no more incidents at the school, but still no word of who'd done the damage. A few more claimed to have seen the man with large hands who could have been Jem Carter's killer, but still no one could name him. Each day left the Constable more frustrated. He felt like a fool, unable to find someone who should stand out so easily.

When the bell rang for the start of the cloth market he paced up and down Briggate. He'd completed three circuits, not really paying attention to what was happening, when a hand tugged at his sleeve.

'Richard.' He turned, seeing Tom Williamson smiling at him.

'I'm sorry, I was thinking.'

'I've been trying to attract your attention.'

'Is something wrong?'

'No, nothing like that.' He drew Nottingham away. 'I just

wanted to tell you the Corporation's decided not to rebuild the workhouse. It's what we suspected.' He hesitated, then asked, 'Any word on who started the fire?'

'No.' The Constable shook his head, not saying he'd done nothing to look. 'No one's going to admit that. Can you blame them?'

'I suppose not.' For once the merchant was soberly dressed in a dark grey coat and breeches, workaday shoes on his feet. He saw Nottingham looking and grinned. 'I was dressed and out before Hannah was up. I feel much more comfortable like this.'

'Tell me, can you think of a big man with large hands?'

'What?' The question took Williamson aback for a moment, then he thought. 'Not really. A few who are tall or broad, I suppose, but you know most of them. Why?'

'Someone I'm trying to find, that's all.'

'Is this to do with the school?'

'A killing. But we haven't forgotten the school, don't worry about that.'

'I have faith in you, Richard. Now I'd better see about getting this cloth I've bought to the warehouse.'

At least someone had faith, Nottingham thought as the merchant walked away. He was fast losing his.

By dinner he'd stopped three men to question them, each one towering above him. Two had been poor, their clothes more covering than decoration. The third had an expensive coat and breeches, his dark hair carefully dressed, and for a moment the Constable let himself believe he'd found his man. But he was a cloth agent, a man who made his living on the road, with signed documents in his pocket to show he'd been in King's Lynn the night Jem Carter was murdered. With an apology he'd let the bemused man go.

At the White Swan he brooded over his meal, drinking and picking at the food. Clouds had drifted in during the morning. No promise of rain but they were enough to clamp the heat close to the ground, making skin prickle and tempers fray.

Rob appeared and sat on the bench. He pushed a hand through his hair so it stood on end. 'The bastard's some-where.'

'We'll find him. Even if it takes a while,' Nottingham said with a confidence he wasn't sure he felt. 'We do what we can. Even a new deputy can't solve everything immediately.'

Lister pursed his lips. 'Boss, I'm not sure I'm the right person for the job. Not after Mr Sedgwick.'

Nottingham smiled gently. 'I think you'll become a fine deputy.' He chose his words carefully. 'I know you're not John. Don't try to be.'

A sudden cry made them sit upright and glance out of the window. A man was running down Kirkgate. A big man in good, dark clothes.

'Go!' the Constable ordered.

His lungs were burning. His feet pounded on the ground. Rob had chased the man past the Parish Church and over Timble Bridge. He'd gained a few yards but the man kept on moving, glancing over his shoulder as he crossed the fields and began the scramble up Cavalier Hill.

Rob picked up speed as a second wind coursed through him. He drew close enough to make out the man's features when he looked back, frantic fear in his eyes.

The man stumbled, reaching out to clutch at the grass and pull himself quickly upright, near the top of the hill. Rob pushed himself harder. He could hear the man panting now and smell the sweat from his body. He reached out, fingers closing around the man's ankle to send him tumbling and spinning helplessly down the far side of the hill. He didn't try to rise again.

Rob bent over, hands on his knees. His breeches were dusty, legs shaking. He unwound the stock from his neck and wiped his face with it, keeping his eyes fixed on the man, ready to pursue if he tried to move.

After a minute he began to ease down the slope. He circled the man carefully, ready for any sudden movement, but he remained still, eyes closed. Finally Lister knelt, shaking the man's shoulder. Nothing. He placed his fingers against the neck, feeling the beat of blood strong in the veins. Reaching in the deep pocket of his old coat he found a piece of rope and tied the man's hands behind his back. Then he sat, waiting for him to come round.

Two farmhands had joined him by the time the man finally moaned and tried to stand, collapsing back when he couldn't move his arms. He jerked his head around until he spotted Rob.

'I'm going to kill you,' he said, spittle on his lips. 'Let me go.'

'Give me a hand to get him upright,' Rob asked the men.

'He's a reet big bugger,' one said.

'They's none of 'em so large when they're on t' ground,' the other laughed. But together, hands under his arms, they pulled him up.

'What's your name?' Lister asked.

'Why?'

'I'm the deputy constable and I want to know. That good enough for you?' It felt strange to use the title, as if it didn't fit yet.

The man glared. 'Jackson,' he replied grudgingly. 'Ralph Jackson.'

'Why were you running, Mr Jackson?'

'I was late,' he smirked.

'Then I'll make sure your appointment can find you at the jail.'

'And if I don't want to go?'

Rob nodded at the labourers. They took hold of the man's arms and started to march him towards Leeds.

In the cell he made the man stand with his back towards him before he'd untie the rope and Jackson massaged his wrists slowly. He was a good two yards high, with a wide chest, but his hands weren't especially large.

'The Constable will talk to you when he's back.'

'And what am I supposed to do until then?' the man asked.

Rob smiled. 'I'd suggest you sit and gather your wits, Mr Jackson. You might need them.'

Let the man stew a while, he thought. The weather was close and the cells were hot. It might put him in a more talkative mood later. He poured himself some ale and drank deep.

An hour passed before Nottingham returned. He hung his coat on the nail and sat behind the desk.

'You must have caught him, you look pleased with yourself.'

'In the cells.'

'Why was he running?'

'Late for an appointment.' Rob said, raising his eyebrows. 'That's all he's said.'

'Does he have a name?'

'Ralph Jackson.'

'What do you think?' the Constable wondered.

'He's hiding something, I'm sure of that. But his hands aren't that big.'

'I believe I'll have a talk with Mr Jackson, anyway. Have you given him something to drink?'

'Not yet.'

Nottingham nodded, poured two mugs of ale and carried them through to the cells.

'Mr Jackson, I'm Richard Nottingham, the Constable in Leeds. Some ale for you, perhaps?' The man took it gratefully and drained the cup in a single swallow as Nottingham stood by the door. 'You were running at a fair pace earlier.'

'I told your lad, I was late.'

'Who were you meeting?'

The man looked directly at him. 'I can't tell you,' he answered.

'So it's a mystery,' the Constable mused. 'Turn out your pockets, if you will.'

There wasn't much, a purse with a guinea and some smaller coins, a square of linen and a comb.

'That lad took my knife when he tied me up.'

'I should hope he did,' Nottingham said with amusement. 'You have some money, your clothes are cut well. They'll have cost you a penny or two. But I don't know you, Mr Jackson. I don't believe you're a Leeds man.'

'I'm from York,' he answered after a hesitation.

'And do people in York always run to their appointments? I've never noticed it when I've been there. Or perhaps you were running from something.'

'Did you see anyone coming after me?'

'That doesn't mean much. What's your business in Leeds?'

'I'm here to see someone.'

The Constable sighed. 'That seems to bring us in a circle. Who were you here to see?'

Jackson pushed his tongue around his cheek and stared straight ahead. 'I can't tell you.'

'Admirable discretion, Mr Jackson, but not helpful. We've been searching for someone who looks like you. We think he committed a murder.'

The man began to rise, then sat on the bench again. 'I haven't killed anyone,' he said quietly.

'That's an easy claim to make, Mr Jackson. But I'll need some more proof. How long have you been in Leeds?'

'A fortnight.'

'A long visit,' Nottingham mused. 'Where have you been staying?'

'The King's Arms.' The Constable knew it well, on the corner of Briggate and Currie Entry. Close to Megson's Court, where Carter's body had been dumped, and the man had been in town the night of the murder. 'Ask the landlord, he'll vouch for me.'

'I plan on it, Mr Jackson. In the meantime I'll leave you here to think about what else you want to tell me.'

The building had once been the home of John Harrison, the rich wool merchant who'd built St John's and the grammar school and given Leeds its market cross; that was what Thoresby had told him years ago, anyway. If it was true it must have been a grand place when Harrison was alive, bigger than any of the new mansions at Town End, a rival to the brick Red House on the Upper Head Row. But Harrison was long dead and the place had been the King's Arms as long as the Constable had been alive.

He found Benjamin Barton, the landlord, inside, watching as a serving girl waited on a pair of drovers still dusty from the road. He was a small man with a harried, hunted face, as if the world was too much for him. From all reports it was his wife who held the power in the place and her money that had purchased it, as she reminded him often.

'Mr Nottingham.' Barton gave a nervous, greasy smile and wiped a hand across his mouth. 'Not often we have you in here. Is there a problem?'

'Just one or two questions, Ben.'

'Ask away. Ask away.'

'Do you have a man named Ralph Jackson staying here?'

'We do, we do. Two weeks now, close enough.' So he hadn't been lying about that, the Constable thought.

'How has he paid for his lodging?'

'It was cash when he arrived.' No landlord would forget that.

'For how long?'

'Until Monday.'

'And has he caused any trouble? Been out late or anything like that?'

'Not that I know of.' He looked suddenly worried. 'What's he done?'

'He's not accused of anything,' Nottingham answered carefully. 'Has he met anyone that you've noticed, or mentioned anyone?'

Barton scratched his head. 'I've seen him with a fair few folk in the bar,' he said. 'And he's been going off here and there.'

'Do you know where, or what he does?'

'No,' Ben answered with a chuckle. 'Can't be asking them that, can I?'

'No ideas?'

'None, Mr Nottingham. He's always polite, dresses well. He must have paid a fair price for that horse he has back in the stables. Not short of a guinea or two, I'd say.'

'Thank you.'

The Constable went back into the heat with more questions but no answers. Jackson had enough in his purse to keep himself until the next day. Why wouldn't he say who he was meeting? And what had he been doing in Leeds? Business?

He seemed an unlikely murderer but the Constable had known stranger ones before, men as innocent as buttermilk who turned out to have violent, vicious natures.

'You look vexed, laddie.' Tom Finer stood there, well wrapped in a heavy coat regardless of the warm weather, looking oddly heartened for someone who'd just lost his workhouse. 'Troubles?'

'They're my job, Mr Finer. As I'm sure you know.'

'And what have you found out about my troubles, I wonder? Discovered who burned the place down yet?'

'Not yet.'

'I daresay you've had other things to think about. At least you killed the one who got your deputy. Didn't give him a chance from what I've heard.' He nodded his approval.

'I did what had to be done.'

'You got something for the widow and children, too. You've learned well, Constable.'

'What about you, Mr Finer? Are you keeping clear of business for a while?'

'You never know when an opportunity will come.' He tapped a finger against his nose. 'You have to stay alert, laddie, and ready for the possibilities.'

TWENTY-NINE

All day his mind had been elsewhere. Even as he chased Ralph Jackson, Rob had been thinking about Emily and the baby inside her. Their baby. The idea seemed so big he believed his head would burst. Between that and what had happened to John, his world had turned into a strange, unknown place, so different from what it had been just a few days before.

He was waiting near the school for the girls to rush out like a river then trickle away into the distance. Once they'd passed him, laughter and shouts rising into the air, he strode into the room. Emily was cleaning, bending to pick up pieces of this and that. Without thinking, he joined her.

'They seemed happy when they left.'

She laughed. 'Weren't you when school finished for the day?'

'I was just glad to leave.' He smiled. 'But they looked as if they enjoyed it more than I ever did.'

'Maybe they have a better teacher.' Emily grinned and he put his arms around her.

'A lovelier one, anyway,' he allowed. 'I'd never do this with Mr Brown.'

'I should hope not!' Playfully, she pushed him away, her eyes twinkling. 'Come on, it's too stuffy to stay here.'

She put her arm through his as they walked. Women stopped to talk to her about their daughters and men raised their hats in greeting. They needed her here, they valued her, and he knew what he had to do.

At Timble Bridge he stopped, leaning over the parapet to look down at the clear water flowing gently over the rocks.

'What are we going to do?' he asked.

'I don't know.' She stooped, picked up a pebble and tossed it into the stream.

'Could Lucy look after the baby while you teach?'

Emily turned slowly and cocked her head. 'Why?'

'Because what you do is important.'

'You know what some people would think.'

He nodded and took a deep breath before speaking. 'Folk are going to think what they want, anyway. They're always going to talk. This way, at least they'll have something good to talk about.'

She looked into his eyes. 'That's not what you said before.'

'I know,' he admitted. 'But I've seen the way they treat you. You're right. You can't stop now.'

'Thank you.' Emily reached out and squeezed his hand. 'But the Williamsons might not like it. They might decide not to support the school.'

'They're the ones who have to decide that.' He hesitated. 'We will have to get married, though.'

'Yes.' It was a small word that said so much, a reluctant acceptance of the situation and his proposal.

'I'll make you happy.'

'I know. I just wish . . .' She threw another pebble, watching it land and the ripples spreading before shaking her head. 'But wishes aren't horses.'

'We'd better tell your father.'

'Yes.' She agreed joylessly. 'I wish Mama was still here. She'd have loved to help me prepare for my wedding.'

'I'll talk to the vicar and have him read the banns.'

'I didn't want it to be like this, Rob.'

'I know.' He held her hand as they walked up Marsh Lane. 'But we'll just make the best of the way things are.'

The Constable returned to the jail at the close of the afternoon. The heat seemed to press down on his flesh and he felt as if he was basted in his own sweat.

'Well, Mr Jackson, you didn't lie about staying at the King's Arms.'

'Why would I?' the man bristled. 'Do you have more ale? I'm dry as dust.'

Nottingham poured him a mug. 'But I still don't know why you were in Leeds. Two weeks is a long visit. There must have been a purpose for it.'

'I'm not your murderer.'

'Perhaps you're not,' the Constable agreed breezily. 'But unless you start giving me some truth, how can I be sure?'

Jackson seemed to think for a long time. 'I'm a buyer for the government,' he said finally.

'Are you now?'

'I've letters in my pack to prove it. They're at the inn.'

'It's an honest enough occupation. Why do you need to be so secretive about it?'

'I'm negotiating contracts,' the man told him, 'and my job is to find the best prices. If everyone knows what I'm doing . . . well, you see?'

'I'll need to check your papers.'

'Of course.' The man gave a quick bow.

'Work like that doesn't mean you're not a murderer, of course. And it still doesn't explain why you were running.'

'I was late, I told you.'

'Not for business, I'm sure of that. A lady, perhaps?' Jackson stayed silent and the Constable sighed. 'If you won't say, you have to stay here. I don't trust you.'

'As you wish,' the man said. 'I warn you, though, once people learn I'm in jail they'll be coming to see you.'

'I look forward to it.' Nottingham raised his mug in a mock toast and left.

He doubted that Ralph Jackson had killed anyone. He didn't have the air of a murderer. And his hands didn't fit with what they knew about Carter's killer. But he was still the best they had, and he refused to account for himself properly. John would probably have already turned him out with a warning, he thought. He wasn't ready to do that quite yet. Instead he arranged food and drink for the man and set off for home, weary to his core. They needed to keep looking.

He was distracted as they sat around the table to eat, wondering how to pry the truth from Jackson. He'd check the man's pack, but he was already sure of what he'd discover. What he needed was the rest of the tale.

'Papa,' Emily said, drawing him out of his thoughts. He looked up to see them all staring expectantly at him, his daughter, Rob and Lucy.

'What?' he asked.

'We have something to tell you.'

He glanced from one face to the others, all of them bright with a secret. 'What is it?'

Rob took hold of Emily's hand. 'We're going to get married,' he said.

For a moment he thought he'd misheard. She'd always said she'd never marry. He'd come to accept it, although he'd always hoped she'd change.

'I'm going to have a baby,' Emily told him. 'You're going to be a grandpapa.'

Nottingham began to grin, a smile that filled his face before turning to laughter.

'That's wonderful news,' he told them, feeling the joy well up inside. Lucy was smirking, and he said, 'You knew, didn't you?'

'Miss Emily asked me not to say anything.'

His little girl, married. He'd seen her sister wed before she'd taken ill and died. Now he had to hope that Emily would survive the birth and that the child would be healthy. More than anything, he wanted her to be happy, but as he looked into her eyes he wasn't so certain that she was.

In bed he stretched his arm out across the sheet, imagining for a moment that Mary was there, thinking of all the things she'd say at the news, her excitement and joy. She'd have already been making plans, a new gown for the bride, talking about this and that until he couldn't keep his eyes open.

But the only words she spoke were in his head, and he stayed wakeful long after the rest of the house was silent, caught between the pain and pleasure of too many memories.

The Constable completed his Monday rounds. The Sabbath had been quiet. After church he'd stopped at the graveyard, giving Mary and Rose the news, letting the silence of the place fill him.

Jackson had offered him nothing more. He'd been to the King's Arms and examined the pack; everything was as he'd claimed. But before he set the man free he needed to know why he had been running.

He walked to the bridge, turned and began the climb up Briggate. Clouds still covered the city, making the air close and thick. As he reached Boar Lane a boy darted out from a court, his eyes hopeful, a letter clutched in his dirty fist.

'I was told to give this to you, sir.'

'To me?' He looked around. 'Who told you to do that?'

He shook his head. Nottingham brought a coin from the pocket of his old breeches and gave it to the lad.

'Thank you, sir,' he said and scurried off quickly.

The Constable broke the plain seal on the note.

You have a gentleman in your jail. He was on his way to see me. If you come and meet me now I can vouch for him. I shall be at Timble Bridge.

It was a woman's hand, flowing, educated. More mystery. He put the paper in his coat pocket and began to walk towards Sheepscar Beck.

She had her back to him, but from ten yards away he knew who it was. He'd seen her often enough at church. His boots rasped on the wood and she turned quickly at the noise.

'Mrs Williamson,' he said, and gave a small bow.

She glanced around nervously. 'I hoped the boy would find you.'

'He did. You've something to tell me?'

'I'm going to have to trust you, Mr Nottingham. Please don't say anything to my husband.' She was trying to keep her voice steady but he saw her hands shaking. 'I know he's your friend.'

'We all have our secrets, Mrs Williamson. Not all of them need to be told.'

The woman nodded. 'Mr Jackson was on his way to meet me. You . . . I'm sure you don't need me to give you details.'

'No.'

She took a deep breath. 'I hope what I've said is enough for you. Now I have to pray you're as good as your word.' Hannah Williamson stared at him.

'I'll say nothing,' he promised.

'Thank you.' Relief flooded into her face. 'I ought to get back, I told the governess I'd only be a few minutes.'

'Of course.'

He watched her walk away, knowing the courage it had taken to speak up. And for Jackson to have remained silent. Once she was out of sight he returned to the jail and unlocked the cell.

'You're free to leave, Mr Jackson.'

'Decided to believe me?'

'You could say that. Just in time for you to start your journey home, too. York, wasn't it?'

The man smiled. 'That was what I said. I'll bid you good day, Constable, but I hope you won't mind if I don't thank you for the hospitality.'

As the man reached the door Nottingham said quietly, 'Your discretion does you credit.'

For the briefest moment Jackson hesitated, then walked on.

They were back to nothing, no one in custody, not even a suspect. And no one in mind for the damage to the school. Ten years before this wouldn't have happened. He'd have had them all under lock and key instead of feeling like a man fumbling his way through the darkness with no path to guide him.

THIRTY

Rob wanted to tell people. He'd visited the church and talked to the curate; the banns would be cried for the first time on Sunday. He felt that the news was written on his face; if anyone looked close enough they'd see his expression, overjoyed but full of trepidation and make their own guess.

Emily had asked him to say nothing about the baby yet. Too many things could go wrong; for now, silence was the best course. But once the school day was over she'd go and talk to the Williamsons and tell them everything. Then she just had to hope they'd be willing to keep supporting the school.

He walked out along the riverbank. The camp had been cleared for the day, only the charred circles of the fires remaining. Bessie was under her shelter in the trees, needles clacking as she knitted.

'I hear you're the deputy now, Mr Lister,' she said as he approached.

'I am, Bessie, although I'd rather it wasn't that way.'

'We'll all miss him. Not as much as his lass and their little 'uns, though.'

He nodded. He still hadn't been to see Lizzie again. He didn't know what to say to her. Every sentence he formed in his head never seemed enough.

'Your folk must be breathing easier with the workhouse gone,' he said.

'They are,' she agreed. 'We've had a few drifting back now that word's gone round. But like I told the Constable, I don't think any of them set that fire. I'd better not hear that they had or I'll be bringing them to the jail. I won't tolerate that, Mr Lister.'

Rob smiled. 'Do you know anything about a big man with dark hair and very large hands?'

'That's a strange question,' Bessie said, looking at him curiously.

'Hands so large you'd notice them,' he prompted her.

'I've seen someone like that.'

'Down at the camp?'

'No, not here.' She looked into the distance across the river, trying to recall, then shook her head. 'I don't remember exactly where. I'm sorry. But I remember his hands.'

'When was it, do you know?' He was desperate for any information that would bring them closer to the man. All Bessie could do was shake her head once more.

'The days all get mixed up, Mr Lister. I wish I could tell you.'

'Thank you, anyway.'

She looked at him again. 'You look like you've had good news.'

'Me?' he asked, reddening.

She grinned. 'Aye, you. You can't hide a thing. It must be to do with that lass of the Constable's.'

'Maybe.'

Bessie smiled and winked. 'Whatever it is, I wish the pair of you well.'

Nottingham marched down Briggate, greeting all the faces he knew. Crossing the bridge he dodged between carts and the piles of stinking horse dung on the road, before threading his way into the small streets. He'd been reluctant to return here, to ask for help once more. Now he felt as if it didn't matter. All he wanted was for this business to be done so he could leave this job.

A grinning Henry, his dark skin shiny with sweat, opened the door.

'Get thisen inside, Mr Nottingham,' he said. 'I'm in the kitchen cooking, but Mr Buck has a cool room. Go through, tha knows the way.' He hesitated. 'I'm reet sorry about Mr Sedgwick. He was a good lad.'

'He was indeed, Henry.'

Joe Buck was in the parlour, reading; the shutters were partway closed and the window open to catch the hint of breeze that came along the river. He was in his shirt, stock unwound.

'Constable.' The fence rose easily, a ready smile on his lips. 'Sit down, it's too hot to be standing. Some ale? You must be dry.'

'Thank you, Joe.' He shrugged off his coat and lowered himself gently on to the settle before taking a long drink.

The man stared at him. 'You're welcome to stop here a spell, Mr Nottingham. But you don't look like you've just come for the company. And much as we both miss him, I don't think you're here to reminisce about Mr Sedgwick, either. So what can I do for you?'

'Have you had any word on the school?'

Buck shook his head. 'I'd have told you if I had. No one's said anything and they know better than to lie to me.'

'Doesn't it seem odd to you that there's not a whisper on it?' the Constable asked quietly.

Buck frowned. 'It depends. If there's a lunatic out there, I could see him not telling anyone.'

'That's what worries me, Joe – a lunatic. You can never guess what they're going to do next.'

'I hear you have a man inside the place all night now.'

Nottingham nodded and smiled. Little escaped Buck's sharp eyes.

'I want this man. I might be willing to forgive and forget quite a few things if anyone can help find him.'

'That's a generous offer.'

'I'm serious about this. I want him soon.'

'I'll pass the word, Mr Nottingham. I'm sure there are folk who'll be interested.'

'Good information only, Joe.'

'I'll make sure of it,' Buck said with a grin. 'You've not taken anyone for that murder yet, either.'

'I know,' the Constable replied. 'What do you know about a man with dark hair, big, well-dressed, very large hands?'

'Doesn't fit anyone I know. Is that your killer?'

'Yes.'

'You think he killed the girl, too?' He raised his hand before Nottingham could say anything. 'We both know there aren't many secrets in Leeds. Let's not pretend there are.'

'Possibly,' Nottingham acknowledged.

'Someone will know. Happen you'd be grateful for that, too?' He raised an eyebrow questioningly.

'Maybe I would.'

Buck nodded. 'I'll tell folk.'

Lister waited patiently, close to the Williamsons' house on Briggate. He'd found a patch of shade on the far side of the street but the air was still too hot. If it remained like this all the crops would be withering in the field long before harvest came.

Emily had been there for close to half an hour. He'd walked over with her and pressed her hand as she knocked. He'd even offered to escort her inside, but she'd refused; this was something she had to face on her own. The school was hers and she needed to make her case.

Finally the maid showed her out and she stood blinking in the sunlight. He hurried across, sliding between the carts that moved quickly up the street.

'What did they say?' he asked.

'They're going to stay with the school,' she answered slowly, almost in shock. Her eyes widened and her hands clutched the sleeves of his coat, jumping up and down like a child. 'They're really going to do it! I was sure they'd say no.' Emily bit her lip. 'I can't believe it. Mr Williamson looked embarrassed when I told him, but Mrs Williamson just took over. She said she thought I was being very brave. She surprised me.' She grinned at the memory. 'She didn't even give him a chance to speak. She said they'd be happy to keep on paying the bills of the school and that if there was anything she could do, she would. She even wants me to call her Hannah.' She smiled again.

'You've an important backer there.'

She began to laugh. 'I was so scared. I thought it would all go back to the way it was, just me, on my own. They're wonderful people, Rob. I hope Papa isn't late home, I can't wait to tell him.' Her eyes were sparkling and the broad smile on her face made her look younger. 'I'm so happy, I feel like I can breathe again.'

Rob watched her as they walked, imagining how her belly would swell in the months ahead. It scared him to his heart, but he wanted it. He wanted Emily as his wife, the mother of his children.

He left her at the door of the house on Marsh Lane and walked back into Leeds. Nothing was the same, it never would be again. He breathed deep as he clattered up Kirkgate. Everything was changing. As he passed the church he tried to picture the wedding, wondering whether he should invite his parents.

He'd left their home because his father couldn't accept Emily. Her grandmother had been thrown out by her merchant husband and she'd had no choice but to whore to support herself and her son. Never mind that the boy had grown up to become Constable; that history would never make her acceptable to Rob's father. At a Sunday dinner he'd tried to humiliate Emily. He'd failed; she'd turned the tables on him. But Rob hadn't spoken to his parents since.

How would they take the news? They'd hear soon enough, the word would spread. Rob sighed. Whatever had happened, he owed it to his father to tell him before that. He returned to Briggate and paused at the door where the sign announced *Leeds Mercury*, looking through the glass at James Lister bent over the desk, scribbling away furiously. He pushed down on the handle and entered.

The smells were immediately familiar, ink, metal and polish. 'Hello, Father.'

James Lister looked up, squinting behind his spectacles. 'Robert,' he said, sitting back, a self-satisfied grin on his face. 'This is a surprise. Sit down.'

Rob settled himself on the hard wooden chair. 'Everything looks the same.'

'There's no need for it to change,' Lister told him. 'It suits me, you know that.'

His father looked much the same, Rob thought. Rounder, perhaps, his face more florid, a little less hair on his head.

'I was sorry to hear about Mr Sedgwick. By all accounts he was a good man.'

'A very good man,' Rob replied firmly.

'And you're the deputy now, I gather. You've risen well, Robert. My congratulations.' He looked bemused. 'Is this visit official or personal?'

'Personal. I wanted to tell you that I'm marrying Emily Nottingham.'

'I see,' Lister answered slowly, then looked at his son. 'Tell me, is there a baby involved in all this?'

'There is.'

'I'm sure your mother will be happy to know she's to become a grandmama.' It was as much as he'd allow.

Rob stood. He hadn't known what to expect when he came in, but he'd hoped for something more than this. 'I thought you should know, that's all.'

'I thank you,' his father said. 'I wish you the joy of a son to carry on the family name.' He lowered his head to read over the words he'd written.

Back out in the heat, the happiness he'd felt earlier deserted him. His father could do that so easily, leech the joy out of the world to leave it dry and empty. He was a man who held his grudges close, and to be defied by his own son was the gravest insult of all. It had been pointless to go. Still, he'd done his duty, he could always say that.

He began to amble up the street, thoughts dashing off in all manner of directions, then something caught his eye. A man, ten or more yards in front of him, fully half a head taller than those around him, with dark hair and dark clothes. Rob started to walk faster, pushing through people, hearing the protests as he pushed them aside but paying no attention. His eyes were fixed on the man, trying to catch a glimpse of his hands.

Something must have alerted him. The man glanced over his shoulder then began to run, forcing folk aside; a pair of women toppled over. Rob followed, dodging and sliding between the bodies. The man turned into one of the yards that ran back off Briggate. Rob had to stop, edging around a hand-cart outside the leather merchant, a few precious moments lost before he could duck through the entrance and into the cramped space of the court.

There was no sign of the man. He stopped, listening for the sound of feet but hearing only his own breathing. A path led through to a ginnel which joined a network of tiny alleys that fed out into the orchard above Holy Trinity church. The man could have gone there. Or he could be in any of the buildings in the yard, waiting, hiding.

He looked around, hoping for some sign, any indication at all. A door not closed fully, a shadow in a window. But there was nothing. On his own he didn't have a chance. As soon as he went in one direction the man would be away in another. It was hopeless.

'It was him. I'm sure of it, boss.'

'I'm sure you're right,' the Constable agreed. 'Did you see his hands?'

'No.' All the way back to the jail Rob had been cursing

himself, thinking of the things he should have done. 'If I'd just followed him instead of running . . .'

'You did what came to you. I'd probably have done exactly the same thing.'

If the words had been intended to console him, they didn't work. 'I'd know him if I saw him again.'

'We're getting closer. That's something,' Nottingham mused. He frowned. 'The problem is, now he knows we're after him, he'll stay out of sight.'

'I'm sorry, boss.'

'It's not your fault, lad. You did the right thing. A little luck and you'd have caught him. Luck just hasn't run our way in any of this.'

'What do we do now?'

The Constable thought for a long time before speaking. 'Apart from the Rose and Crown he's been seen on Briggate and out by the tenter grounds. I want you to start asking in all those courts off Briggate and out along Swinegate. Maybe he lives along that area. Take two of the men with you. Ask about a big man, maybe with a sister.'

'Yes, boss.'

We're going to find you, Nottingham thought after Rob had gone. We're growing closer, and you'll pay with your neck. He could begin to believe that it was just a matter of time now. And once they had the murderer, he'd give all his attention to the other matter. The school.

THIRTY-ONE

By evening Rob and his men had gone through three of the courts, knocking on doors, asking their questions so often they'd lost count. But no big, dark-haired man with large hands. No one knew him, no one cared; they had enough to do simply living their lives.

He bought the men a jug of ale and drank a mug with them, the liquid sweet on his throat, washing away all the dryness and the words. With the long shadows the worst of the heat had gone. He hung his coat over his shoulder as he walked back down Kirkgate and home to Marsh Lane.

The Constable looked at him hopefully as he entered but all he could do was shake his head. Emily was working, searching for something in a book, frowning until he kissed the top of her head.

In the kitchen, Lucy had cleared everything away except for one plate sitting on the table.

'I dished it up when I heard the door. It's still warm.'

'Thank you.' He began to eat, barely noticing the taste.

'You look like you haven't had a bite all day.'

'I don't know that I have,' he said with a grin.

'You're still a growing lad, you need your food. And you look like misery.'

She'd become a mother to them all, he thought.

'I went to see my father today.'

'Not a happy visit, from the look of it.'

'No,' was all he said.

Lucy stared at him, her arms folded. 'You can't choose your family, you know. And just because they're related doesn't mean you have to love them.'

'I thought I had to tell him.'

'With some folk, saving your breath can be the best thing. You've got a family here, any road.'

It was true. And soon enough he'd be a husband, then a father, more at home in this place than ever. He finished the meal and she took the plate from his hands.

'You go and spend time with Miss Emily,' she told him. 'I need to start tomorrow's bread. The way you lot go through it you'd think it came out of thin air.'

'I want you back covering the yards today,' Nottingham told Rob. He'd finished the daily report, ready to deliver to the Moot Hall. The morning air seemed fresh, enough of a breeze to stir things and cut through the closeness.

'Yes, boss.'

'He's back in there somewhere.' He clenched his fist. 'I can feel it. Someone knows him.'

Rob nodded. 'What did you think of Emily's news?'

'Grand. Useful, too. She can hold on to her money. You'll need it with a baby on the way.'

'You know, Mrs Williamson surprised me,' Rob said. 'She always seemed like a prig to me.'

'Folk have hidden depths, lad. They can do things you'd never believe. Off you go. I'll take care of the morning rounds.'

The Constable had almost completed his circuit, finishing with the stretch along the Head Row to Burley Bar. He passed Garraway's, the smell of coffee strong in the air, just as Finer emerged from his lodgings, gazing around at the view.

'All well in Leeds, Mr Nottingham?'

'There's nothing new, if that's what you mean.'

'Be grateful for it, laddie.' The man grinned.

'I always am.'

'Where are you going?'

'Back to the jail.'

'I'll walk down Briggate with you.' Finer fell in beside him, Nottingham slowing his pace so the man could keep up. 'I hear that boy of yours was after someone yesterday. People were talking about it last night.'

'They'll talk about anything.'

'I know that. I've heard what they say about me. You'd think the devil himself had come back to Leeds.' He grinned again. 'But you still have murderers to catch.'

'We'll catch them. And what about you, Mr Finer? What's keeping you busy?'

'This and that, laddie, this and that.'

'All of it legal, I trust.'

'Would it be anything else?'

The Constable snorted. 'We both know better than that.'

'In the past, laddie.' He waved away the thought. 'You don't want to believe me.'

'I saw what happened with the workhouse.'

'Business, not crime. Two different things.'

'Not so far apart at times,' Nottingham told him.

'Except one won't end up in court.' They'd reached the corner of Kirkgate. Finer lifted his hat. 'I'll wish you well. I'm off to enjoy a grand day.'

The next Constable would need to keep his eye on Finer, Nottingham thought as the old man shambled down the street.

He'd had one iron in the fire with the workhouse; he'd have others, too. But at least it wouldn't be his worry.

He unlocked the jail and picked up a letter that had been pushed under the door. The paper was grubby, as if it had passed through many pairs of hands before it was delivered. He pulled back the seal and unfolded it.

The writing was cramped and awkward, many of the letters so badly formed that he had to read it three times before he could gather the sense of it.

Mr Sedgwick,

In reply to your letter, we did indeed have an incident in Whitby earlier this year that we've never been able to resolve. Mr Marlowe, one of our good merchants who lived on Baxtergate, was discovered dead when his servant returned after two days away. All his money had been taken and other valuables, too.

Our apothecary examined him and declared he'd been poisoned. He'd been keeping company with a young woman, Anne Briggs, who'd lately moved here with her family, and they were just as you describe them, a mother who claimed to be a widow, another daughter and a son. But they vanished the night of the killing, leaving their lodgings and we haven't been able to trace them.

From all you tell me, I'd like you to take Anne Briggs, or Anne Wade as she appears to be now, into custody and send her here to be questioned for murder. I have no evidence against the others but you should watch them carefully.

Your servant,
Charles Meecham
Constable of Whitby

Nottingham laughed. So John had taken it on himself to write to Whitby about the Wades. It was probably the first letter the man had ever composed, and the last. And he'd found a murderer; those suspicions he'd had, that feeling had been right. Even though he was dead, the man was still helping.

Poison, he thought. That would explain the girl they'd found buried. No marks on her, just the faintest smell of something in her mouth. It all fitted.

The Constable shook his head. He should have seen it himself. He should have asked more questions. He should have listened to the deputy instead of dismissing what he'd said. More and more, it seemed, retirement was the right decision. One thing was certain, he'd take no chance with this. Not now, not when he was so close.

'I want you to gather four of the men,' he told Rob as they sat in the White Swan eating their dinner. 'Have them at the jail in half an hour.'

'Yes, boss. Where are we going?'

'To bring in someone suspected of murder in Whitby.'

'Whitby?' Lister's head jerked up. 'You mean one of the Wades?'

'One of the daughters,' Nottingham explained. 'They think she poisoned someone and they want her for questioning.'

'It won't take six of us for that.'

'Better to be safe,' he said. 'And she might be responsible for one of our murders.'

'The girl?'

The Constable nodded. 'Yes – I smelt something when I opened the mouth, and the killing in Whitby was poison. We have Mr Sedgwick to thank. He wrote to the Constable there.'

Rob raised his eyebrows and lifted his mug in a silent toast.

'I'll want you in with me, armed. Two men at the front door and the others at the back. There's a yard that leads to a ginnel, put them at the back gate.'

'Yes, boss. Are we bringing all of them in?'

'We are, but there's nothing against the others so far. I want the house searched, too. Look for poison.'

'What about the whores there?'

'Question them. I'll take the family.'

The Constable waited until everyone was in position. The sword hung from his waist, the pistol primed and loaded in his coat pocket. Rob stood at his side, and the men gathered loosely around. Nottingham raised his hand and brought it down hard on the wood, continuing until one of the daughters answered the door, her eyes blazing until she recognized him.

'Mr Nottingham,' she said, swallowing her anger. 'What can we do for you?'

'I'd like to come in if I may, Miss Wade.'

'Of course.' She'd dressed hurriedly, with no powders and potions on her face and her hair loose. 'I'll fetch Mama.'

'I need to see all of you.'

She hesitated then nodded, guiding them through to the parlour.

The long clock ticked, seconds passing slowly. The Constable looked around the room carefully, eyes taking in everything. Here and there he picked up an item to examine. Rob opened his mouth to speak but Nottingham shook his head; anyone could be listening.

Fifteen minutes passed before Mrs Wade swept into the room. She'd used the time to dress and prepare, wearing an expensive gown, hair neatly pinned under a cap and her face made up.

'Constable.' She stood inside the door, hands on her hips. 'I hope it's something important that brings you here. We keep late hours, I've told you before.'

He gave a small bow. 'It is important. As I told your daughter, I'd like your whole family here.'

'You'll have me until I know what you want.'

Nottingham smiled, keeping his tone gentle. 'I'm sure I don't have to remind you that I'm the Constable here in Leeds, Mrs Wade.'

Grudgingly, she nodded, disappearing again to return five minutes later with her daughters.

'Might I ask where you lived before you came to Leeds?' Nottingham began.

'Why does it matter?' Mrs Wade countered.

'Indulge me, please.'

'York,' she answered.

'Not Whitby?'

'Whitby?' she asked incredulously. 'Whatever gave you that idea?'

'Two of your children were heard talking about it.'

She shot a glance at her girls, then said, 'I wouldn't know about that. But we've never even been there.'

'Do you know a family called Briggs?'

'Briggs?' She frowned and he kept his eyes on her, watching for any glimpse of fear. 'No, I don't. Why?'

'There was a family in Whitby by that name. A widow with two daughters and a son. You have a girl named Anne.'

'I do.'

'That's curious. Mrs Briggs had a daughter named Anne, too.'

She shrugged. 'Coincidences happen, Constable.'

'They do,' he acknowledged. 'I don't see your son.'

'He'll be down shortly. Now what's all this about? You didn't come here to compare names.'

Nottingham turned to the fair-haired daughter, the one who had let them into the house.

'You're Anne?'

She looked towards her mother then nodded.

'I need to take you into custody to be sent to Whitby, Miss Wade.'

'What for?' her mother interrupted.

'Suspicion of murder.'

'No!' Mrs Wade shouted. 'My Anne would never do anything like that.'

'Then perhaps you did, or maybe her sister. I'll need to take you all to the jail; Anne will be sent on to Whitby.'

The room erupted in a babble of female voices. Then the door opened and a young man entered. He was tall, shoulders very broad, hands down at his sides. The son, Nottingham thought. Mark Wade.

'What's all this about?' he asked, his voice raised. His dark hair was combed and he'd taken the time to dress well in a fashionable black coat.

'I'm sending your sister to Whitby to be questioned about a murder.'

'Be damned you are.'

'I am,' the Constable told him firmly.

'Boss,' Rob said quietly, directing his gaze. Nottingham stared at the man's hands. They were large, far larger than normal. He looked at the man's hard eyes. 'And I'm arresting you for the murder of Jem Carter.'

'Who?'

'Enough!' Mrs Wade cried. 'First you want my daughter, now you want my son. I have friends among the aldermen, Constable, I warn you.'

'I'm sure they'll visit you in the jail and listen to your

complaints. Rob, tie Miss Wade's hands and then Mr Wade's.'

Lister took rope from his pocket, wrapping it around the girl's wrists as she looked beseechingly at her mother. He moved towards Mark Wade. In a quick movement the man pushed a big hand into Rob's chest, sending him sprawling backwards into the Constable.

Wade ran. Nottingham heard shouts from outside as he picked himself up, followed by silence. Mark Wade hadn't managed to go too far, it seemed.

Anne stood against the wall, weeping softly. The other women had vanished.

'I'll take this one,' he told Lister. 'You make sure the men caught everyone.'

'Yes, boss.'

The Constable leaned close to Anne's ear and whispered, 'We both know you did it. It'll be better for you if you tell me everything.'

The girl just shook her head. He took hold of her arm and guided her out into the sunlight. Mark was there, heavily bound, cuts on his face, held still by the men as he tried to force his way free.

'Where are the others?'

'It took both the men to subdue him. They must have slipped out,' Rob said with embarrassment.

Nottingham said nothing for a moment, surveying the scene.

'Take him to the jail. I'll bring her.' He turned to Lister. 'Get the men searching all the roads out of Leeds. I want them taken. After that I want you to talk to the whores upstairs. They'll know more.'

THIRTY-TWO

The Constable saw them into the cells, Mark Wade ranting and cursing, his sister quiet and subdued. He left the ropes on their wrists, leaving them to feel the oppression of their surroundings.

Christ, how could Mrs Wade and Sarah have escaped? He'd been stupid, he hadn't anticipated that the women would try to run. Now he needed to find them quickly.

What would he do in their place? Where would they go? Out of Leeds, he thought, as far and as fast as possible. Even with nothing, being alive was better than what would face them. They were all guilty. If he hadn't been certain of that before, he was now.

Nottingham could feel every muscle in his body aching with the strain. Soon he'd begin asking questions of both prisoners, seeing what answers he could find. Anne would be the one to talk. She was scared, feeling alone and abandoned.

He poured a mug of ale, forcing himself to sip at it slowly, hoping for some report from the men. But by the time he'd finished no one had come. The Constable brought Anne from the cell and seated her on the chair across from him. All the colour had drained from her face and tears had left tracks on her cheeks. She didn't look up to face him, but kept her head bowed.

'You were in Whitby, weren't you?' he asked, and saw her nod slightly. 'And you knew a merchant named Marlowe.' She dipped her head once more. 'You killed him and robbed him.'

'I didn't kill him,' she said, her voice so small it almost wasn't there.

'Then who did?' he pressed.

'Mama.'

'Your mother?' he asked in astonishment.

'Yes.'

For a moment he didn't believe her. But her gaze was straight and honest. He wiped a hand across his mouth. 'How did she kill him?'

'She put poison in his drink.'

Poison, he thought, a woman's weapon. Then he thought of the girl they'd found buried and the faintest whiff of something when he'd opened her mouth.

'Has she killed in Leeds?'

'Two of the whores.'

'Two?' he asked, his voice sharp.

'One of them tried to leave.'

'Is that the one your brother buried?'

'Yes.' She whispered the word. Now he knew who'd been responsible for that death.

'What about the other one?'

'He put her in the river so it would look like she'd drowned.'

Jenny Carter. It hadn't been suicide after all. He closed his eyes for a moment then said, 'Who has your brother murdered? Peach well enough and it could save your neck.' He poured her a cup of ale. She held it awkwardly, hands shaking.

'I . . . I don't know.'

'Are you certain, Miss Wade?'

'I'm sorry.' He'd seen the fear in her eyes and the way her hands began to shake when he'd mentioned Mark Wade. She was terrified of him.

'Where would your mother and Sarah go?' He kept his voice gentle, trying to calm her. 'They're leaving you to hang. That's not showing you love, is it?'

She shook her head. He was willing to believe that she truly didn't know.

Rob hurriedly searched the brothel, taking the money from the strongbox and a ledger from the desk; that way no one else could steal them. Then he unlocked the four whores from their rooms, each of them frightened and bewildered. He sat them in the parlour and waited until their eager voices dropped to silence.

He doubted that any of them were older than Emily. It didn't take long to hear their stories, each one much the same. In return for Mrs Wade providing board, lodging and good new clothes worth five pounds – a handsome sum – they'd agreed to work for her until their debt was paid. They'd all made their marks on a contract. But as soon as they wondered what they owed, asked for an accounting and talked of leaving, the woman had threatened them with the law and debtor's prison. They hadn't been allowed out of the house, not even into the yard. Slaves, he thought, that's all they were.

Jenny Carter had been there, the girls told him, but only for a few days. Just after the place opened she'd disappeared. Mrs Wade claimed she'd been allowed to leave because she didn't like the life. It let them hope that she might let them go, too. Then Violet, another girl, had vanished. She'd been

unhappy and had talked of escaping. One morning they'd
awoken to find she'd gone, and no one was willing to answer
their questions.

Every one of them had lived in fear of Mark Wade. He used
them when and how he wanted, never caring if he hurt or
bruised, taking pleasure in their fear.

One girl rolled up the sleeve of her shift to show the bruises.
She was the youngest of them all, her arms and legs like
sticks and her face like a child's, but eyes far older than her
years.

'He did that, mister. Enjoyed it, too.'

'He's in jail now. He can't hurt you again.'

'What's going to happen to us?' Frances, the one who
seemed to look after the others, asked.

'You're free to go,' Rob told her.

'Go where?' she asked, her eyes hard and opaque. 'You
think we'd be here if we had somewhere else?'

He took out the money he'd hidden in his coat and divided
it between them. God knew they'd earned it.

'That'll give you a start.'

'What about the clothes?' Frances wondered suspiciously.

'Take them. Take whatever you want.'

He left them to start their new lives. The folk round here
would soon strip the place of whatever the girls didn't carry
off. For now he needed to find Mrs Wade and Sarah.

'No one's seen them on any of the roads leaving town,'
Nottingham said. Rob had told him what he'd learned.
There'd been nothing in the papers or ledger to show any
new destination.

'They're still in Leeds, then. They'll probably try to leave
once it's dark.' Rob glanced out of the window. From the
brightness it was still only midday. 'I put a man on each of
the roads. When it's dark, though, there are so many ways
they could escape.'

'We'd better find them before evening, then.' Nottingham
said, pacing around the room. 'Rouse the night men. I want
everyone out. Put them in twos and give each pair an area to
search.'

'Yes, boss.'

'Once you've done that, you and I can take the stretch along the river.'

The Constable stood in front of Mark Wade's cell, watching him through the bars. The man knew he was there, but paid no attention, sitting quietly with a smirk on his face.

'I'm going to hang you for murder,' Nottingham announced. Very slowly, the man turned his head.

'Are you now?' Wade asked calmly.

'And for helping in another.'

'You'd better have your evidence, then.'

'Don't you worry about that.' He smiled.

Anne came out meekly. As they passed the other cell her brother called out, 'You'd better not tell him anything. You know what'll happen if you do.' She tried to stop but the Constable urged her on. 'You know what I can do,' Wade shouted.

She was shivering as she sat in the chair.

'He can't hurt you,' Nottingham assured her. 'I'll move you to the prison under the Moot Hall until I can send you to Whitby. You'll be safe there.' He took the document he'd prepared. 'Can you read and write?' She nodded. 'This is what you told me earlier. If it's all correct, sign it for me.'

'Will it save me?' she asked softly.

'I can't promise that,' he said honestly. 'But there's a better chance with it. I'll send a letter saying you've helped. It'll be up to the magistrate; it could make a difference.'

She looked at the page, dipped the quill in the inkwell and signed. Anne Briggs, he noticed, not Wade.

THIRTY-THREE

Rob heard the Parish Church bell ring eight. They'd been covering the ground since noon and now evening was creeping around, the shadows lengthening, the fierceness gone from the sun as it started to slip away. Emily would have waited a while for him at the school then made her way home. She'd understand; she'd grown up with all this.

There'd been no sign of Mrs Wade or Sarah. He'd gone to the camp and talked to Bessie, and to folk in the warehouses along the Aire. Nothing. But there were so many places to keep out of sight. During the night they could slip away unnoticed through the fields, never to be seen again in Leeds. He'd done all he could: put men on the roads, told everyone he could to watch for the women.

The Constable had said little over the last few hours, locked away in his thoughts. He'd issued a few orders, vanished at times to check on the others only to reappear frowning more than before.

Finally, once it was too dark to see more than a few yards, Nottingham said, 'That's enough out here. We'll go and try around the yards.'

'Yes, boss.'

'Find yourself some food and something to drink first. Come to the jail when you're done.'

Nottingham sat at his desk, the mug of ale in front of him. He was hungry but he couldn't eat. John had given him a gift from the grave and he'd been too stupid to use it properly. He simply hadn't believed the women would run. He'd imagined Mrs Wade would give herself up to justice once he had her daughter. Now he had to make it right.

He heard Mark Wade stirring and walked through to the cell.

'Can I have some ale and something to eat?' the man asked. He looked calmer, all the fire gone from his voice.

'I'll have the inn next door bring something over for you.'

Wade held up his wrists. 'And untie me, perhaps?'

'No,' the Constable answered bluntly. 'Not yet.'

By the time Rob returned he was ready to lead the way through the yards and courts that squatted behind the houses of Briggate and the Calls. Some were respectable, homes to artisans, clean and well-kept, while others stood dirty and dank, the air heavy with the stink of decay. He tried doors, shining a lantern inside whenever he found one open, went into corners the sun might not have reached in years, and worked his way through to cramped spaces half-remembered from his youth.

Leeds went to sleep around them. They questioned the whores on Briggate whose work filled the dark hours, the girls Rob knew from covering the nights, but none of them had seen a pair of women together.

He sent Rob off to check on the others as he continued to search. The only consolation was that Mrs Wade didn't know Leeds well; she'd be hard pressed to find her way out without daylight. If God was giving him luck for once, she was still here.

The first fine, pale strands of light appeared on the horizon. He was weary, but not ready to give up yet. He'd push on until he found them, and he'd make sure the men saw him; he couldn't ask them to do anything he wouldn't undertake himself.

At the jail he peered in on Mark Wade. The man was asleep, those large hands cradled under his head like a child. Enjoy it, he thought, soon enough you'll have the rope around your neck.

Rob had settled back in the chair, eyes closed, resting while he could. The Constable sat and pictured Leeds in his head, every street, each nook and cranny, trying to picture the Wades in one of them, hiding. They had no money, they wouldn't have eaten or drunk anything more than they could scavenge. They wouldn't have dared sleep for fear of being discovered. This morning, this morning he'd have them.

'Come on, lad,' he said finally. 'You try out along the Calls and the warehouses again. I'll stay and hear the reports from the men.'

Rob started out on Call Brows. From there he could look down to the water and see if anyone was trying to keep out of sight. He followed the road all the way past the bend in the river, seeing nothing unusual; the only women were the ones who made their living washing clothes in the Aire.

He turned back to make his way along the Calls, ducking briefly back into each of the yards as he passed. They could be anywhere. He had a nagging feeling in his belly that they'd already fled Leeds and all this searching would be fruitless.

He moved along the street, methodical and cautious, then glanced up, worried to see a group of women standing outside Emily's school with their young daughters, all talking among themselves.

'Is something wrong?' he asked.

'It's still all locked up,' one of the women told him. 'That's not like Miss Emily.'

The shutters were tight, the door closed.

'She's probably just late,' he said with a smile. 'You know what she's like.'

The woman kept her hand on the shoulder of a girl and looked at him steadily. 'No, love, she went in five minute back. I saw her from me window.'

Rob's stomach lurched.

'Have you seen two women around here this morning?' he asked urgently. 'One of them older and big, the other younger?' He raised his voice so they'd all take notice. Some just shook their heads, then one, a mousy, timid woman at the back of the group with her hand protectively on her daughter's head, answered, 'Aye.'

'Where were they?'

'Just up there.' She pointed at a passage a little further up the street. 'I went down to t' pump and saw them.'

'How long ago was that?'

She shrugged. 'Quarter of an hour, mebbe.'

'I saw them go in the school,' the first woman told him. 'Right after Miss Emily. I were just coming out over there. Then I heard someone lock the door. That's why I was wondering.'

Jesus. They had Emily.

He took a deep breath, ready to send someone for the Constable, then his head turned quickly as he heard someone running. He saw Lucy dashing up the street, skirts flying around her ankles.

'What is it?' he asked.

She held up a book. 'Miss Emily left this. She was late, all at sixes and sevens with you not there.' She looked around at the women. 'What's wrong. Where is she?'

'Go to the jail,' he told her. 'Bring Mr Nottingham.' There was a thud inside the building, something knocked over, a desk or a table. 'Now!'

The men had returned in dribs and drabs. He'd no doubt that some had stopped on the way to slake their thirst. He'd despatched a few to keep an eye on the roads and sent the others to search in different parts of the city. The last four were with him, Holden and Todd among them, and he was giving them their orders when Lucy pushed the door wide and ran in, her eyes wilder than he'd ever seen them.

'What is it?' he asked urgently.

Her words came out in a jumble. 'She was late to school. Mr Rob is there. There's noise inside and it's all locked up.'

Oh Christ, he thought. The Wades had his daughter.

THIRTY-FOUR

The Wades have her. The Wades have her. His footsteps kept the rhythm as he strode along Briggate. Lucy hurried to keep in step beside him, Holden and three more of the men close behind. At the jail he'd taken two swords, then loaded and primed a pair of pistols.

'What are you going to do?' Lucy asked.

Without hesitation he replied, 'I'm going to keep her alive.'

She was all he had left. Mary was dead, Rose was dead. He couldn't lose Emily. Not now, with marriage and mother-hood ahead of her. He picked up his pace. At the corner of the Calls he paused a moment, directing two of the men out along Call Brows to the back of the building. 'I want you in the yard in case they try to get out that way,' he said.

At the school he looked at the door and the closed shutters before drawing Rob aside. 'What do you know?' he asked.

'Emily was late. Some of the women saw her arrive. It looks as if Mrs Wade and her daughter were waiting in the entrance to one of the courts. They went in right after her and locked the door. I heard something crash down right before I sent Lucy for you.'

'Any voices?'

Lister shook his head.

Nottingham needed to think clearly. He handed Rob a sword and one of the pistols. 'Use it,' he ordered.

The Constable's mind was a tangle. 'Why?' he wondered. 'What do they want in there?'

'Revenge?' Rob asked.

He didn't know, but it made as much sense as anything. He'd taken two of her children so she'd take his. He'd left Mrs Wade with nothing, no home, no money, so she was going to take the only thing he valued. Then he understood, as clearly as if someone had whispered it in his ear. The Wades had done the damage to the school. They'd pushed his attention to something he wanted to protect, and away from them. The woman had played him like a fiddler with an old, favourite tune.

'That crash I heard was just behind the door, boss. They might have set up a barricade.'

'We need to be in there.'

He had to see that Emily was still alive, to make sure nothing happened to her.

Lister shook his head. 'We'd have to force our way in. They'd have all the time they needed.'

Nottingham tried to push the freezing fear out of his mind. The woman would want him in there; he was certain of that. She'd want him to see what she had planned. And Mrs Wade was no fool; she'd know there was no escape for her now. She had nothing to lose. He took a deep breath.

'This is the Constable,' he shouted, his voice rising easily above the noise on the street as the women talked among themselves. 'Let me in.'

He exchanged looks with the Rob. Moments passed slowly. His fists were clenched so tight that his knuckles were white, fingernails digging deep into his palms. He hardly dared to breathe. Finally he heard the rasp of something being dragged across the floor. It stopped then began again, a slow, desperate sound.

'I'm going in with you, boss.'

He hesitated, then nodded. Emily was going to be Rob's wife, the mother of his child.

'So am I.' Lucy had appeared at his side, the small knife in her hand.

'No,' he told her.

'I'm not scared of them.'

'I know you're not,' he said quietly. 'But Rob and I are going in alone.' Defiance blazed in her eyes, and he thought quickly. 'I need you out here, to organize the women to stop them if they try to come out.' He turned to the men. 'You know what to do. Keep everyone back. If you hear anything strange, anything at all, come in.'

They heard the key turn in the lock. He moved forward, pushed down on the handle and slowly opened the door.

The room was dim, a maze of hot shadows. He stood in the doorway, letting his gaze adjust to the gloom until he could make out Emily sitting behind her desk. Her eyes were open, pleading at him, her hands gathered in her lap, fingers clasped tight together. Mrs Wade stood behind her, a knife to the girl's throat. He picked out Sarah in the corner, her face hidden in the shadow.

'Just you,' the woman said. 'Not him.'

'He's courting my daughter,' the Constable answered, and waited until she gave a brief nod. 'What do you want?' he asked. His mouth was dry. He looked at Mrs Wade, seeing the hatred on her face.

'You know well enough,' she answered, pulling hard on Emily's hair. He drew in his breath and clenched his fist as the girl cried out, her head yanked harshly back.

'Let her go.' It was part order, part pleading.

'What are you going to say next?' The words were a taunt. 'She's done nothing?'

'She hasn't.' He could hear the desperation in his voice. 'You know that. You're the ones who killed people.' He glanced across at Sarah, still unmoving in the corner. 'All of you.' The Constable paused. 'Why?'

'To survive,' Mrs Wade replied simply. 'That young man, he came when we opened, and saw his sister. Mark took care of him before he could start a fuss.'

'The girls? Why did they have to die?'

'I needed to be rid of Jenny before you began asking too many questions. And the other one tried to leave. I couldn't allow that.' She shook her head, no more emotion in her description than a shopkeeper describing damaged stock. 'I underestimated you, Constable. I thought you'd be as stupid as all the others I've seen. You're persistent.'

'You like to use poison, don't you?'

'So much less violent, and so pleasurable after they realize what they've drunk.' She smiled.

'I'm going to give the people you murdered some justice.'

'But not before I have mine for my son and daughter.' She laid the flat of her blade against Emily's neck. The girl flinched, scarcely daring to move. 'What's she worth, Mr Nottingham? What's she worth to you?'

'You're not going to go free.'

She chuckled. 'That wasn't my question, was it? I know I'm going to hang.' She twisted Emily's hair again. 'So one more body won't matter, will it? Or would you rather take her place?'

'Yes.' He didn't even hesitate, but sensed Rob stiffen beside him.

'Now that's real love, Constable, giving up your own life for your daughter.'

'Let her go,' he said again.

'No,' she answered. 'Tell me, is this what you want, to sit here and have everyone watch while I slit your throat?'

'As long as you let her live,' he replied. The blood was beating furiously in his head. The room was stifling behind the shutters but he felt chilled. The woman seemed to ponder for a long time.

'Take off your sword and your knife,' she ordered. 'And put down the gun.'

He did as she commanded, letting them fall to the floor.

'Move forward.'

He took two paces towards her.

'Stop,' she said.

He halted. Mrs Wade tugged Emily's hair, dragging her upright. The girl opened her mouth, swallowing hard, her eyes refusing to cry. The woman pushed Emily forward, the blade still against her neck.

'Three more steps.'

He was close enough now to make out every line on her face, to see the thin sheen of sweat on his daughter's skin.

'Now come to me.'

When they were just a pace apart Emily reached out for his hand. He grabbed it, and with one swift movement pulled her down, throwing himself on top of her. Please, he thought, Christ, please. He had to hope Rob had the brains and the speed to do something.

Time seemed to hang as he waited. Then the explosion filled the room, booming in his ears. He kept his arms tight around Emily, holding her still and praying he was keeping her safe.

Then there was a quick madness of voices as the men stormed in, shouting and yelling, a thunder of noise that slowly faded away. Very cautiously, the Constable raised his head, cradling Emily, feeling her sobbing without making a sound.

It was over. Lister had Mrs Wade under guard, his sword drawn. His shot had missed; the ball was buried high in the wall and a shower of plaster sprinkled the boards, but it had been enough. The men were already bundling Sarah away.

The woman had dropped her knife. Nottingham reached for it as he stood up, helping Emily to her feet. She clung to him, shaking, and he began to move away, his arm fast around her.

'Bring them to the jail,' he said and turned his back on the scene. He felt drained, barely able to stand, everything gone from him. Then, before he understood what was happening, Lucy was there, running, her teeth bared, pure anger on her face. He followed her with his eyes, seeing her leap and bite down so hard on Mrs Wade's arm that the woman screamed in pain. The bottle she'd pulled from her pocket tumbled and shattered on the ground, the liquid making a small, dark puddle on the wood.

Rob grabbed Mrs Wade by the hair, tightening his grip until she howled as he dragged her out of the building.

'It's over now,' Nottingham whispered in Emily's ear, stroking her hair as he gathered her close. 'It's over. They can't ever hurt you again.'

She was crying, letting the tears flow freely. He could feel Lucy next to him, hear her breathing, but the only thing he cared about was Emily.

'Papa,' she said, trying to gulp back the sobbing, 'I hurt inside.'

'They cut you?' He didn't understand. He'd seen nothing on her. Now, as he glanced, he could see blood colouring the back of her dress.

'The baby.' She clutched her belly, and her eyes were wide and fearful as she looked up at him. Before he could speak, Lucy edged him aside, gently guiding Emily out of the door, where the women were waiting.

The Constable stood alone in the room, feeling the silence weigh down on him. He bent to gather up his weapons. He'd never need them again. It was finished. If he'd done his job properly, if he'd *thought*, it would have ended before all this. Now Emily might still die.

He turned at the tentative footfalls. 'How is she?'

'They've sent for the midwife,' Lucy told him. 'One of the women has taken her in.'

'Will she . . .?' He couldn't finish the question.

'They said she should be fine.'

'The baby?'

'No.' Her mouth crumpled as she said the word.

'I want you to stay with her,' Nottingham said. 'I'll go to the jail and send Rob down.'

He started to walk out, one hand on the door, when Lucy said, 'Mr Nottingham.'

'What is it?' He wanted to leave this place, to smell air that didn't stink of gunpowder.

'You're not going to do this any more, are you? I can see it in your eyes.'

He had to smile. How could she be so young and understand so much? At times he wondered if she had something of the fey in her, the way she sensed things that were thought but unspoken.

'You're right.' She opened her mouth but he held up her hand to quiet her. 'But not a word to anyone yet. Don't worry, you'll still have a job. And a home. Thank you for what you did today. How did you know?'

'I just did.' She shrugged her thin shoulders. 'There's evil in that woman. I want her to suffer for what she did to Miss Emily.'

So did he.

THIRTY-FIVE

I t was rare enough to hang one person up on Chapeltown Moor. Three of them together, and a family at that, made it feel like a holiday. The anticipation had been growing for a week, ever since the sentences had been handed down. There would be horse races in the afternoon, drawing people from all around, all capped with Sir William Milner competing against Mr Arthington, twice around the circuit for the Hunter's Plate. Hundreds of pounds had already been wagered on the outcome and there'd be hundreds more before dinner. Folk had their stalls open early, ready for the crowds, selling hot pies or mugs of ale, while women offered their baskets of lucky heather and a patterer told the tale of the killers in exchange for coins.

Anne had been sent off to Whitby to face her own justice; the Constable had no doubt she'd soon find her fate there. On the first Monday in July as the bell at the Parish Church struck seven, he escorted the Wades from the prison under the Moot Hall to the cart that would take them out along the Newcastle road. Mrs Wade and Sarah were in the only clothes the whores had left them, hair covered in newly laundered caps, and Mark Wade wore his best dark suit. All three of them were defiant, standing together as they were shackled into the wagon and holding their heads high as the cart edged up Briggate and out of Leeds.

The Constable led the procession, Rob by his side. Crowds lined the street all the way past Town End, then fell in behind. Lucy was somewhere back there, eager to see the spectacle. Emily had stayed at home.

After they'd taken the Wades to the jail he'd sent Rob hurrying back to the Calls, then stood and looked at the cells. Mrs Wade sat with her arm around Sarah, Mark at the edge of his bed, whispering quietly to them through the bars. There was nothing the Constable wanted to say to them. There were no words for what he felt.

Instead he locked the door and walked to the house on
Lands Lane, waiting as a baby wailed and footsteps moved
towards the door. Lizzie had Isabell on her shoulder, her hand
rubbing circles on the girl's back.

'Mr Nottingham,' she said in surprise. Her hair was lank,
her face drawn and tired. 'Come in, please. Sit down.' She
gestured towards the table. 'I . . .'

'It doesn't matter,' he told her with a smile. 'She's more
important.'

Lizzie sat across from him and he could see all the questions on her face. Why had he come? What did he want?

At least he couldn't hurt her with more bad news, he thought.

'I wanted you to know that your John helped solve
something.'

'John?' she asked in astonishment. 'You mean those women
you were looking for?'

'Yes,' he said and told her everything, the deputy's idea,
the letter he'd written and what it had all meant. When he'd
finished she sat back, shook her head and gave a small laugh.

'He could be a dark one at times, couldn't he?'

'But worth ten of most people.'

'They're going to hang?' she asked.

'There's no doubt about it. And soon after that I'm going
to resign.'

'You?' She looked at him in disbelief. 'Why?'

'Because it's time.' It was the best he could offer, a small
sentence that seemed to say everything. 'But I hope you'll
still be a friend to us all. James and Isabell, too.'

'Of course.' She grinned and he caught a glimpse of how
she'd been before her man died. 'But only if you promise not
to be a stranger here, either.'

The school remained closed for a fortnight, long enough for
Emily to regain her strength. She'd been taken home, to rest
in her own bed, and Lucy had seen to her needs until she'd
had enough of being waited on like a lady and was eager to
do things for herself once more. Rob had been with her whenever he wasn't working, attentive and asking what she needed
until she finally snapped at him to leave her alone. That was
when the Constable knew she was ready. The day the school

reopened the girls brought in small bunches of wildflowers they'd gathered to give to her. She wasn't going to stop teaching, he knew that, she wasn't going to let herself be pushed out. The fear was still there, it would always be there, but she'd never let it show, she'd keep it locked away, hidden from sight; she took after him that way.

The new books arrived and the smile slowly returned to her face. She didn't say anything to him about what had happened, but he knew she and Rob must have talked. In the evening she devoted less time to her work and more to her young man. They still planned to marry; the banns had been read for the first time the previous Sunday. They'd decided that it seemed the right thing to do.

The Corporation voted Nottingham a pension as gratitude for his bravery. Money to keep him, he thought as he sorted through a chest, finding one of Mary's old dresses. He held the garment close to his face, taking in the scent of her that still lingered faintly in the material, picturing her face, the texture of her hair as he stroked it, and loving her as much as when she'd lain next to him.

The moor was packed with people; most of Leeds and the villages around had come out, it was an event few wanted to miss. The members of the Corporation, all in their finery, had ridden the three miles out to Chapeltown after the cart had arrived and the prisoners taken up to the gallows, hands bound behind them and the nooses around their necks. The vicar moved between them, urging repentance and saying his prayers for their souls.

Finally, as the small bell of St Matthew's church tolled nine, he stood back. The executioner checked the knots and nodded to the Constable. The crowd fell silent, craning for a good view of the end. Before he could give his consent, Mrs Wade spoke out, her voice loud, 'I damn Constable Richard Nottingham and his family.'

The trapdoor opened and the bodies fell suddenly so all that was left above the platform were heads and shoulders. People surged forward, noisy, excited, eager to touch the feet as they dangled close to the ground. A few more minutes and the hangman would be busy selling lengths of rope and the clothes of the corpses, cut into small squares, as the bodies were taken off to be buried.

'A good hanging, Richard.' Tom Williamson stood, a peacock in his finest clothes. As an alderman he had to be there. 'But her words can't hurt you.'

'I know.' He managed a sad smile. They'd slid off him, just one more curse among so many over the years. But there had been too much dying, too many deaths.

The week grew into the next and the weather turned sultry, a patchwork of storms and prickly, fretful heat, sun blazing one day, rain pouring the next.

The Constable was at his desk, noting down expenses, gathering together small notes and adding up totals. The windows of the jail were open wide and he was in his shirt, still sweating as he worked. He opened the drawer and glanced at his letter of resignation again. At the middle of the month he'd give it to the mayor.

He'd almost finished his work when Rob returned from his early rounds.

'Did you know they're starting to clear that old orchard on Lady Lane where it runs down to Sheepscar Beck?'

'The one by Vicar's Croft?' he said with interest. 'What are they doing?'

'I talked to the foreman. They're going to build houses.'

'There?' He knew the city owned the land; it had been bequeathed to them years before.

'I asked who they were working for. He said it was Tom Finer.'

He found the man where he expected, sitting in the corner at Garraway's Coffee House, reading through the London papers that had arrived the night before. Finer looked up and waved the Constable to the table, smiling slyly.

'I had a wager with myself that you'd come looking for me before dinner.'

'How long have you owned the land?'

'Patience, laddie.' He lifted his hand and nodded his order for another dish of coffee. 'You thought the workhouse was what I was after, didn't you?'

'Wasn't it?'

Finer allowed himself a satisfied grin. 'You saw that and it was all you could think about. But you should have dug a little deeper. It was only one part of my arrangement with the Corporation. The rest involved the land. Plenty of room for building there, and a pretty penny to be made from it. I told them I'd renovate the workhouse and run it if they sold me the land cheaply.'

'Then the workhouse burned down,' Nottingham said.

'So it did,' Finer agreed blithely, cocking his head. 'So it did. Unfortunate, wasn't it? Still, we'd already signed papers on the land. To tell you the truth, I didn't mind about the fire.'

'You wanted the workhouse.'

'Did I?' The man raised his eyebrows. 'I'd have made a little from it, but that's all. Hardly a fortune and there'd have been plenty of effort. The real money's in land and building these days, laddie. That fire turned out to be a blessing.'

'A very handy one. Did you start it?'

Finer sat back. 'I'd be very careful with questions like that if I were you. I wouldn't ask them too loudly. A little too far and they come close to slander. I doubt my friends on the Corporation would like that.' He sighed. 'You saw what you wanted to see, laddie. Or what I wanted you to see. You just never understood it was only one part of the picture.'

'It seems I didn't,' the Constable agreed.

'Amos might have taught you a thing or two but he was never a man for subtlety. You might think you are, but you've still plenty to learn, Constable.' He picked up the newspaper and began to read again.

Nottingham stood. As he opened the door Finer called out, 'Think on for the future, laddie.'

The Constable walked out into the harsh sunlight.

ACKNOWLEDGEMENTS

There was a workhouse in Leeds. Originally opened in 1638, it was in use as a school between 1705 and 1725. Then it was decided to re-establish the workhouse, and it operated for three years, with the wonderfully named Shubaal Speight working there. It closed in 1728, in debt from a lack of contracts. The real workhouse wasn't destroyed by fire; that's purely my invention, as is Emily Nottingham's school.

I'm grateful to Kate Lyall Grant, whose words helped transform the book entirely, into something that I hope is deeper and richer; to all the staff at Severn House, and to Lynne Patrick, a wonderful editor and friend. To my agent, Tina Betts, and to Thom Atkinson, a superb writer himself, whose reading of my work and suggestions are always perceptive. My thanks, too, to Linda R. Hornberg for the map. To Penny for her constant support, and to the friends who believe – you know who you are.